THE
LADY
WAITING

Magdalena Zyzak

/////////////////////// RIVERHEAD BOOKS   NEW YORK   2024

RIVERHEAD BOOKS
An imprint of Penguin Random House LLC
penguinrandomhouse.com

ISBN 9780593542941

Printed in the United States of America

BOOK DESIGN BY MEIGHAN CAVANAUGH

For Zachary

Blessed are the simple rich for
they inherit the earth.

F. Scott Fitzgerald

LOS
ANGELES

1

A woman in green chiffon stood on an island on the 101. She held her arm aloft—her jewelry flashed—like someone proposing a toast. I don't know why I stopped. I'd never picked up a hitchhiker before and never would again. She moved toward my slowing car, bizarrely fluttering her fingers. Here are some roles I would play for her in the coming months: her help, her thief, her lover, her lover's lover.

"Well, hello. What time is it?" asked the evening-gowned hitchhiker as she flopped onto the seat. It was two p.m. "Just look at this." She put her feet up on my dashboard—I didn't mind, my car was old—and pointed at the brown stain on her stomach. "Is it coffee? Blood?"

Heat emanated from her, as if, after many hours in the sun, she now possessed the freeway's qualities.

"What do you think?"

"Excuse me?"

"Blood or coffee?"

Was she drunk? Or injured? Yes. And maybe. But if so, not very badly. Cautiously, I pulled back into traffic.

"Take your pick. The bar's wide open." She opened the sun visor mirror and rubbed her eyes, smearing her already smeared mascara. Some of it got on her forehead. "Is today Ash Wednesday?"

"Umm, I think today is Monday, and not February."

It was May 2018.

"You're a Catholic!" It sounded like an accusation.

"You are okay? You are bleeding, your elbow," I said.

She adjusted her hair, examined her elbow. "Yep! Well, what do you expect? I jumped from his car. Sometimes there's just nothing else you can do, don't you think?" Her eyes shone as if from laughing or crying. I could smell her distinctly, perfume and whiskey, then a different whiskey, bad but good, as if a bottle inside another bottle had come uncorked.

"You mean, someone stole you?" I inquired, intimidated, suddenly a little drunk myself. My verbs, under stress, swooned and scattered in my head. Back in Poland, I thought I spoke English. In Chicago, where I'd spent the last year working at a restaurant, I learned I barely did. Here in LA, I had been strenuously faking fluency and failing to find a job.

"So I should take you to police? The hospital?" I said.

She effloresced in my peripheral vision in her ultra-green dress. The diamonds on her bracelets fired scattershot light all over my car's cheap upholstery as she piled her hair on her head, then let it fall between her knees, her pumps on my dashboard.

"Luckily, he was already pulling over," she said, licking her elbow. "Otherwise, I would've skinned my face. One time, I asked him if he'd still like me if I was disfigured, and he said, 'Yes, in the dark.' I thought that was sexy and honest. Don't you think that's sexy and honest?"

Cars passed on both sides. A sports car cut in front of us. I had a sense we were in a race and losing.

"But who other than my grandma wants sex in the dark?" She shrugged. She had a tremendous amount of blond hair. A bobby pin hung loose against her cheek. She paused, then chattered on. "Moonlight sex. Corporations are dividing up the moon. They already own the sex. I'll sell you two acres of moon for your ass. The moon is the new Wild West, did you know that?" Her words frayed at the edges. She was drunk. "The boys want to possess the moon. Anyway, I'm glad I jumped. Otherwise, we'd be in court right now getting a divorce. Divorces are such a mess. I hate them. Do you have any music? My phone's dead. My fucking husband says no one can feel anything anymore without a pop song playing."

She spoke with her eyes closed. She almost resembled one of those sleeping Buddha masks that nobody buys from the knick-knack stands on the Venice Beach boardwalk.

I said, "Excuse me, but . . . where should I take you?"

She was quiet. I waited. "Are you asleep?"

The hills of Hollywood flew by to either side.

"Forget what I said about divorce," she said, gathering a compact from her purse, powdering her nose, then shaking the sun in the compact's mirror. What was she doing, blinding drivers behind us? "We could never live apart," she said. "We're a four-legged hermaphrodite."

I didn't ask what a hermaphrodite was. Then she actually fell asleep. Neither my questions nor the radio—not even an ambulance passing—woke her.

In Los Angeles, you saw women like her on billboards above the boulevards and on the boulevards below the billboards. Magazine hair, designer purses. Out of the back doors of black cars, into restaurants. Some man's girlfriend, some other man's daughter. Somebody's prize and worry. Nobody worried about me. I was completely alone in this city, country, continent. My loneliness was a radiating force. The year before last, I'd left my family in southern Poland. My mother, barefoot on her knees, bursting out of her slip, cleaning the floor. My cousins, pushing baby strollers, sitting behind cash registers, registering nothing.

I had a teaching degree, though nothing to teach. If I was at all like the women on the billboards, it was only inasmuch as I, too, didn't like to speak. When I did, it was in questions and ellipses. I thought I was shy, but my oldest brother liked to call me *nieprzystępna, zuchwała*—standoffish, impudent.

I pulled off the freeway and into a gas station, not knowing what else to do. Her beaded clutch, her gown, the satin shoes—one on the floor, one on the dashboard—had to be worth together at least two thousand dollars. Each wrist had a dozen ropes, each with perhaps twelve tiny stones, each stone, I guessed, worth a few hundred dollars, maybe a month's salary for a teacher in Poland. If you had so many, would you miss one? Maybe I was undervaluing the diamonds. I had always been undervalued. Do the rich suffer loss less than the poor?

She murmured something in her sleep.

Most people I'd become acquainted with in service jobs, in Poland and Chicago, hated or at least disliked the rich. I was confused about the rich. Disliking them meant not desiring to become them. Self-loathing wasn't in my constitution. If I became the rich, I thought, I'd like myself. Time, freedom, luxurious foods. I was bland. I blandly understood this, but with money I would have a flavor. Yet I had no idea how one got money. I did not know I'd just met my unsentimental guide to loss and gain.

"You seem nice. Could we go to *your* place? I just need a nap so badly," she said, awake.

She had one of those faces you couldn't define. A dash of mercury beneath the skin. The only constant in such faces is a promise—nudge a feature a few millimeters, it falls with the others into a striking arrangement. That promise made her beautiful. She had a strong jaw, a prominent forehead. Her right eye had the tiniest rip in the iris, a little lava leaking out. One fake eyelash had come undone. Bare, this eye regarded me sternly, its winged sister soft and vain.

"My place?"

"I'm sorry. You must think I'm, like, a terrible person. You have better things to do."

I smiled and said, "That's okay."

"Do you?"

"What?"

"*Do* you have better things to do?"

"No." It was the truth. "No." No job interviews. No friends to see, that day or ever.

"So I'm not a bully. It's so hard to find something *actually* worth doing, isn't it?" She laughed. "Let me see . . . what's worth doing? Getting your hair done? Then it rains on your way home. You've wasted your time and look like a wet dog."

"Maybe you go to the toilet to wash." I pointed at the stain. "It's a beautiful dress."

"I need a nap so badly."

"Actually, I'd rather go home," she said thirty minutes later when we were on La Tijera, almost at my place. "Back in the Hills, off Mulholland. Sorry! Do you mind? My phone's out of battery, and my husband will kill me if I don't get home soon."

"He will hurt you?" I asked.

"Not unless I ask him to, but I'm not into that these days. Although sometimes I like to be spanked with a hairbrush," she said. "Usually not, though," she added blithely.

So I made a U-turn, feeling no exasperation, just relief. I didn't want her to see my place.

"Do you have a phone charger?"

I didn't.

"Tell me where you're from at least."

I was from Straconka—once a village, then a district of Bielsko— its name derived from the Polish infinitive for *to lose*. The lost (*stracency*), the condemned. Historians claimed that the village was named after prisoners executed there in the mountains during the war. Geographers argued that the village took its name after the river, which got lost in the mountains.

"I'm from noplace," I said.

"Noplace? Never been," she said in a serious tone.

"Where are you from?" I asked.

"Made in Poland," she said, picking up her Italian shoe and shaking a crumb out of it.

This wasn't much of a coincidence. Polish people were everywhere in 2018. Could she tell I was Polish? Her being Polish, too, upended everything. My admiration for her jewels and shoes became resentment. My car had never looked as meager as with her inside it. Scrapes along the gearbox. Odors of spilled gas and cigarettes smoked years ago and not by me. How could she be Polish and so much better off? Was she from Warsaw? I wanted her out of my car. I wanted a better car with her in it.

"I came here for college," she continued. "*So* long ago. I'm like Maria Callas."

For college? So she'd been rich before she came? Was that better or worse?

"You sing?"

"Never."

"But you said you are like Maria Callas," I said, changing lanes.

"Oh, I just meant my accent's muddy, like Callas's was. International, you know. I learned English in Switzerland at boarding school, but all my friends were Turkish. My English teacher was American, though, except my very first teacher was Australian, and she was married to my dog's vet, not the dog I have now, but my accent's Turkish-Swiss-Polish-American-Australian. I'm an accent slut. Better than a slut with an accent, don't you think? That's not my line, by the way. It's Lance's. I don't mind stealing his lines, though. What's his is mine. My name's Roberta, but I go by Bobby. I was almost named Dominika, actually. You know, *dominica* means *Sunday* in Latin. My mom had a hunch about me——she knew I was a Sunday child. A lazy child. But my dad was the one who filled out the form, and he wrote *Roberta*."

"And who is Lance?"

"Not my husband!"

"Ah. And your husband—"

"Sleeper? He's the best," she said with genuine, bewildering affection. "What about yours?"

"I don't have a husband."

"No, I meant your name."

"Viva," I said. My name was Wioletta, anglicized into Viola. I'm not sure where *Viva* came from. It was born just then, with oil derricks passing in the window as we traveled north again.

La Cienega and up into the Hills. Sinuous roads, SUVs. Bobby spoke less and less the higher up we drove. Facades of houses through foliage. I imagined their inward lazy sprawl, tall women reclining on sofas and beds. Earthquake-proof buildings harboring salt-of-no-earth inhabitants. I drove carefully. A group of slim, good-looking people got out of an SUV, holding babies in baskets and baskets in cellophane.

We stopped in front of a gate. Except for a bit of the mansard roof and terrace, the house was hidden.

"Thank you very much! *Merci*." Shoes in hand, a swoop of green, out of the car—her departure was as abrupt as her arrival. I was a little shocked but put the car into reverse.

A tap on my window. Relieved, I rolled it down.

"Can you write down your number? Oh, and, like, your address, in case I lose your number? I don't do social media and hate writing emails and want to send you something."

I wrote my phone number and address on the base of a polystyrene cup. She grabbed the cup and kissed my hand—the way men from my mother's generation kissed women's hands—and opened the gate with a fob from her clutch.

Above the gate, between the trees, I saw a shirtless man, powerfully built, appear on a terrace, then disappear behind a grapevine-covered wall.

Bobby turned and yelled in Polish, "Usually I don't like Polish girls abroad, but you're—"

The gate clanged as it closed, eclipsing what she thought of me. Another shirtless man, of slighter frame, passed on the terrace.

2

Six days later, I still hadn't heard from her. Nothing exciting had happened to me since I'd come to LA. Until Bobby. Though coincidental, her being Polish felt symmetrical, a sparkly event. And I had no friends. So I checked my phone for messages a hundred times a day. I'd drive to a job interview or the ocean, absurdly scanning freeway shoulders for figures in green.

In offices, people spoke English full of incomprehensible slang. On the beach, more people spoke Spanish than English. This freed me from the pressure to understand. I watched happy families, happy my family was absent.

Back in Straconka, I used to read novels about teenage rebellion, runaway girls, girls who went to psychiatric institutions. I was not the least bit disturbed. My situation wasn't decadent enough to allow for disturbance or rebellion. There were no authorities to rebel against. There were teachers we mocked until we became them, priests who masturbated in confessionals as we generously fed them outrageous fictional sins, politicians on TV, gray, small, like people's fathers. I had no father to resent. The man who "raised" me was an exterminator. He drove a van with a roach painted on it. The man who had impregnated my mother in a rape-seed field—not a metaphor, a major Polish crop—had ridden a motorcycle. He was gone by harvest. For a long time, when I saw vans, I thought of weak men. When I saw motorcycles, I thought of absent men, men of windy nightfall, men so obscure they barely existed.

My tenth interview that month was on one of those dismal LA streets where everything—dry cleaners, beauty parlors, shops, offices, parking lots—seems engineered for easy collapse and equally easy reassembly. This readiness for wreckage, for the earth to move or hills to burn, imposed a permanent impermanence that dryly mocked the glamour one expects to find. It took me a long time to understand that most of LA had the shabbiness of a movie set, a great backstage in which performance was to be not enjoyed but prepared. And if there were enclaves of glamour—houses, restaurants, clubs where beautiful beings strolled in dresses that cost five years of my family's combined income—these weren't accessible to immigrants like me. I thought of Bobby in her dress and her house, tucked in the hills.

I locked my car and crossed the potholed street. I imagined myself in a long green gown. It was morning. I felt warrantlessly optimistic about getting this job.

Inside, a woman with a rumpled mouth like a drawstring neckline asked me to sit down and list my weaknesses and strengths.

"Unexperienced," I said. "Scared of people. Manipulating, but so sometimes I don't know I'm manipulating."

"The word is *manipulative*."

"I'm still working on my English."

Not for us, her eyes were saying.

"But I didn't tell you my strengths. I have strengths."

The drawstring had pulled shut.

"I did not get this job," I said to her, as she, after some small talk, showed me out. The hall was windowless and gray, the color of machine-made madness, and it matched the woman's suit.

She shook her head. "We have too many candidates, some with much more extensive experience in the field."

The "field" was filing, hard copy and electronic.

"A word of advice," she offered. "What you said about being manipulative . . . We don't admit to such things so much here."

I wasn't sure if she meant her office in particular, or Culver City, or the United States.

"Also," she added in a theatrical whisper followed by a wink, "that's not really a weakness. As long as you don't talk about it."

"But in Poland, I am high school teacher, you know?" I meant I was overeducated for the job, therefore I should get it. I wasn't sure how to say it in English. *I'm emotionally unstable*, my eyes were saying. It wasn't true.

"Are you okay?" She was more concerned about appearing concerned than about me. "I'm sure you'll find a job soon. Good luck."

"No, I will never, ever find nothing," I said and willed my tears to stay in my head and turned to go, rejecting the handshake she'd offered.

On the freeway, I mocked her. "Are you okay?" On the radio, a woman sang about breaking up with some idiot. I'd never particularly wanted to leave Poland, but you don't win the green card lottery and not use the card. That's what everyone in my family said. That's what the sensitive computer engineer who had made me apply for the lottery said. He lolled on my bed, talked left-wing politics, installed things on my laptop. I was twenty-one, about to receive my teaching degree, and Poland was back on the green card lottery list, a program that made fifty thousand visas available per year for immigrants from certain countries. I applied, and cried when I won. Leaving my puny life full of troublesome brothers, laundry bisecting the living room in winter, crotchety women crocheting, vodka, disco polo—leaving all this shabby comfort suddenly seemed a sacrifice. And so, less than a year later, with a suitcase with one busted wheel, bad jeans and sweaters, paperbacks, an aged laptop, and the address of a distant cousin in Chicago, I was on a plane. At least you can't say I "followed a dream." Where I'm from, fantasies tend to be about revenge, not aspiration.

"Are you okay?" I mocked not only the woman who wouldn't employ me but her whole nation, obsessed with the question.

My building, by the airport, under the constant roar, had an open-corridor design, like a motel. I parked my car and crossed the courtyard. A deliveryman heaped flowers near my door.

"You Viva?" he asked.

Cellophane and chrysanthemums—maybe a dozen bouquets—had turned my door into a Polish grave, or the site of an accident in America. The place of someone who wasn't okay.

"Yes," I said.

"I should've rung the door first, but I thought, like, why not carry some of the bouquets up while I'm at it? Should I bring them inside?"

I resisted asking him if there were any openings at the florist. "You are sure they are for me?"

"You Viva?"

Together we doubted my identity for a moment. I'd never gotten flowers before. Flowers overfilled his arms; they rustled by our feet.

"From who are they?" I said and unlocked the door. "Come in."

Chrysanthemums, piled in his arms in their cellophane crowns, disdained my poverty, their mindless yellow, purple, blood-orange heads shaming the fecal brown of the carpet.

"Can you put them on the bed? I don't have——" The word for *vase* escaped me.

The card, when I unpinned it from the largest arrangement, which he'd laid upon my evil, bony sofa, read, *Thanks for saving my life. I'll text you, but in case I forget, meet me for lunch at 2 pm at Erő on Canon in Beverly. Something important to discuss. Bobby.*

"Guess I'll be going." He didn't move, apparently mesmerized by last night's chicken bones in the take-out box on my nightstand.

Then I remembered what country I was in. "Oh, wait." I fumbled in my purse but found only a single twenty. "Oh, I have only . . . but, oh, but I——" I flushed.

He flushed. We could've delivered many packages together, worked well and unhappily together.

"Take a bouquet," I said to him. "Please, take . . . for someone," I whispered and forced one of the smaller bouquets into his hands. With traffic, I'd hardly make it to Beverly Hills by two o'clock.

I ran a bath for the flowers.

"Welcome. How can we help you today?" The hostess, sheathed in white elastic, her Afro stop-sign red, exuded unwelcome. Beyond her station, against a bizarre wall made of something like woven tinsel, groups sat at wooden tables under exposed bulbs. The layout resembled a lab. In Poland, places and people resembled them-

selves. In LA, places, people resembled somewhere else, someone else.

"I'm meeting a friend. She invited me. I think she reserves a
table."

"What's the name?"

"Bobby. Or Roberta."

She tapped her tablet. "We don't have either on the list."

"I can look?"

She nodded. In the dining room, I scanned in vain for Bobby.
Some women were dressed expensively, in bouclé blazers, blouses.
Others were expensively shabby. Faded jeans, translucent thread-
bare tees. Legs in leggings, heads in hoodies. Leisurely people
dressed for physical work. Bare midriffs, wrists loud with bracelets. All the genders, all bejeweled, poking at poké, drawing with
provided crayons on white paper placemats. The waitresses also in
white. Any job openings, girls?

"Maybe it is another name and she still comes," I said to the
hostess. "I can wait?"

"You can wait in the waiting area."

"On the street?"

"In the waiting area."

The waiting area was on the street. A discreet line formed behind a velvet rope. People read menus and phones. An alley led
behind the restaurant—fruit crates, trash cans, exposed wires,
sleeping bags, an upturned shopping cart. In front of the restaurant, the valet ballet took place. Men in white jumped in and
out of cars, capered with keys and tickets. Any job openings, boys?
Their faces were empty. I understood. In Chicago, for nearly a
year, I had stood by a sink in a trash bag with armholes and called
it a profession.

After seventy minutes, I found myself at the front of the line, then at a table for two. I sat with a glass of tap water, tapping my cheap ring against it for most of an hour. The rhythm of disappointment. I grabbed a crayon from the jar on the table. My mother's aphasia had gotten worse just before my departure to the US, and I'd been marking items in her house with sticky notes. *Lodówka*, I wrote on her refrigerator. *Okno*, said the note on the window. *Telefon*, said the phone, though I knew my mother wouldn't call.

Fuck yourself Roberta, I wrote in Polish with a crayon on the placemat. On my way home, at a drive-thru, crying into a cheeseburger, I realized no date had been indicated on the card and that I'd be desperate enough to go back to Erő at two every day for weeks.

"At any given moment, half the population of LA is giving therapy to the other half," she said on the fourth afternoon. In a black turtleneck and high-waisted pants, she swiveled a lipstick back into its tube. "Fifty percent of LA is depressed. Only five percent of Bhutan is. You ever been here?" she asked. "The hamachi salad's yummy." She threw the lipstick into her shoulder bag and, leaning across the rope into the waiting area, hugged me like Americans do.

"No," I said.

I was pathetically delighted.

She pulled me out of line, into the restaurant. The hostess called her Roberta, gave her a kiss on each cheek and me a look of thinly concealed contempt, or maybe it was simply vague recognition.

"Hope you didn't wait too long," Bobby said, as we were seated. Truth or mockery? I couldn't tell.

"Look. No more blood!" She pointed at her stomach. "Hello, Carl!" she greeted the waiter bringing a bottle of pink wine. Two servers followed with multiple plates of colorful food.

"Cauliflower in blah sauce, sea bass with whatever, balls, like, fake, vegan balls, anorexic supermodel shrimp," Bobby narrated for my benefit. "I called in the food in advance. I hope you don't mind. Hate meeting people on an empty stomach. Hate waiting in general." Smiling, she turned to the waiter. "Is that *my* rosé? What's it called—from Puglia?"

Carl assured her that it was. "People hate rosé," she told me, "but I love it. Do you mind it?"

"I—"

"Doesn't give you as much of a headache, as long as it's a quickie, not an affair. Never date a socialist unless he's the champagne kind. Oh, hey, socialism! We're going to share all the plates!"

I smiled, barely following.

"Speaking of sharing, I couldn't park anywhere. All the spots are taken by BH housewives with BV. What about you?"

"What's BV?" I said.

"Bacterial vaginosis. A real plague in Beverly Hills, or so I'm told by Lance."

"Who's Lance?"

"My live-in biographer. A fellow Marxist. Groucho Marxist— do you know what that is? It means he won't join any club that would accept anybody as awful as he is. Oh my god, spit it! Right now!"

"What?" I said through the shrimp I'd just put in my mouth.

"Spit that shrimp out now!" She extended her hand, and I, to my shock, spat into it.

A woman, possibly with vaginosis, who had possibly taken Bobby's parking spot, looked at us archly from a neighboring table. Bobby placed the chewed-up shrimp on the edge of her plate, then reached for a fresh shrimp and ate it.

"What is wrong with shrimp?" I whispered.

"Oh, nothing. It's just you're not titrating right. You aren't *drinking* fast enough. It's crucial to have the first glass on an empty stomach." She filled my glass to the very top and raised hers to mine. "Drink! Celebrate! You were on that stretch *just* when I needed someone to save me." The universe, I would learn, was Bobby-centric. All events led indirectly or directly, via multiple improbable coincidences that did not amaze her, to her.

"What about you?" she said. "How come you were on the 101 heading into the Valley? Don't tell me you live in the Valley!"

"You know where. I live near airport," I said.

"Burbank?!"

"No."

"What are you doing in America, dear?"

"I am because I won the lottery," I explained.

She rested a shrimp tail on her plate's edge and leaned forward, attentive. "How much?"

"No. Green card lottery."

"How does that work? You pick some numbers and the balls spin and poof, you're in America, legal and all that?"

"Something like this," I said, laughing.

"Incredible. I always wanted to meet someone lucky. So far everyone I've known has been unlucky, including myself."

"I won, but I'm still poor." A blush spread through my body, blood mixing with wine, as if I'd just committed a courageous act. I was ashamed of my economic situation, but my bad English helped me be direct. Later I'd learn Americans preferred to say *low income*. But Bobby liked that I'd said *poor*. She liked to say it, too.

"My *poor* lottery winner," she said, "I'll *pour* you some wine. Poor winner, you're a poor, moronic oxymoron. I want to know everything about you."

More food arrived. She drank her wine, then mine, and the inverted bottle in the ice bucket, the missile in its silo, was replaced. She moved her chair next to mine. The room murmured around us, packaged us.

"Why is your English so good?"

"No," I said. "No." I laughed.

"So good!"

"In Poland, I was teacher. *A* teacher," I corrected myself. "Articles. I always forget."

"Articles! Don't you hate them? What kind of pedantic sadist invented articles? If articles were articles of clothing, they'd be G-strings. It was definitely a man who invented articles, some puritan who married a merkin. When I first learned English, I refused to use them, too, but then I realized articles are like accessories. And accessories *are* important——in language, in fashion, in sex. Actually, in sex, not really. Who needs toys when your guy has a big one? No, sex rarely needs an article. I want sex, not I want *a* sex. You have no idea what I'm talking about, do you?"

I laughed and nodded.

"I want *the* sex!" she announced to the room. "Now you tell me your story. You came directly from Poland to LA?"

"First I worked at *a* restaurant, then for *a* rich lady in Chicago. But she killed herself."

Bobby leaned across the table, bumping the butter dish with her breasts. "She really killed herself? Tell me more about this dead rich lady."

"Oh . . . she was ill and old."

Her mouth twitched, as if insulted by the combination. "Was she Polish?"

"Yes."

"Did she have cages with birds?"

"No."

"Parrots that said '*kurwa*' when guests came over?!"

Kurwa is the most versatile curse in the Polish language. It means just about everything rude.

"No, she had a dog," I said in English. "And he never said a word and then he killed himself, too," I finished in Polish. It was the first time I had joked about the event. To do so felt a bit like relief but a bit like betrayal, too. But whom was I betraying? Elms shading the window over the sink. The oven, obscenely open. The smell.

"His name was Kazio," I said in Polish. "He was a hairy moustache dog, you know? I found them both dead in the kitchen."

"Like Romeo and Juliet!" Bobby exclaimed. There was no mockery on her face. Later I found out she didn't hold many things sacred, except maybe her love for her husband and the connection between a woman and her dog. "Did she leave you a bag of money?"

"I don't know."

"Oh, come on. Nothing to be ashamed of!"

"What makes you think she left me any money?" I asked her in Polish, uncomfortable.

"Practice your English. Why wouldn't she leave you money? It's universal, like a love story. It *is* a love story, kind of, a platonic one.

It's Dickens but without the dick. An older, ailing, childless lady takes a liking to a poor ingenue, leaves her an unexpected fortune. But of course she didn't leave you quite enough. She donated most of it to an obscure charity."

"I used money to move from Chicago to LA. The money," I corrected myself.

"Baby!" she exclaimed, "You've been through so much. And all by yourself!" Bracelets clinking, she reached and clutched my hands. To my surprise, I felt like crying.

"This is LA," Bobby said. "Let's not be so dark anymore. Let me tell you all the unimportant things that happen here."

She traded one of my hands for her glass as she spoke, but the other remained. I was the younger foreigner, open to the local's advice. The guide beguiles the guileless.

"No, wait. I'll tell you all about my childhood."

But the story she told me was about her father. She and her mother were minor characters. Unlike mine, Bobby's childhood had been "privileged." This was rare under communism, in the eighties. Some obtained wealth but at great risk. Bobby's father's henchmen drove clandestine truckloads of Austrian products through Czechoslovakia: juices, chocolates, clothes, appliances.

"In those days," she said, "if a guy gave you a blender, you'd marry him. You'd fuck him, at least!"

I knew this but didn't. When I was born, fourteen years after Bobby, communism was five years gone.

The communists had suspected Bobby's father of being a spy. And maybe he was. He was a multitude of things: a skiing champion, a manufacturer of machines, a builder of Baltic beach hotels. An untamed alpha male who'd pulled himself out of world war poverty, who'd started, lost, and reinvented companies. His worst loss was in Transnistria. His architectural company there went under because of the war in 1992. Women hated and admired him. Bobby's mother had been his mistress for ten years, waiting patiently for him to leave his wife. Theirs was a great love story, Bobby told me several times. Bobby was a love child, a "child of sin." In Catholic kindergarten, the teachers had told her this. Child of sin, conceived before marriage.

"I'm a child of sin, too," I said in Polish, "but not of love."

She let go of my hand.

"English, dear. You need to practice. I always knew I'd go west. I mean, where else can you go but west? I wasn't going to Moscow! Though I considered it, briefly. Oh shit." Her hair was in her water glass.

She tossed her head and made a pony sound. "Even my mane came west. Hair extensions. First-class Ukrainian import. Don't you dare look at my tits! They're as real as real estate. I even tried to get rid of them once, when I was young and stupid. For months I ate nothing but cotton balls, but the tits went down only to a C. I wanted to be a model. Not like an underwear model, but a proper *fashion* model. I *love* models. They're reminders of both."

"Both what?"

"Perfection and death." She laughed, took off her rings, and placed them on the table in a semicircle. "Then I read how Maria Callas got a tapeworm and was thin forever after that, but I didn't know where to buy tapeworm eggs. I hardly know where to buy, like, hen eggs. I think I just wanted to spite my dad."

Profiteroles arrived. We ate them. She never stopped talking.

"Anyway, Sleeper *loves* my tits. I love Maria Callas."

"What do you do now?"

"I run a gallery."

"Where? I'd like to see."

She wrinkled her nose. "You can't *see* art. This isn't the twenti-eth century. Art is *invisible*."

"Invisible?"

"My gallery isn't, like, even a set of walls. It's a concept, a cura-torial vision, not an office space. So no, you can't just, like, go see it." Bobby sighed, stacked her rings back onto her fingers, leaned back. She seemed annoyed. The room had emptied, except a few tables. Lunch was over.

"This restaurant is such a cliché. To even say it's cliché is cliché. I bet you everyone here is saying just that," she said angrily. She clicked her tongue, cooed at a waiter rushing by. "Excuse me, can we have more bread? And can you tell Carl to bring the check?" From her bag she fetched a few multicolored jars, a lipstick, and a compact and lined them up on the table, began working on her face.

"Is everything okay?" I asked her. She didn't respond at first. Her attention had burst, bent inward.

"I have to ask you for a favor," she said, adding kohl to her eyes, "since you're lucky."

"What is it?"

"Will you do it?" She applied something glossy and sweet to my lips with a finger. The waiter brought bread.

"Here's my little stretch-marked lamb," she said to her wallet, giving the waiter her card.

"What favor?"

"Just tell me if you'll do something for me." She wanted my commitment before the favor was revealed. I should have under-stood this as a warning sign, but she was radiant again, bad mood forgotten, lips freshly red. She scooped more of the gloss and applied it to herself with small precise motions, an android eating synthetic fruit. My new friend. Of course I would. I put on my hat. She emptied the contents of the bread basket into her bag.

"I love this bread, don't you? And who wants to go to a grocery store, anyway."

3

The alarm went off as we went in.

"That's me! I cause alarm wherever I go," Bobby informed the sales assistant, the mannequins guarding the entrance, and the black-suited man guarding the mannequins. "I'm a Chernobyl child. Radioactive. No, *really*. When I was a kid, it exploded just five hundred miles away. I was popping iodine pills and sucking thumb. Now I pop Xanax and suck dick." She cackled.

It was the kind of store I'd never dared enter. A temple of iron and stone, a few dozen gossamer items hanging from industrial rods. The sales assistants knew immediately if you belonged. And yet it seemed I'd been mistaken for another woman, because a sales assistant—pixie haircut, blazer over naked flesh, big blocky glasses—asked, "What size, please?"

"What size?" Bobby repeated, looking at me.

"What, me?"

"Yes, if it's not too annoying. I need to buy a dress for a friend of mine, and she has your exact body type."

So this was the mysterious favor. The size of it disappointed me.

"Extra small," I said. Who was this friend, my doppelgänger, and why was Bobby buying her expensive dresses?

In a black marble fitting room larger than my apartment, I stood in my underwear. My mother had brought us up always to wear good underwear, in case of accident or death. Untidy underwear dishonored not just you but everyone. My mother cared about the priest, the doctor, the mortician. She had forgotten that before death there were other moments to disrobe before an audience. Sex, for example, or shopping.

Bobby studied my figure with unabashed focus. I didn't mind. My body was one of the few things I had to show off—you should see me now! Sixty-one years have passed, but in 2018, I was compact and composed. Arms, ass, legs, belly, hips, all neatly integrated, like an astute thought.

I stepped into the dress with a little sales assistance, a sleeveless design in braided shades of iron and stone, with a red tulle detail fanning open at the hip.

"Hot shit," Bobby noted from the geometric bench where she was perched, drinking from a bottle of complimentary Swedish water.

She was right. The dress was a passport to places you needed a password to access. I couldn't pronounce the designer's name. Poor girls from Poland, Russia, Ukraine in my generation had little to no inoculation against luxury products, communism having wiped out most hereditary wealth. We'd kill for a pair of designer shoes. My greed was childlike, tactile. I kept touching my stomach and legs in the dress, imagining Bobby's friend wearing it. How did she look, this friend?

"I don't know how many cotton balls I'd have to eat to be like you," Bobby said. "You could be a model if you weren't so average height. You're svelte! You don't even *need* a tapeworm."

Bobby was not unslim but gave a primary impression of solidity. At five foot nine, with a big ass and breasts, she dwarfed the cube on which she sat. You could imagine her climbing mountains, swimming rivers. Not that she ever would. She hated effort, considered the countryside an uncivilized place.

"It suits you."

"Thanks," I said, feeling covetous and lost.

"Is it organza?" she asked the assistant, who listed a few other fabrics. "How much?" Bobby asked.

"Nine thousand one hundred ninety-nine dollars."

"That's *ridiculous*," Bobby snarled. "Even for your store."

This was sacrilege. Bobby knew, the assistant knew, even I knew, with a knowledge that precedes experience, you weren't supposed to comment on the price. You were supposed to say a shy "Thank you, I'll think about it." Or, better, "I'll take it," preferably without having asked the price, and extend your card with suicidal bravado. Only then did you belong.

The assistant's face indicated a *faux pas* had indeed been committed.

"I bet it was still made in Bangladesh by sweatshop slaves," Bobby said. "Your employers' profit margin must be very impressive."

"All of our dresses are handmade in Italy." The assistant smoothed the material on my hip with the subdued violence of a nun. I wouldn't have been surprised if she'd pinched me.

"So you're saying your company is, like, too moral to support the desperate women of Bangladesh?" Bobby said. "These women need jobs!"

I felt awkward, a bride forgotten at a wedding.

"This dress was made in Italy," said the uncomprehending assistant, "not Bangladesh."

Bobby squatted to brush the hem. "You know, Bangladesh will soon be completely flooded. Sea levels, you know. Imagine, a whole country of dressmakers almost entirely underwater. Venice Beach will drown, too. Also Venice, Italy. Also Santa Monica. I won't miss Santa Monica. They can all float belly-up. Vietnam, parts of Thailand. Half the world will be the new Atlantis. Do you ever worry about, I don't know, a really really really big wave?"

Bobby loved disasters. How fitting that one day she herself would suddenly disappear.

I reached for the zipper on my back. "Should we go?"

The assistant approached, armed with a hanger. "Please, let me help you," she said, her voice shrill with triumph. Having not sold the dress, she'd done the next best thing—defended the honor of the brand.

I stepped out of the pool of fabric, pulled on my T-shirt.

"Hold it. We just got here," Bobby said to me. To the assistant: "There are a few things *I'd* like to try. Actually, I'd like to try every single thing in the store."

"Every single one?" A smile like a sneeze twitched the assistant's nostrils.

"Yes. You've persuaded me. This company is great. Can you help me with sizes? I'm usually a forty. A forty-four in Italy, the land of petite women packed with pasta. Oh, and please leave the dress in the fitting room. My friend's still thinking about it."

"Oh, but it's not for me," I mumbled.

Bobby stood and glared at me. She was imposing, furious. She would save nations by expanding other nations' wardrobes.

"Please show me which items you'd like to try." The sales assistant had been cowed into cordiality.

"All of them. I love them all," Bobby exclaimed with an enthusiasm that sounded somehow genuine and satirical at once.

"Well, I don't know if we have them all in *your* size," the assistant told her.

Five minutes later, the woman returned with "everything."

"Oh, and that blue suit on the mannequin." Bobby smiled. "I love it."

"That's the last one."

"All the better. I want that mannequin stripped naked." To me she spoke in Polish: "Do you want to add some coins into the meter outside and wait for me in the car?"

We'd left the restaurant in Bobby's car and parked directly in front of the store—a bit of luck that Bobby said was clearly mine, because her "parking luck is fucked." My car was probably just now getting a ticket. I'd forgotten about it, and now it was too late. The hours had rolled by, round as coins. She put a few into my hand.

"Keep the engine running," she added in Polish. "For the air-conditioning."

I didn't point out we'd been driving with the top down.

In the showroom, the guard watched the sales assistant disrobing and dismembering the mannequin. At the door, I didn't cause alarm. I'd been born years *after* Chernobyl.

Coins in the meter, I sat in the driver's seat and hesitated, wondering if I'd misunderstood her, but I turned the key in the ignition. From the stereo, a girl strummed acoustic guitar and sang in French. The street pulsed with the urgency of dusk, of people going home and out to eat, the storefront shutters rolling shut. Two men holding hands regarded an hourglass in the home décor store-front next to the boutique with Bobby inside it. The beautiful car's beautiful nose pointed west into a nosebleed of a sunset. In this moment, it was my car. Was half of LA actually depressed? If so, I realized I belonged, for the first time in a long time, to the happy half.

She emerged without apparent purchases, purse swinging from her elbow, the alarm again sounding. She waved goodbye to the sales assistant. Barely a turn of the wrist. A first lady greeting a crowd of two. The sales assistant, marionette-stiff, raised a hand. She wanted Bobby gone. The security guard nodded. I think he liked that we'd made the assistant suffer.

"Okay, let's drive." Laughing, she knocked my hat off. "Drive!"

I drove north, then east on Wilshire Boulevard. Never had I driven anything so unstained and odorless and quiet.

The car was quiet, not its owner: "One thing I won't tolerate is the tyranny of salespeople. They borrow attitude from the outra-geous prices. It's like they forget they're there just to sell shit. They didn't actually make any of it, and couldn't afford it if they wanted it, but they act like they own it and you can't afford it." Legs on the dashboard. "You're a good driver. Not like these LA somnambu-lists. Let's go to my house! I need to ask you something. This time for real. Oh, and please obey the traffic rules. Lights and whatnot. We don't want to be pulled over just now."

"Why?" I asked.

The light turned green, and my hat soared from her lap onto the road.

"Just drive. I'll get you a better one." Her flippancy made me laugh, relieved. We'd see each other again. We'd shop for hats. I drove, and the end of her ponytail whipped my face.

"Actually, can you hop onto my seat? I want to drive."

At the next red light, she put the car in park and pulled me onto her lap. The cars behind us honked. Limb by limb she wriggled out from under me. She smelled terrific—smoked vanilla, also something hard to place, a masculinity, but masculinity from a bottle, woman-made, made in some lab.

"Listen to that phony honking symphony. People need to get a life. Quick, though. We can't be pulled over!"

"Why?"

"I can only talk to cops when I'm, like, in my cups. Can't you find a better song?" She threw her phone at me.

At a yield sign, she contoured her cheekbone. I put on a playlist called "Postcoital." Others on her phone included "Hair" and "Fuck off Lance." She was unable to obey the rules. Each yellow light unleashed in her a civil war: she stomped the gas, braked, stomped the gas, braked, plummeted through the intersection, laughing. The postcoital playlist, mostly seventies British rock, propelled us up into the hills and the night.

The air by the house smelled of Bobby and jasmine and resin. We stopped at her gate. The house's hulk, punctuated by spaced-out lights, had the vagueness of an image, not an image seen but one imperfectly remembered. Shreds of words, incomprehensible, drifted down through eucalypti and the gate.

"Okay, we made it. I'm going to ask you now." She turned the engine off, dabbed with a brush at her cheek in her lit visor mirror. "I don't know what your situation is. What anyone's situation is. And what the fuck it even means, a *situation*. English is a fucked-up language." She laughed, closed the mirror. "Anyway, I know you're kind of new to, like, America, and you said you're looking for a job, and we need someone to, like, help us. Seriously, we can barely survive. Last year we didn't go to a store for, like, a month, and then we both lost our wallets, like, both at the same time, and for days we had nothing to eat, no money, no IDs. I was thinking to steal bread from those ducks in Echo Park, but I was in heels. Instead I picked prickly pears from a cactus and microwaved them. They were gross. We need someone to run errands, someone to cook something. I can cook tea in the microwave, but that's about it. I have aspirations, so far mainly theoretical. I'd like to make casserole à la normande, but will I? I doubt it. Sleeper says our household needs a wife. We're terrible, messy, awful people. Once you get to know us, you'll quit, but we can pay you a thousand a week, cash if you want, and you can live with us, and we'll feed you, if you buy the food or order it, or whatever. The house is big." She rushed through the details, never breaking eye contact. She leaned forward into the halo of the gate light. "So?"

"Yes, but . . ."

"What *but*? But what?"

"If you don't even have money for food," I said in Polish, "do you really have a thousand a week to pay me?"

"English, bitch!" She cackled. "Is that what you said to the lady with the dead dog?"

"What?"

"Your Chicago granny. Did you ask her if she could afford you?" She had closed the visor light, and now I couldn't see her eyes. Her laughter in the dark was like a question mark at the end of an affirmative sentence. "Baby, I'm just torturing you. Reciprocal torture is allowed in our house! And no pouting. You can call me 'bitch,' too."

"Okay, bitch."

She laughed again. "But seriously, we had no food. I mean, we have a few friends who own restaurants, but I wanted fresh food in the fridge. It was a shitty week. Until I remembered the cash in the wall."

"You have this in the wall?"

"Doesn't everyone? So what's the answer?"

"Yes." I laughed. "Of course I will like to work for you." So we won't be friends, I thought. Who cares. I was so happy to have found a job.

"Really? Real yes? Not a Polish yes?"

"What is a Polish yes?"

"You know how in Polish *no* means *yeah*? When an American in Poland hears us saying no, they learn we're saying yes, but then they come back here, and then it's, like, confusing during sex." She laughed her raspy, scratchy laugh again. Someone else was in there, scratching at a wall behind her laugh, trying to get out. "So it's a *yes-yes*. I was worried you'd be insulted."

"I should be?"

"Because in LA nobody ever wants to work for anyone else."

"I'm not from here."

"Of course, we've *had* assistants. But they don't work out. They're all so . . . normative, so indiscreet."

"You'll be glad with me, I promise. You're a first nice person I meet here, or anywhere."

"Really? You think that? I've never heard anyone say that before. So, the truth is, I'm not nice, really. I need you to know it."

"Okay."

"Say it."

"Say what?"

"Say 'You're not nice.'"

"You're not nice."

"Promise you won't hate me one day. I mean, I've *told* you I'm not nice, right at the beginning. You can't hold it against me later."

"I will not."

I should have run then, for her sake more than mine. Instead, I shook her cool, long, ringed hand. A transaction in the dark.

"Uff, I'm glad that's over with. One thing about me is I hate being criticized. Even by myself." She reached into her purse and slipped a metal object into my hand. "The spare key to the house. Now come meet everyone."

The house was tremendously long. A tower with a terrace jutted from one end. A front door soared from marble flagstones to the base of the mansard roof. Bobby wanted to show me the grounds. We walked under the vine-veined windows and white balconies, shoes sinking in gravel and moss.

"The house is hemophiliac," she said.

"What does it mean?"

"It leaks, it bleeds, it faints. A few years ago one of the balconies crumbled during a small earthquake, and the railing fell and crushed a rat. Or maybe it was an assistant." She clutched my shoulder. "Just kidding. Careful here. There's a plank that knocks you out if you step on it."

We crossed a little garden bridge. Below us, in the dark, the lawn blended into an algal pond, which stank of health food stores, old veggies, rotten health. Blue lilies in the sludge like frayed black suns.

"I probably shouldn't be showing you everything in the dark. But it's always the arrivals that matter. The first nights, you know? You remember those." She braided her hair as she walked.

Nooks, bowers, a tennis court with a wilted net. The house had everything; it was in the process of losing it all. She pointed out every flaw. The court was mossy. Glass doors to some lower rooms didn't close. Some windows didn't open. The sculpture in the courtyard had lost its nose out of "loyalty to glorious tradition."

She was hospitable, assigning future pleasures. A ravaged sofa stood amid the "rose garden or what's left of it." She used to nap there. I could nap there, too, drink some wine, she let me know. Was she expecting me to stay the night? I worried about my car, surely soon to be towed, down in Beverly Hills.

"You can sit here and read or whatever," she said by a bench beneath an avocado tree. "I don't read much anymore. Too hard. Each time I read something, I need to read it aloud to Sleeper. It's exhausting to be one person with two brains and bodies."

She grabbed my hand and looked at my palm, a fortune teller with no fortune to tell. A fortune squanderer. "Come. I'll show you something, but don't tell Sleeper I showed you."

Her hair, now braided, still reached nearly to her waist. It stood behind her like a second spine.

"That's it." She pointed at a little fenced-in island in the garden, a bedroom-sized plot full of broken glass, stones, bottles stuck on rods. "I'd let you in, but the gate squeaks."

"What is that?"

"Sleeper's biergarten. He goes in there to smash bottles. He works on it only when he's drunk or angry. I wouldn't go in there if I were you. You could almost call it a work of art, except he's no longer an artist." She plucked a champagne bottle from the garden path and tossed it into the enclosure, where it struck a rod and did not break.

"What is his job?"

"Retired film director."

"How old is he?"

"Sixty-nine."

"Sixty-nine?" I said, surprised.

"Yeah, thirty-nine. Practice your numbers in English! He made sure to retire before getting famous. His last film was *Death of a Sales Rep*. Of course, no sales rep would touch it." She laughed.

We came to a swimming pool of irregular shape on a travertine terrace. A few metal chairs lay on their backs along its edge.

"The guy who designed it was into surrealism. We call it Tanguy's wet dream."

I didn't ask her what she meant. I had too many questions. She was already walking off, past oak trees, up the hill.

"There's a tiny orchard, and over there a gazebo." We stood at an unlit back door to the house. "You have to be ready when you come in. The hat stand always swings toward your neck when you open this door."

"Maybe move the hat stand?"

She seemed confused by the suggestion. The stand swung. She caught it. We entered the Sleeper residence.

A storage room, a laundry room, a shadowy hall. A panel at the hall's end, printed with jungle scenes, folded open when she pushed on it. We entered a frescoed room. Giant women with tigers' eyes rode horses and hunted tigers with women's eyes.

"My Neo-Pre-Raphaelites," she said. "The painter who did it is

such a double-fisted wank—" She struggled with a cut-glass doorknob on a stained-glass door with patterns of fern and liana.

Rooms absorbed us, some furnished, some half-furnished—
seafoam sofas, rosewood credenzas, zebra rugs, mismatched dining
room chairs. One room with only a long mirror. We entered, saw
ourselves, and moved on into a room with a chessboard floor, empty other than a chair with a black dress tossed over it. Another
room had only a loveseat and a row of candles melted into the
floor. The house had a sense of adolescents having squatted there
for years, their parents, silent movie stars, having left on a PR tour
for eternity.

A pell-mell scratching, scrambling sound came from the hall
ahead. "Here comes the love of my life!" Bobby got down on all
fours.

A chestnut dachshund sprinted from a narrow archway.

It thrashed around her, licked her face. "This is Baggywrinkle
Sleeper."

I squatted and patted the velvety forehead between the dog's
paranoid eyes.

"*Dobry chłopak*," she said to him. "He doesn't speak English.
He's the only pure dog on earth. He's never been on the internet.
Hello! Where's everyone?"

"How many people live here?"

"Except for Baggy, Sleeper, and myself, just Lance."

"I don't live here. I just use the amenities," said a nasal, melancholy voice. We followed it into a dim sitting room. A man lay on
the rug, shoulders and head obscured beneath a coffee table. He
wiggled his hips and a tennis ball shot out from underneath him.

"This is Lance. Lance! Viva's our new assistant!"

Lance's large head emerged. He groped for the tennis ball and reinserted it under his buttock. "I have assbram." He wore a pastel blue robe. "Did Bobby tell you about assbram?" A hand with a coral ring floated up toward me. "Assbram, also known as assbramović, is what happens to your ass when you sit on it for weeks, like I just did when I wrote a play, or like Marina Abramović for *The Artist Is Present*."

"What is this?" I asked.

"Marina Abramović! For two months she sat on her ass at MoMA, without getting up or speaking, while people lined up to take turns sitting in a chair in front of her. She'd just stare at them, all day long. For that, she was glorified and declared a saint by the art gays, the male gays." He winked. "The populace seems to have forgotten everyone else *also* sits on their asses all day—in offices, not museums. I don't know about Marina, but I use the tennis ball to force my gluteus to relax, on the recommendation of my physical therapist, Jimmy." He leaned out from under the table and squinted through tortoiseshell glasses at me as I shook his fingertips.

"Ignore him," Bobby said.

"Hi," I said. "Nice to meet you."

The ball again shot out from under him, and Baggywrinkle ran after it.

"May I ask you for an honest appraisal of my face?" Lance said.

"What?" I was comprehending less than half of Lance's chatter.

"Yeah. What do you think of it?"

"Where's Sleeper?" Bobby said, placing her purse on an aerodynamic beige couch.

"Who knows. I want to talk about *me*," he whined.

This room, more modern than the others, still obeyed the house's odd code of nostalgia. Low chests on spindly legs, boomerang-shaped tables, bolted-together chair-pairs like seats on planes—the past's vision of the future, a retro space station, nostalgia on the moon. Lance's face, long and longing, belonged in here.

Having grown up with brothers, I knew second best to a witty response was silence.

"I'm *serious*," said Lance. "If she's going to live with us. What do you think?" Both hands pointing at himself. "Handsome, kind of, at first glance, but the handsomeness doubts itself around the chin and panics at the chest? I have no 'muscle mass.'" He made elaborate air quotes. "I'm thinking of being like everyone else and growing a beard. What do you think? I'm already Bobby's beard. I'd be a beard with a beard. *Pars pro toto.* A walking synecdoche."

"Don't pay attention to him. He's depressed. Lance, where's my husband?"

Lance pushed up his silk sleeve and presented a fragile arm for my assessment. He was one of those people who make themselves unignorable. His eyes had the slow alertness of lemurs' eyes in nature videos.

"I guess you can try sports more," I said.

"Sports more! See? She agrees with me. No attempts to save my pube of an ego. I like her." He guffawed. "Wait till you meet Sleeper," he continued. "He's like Lytton Strachey. I don't mean he's intelligent or particularly Victorian, but that his face 'enrages the common man on sight.' Apparently that was a problem for Lytton, even in a society less democratical and *far* less facially symmetrical than ours."

A tall man in another silky blue robe entered, carrying a tumbler of whiskey.

"Greetings."

"There he is." Bobby kissed him on the mouth. It was an arrogant mouth, used to accepting gifts.

"Look! Meet Viva. She's our new assistant. She's promised never to start hating me."

"Vain hope." He smiled and shook my hand. His other hand held Bobby's. "I'm Sebastian. Everybody calls me Sleeper."

"Who wants to wear pants? I'd rather just not meet new people," Lance said. "Hey, do me another favor and kick that ball my way?"

With my shoe tip, I nudged the ball out of a corner and kicked it to Lance, who put it back under a buttock.

"Sure you want to work for us?" asked Sleeper. "I wouldn't want to. I know something about it, because I've been helping myself lately, as it were."

"I want to. Thank you very much," I said, and Lance guffawed again.

"What have you done to this woman, Bobby? Did she roofie your drink?" he asked me.

"No," I said, uncertain. "I just drunk my drinks."

"I'm a drunk. You're a drunk. She's a drunk," Lance conjugated.

"*Would* you like something to drink?" Sleeper's eyes stayed on me, not exactly how a person looks at a person, more like he was reading, memorizing me. I felt like text.

"A glass of water, please," I said.

"How about a dry martini?" Sleeper said. "Thou shalt not drink what shalt not alter thy state of consciousness. Rule of the house."

Maybe he enraged men, but he was the kind of man women like. It was a quiet fact in his face, as apparent and objective as the room's expensive furniture. Availability was the issue. Some chairs were taken. Some people, like Lance, had fallen over.

I said, "Yes, please."

Sleeper stooped over a low bar and poured transparent alcohol into a crystal shaker. "Martini, the only American invention as perfect as the sonnet," he murmured, stirring with a long thin silver spoon. I sat next to Bobby on the couch.

"He's a bat," she said, holding Baggywrinkle's long ears open by their tips.

The dog leapt off her, ran past a ziggurat of books supporting a tray of tea and coffee cups and out the French doors into the dark garden.

"Make me one," Bobby whined at him as he passed me the martini. To me she said, "Do you want to show Sleeper what we got for you?"

Later, I found out she used the phrase *Do you want to* not out of politeness, but to subtly dominate. It wasn't enough to fulfill her demands. You had to *want to.*

"What do you mean?" I asked.

"The dress," she whispered, digging in her purse.

The dress flew toward me. I tried to catch it, spilling the martini on my shirt.

"Oh god," I said. "I'm sorry. I spilled."

Baggywrinkle sprinted back into the room, and Bobby barked at him.

"Sleeper will make you another martini," she said. "Now you *have* to change into the new dress. You're all wet."

"Getting ice," Sleeper said, leaving. "Let's see the dress!" he yelled from the hall.

"You bought this?!" I dabbed myself with pastel napkins she kept handing me. Then I saw the little mushroom cap of the safety tag on the hem.

She saw me looking. "Nothing two forks won't solve." She promptly gathered two forks from the tray atop the books. "Don't worry, it's not the kind with ink. The ink thing is mainly a myth, like your pee turning red in the swimming pool."

"Now you know not to swim in our pool," Lance said.

4

"You stole again." Lance seemed to approve. He'd risen and was sitting on the sofa next to Bobby. He poked one of her breasts. "You scheming slut!"

"Stealing a dress is only a misdemeanor." She stood up and lifted the dress in the air in front of me. "Plus, I didn't *really* steal it."

"Well," said Lance, "if the dress is worth more than nine hundred fifty dollars—"

"Barely!"

"—you could be charged with a felony, but whatever and well done."

"Penile code." She poked Lance in the forehead.

"Why did you steal it?" I asked.

They both looked at me as if surprised by my presence.

"Because I could afford it," Bobby said, tossing the dress over her shoulder. She collected the wet napkins from my hand and threw them onto the floor.

"What? This I don't understand."

"Baby, I could've bought it for you, but then it wouldn't be a sacrifice. It'd mean nothing." She looked at me so intensely I had to look away.

"You said it was for a friend."

"What was I supposed to say?" She was almost aggressive. "That my only friend is this here?" She threw the safety tag at Lance.

"Don't tell Sleeper," Lance told me. "He'll divorce her if she steals again."

"Well, we can't return it, can we? Like, go back and say, 'Hey! Retail bitch, we've changed our minds. We're unstealing this beautiful dress!'" Then she leaned right into my face and said, "I want *you*. To be my friend. I stole it for *you*."

So we would be friends after all? Who knows, I thought. I understood that much was hidden inside *you* and *friend*, these empty American words—Russian dolls, each emptiness containing smaller emptinesses.

So much that followed would echo this stolen dress. I would be allowed illusions of choice, of agency, only later to learn it was all a fait accompli. Sure, there is no fate, but a certain kind of woman in one's life can act a lot like fate.

I said in Polish, "But doesn't this make me complicit, kind of, in a crime?"

"I know, right? Thieves together! Thieves like us! Theft suits you!" she shrieked in Polish, shaking the dress at me. "You look different now that you know you're a criminal," she said in English. "Doesn't she, Lance? No longer so overwhelmed by, by—"

"I can lose my green card," I said in English.

"Lance will marry you! In the US, when you marry, your crimes are forgiven."

"Not quite," Lance said. I wasn't sure if he was referring to the laws or our marriage.

"Come on, I want to see it on!"

I was too excited to be frightened and too frightened to be smart. I could have left. Instead, I went into the next room and put on the dress, leaving my jeans and shirt on the floor next to the melted candles.

As I struggled with the dress, I heard Lance yelling. "Bobby stole a twenty-thousand-dollar dress, and it's all on CCTV!"

Sleeper's response was muffled.

"There was no CCTV!"

"There's always CCTV."

My older readers will remember, facial recognition software in 2018 was imperfect. You could still be recorded and not identified.

"We'll just never go to that block of Beverly Hills again! There are plenty of places it's dangerous for us to go to, like, like . . . Syria!"

"It's not next to the brunch place, is it?" Lance asked.

"Bobby," I called through the door, "can you help me?"

She came in. Like before, in the store, she wasn't simply looking—her eyes were like a man's eyes but bolder, without inhibition or propriety.

But she didn't touch me, not even on the shoulder, as she pulled the zipper.

"He's going to love it," she said.

I didn't ask who, and followed her back to the sitting room.

"You're first-rate," Sleeper said, the fresh martini in his hand. Or maybe he said, "*It's* first-rate." I would learn he never called women *cute* or *hot*.

"Isn't she?" Bobby held my hand proudly, possessively. I thought maybe she wanted to exaggerate the effect of the dress to avoid discussing the theft.

"*Boner and Clit . . .*" Lance crooned to the tune of Bardot and Gainsbourg's "Bonnie and Clyde," a song I would come to know well from both the "Postcoital" and "Fuck off Lance" playlists. He said, "Huh . . . couture really lends one a unique aura," regarding me with interest. "It almost makes you believe we're all not mechanically reproduced."

Sleeper didn't seem angry at her. I didn't know he'd never show anger in front of a guest. I was a guest tonight. Tomorrow I'd be help. Their relationship was full of witting and unwitting betrayals, but one rule was to keep a united front. Honor among married thieves.

"She steals for charity," he said to me. "Roberta Sleeper's fund for self-maintenance and general extravagance. It's nice to see her include others."

He passed me my martini.

"After all," said Lance, dry as my drink, "what's more criminal, to open a boutique or rob one?"

Bobby insisted Sleeper drive me to my car. Had she noticed I found him attractive? A sixth sense for sex. She'd had me undressed, dressed, undressed, and dressed again. I was to drive home and collect my few belongings, then drive back and move into their house that very night.

Mulholland Drive was empty, windy with desert-night cold. Sleeper laid his jacket over me. The gesture was simple, gentlemanly, and yet an additional meaning wove through the cloth: possession, sensuality. He, too, was dressing me.

"Should I put the top up?"

"No, thank you."

"Don't worry about Bobby," he said. "She's harmless, theoretically. Her talent lies in the ability to keep you right at the edge of what we used to call, in prep school, 'the abyss.'"

"What does it mean?"

"She keeps us safe from complacency, safety, seriousness, the smug self-righteousness people in LA have. She makes us misbehave, controlled misbehavior, misbehavior in a lab."

Had I been recorded on CCTV, a getaway driver? Had Bobby already cost me a green card? To see how little they worried was liberating. The more reasons they had to worry, the less they did. Or was it a contest? Who could be the blithest of the blithe?

I, too, was blithe. Blithe miles away from the sadness and frustration of the last few days. I liked that Sleeper spoke to me about her without her. He drove, and I studied his profile. The eyebrow had an ironist's peaked arch. The face of a man who had "seen it all." Quiet domination over rooms, roads, people, not through violence and imposition but ease. With equanimity, he would accept rips in reality. His wife in a party dress walking the freeway. Financial windfalls, bankruptcies. The road's spontaneous end, its reappropriation by the desert.

He looked over at me, more than once. "Sure you don't want me to put the top up?"

"No, thank you."

My first time alone with each of them was on the road. Some law of larger personalities stated they had to be encountered at high speed.

At a red light on Coldwater Canyon, he adjusted his jacket on my shoulder. Who says you can't borrow a life or steal it?

I didn't want the drive to end. By the time we had descended into Beverly Hills, I no longer felt like an uninvited guest. Bobby was right: I had already developed hints of a new attitude. A petty criminal's confidence. All lights were green, the red ones especially. We found my car. I didn't have a parking ticket.

I drove drunk, feeling sober. I packed everything but the chrysanthemums. I left them rotting in the tub.

THE
HILLS

5

Barefoot, I stood at the foot of my new bed, facing a rounded window with a shade you controlled with a button. I pressed it, unveiling a pear tree in the garden. The tree's trim shape imperfectly mirrored the woman in the lone print on my wall. Naked except for ankle socks and sneakers, she gestured with a cigarette holder at a winding stair behind her. I had a vanity, a big bed, an armoire, three little tables. Three tables seemed a lot, a decadence of surfaces. Would I have enough activities and objects to fill them?

Photographs, mostly black-and-white, leaned against the walls in the hall, as if someone had taken them down for a move but never moved. This hall also had jungle frescoes, paler than the ones downstairs, fewer animals, more Venus flytraps and women. Multiplied by multiple mirrors, I made my way toward the house's central staircase. My room was above the kitchen, in the east wing. Downstairs, in another extra living room, between two skinny sofas on a zebra rug, I found Lance in a new robe, this one neon pink, badminton racket in hand, practicing his serve.

"Hello," I said.

"Who are you?" he said. "Excuse me while I get my shuttlecock."

"I'm good, thank you," I said.

He fished what I determined was a shuttlecock out of a giant vase.

"I'm glad you're well. Who is well?" he asked. He smacked the shuttlecock against a wall.

"What?"

"Sorry, I don't recognize you. Have we met?"

I figured he was hazing me, but just in case he'd been inebriated, I said, "Viva. We met yesterday."

"Right. I remember now. You've taken off your dress. I didn't recognize you in your own bad clothes."

"Where is Bobby?" I said.

"She's doing the leafy."

"What is . . . the leafy?"

"It's when you swim in a pool full of leaves because nobody's cleaned it. There was so much wind last night. She offered me the pool-boy job at some point, but I said, 'Fuck off.' I can't pool-boy. I haven't been to rehab."

"Rehab?"

"Yes. Our pool is leafy because our pool boy's gone to rehab. Ergo, if you haven't gone to rehab, you can't be a pool boy. That's the kind of circular-jerk logic that passes for whatever here. Bobby-logic. You'll get used to it. It has the reassuring qualities of childhood, or, you know, the nightmares you get after eating a massive lamb chop. Chop, chop," he said, leading me down the hall.

"Hey there, stupids!" cried Bobby, coming through the glass

doors in a tiny gold bikini and an open brocade gown, a towel wrapped around her hair.

"Cover up, woman!" Lance closed his eyes. "I detest the abundant female form in its modern skimp."

"Viva. How was your first night?" Without makeup, her eyes looked naked and vulnerable, as if they'd forgotten all their secrets. "Do you have everything you need? Would you like some breakfast?"

"Breakfast! Do you mean to say there's breakfast today?" said Lance, brandishing his racket.

We followed Bobby, presumably toward the kitchen.

"What do you usually have for breakfast?" he asked me.

"I usually make the oatmeal or the toast," I said.

"Well, well," said Lance, "Booby and I aren't too familiar with the kitchen, but what I do feel capable of is introducing you to our condom-ments!" said Lance. "We have them all. Dijon mustard, honey mustard, jalapeño jelly, silicone jelly, edible lube, Parisian butter, tossed-salad dressing, cilantro dressing, Chinese mustard, ginger mush, lemon turd, plum jam, apricot preserve, fetus preserve, pickles and cornichons, truffle paste if the truffle pig hasn't snorted it all . . ."

The kitchen was large, pristine. Pots hung from hooks around the kitchen island. Bobby and Lance mounted barstools between the island and the window. They regarded me with expectation.

"Would you like I will make this?" I asked.

"Yes, please!"

"Me, too!" Bobby said. "I didn't want to ask. I know I hired you, but now I feel weird asking for things."

"The queen has boundaries!" Lance snickered. "Don't be fooled, Viva. Soon you'll be on your knees polishing floors."

"Don't listen to him. We do have a cleaning lady, Lana. Normally she comes twice a week, but she and my bikini waxer are on tour with their garage band right now. Make me a fried egg, too."

I located the ingredients, then boiled the water and oats. In another pan, I cracked an egg into a spot of oil.

"Wow, may I see how you scoop oats again?" Lance asked. "I love watching women in domestic environments. So comforting."

I served him a bowl with apple, nuts, and raisins.

Lance: "This is delicious!"

Bobby: "I told you she's special!"

Lance: "Homemade food!"

I looked at them to see if they were mocking me, but they ate my simple oatmeal quickly and with appetite, sitting close to each other like two obedient, hungry children. Bobby ate the egg. I didn't ask where Sleeper was, or if I should make him breakfast. I wanted to make him breakfast.

"Coffee!" Bobby yelled in Polish. Cursing, pulling at the levers of a complicated espresso machine that released steam, milk, coffee, and water from various orifices, she said in English, "I hate this machine. I have to have coffee before I can show you how to make coffee! Can coffee be one of your jobs?"

"Steve Jobs!" yelled Lance, pulling his collar up over his mouth into a makeshift turtleneck.

Caffeinated, Bobby took me back to the room where I'd modeled the dress last night. She handed me a wad of papers. "I don't know where to start, so let's start here." From the floor, she gathered another messy wad of unopened mail. "So much information! Who can read it all? Can you? Like, are there bills to be paid or ignored or whatever?"

Whatever turned out to be an ambiguous category involving

haggling over bills for services Bobby didn't remember getting, calling various front desks and saying, "My boss does not think Baggywrinkle had a doggy facial, or a shimmer spray, or . . ." Bobby, bicycle-kicking her stilettos on a sofa, would yell, "She's lying! I never ordered that!" or "I never ever called Hong Kong on that phone!" Eventually, her memory would return—"Oh, shit . . . on second thought . . ." Instead of apologizing she'd turn indignant: "God, these small-minded, petty losers!" Penitent, I dictated her credit card numbers to irate service people. I had a suspicion her objective wasn't to save money but to insert belligerence into professional transactions.

She overspent heedlessly. I carried her bags, received her packages. Sometimes weeks went by before she opened them. New boutiques, pop-ups, leather repair stores, dry cleaners, beauty treatments—I researched them all. I arranged food deliveries, triaged bags of eyeliners and lipsticks, called restaurants where Bobby thought she'd left a blazer or a credit card. I'd trawl the house and grounds in search of earrings. Handbags, beads, jeans, miniskirts, shorts, skorts—I was their shepherdess. Stockings, twisted into ropes, entangled bangles with bra straps. I spent hours untangling them.

Although the errant cleaning lady finally returned from tour and, trading microphone for mop, furiously cleaned the house, blasting Romanian pop, her efforts barely minimized the disorder. She cleaned and replaced objects where she found them. Clean broken table legs remained on tabletops, and teacups atop bookshelves. Bronze statues, dusted, were rewrapped in shearling coats. An antique Ouija board continued to haunt the ironing board. I alone had sanction to rearrange Bobby's objects. I made lists and catalogs, photographed wardrobes and storage rooms.

The only place Bobby kept perfectly neat was the shoe closet. Multitiered, with cones of light illuminating shelves, it was a museum of nights out, tipsy afternoons, appointments kept and missed. Pumps, clogs, mules, platforms, boots. I'd only ever had two pairs of shoes at once, a good pair and an everyday pair. Bobby taught me all the names and variations. Objects of worship in a reliquary. Most of them hurt your feet. It was my job to break them in for her. Agony was essential, Bobby claimed, examining the blisters her shoes left on my toes.

But my agony wasn't physical. Trying on a pair of Bobby's black-and-white calfskin boots, I felt desire to own them that was akin to lust or hunger. The discovery shocked me—the human body could be fitted into such superior, expensive forms, forms that were like a new anatomy, a new autonomy, a shell into which you remodeled and remolded yourself.

She and Sleeper went everywhere together. He often joined her for her appointments, for such trivialities as nails and hair. What man in Straconka had ever entered a nail salon with his wife? They would sit side by side for hours on their laptops, their silence the opposite of boredom and as intimate as a shared bedroom. I began to wonder whether my presence wasn't both an intrusion into that intimacy and its intensifier.

There were many "rules" in the Sleepers' house, but no one remembered them for long. One rule everyone obeyed was *spritzatura*: each dusk you had to drink a Spritz Veneziano in the hot tub.

"*Spritzatura*," Lance said, "from the Italian *sprezzatura, the art of studied nonchalance.*" His glasses fogged up, chin in bubbling water. "Not to be confused with *spazzatura*, Italian for *trash.*"

"Canadian trash!" yelled Bobby at Lance.

In the new blue bikini Bobby had bought me, spritz in hand, I joined them.

"Anything well planned that looks accidental is sprezzy," Sleeper said, making space for me on a small underwater shelf. I looked past his shoulder at boulders and other rich houses. The tub perched at the cliff's edge in a ring of laurel sumac. I could lift my hand and touch the flowers. I could drift an inch and touch him.

Of course I liked him within the safety of his position: my boss's husband. As much as they lacked the professionalism of employers, he lacked the tameness of husbands, that mild steer-like melancholy of taken men. What in other men's eyes was dormant—or torturously stealthy and therefore pathetic—was alive in his and left a stamp of sexuality on our interactions. He was not lecherous or predatory. His eyes said, casually, "You are a woman, I am a man." With gentle insolence, he seemed to both acknowledge and mock that fact. In doorways, in corridors, in the kitchen, it was a possibility, but a permanent one, not to be realized.

"Gowns with tennis shoes or dress shoes at the gym are sprezzy." Bobby stroked Baggywrinkle's chest. Standing at the tub's edge, he lapped the chlorinated water. "Neckties with robes. Girls in boyfriends' shirts. What else?"

Sleeper: "Reciting Lu Xun in the original to your Chinese friends without having mentioned you speak Chinese."

Lance: "Stealth wealth is sprezz."

Sleeper: "That depends who's doing it. If you're a public figure obviously stealthing, no sprezz."

"Having a vast but shitty vacation home is sprezzy," Bobby said. "If the building itself is nice, at least furnish it with a hodgepodge of cheap, bad furniture. You get it?" she asked me, reaching out of the tub into her crumpled robe for her vanilla cigarillos. After a puff or two, she'd let it burn between her fingers. At this rate, I thought, she'd never get cancer. Was that sprezz, too—to smoke without smoking?

"I think so," I said.

"Once she truly gets it, she'll leave you," Lance told Bobby. "You can't have sprezz and be domestic staff."

"Of course you can," said Bobby. "You, for example, could never be fully sprezzy. That's why you stick around, Sir Lanceabutt."

"Excuse me, *what*?"

"Sorry, darling. It's because of your play. To have true *sprezzatura*, you'd have to give up either writing or drinking, you *know* that. What's the rule again?"

Sleeper recited, "One can either work and be sprezzy, drink and be sprezzy, or work and drink. One cannot work, drink, and be sprezzy." He raised his spritz.

"Who says?" demanded Lance. "Not Castiglione!"

"Lance is the only person around here who does *something*," Bobby explained.

"Do I, really, though? Does dramaturgy truly count as work? I mean, I spy on you. I take some notes, I write a few lines, but I *never* get paid. I have no contract for the play, no plans to have it published or produced. I'm purely a dilettante living entirely off family and friends." Lance finished his drink, slid an ice cube into his mouth, and let it distend his cheek. "Most families appreciate the quiet dignity of failure, a kind of modern revival of the prodigal son archetype. Of course, this paradigm is only emergent in overabundant and decadent societies. Not an attitude you illegal immigrants would understand," he informed me.

"I'm not an illegal immigrant."

"I know, dear, you won the lottery. You're barely legal, as far as I'm concerned."

He smiled at me and swallowed the cube. Simply disliking him would have been too simple. He jousted with everyone. During those first weeks at their house I tried to withhold my judgments. My bad English allowed me to give multiple benefits to many doubts.

"Trash," said Bobby ambiguously. "If your family looks down on you, not sprezzy."

"Sprezz and families are antithetical anyway," Sleeper explained. "The problem with family and close friends is they know you too well. No one fully known is sprezzy."

Lance: "Well, not everyone can be lazy annuitants like you two."

"What's annuitant?" I asked.

"Disgusting individuals like Booby and Sloppy here, who live off investments."

Sleeper: "Just like the Industrial Revolution created the proletariat, the Digital Revolution is creating a new class, the useless class, one job at a time. Drivers and shop assistants go first. Then lawyers and doctors. The creatives are supposed to go last, but somehow we went first. I guess we're just ahead of the curve." He shrugged a little sadly.

"You're both ahead of the curve and touchingly behind," said Lance. "You're like the nineteenth-century aristocrats. Today, the rich are no longer supposed to be lazy. The top five rungs of society are busier than the bottom ones. The CEOs, the technocrats, the lawyers work around the clock. Those who can't get a job and those with part-time jobs are the last guardians of leisure—an average waiter today, or . . . Viva here. If we agree that free time and leisure are worth more than money, you have an objectively better life than your permanently jet-lagged, prematurely balding, ulcerated Silicon Valley CEO. Sure, you work." He looked at me intensely, without humor. "But, having spent a few weeks here, you'll admit you have lots of free time. I see you sitting around reading books, swimming. I hope you see my point. For once, I'm not trying to offend you."

"No, I think you have right," I told Lance. "I have better than CEO, but you have better than I have."

They all laughed.

"Shrewd as a shrew," Lance said. "I like her."

"No, *I* like her," Bobby groped for my hand underwater. I was thrilled by this small, ambiguous act of possession.

Lance reached into the ice bucket. "Oh, *dommage.* Um, Viva, ha, well, now that we've fraternized, would it be inappropriate to ask you to bring more ice? That's one commodity that's always missing here. It's here, then not."

"Schrödinger's ice," Sleeper said.

"Schrödinger's assistant," Lance said, as I climbed out of the tub.

I was there, I wasn't there. The pool boy was still in rehab, so I cleaned the pool, and nobody, not even Bobby, noticed. I enjoyed doing things she didn't ask me to do, and often she forgot to give me tasks, and it was up to me to keep myself occupied.

In an old T-shirt with a cartoon pelican advertising a local gourmet fish market, she dipped her toes in the water.

"Baggy!" she yelled, kicking a rotten apricot toward her dachshund, who, sniffing a turd I hadn't cleaned up yet, haughtily ignored her.

"What a boor," she said. "Do you want to take that package to the post office and then lay out?" She hopped on one leg, arms akimbo. "We need to have a serious discussion."

"Okay."

To *lay out* was a term women—especially in LA—used in the teens and twenties, before sunbathing went the way of sex and cigarettes, nitrates, plastic food containers.

"About what?" I asked.

"What does one really ever talk about? The future!" In her ratty shirt and old hat, she had a dreamy, just-awoken look, like Bardot on the cover of the *Bubble Gum* EP I'd just reshelved for the thirteenth time this month. Was this look sprezz?

When I got back, she was on the stairs in a bikini. We *laid out* in loungers on the lawn. She had me slather her in sunscreen, and it smelled like every vacation I'd never taken.

"So what's your plan?" she asked.

"What plan?"

"Well, you can't be an assistant forever."

This statement might have been distressing, had her face not looked so merry.

"Oh, I will credit my diploma here. I have to make still a few credits. So I will enroll at college."

"Yeah, sure," Bobby said, "it's good to study. So my father always said. Until you come to LA and realize there are so many other important and useful things."

"What things?"

"A huge number of things, most of them useless." She sighed and turned onto her back. I closed my eyes, but she was not so easily banished. Red-orange Bobby copies stayed against the black insides of my eyelids. "I want to achieve something but with minimum effort." She raised herself on her shoulder and drank iced tea. A slice of lemon rose and fell in the glass, a slice I'd sliced and placed there. "I want to do something that will impress Sleeper. Something of *this* era—and this era is, like, all about money. Money is the art of today. We only worship people who make loads. There are a few options for women like *us*," she continued, looking serious beneath her massive hat, and I felt a thrill of inclusion.

"You can't, like, make money just by *working*. We live in the knowledge economy. If you can't invent something, like an app or a medicine, all you have left is showing your tits on the internet. But then how tedious, how conformist, just to sell yourself! It doesn't even give you notoriety. Even if you wanted to be just a slut, some liberal librarian will inevitably call you 'sex positive,' and pretty soon everyone—except for, like, a few incels in their cells—will agree and turn you into a civil rights heroine. Blah! It's so hard to be bad nowadays."

"Slut!" came a weak cry from above. I looked up at Lance gyrating in a window, waving a sock at us.

"Anyway, I want Sleeper to be impressed." She squirted a teardrop of sunscreen and spread it on her neck, tilting her chin up.

At the mention of his name, my chest felt hot. Manzanitas sheltering the pond beyond the pool stood in their sunlit stillness. Higher up the hill, mansions looked small, uninhabited.

"Money, time. These things get spent. Lance says I still have about four years," she said, lifting her arms and looking them over. "You have more. In ten years I'll be forty-seven, slouching toward fifty. You'll be basically where I am now." She was whispering, conveying the mysteries, priestess to acolyte. "You can look toward the previous decade, but at some point your neck gets too stiff. There's, like, a brace around your neck. And no point looking back and pretending you're in your fifties when you're, like, sixty-two and no one wants to fuck you, no matter what feminists say."

It was strange. I hadn't known Bobby agonized about aging. She seemed above entropy, frozen ripe off the vine. She had been thirty since she was eighteen, she'd said many times.

"I was a feminist once, when I was younger than you, when everything was sexist. Now that everyone's a feminist, feminism's too conservative. I'm into chauvinism these days." She laughed. "The truth is, there are many things *you* need to do even before your thirties, extraordinary things, but you need money."

"I need money," I agreed.

"Yep. *Das Kapital.* I know about something that will solve your problem." She was whispering again. "I'm still learning the details. Are you up for it?"

"What is it?" I asked cautiously.

Baggywrinkle walked up to Bobby's lounger on his four-inch legs. She pulled him onto her lap and stroked his belly with her fingernails. She spread his shiny black claws on her thigh.

"Should we make key chains out of your feet?" she asked him amorously. "You like my bracelet?" she asked me in the same voice, her voice for dogs. "I always see you looking at it. Now it's yours!" She let go of the dachshund, unclasped the bracelet, and dangled it over the grass. A bribe. Baggywrinkle glanced at it, ears up.

"I can't," I said.

"Oh, don't talk like a person in a movie. You don't mind having my husband, so why not have this?" In her fingers, the bracelet slithered and turned. "Or have you not yet?"

"What?"

"Oh, stop. Don't flatter yourself! It was my idea! You're just good-looking enough for it to turn me on. Women like men other pretty women want to fuck. This is old, genetic, boringly true, something we can't control. We have to take our pleasure wherever we find it. Pleasure's limited, like all resources."

I was shocked by this blunt articulation of my desire. Was it even *my* desire? Though I was quite aware of Sleeper's attractiveness, though I had a "harmless crush" on him, I'd never come close to imagining anything might ever actually happen. Sure, I'd fantasized around the edges of it, but so vaguely—a back, a profile, a bed behind a barely open door. Her sudden opening of this possibility was violent. From behind this door came a lust that shocked me. Had she hypnotized me? A minute ago he'd been my employer, and now he was what I required—more than money, but inextricable from it, made of it and America and all this comfort. He was mine, he wasn't, and this was a violent, near-physical pain.

I kept my eyes on the pool. "I don't . . ." I could summon no appropriate verb. ". . . about your husband."

"So it hasn't happened yet," she confirmed. "Okay, that's interesting. But you're so pretty." Was this perhaps permission masquerading as dismissiveness? "Far too pretty not to have this." She rolled from her lounger and knelt by mine. Her face had a brutality, concentrated in the mouth. She raised her hand. I thought she was about to hit me.

She clasped the chain of diamonds on my wrist. Golden, scheming, she was overwhelming me again, and I flooded with love-warped hatred and resentful happiness. I could take and take and take. Her husband, jewels, clothes, ideas. It's powerful to be the giver.

"So, about *das Kapital*." On her knees, she spoke in a whispery voice. "If you do what I say, you can get a fifty-thousand-dollar nest egg."

"What egg?" I stroked a stone on my new bracelet.

Her beauty was transactional. She could've been a CEO, live streaming a sermon on fiscal deception from her garden.

"Nest egg. Fifty grand," she whispered in Polish.

"Fifty thousand dollars? It will be for me?" I said in English, failing to infuse my question with requisite sprezz. "How does this happen?"

"You have to commit to committing before I can, like, commit to telling you."

"It is illegal."

"It will be . . . neither. More than legal, but not illegal. It will be *egal*. Do you speak German? It'll be, like, neutral legally, and good for art, and therefore good for society. Art's so good for society." She snorted. "Why don't people know that?"

"I don't understand."

"It's an art world transaction, to do with my gallery. We have to go and get an object. An objet d'art."

"I thought your gallery, it doesn't exist."

"Exactly, but with this piece, it *would* exist again!"

"What is it?"

"Something stolen, new, red and blue," she chanted.

What would it feel like to steal Sleeper for a night? The thought was so physical, it was more like a sensation. I closed my eyes again. Daylight hot on my legs. On my eyelids, red, blue . . . his weight on me, his arms. How would it feel to be crushed by him?

"What is it?" I repeated.

She laughed.

"Do you know what everybody has the same here?" I said slowly, assembling the ill-fitting kit of my vocabulary. "Everyone talks about things not important all the time, never important things. Everything is joke or game."

Her eyes lingered on me with their minty detachment. She disdained "important things."

"My hair gets so tangled. Can you brush it?" She fetched a hairbrush from a basket on the grass beside her. "Be careful with Ruslana."

"Who's Ruslana?"

"My extensions." She sat on my lounger. Her oiled back, marked by the lounger's mesh, possessed the obstinacy of inanimate objects, the grid of the confessional. She removed her hat and rubber band, and blonde Ruslana fell into my hands.

"Who do you think she was? I wonder why she did it. Who knows." She switched back to Polish. "In old stories, women surrender their voice and their hair for a man. She probably sold her hair to pay for an abortion. Or a ticket to LA to become a porn star. People no longer sell themselves for love, only for a career. Except for us." Her laughter had tiny subsidiary laughters inside it, bubbles, pomegranate seeds.

I shrugged and brushed faster. The fragility of people's heads always surprises me. I counted the brushstrokes. One thousand dollars, two thousand dollars . . .

"Ouch, you're pulling," she said. "The world's unfair. That's why I want to share things a little with you." She looked at me over her shoulder. "Okay, don't be upset, you'll get frown lines. I'm going to tell you all about your nest egg, your tapeworm egg, but can you get us drinks? It's definitely an I-need-a-drink kind of story."

6

Nine years ago," she said, raising a glass of brut and cascarilla in the sun, "two men in black parkas entered the Gemälde-galerie in Berlin. What would *you* wear to rob a museum? Anyway, it was after closing hours and nobody stopped them. They somehow knew how to get in. One of them had a limp—everyone saw it on CCTV. At least that's what *Der Spiegel* says. They stole two Vermeers, two Rembrandts, and one Degas. They removed them from frames and put them into, like, waterproof containers. Apparently it took the museum people until after lunch the next day to realize the paintings were gone. Can you imagine?"

Bobby sat astride my lounger. Baggywrinkle brought her his rubber hamburger, she kicked it, and he fetched it. It struck me that I was employed, tipsy, newly in possession of some small but solid diamonds, young, in good health, listening to a crime story while watching a hot dog fetching a hamburger.

"The museum was closed that day for inventory. Then later

they scanned the footage or whatever and identified the thieves. They were, like, a zoo cage cleaner and his mommy. This giraffe-dung-shoveler's mom was actually a docent at the museum. She'd organized the heist. When questioned by the police, the museum staff could hardly remember her. They raided her apartment and found bucketfuls of bottle caps and lots of radios, all broken. She was a cat lady with no cats. She fled somewhere, they both did, maybe to Brazil. You can read about it online, of course." She kicked Baggywrinkle's burger into the pool.

"What does it have to do with us?" I asked as Baggywrinkle belly flopped in after it.

"I have this old friend who's old, Seryozha. Loves sudoku, squatted on a diamond mine when the USSR was shitting itself and now he owns the mine . . . you know, typical Russian. Once, he shot a polar bear. I told him he should cool it on the *poshlost.*" Then, strangely, she added a whole sentence in Russian.

"You speak Russian?"

"Enough to order vodka. Anyway," she switched to Polish, "two years ago, this French dude brought Seryozha a painting to repay an old debt. At first, Seryozha was amazed. Like all philistines, he loves domesticated women and thinks he loves"—she finished her drink—"Dutch baroque. Then he did some research and realized the painting he got was one of the Gemäldegalerie's missing Vermeers: *The Lady Waiting.* He thought he could sell it on the black market, until he realized you actually can't sell famous stolen works of art, because, like, almost nobody will buy them. You can't even brag about them at dinner! He's not an art thief, he's a businessman. He wanted to return it, but Frenchie had vanished. Do you *love* French bulldogs? God, I love them.

"Anyway, Seryozha called me for advice, because of my gallery stuff, you know, and I told him, 'Hide the painting for a hundred years, at room temperature, forty to sixty RH, and brush it occasionally with your bimbo's mink, and . . . ' Anyway, after showing it to some shady people, he just gave up on it. Then a month or so ago, the museum put out this reward. Like thirty-five million for the five paintings. Can you believe it? It's, like, unprecedented. I always said you were lucky."

"Me? But what do I—"

She put her hand over my mouth.

"We think it'll be at least *ten* for one Vermeer alone." She'd gone back to English. Her hand slid off my mouth onto my knee. "The museum's very strict about the deadline. It has, like, the logic of a lottery. All or nothing. And of course the person who returns it can't be the thief. You have to present a clean story that can be verified. Best not to be Russian, or so Seryozha says."

"Where the painting is now?"

"Here, in LA. With Seryozha's people. When he was abroad, he got added to the Magnitsky list. He had to leave his house in LA and all his possessions behind. And until now there was no point in bringing the painting back to Russia."

"What's Magnitsky list?"

"Oh, just this list they put rich Russian businessmen on. They don't like them to live here," she said vaguely. "We're going to use a German lawyer. Seryozha says there's a lawyer in Köln who, like, specializes in reinserting stolen works into the market. With our help, he will come up with white lies or gray lies or whatever."

I played with my new bracelet. I adored it. I would adore fifty thousand dollars even more. "Sounds great, but it also sounds illegal," I said in Polish.

"It's the opposite!" she said in English. "We're going to, like, make an illegal painting legal again. We're going to steal *The Lady* from Seryozha. Fake-steal, of course. The story has to make sense, like, perfunctorily."

"And how it will make sense?"

"It will. It will once I learn all the details. Nothing for you to worry about."

The sun was directly above us, and when she gestured, she was nearly shadowless, a puppet freed from strings, from consequences. Fifty thousand dollars was my annual wage with the Sleepers, though I didn't believe I'd stay for a year. What if I could have a whole year in my hand? I extended my hand beyond the burning aluminum edges of the lounger. It, too, had no shadow.

"They'll give me a cut," she continued, "and I'll give you a cut from my cut. A cunty cut for a cut-rate cunt, as they say in the UK." This one she laughed at loudly. "Anyway, that's that. Besides, didn't you win the lottery once? You're lucky."

"Why did he, Seryozha, ask you?" I said, to delay my response.

"Who else could he ask?"

"Anyone. Professional thief."

"That's me!"

There was some truth to it. Just last week, at a restaurant in Santa Monica, a woman had asked if we could watch her purse for a minute. As soon as she walked away, Bobby stood up and took some cash out of the purse.

"What? She had fives. I only took fives. Fives are so hard to find! You need them to tip hair-washers. And does it really *matter* when the rich steal from the rich?"

Other people's things gravitated to Bobby. Pens, soaps, lighters orbited her like a ring of debris. What was everyone's was hers. What was hers was hers and, on a whim, sometimes mine. She lifted her hat from the grass and put it on her head. From under the brim, she looked at me with confidence.

I said, "No. I will not steal it."

"Polish *no*?"

"English *no*. I will lose green card, or I will go to prison. I don't have . . . I'm not you."

I saw myself reflected in her eye, apologetic, small, a faint rip of a person in the bright rip in her iris. She blinked and stood up.

"You're not me? Really? What a profound statement. Did they teach you that at teachers' school? Boring. Whatever. I guess you're less fun than I thought." She Frisbeed her hat across the lawn, dove into the pool, and swam its length underwater.

"Did I mention that the fifty thousand is a bonus? And your participation in the de-illegalizing heist is a condition of your employment?" she said when she popped up. "No police will be involved. I don't like men in uniform. My taste is more evolved."

"No, Bobby," I objected from the lounger. "I really can't."

"Then you're fired." She swam again.

I trotted onto the travertine terrace and stood with my toes at the edge. Underwater, she passed back and forth, long-limbed, cloudy with hair. "Bobby, I can't," I repeated when she emerged for breath at the pool's opposite end, but she wasn't listening.

Ruslana in her eyes, makeup ruined, features running off into the water, she appeared demonic. "Pack up your room," she said, then dove again.

I watched my feet walk and my hands collect glasses and bottles and wrappers from the table between the loungers as if nothing had happened. Is it sprezzy to tidy up right when you're fired? Eucalypti down the hill, the bluish cypresses around the pool with Bobby in it—everything was underwater, under airless air. I carried the things toward the house. I would spite Bobby with the neatness of my departure.

From around the east wing of the house came Sleeper in a blue shirt and white slacks and no shoes, toward me as if out of some nebulous thought, a nice thought, possibly erotic, that had been there under all the other angry, anxious thoughts.

"Vivid Viva," he said. Hair tousled, shirt unbuttoned one too many. Maybe I was also coming out of one of his thoughts. "Looks heavy. Should I carry that for you?"

"No, thanks," I said, suddenly aware that all I had on was a bikini. His eyes, though, did not leave my face.

"Well, I insist. Accept my atavistic instincts."

"It's okay for you when I carry like this when you're not here."

He smiled and took it from me. When he smiled, his facial symmetry was not as alienating. It signaled mischief, in which anyone he smiled at was included. "You've articulated my hypocrisy very well."

As we walked to the house, I listened for the sound of Bobby emerging for air behind us. There was only underwater silence.

"So how is it, being here, away from your family? Lonely? Free? Both? Free but you feel a little guilty? You know this word?" He was the only one here who adjusted language for my understanding.

"I know *guilty*, this word." I thought I might be blushing.

In the kitchen, he helped me transfer glasses from the tray into the sink, and our hands didn't touch.

In my room, I packed my suitcase and, still in my bikini, sat on my bed—or someone's bed. I figured I was probably fired, but maybe she'd been joking, or she'd fired me but would soon forget she had, but I was probably fired and absolutely twenty-three and so it was delicious to be furious and wronged, in tears on my computer, looking at rentals I could afford but could no longer live in, having tasted affluence.

After an hour or two came a knock on my door. I expected Bobby with my final pay in an envelope. I opened the door. On the floor was a large pale pink box with a white ribbon.

"Hello?" I said to the sound of retreating feet.

"Delivery for the assistant!" Lance yelped from the stairs. "The center does not hold!"

In the fall and winter LA gets really cold, said the note under the ribbon. *Expecting my ~~assistant friend~~ assistant and friend at spritzatura. Or else you're fired Polka bitch!* In lieu of a signature, there was a smiley face with one eye, sporting a long, curly eyelash.

The box contained a long black coat, the kind in which you can hide and yet be seen. My relief gave way to resentment. I wasn't so easily bought, I told myself. Still, I put it on over my bikini and did some mirror posing. The bikini was last week's gift from Bobby, and only a few minutes ago, I had spitefully considered leaving it behind, unwashed, on the bed. I took the coat off and put a bathrobe over the bikini.

I could neither stay and work for this *Polka* bitch, nor simply leave unobserved. I'd attend spritzatura, be quietly scathing. Then I'd quit.

I walked downstairs and through a glass door to the lawn. Beyond the apricot trees, I saw the Sleepers in the tub. She sat in his lap, his hands on her exposed breasts.

Did they know they could be seen from here? Had I been pointedly invited to disturb their privacy? And if so, if my disturbance was expected, did I still have the power to disturb? I wanted to disturb, to slap his hands off her breasts. I snuck down the path toward the tub, conscious of gravel shifting under my feet, and they were momentarily lost behind trees.

I reached the tub and stood and watched. First, Sleeper saw me. Without haste, he let go of Bobby's breasts and took his drink. The breasts hit the water and sent rings rippling.

"Sorry," I stammered, "I don't know I—"

Sneaking down the path, I had felt forceful. Now, having intruded on a couple in an act of intimacy, I felt impotent and hardly present. Of course they hadn't planned to be seen. They had, though. I had come to punish her. But I had no experience dominating others. I was too shy. I didn't yet know that dominion can be extracted from shyness, if you subject shyness to experience, money, education. I didn't know yet that confidence was often only shyness grown old, weary, rich, informed.

"You're fired again," said Bobby in a lazy voice, rolling her bathing suit up from her waist, pulling the straps back onto her shoulders. "This time for ogling my tits."

"I didn't—"

"You did. And now you can't unsee them."

"No one can unsee them. They have a remarkable lasting power. They've outlived Western culture itself," Sleeper said, "if my news-feeds are to be believed. Hop in."

They seemed tipsier than usual. Sleeper turned to the tub-side tray and poured prosecco and cinchona bitters as an unexpectedly cool wind scattered scraps of foil off the tray, off the edge of the hill, down into Hollywood.

"It is spritzatura, no?" I asked. "Is Lance here?"

Bobby looked around. "Can't see him."

"Sorry, *pani*, we are out of ice," said Sleeper. I thought he was asking me to fetch some, but then I saw he held a spritz for me above the steam.

This was the first time he had spoken Polish to me. It meant something.

"There are these flamingos that turn pink after eating too much shrimp," Bobby said.

They watched me take my robe off and place it on a garden chair. They watched me descend the slippery stairs of the tub. Bobby's toplessness had set a challenge—a demand or a desire— for me to demand to be looked at as well.

And I got what I wanted. "You have a great ass, Viva," Bobby said.

"Bobby," said Sleeper.

"What?" She laughed, half snort, half neigh.

"Bobby has an underdeveloped inhibitory cortex. She's a human Freudian slip."

I sat on the underwater ledge across from them, and Sleeper passed me my drink.

"I'm a slip without a slip." Bobby played with her necklaces.

I was aware of Sleeper's arms, chin, cheeks. His eyes, pale brown, fluctuated. They were easygoing, present, fossilized, distant. I looked at him and looked away, trusting neither his presences nor distances. Pouting, Bobby got hot and sat on the tub's edge, as ever matter-of-factly outrageous in her shiny flesh and gold chains, drinking from a water bottle. I watched the muscles in his back as he turned to accept the bottle. I'd seen him lift weights while talking to his stockbroker on speakerphone. He did push-ups with Bobby lying on his back, her arms crossed like a corpse, a cigarillo in her mouth.

"Baby had her baptism today," Bobby said.

Sleeper: "Baptism?"

"A little test. She passed."

"What kind of test?"

"A test of will. Of resilience." Through thin steam she gazed at me with secretive intensity.

"I still might be leaving you," I said in Polish.

"Wouldn't that, though, be the most boring solution of all?" countered Bobby in Polish, then in English, "The minute I saw you on the freeway, I knew you needed saving!"

"But it was I who saved you," I said in Polish.

"So what was the test?" Sleeper asked.

"Don't tell him!" She placed her hand on my mouth. It smelled of cinchona and chlorine.

"Okay, ladies, I'd rather not know," Sleeper said. "It's okay with me."

She rolled her bathing suit back down to her waist.

"Here she goes again!" Sleeper said, taking another sip of his drink. "Now your assistant will leave you, citing sexual harassment of the indecent-exposure variety."

"No," Bobby said. "She wants me exposed. She can't wait to know everything about me." There was something innocent, almost childlike, in her reexposing herself. "Let them free, let them see," she said softly, tipsily, to Sleeper. "I think he needs an olive. Viva, can you pass the olives? Behind you." She climbed onto his lap, and he pulled her bathing suit back up.

"His hands are busy," Bobby said. "Put it in his mouth."

I held the olive. "Really?"

"*Ja*," she said, presumably in German, "put it in."

"I prefer to feed than be fed," he said.

I crossed the meter of steam between us and placed the olive carefully in his mouth, not touching his lips with my fingers.

Chewing, he said something inaudible into her ear.

"Bad Sleepy. Spit the pit." She opened her hand beneath his mouth.

Sleeper: "Another round for everyone?"

Bobby threw the pit into the grass, took my glass, and floated it in the water by his stomach. "Viva needs to drink. She's disgustingly sober."

He refilled my drink. I took it from him, and our fingers touched, barely. It was unclear what test of will I'd passed. If I'd passed by refusing to help her steal a painting, was I also expected to refuse to steal her husband?

I returned to my ledge, across from theirs. I had a new drink, new dress, new job, new home, coat, bracelet, bikini.

Bobby had a demanding look, a face that meant possession, of self and of others.

"So how did you two meet?" I said aloud.

Their lack of answer was the answer—impossibly, they had always known each other.

"At a party," Sleeper finally said. "I saw a beautiful woman sitting by herself, with a cabbage in her lap. When I asked the name of her pet, she said she had too many to count. She then told me her husband had refused to come and everyone at the party bored her to death."

"Yeah, I was going to make a cabbage salad for him. I used to cook." The tilt of her glass indicated these days were long past. "But then he got on my nerves, so I ran out and still had the cabbage, but I didn't want to leave it in the taxi, and Łyski—that's the nickname of my ex, Damian Chlebek," she explained, "because he had so much great hair . . ."

"He was Polish?" I asked.

"Indeed," said Sleeper. "Whenever Bobby mentions Łyski, I feel like having a *whiskey.*"

Bobby: "Yeah. Our marriage was on the rocks."

Łyski, pronounced *whiskey,* was apparently derived from the Polish *łysy,* which means *bald.*

"I was a bad wife then!"

Across from me, they looked a bit alike. Tall, high cheekbones, large eyes. What a beautiful couple, I thought. Why did I have to quit if I enjoyed them, being with them, so much? Her whimsicality was infecting me.

"Go sit with Viva," Bobby whined. "You're making me all hot." She pushed him out from under her.

"It didn't come naturally," he said, wading dutifully toward me. "Bobby had to practice to become a good wife. She's reformed now."

"I didn't know you were before married," I said to Bobby.

"I didn't know you were married now," she said.

"I'm not," I said as Sleeper sat beside me on my ledge.

"This handsome fellow next to you is not your husband? How did you two meet?" she asked, extending her glass to me as if it were a microphone. "I understand you've been married for only a short time." I shrugged and giggled. "You, sir. Did you like her as soon as you saw her?"

"Oh," he said into the glass, "I was what sentimentalists call *smitten.* She wore a huge martini stain and then changed into a pretty dress. There was a problem, though."

"What is that?"

"My first wife was to blame for the stain and the dress."

"You mean there are two wives?!" Bobby yelled in a faux-English accent. "It sounds you might be what they call a 'scoundrel' in the West and a 'businessman' in the East. What about you, *proszę pani*? What did you feel?"

"I don't know."

"You must've felt something!" She got off her ledge and knelt before us, water to her chin.

"He was handsome," I said. I liked this game. High on heat and alcohol, on attention, I was violently aware of Sleeper's physical person beside me. Had he wished, he could've touched me underwater. We had never been this close.

Bobby was our conductor. She floated before us, a severed head in a nest of tentacular hair. Then she surged out of the water, arms raised, yelling in her ridiculous English accent, "Handsome! Handsome, yes!" She was composite, bizarre: one-third paparazza interviewer, one-third starched aristocrat, one-third synchronized swimmer asking for applause. "Handsome how?!"

"He's like a . . . actor." I knew it was an idiotic thing to say, especially about a film director. There is, however, honesty in idiocy. Sleeper did possess more than a little of that look so popular on screens since James Dean. Billions love and hate it. Billions are made from its fragments.

He smirked and said to my profile, "I'll take it as a compliment," as if it weren't.

But Bobby was delighted by my answer. "Which actor?"

"I don't know. All, but . . . from old movies. I don't know their names." I didn't yet.

"James Dean. Montgomery Clift. Richard Burton." Her hands

grabbed our knees underwater. "By the power invested in me by the janitor of Hollywood Forever Cemetery, I declare you Richard Burton and Elizabeth Taylor. Okay, get up, you're divorced." She tried to stand up, slipped, and fell between us with a splash and shriek.

"Who's afraid of Roberta Sleeper?" Sleeper said. She went limp on his shoulder.

Her big ass had displaced me from the ledge, so I went to the other one.

"I think I drank too much." She laughed. "I'm going to be sick. Is anyone hungry?"

We were out of the tub now, laughing and tipsy and drying each other. Bobby dried my back and whispered in my ear, "You're a good negotiator."

"What?" I whispered back.

Sleeper, on the far side of the tub, tied a towel around his hips.

"How about instead of fifty," she whispered in Polish, "you can have a hundred thousand? What do you say, baby, one hundred thousand for your little dowry? No bride could say no to that."

Before I could speak, she was giggling, yelling, "Sleepy, I can't walk! Piggyback your pig bride to the pig bed!"

And I watched them lurch away, a hunched, two-headed, swooning beast, behind the apricot trees, past the gazebo, into the house.

7

I imagined holding a small piece of the stolen painting in my hand—my cut, a square of canvas worth a hundred thousand dollars, a ticket to the "American dream" the Sleepers and Lance were always mocking, a small cut of American prosperity in Baroque colors.

I researched the Gemäldegalerie robbery. Bobby had told the truth about the working-class mother and son robbing the museum. They'd never been caught, but their photos online had the severity and implied dishonor of mug shots. After further study, their faces, probably via proximity to stolen Rembrandts, Degases, and Vermeers, carried a taint of sophistication. I knew nothing about art, though, and when I looked at the painting Bobby wanted us to "rescue," I thought mainly of the huge reward. My promised piece would be enough to start *investing*. When his office door was open, I'd see Sleeper leaning on his desk, saying words like *asset allocation* and *risk analysis* into his speakerphone. *ROI* was written on documents on his desk. When I asked Lance what it meant, he said, "Oh, that means *king* in French, why?"

My nonfiduciary fantasies were simpler. I imagined entering their room, standing by the bed. She's on top of him, her hair everywhere. She looks over her shoulder at me, indignant, interrupted. He's just a shape underneath. His arm extends toward me. Her face in its halo of crazy gold hair is roughly rendered, faces from Vermeers and from her jungle frescoes superimposing themselves onto hers; then it's my face on her neck. I'm a young witch, riding a jaguar. He says something graphic and demanding. Then I come and fall asleep.

They were gone in the morning—to Catalina Island, Lance informed me.

Two nights later, well after midnight, a crash of glass woke me. Nights here were quiet, except when Sleeper smashed bottles in his biergarten, but this crash had come from inside the house.

I felt the wall above the bed to find the light switch. I moved slowly, the house's least important person. Cracking open my door, I listened into the hall. I approached the stairs and heard whispers below.

Sometimes there were men at night. Sometimes shirtless, one time naked. Lance met them on apps. I learned to dodge them with a polite nod. One had asked me for directions to the bathroom.

From the middle landing, I looked down into the foyer. In a pair of Sleeper's boxers and one of his old sweaters, Bobby was whispering in a man's ear. Much taller than she, he held a broken vase, the brain-shaped one that lived on the table by the bottom step. He had long hair, large hands, the kind I associated with men at ski slopes and sports rental shops, hands that handle ropes, backpacks,

acrophobic vacationers. I couldn't see his face. He passed the vase
to Bobby, gripped her shoulders.

"It was my sleeve that did it . . ." he was saying—in Polish, to
my surprise. "Come on, you know I didn't come here—" The rest
was muffled.

"I don't care," she said in Polish, shrugging out of his hands
and placing the vase back on its table. "Take whatever, but you
have to go."

"*Kobieto*, Robcia, I'm telling you, it was an accident. I'll pay for
it. Even though that was a gift for our wedding, I'll pay for it."

"It's an Ina Levi-Ono, you cave dweller. You could never pay for
it. It's from my gallery." She bit her nails.

"You have a gallery? You mean that shithole in Van Nuys that's
now a karate studio?"

"How many times have I told you, you can't just come in here!"
She paced back and forth by the door. He scratched at his unbuttoned shirt, revealing a wild streak of blond on his stomach.

"I thought you'd be awake," he said. "You never used to sleep all
night. Party girl! Let's party!"

On the chessboard floor, they had the forlorn quality of two
last pieces, the game nearly over. He transferred his weight from
one foot to another, as if rehearsing his departure and deciding
against it.

"How did you get in again anyway? Did you break a window,
stupid?" I'd never heard Bobby speak Polish at such length.

"Latch on the back door, stupid," he said. "Gotta be careful,
house like yours. Last week a dude came into this chick's house
and shot the chick's dude while the chick was at lunch." This was
the tangled, slangy Polish of poor suburbs, of graffiti, combat boots,
glue sniffers, soccer hooligans. "Happened right on Vine," he said.

"My friend's dude's guitarist knows the chick. She found him in piss and blood when she came home with bagels. Now she talks to his ghost."

"You can't keep breaking in. It's not your house, you know." She was mature and stern, yet she tousled his hair.

"If I crawled under one of those tables and slept twelve hours, you'd never notice."

"Can you leave now?" She patted his head. "Can you *please* leave? You're going to wake up everyone."

"Your dude ever build anything? Doesn't seem like a dude who is good with his hands."

"If you don't leave now—" She saw me. "Viva."

"Is everything okay?" I sensed I'd better speak English.

"Has he built a house?" the man demanded as I came downstairs. "You know I've built a house? A small house in Istebna, in the forest."

Bobby pulled me to her, arm around my waist. She used me as a shield. "We need to get him out," she said.

"Introduce me!" he squawked in Polish.

"Keep your voice down, drunky."

"Me? You're always drunk." He turned to me, pointing at her with a gnarly thumb, and spoke, mostly in English: "This *kobieta* can outdrink a Slovak. Ever tried to outdrink her? Lock her up in a room with a bottle, see who's upright at the end. Upright? Walking on the ceiling. Hair sweeping the floor." He bent and brushed the floor, then looked at me and said, "Who are you anyway?" Up close, he was more or less handsome, blond, physically massive, his face made stubborn by a slight underbite.

"Out, out, out." She let me go and pushed him toward the door.

He took two steps, stopped, then tripped over a standing lamp, which fell loudly, yanking its plug from the wall, and the door opened.

Sleeper entered. Pale slacks, caramel jacket, car keys in hand. Where was he returning from, so late at night?

"Łyski," Sleeper said. "Whatcha doing here, old chap?"

So this was Bobby's ex. "The man of the house!" he boomed at Sleeper. "Question for you, man. You ever planted a tree?"

"No. I once invested in an orchard," Sleeper said, removing Bobby's hand from Łyski's arm, then greeting me with a tiny, chaste pat on the shoulder. "Good investment but illiquid."

"How about a hug?" said Łyski. "Friends meet in the woods in the middle of the night!"

He embraced Sleeper and laid his head on Sleeper's shoulder. There was something awful about this, and Sleeper's stiffness suggested he agreed. No one spoke. They stood like exhausted boxers waiting for the referee to separate them, Łyski clinging in bitter mock love, Sleeper frowning, averting his face. He spoke softly to Łyski. I couldn't make the words out. He was half a head shorter than Łyski, but there was a nimble solidity to him, a physical promise—he could dance, fight. Above him, Łyski's bulk, his slope-shouldered unsteadiness, also suggested combat, but not as a dance, just thuds and thumps and headbutts. I could see the two of them through Bobby's eyes, through eyes of sexual selection. I was also making a selection. Where Sleeper had touched my shoulder, I now felt Bobby's hand.

A bark from the staircase. Lance stood on the landing, Baggy-wrinkle wriggling in his arms.

"Man, I broke your vase. *My* vase . . ." Łyski was saying. "What's yours is mine. What's yours was mine. Be a good host, man. Don't throw me out." Łyski stumbled, whistled. For a second I thought he was going to vomit on the floor.

"Come on, comedian," Sleeper said, almost pleasantly, pulling Łyski slowly toward the door. "The sad thing is, if you break in again, I'm going to have to file a restraining order. And that'll be a pain for everyone. So how about you fuck off for a year or two, and if you've been a good boy, you can make an appointment to visit us in the future?"

"Why hast thou forsaken me?!" Łyski bellowed in biblical Polish.

"Come on, have a little dignity." Sleeper buttoned Łyski's shirt. "Just a bit."

"Tell your sugar daddy to stop trying to get me naked!" Łyski yelled at Bobby, though he let Sleeper maneuver him toward the door.

I looked at Bobby. Her expression was so strange, so disappointed—like a little girl counting presents and finding the number unsatisfactory—but so pure, so sweet that I felt sudden affection for her.

"Łyski tried to kiss me!" she blurted.

He hadn't, not while I was present. The men stopped in the open doorway.

"Did you try to kiss my wife?"

"I didn't try to kiss that *szmata*. Why would I try? We're divorced. Who wants chicken when you can have steak?"

The men made the doorframe look frail. It couldn't contain them. There was, in the air, not an actual smell, but that masculine tang you sometimes feel in crowded bars. Sleeper's face, tense with territoriality, was very close to Łyski's stubborn face.

Then Bobby laughed her scratchy laugh. "Oh, guys. I was *jok-*

ing! He wasn't trying to kiss me, he was just sniffing his upper lip, like, snorting it. Don't overdose on your upper lip, Łyski! *Adieu*, idiot!" She let go of me and stomped up the stairs, sneering in passing at Lance, who asked her if she had a Xanax.

"I'm going to call a car for you," said Sleeper, pulling out his phone. "You're too drunk to drive. But pick your car up by noon tomorrow or I'll have it towed. And when you come, don't ring the gate. You're banned for two years, got it?"

"Don't believe her when she says she loves you," Łyski told him.

Later, Lance and I walked laps around the lawn, watching Baggywrinkle dig a hole. I couldn't sleep, neither could Baggywrinkle, neither could Lance.

"It was nice to see that drunken piece of shit," said Lance. "Reminded me of the old party days, the drama days." Lance retied his robe.

The first few cars proceeded down the hill. Who drives down from the Hollywood Hills at five a.m.? Cinematographers, doctors?

We crossed the bridge, through the stink of the pond.

"Bobby has inexplicable power over hetero males. It goes beyond mere tits and ass. Poor Łyski can't get over her. If he comes back, or should I say *when* he comes back, there's going to be fisticuffs and blood and men in uniform."

We stopped by the gate of Sleeper's biergarten. Raw early light transformed the rectangle of trash into a garden on a different planet, where plants arose from melted sand—jagged roses, translucent and delicate.

"Why did Bobby say he tried to kiss her when he didn't?" I said.

"She wants men to fight for her," Lance said, reaching over the fence to peel a label off an old Chablis. "Normally, she's a perfect wife for Sleeper. But she's also a sleeper agent for the Committee of Chaos and Marital Disorder, all blow jobs and affections until she's woken up, you know, activated."

"What is sleeper agent?"

"Oh, that's espionage talk for an undercover agent who's dormant in a foreign country until she's 'woken' by her sponsors and becomes an active asset. In Bobby's case, she's woken monthly by Estrogen Esquire and causes havoc. Needs an endless climax, a continuous replaying of hetero melodramatics. Toxically feminine, so to speak. Łyski thinks he didn't get enough in the divorce, and now and then he has twenty beers and remembers that Bobby 'owes him' and comes snooping around the house. Occasionally he steals a thing and two, usually worthless. The house is all brick and bric-a-brac, with an occasional Braque. What does love have to do with marriage?" Lance continued. "What do I *really* know about my straight friends? I'm just Bobby's depressed gay friend. I'm 'the gay friend.' How fucking typical is that? I'm like the sick aunt in a Bergman film, the fairy godmother . . . just a dragqueenfly."

He strolled off into darkness under the acacias. Above the terrace, in the tower window, the curtain distended and curled outward. Were they up there fighting? Had they fallen asleep?

"I once crossed the Mexican border in this trunk," said Bobby as I padded the trunk of her car with pillows and pelts. "It wasn't as bad as you'd think."

"Why you were in the trunk?"

"Just some visa bullshit. Did you pack the wigs?" She was excited. I could tell from the subdued way she spoke.

"Wigs." I pointed at two plastic bags in the back seat.

We told the boys we were off to try a new Pilates class. The plan was to drive instead to a restaurant and change there. "We can't risk Lance and Sleeper asking why we're dressed like French queens," she'd explained.

"Why it is a costume party?" I asked as I shut the trunk.

"I have no idea. You know, they're Russians." She got into the driver's seat. In black spandex, her braid pinned to her head, a mangled cigarillo in her mouth, she did look like someone who'd sneak into a home through a window.

"How do you know the Russian who wants that you will fake-steal for him? This . . . Seryozha?" I settled next to her.

We drove out the gate, into the canyon.

"How does anyone know anyone? People just appear one day, in the living room, at the table, in the pool, in bed. Who knows where they come from? Seryozha's reliable. A good skier. We did some black diamonds at Cortina d'Ampezzo together."

"In Russia, doesn't having a diamond mine basically mean you're mafia?" I asked in Polish, a question that had been on my mind for a while.

"Yes and no," said Bobby. "You know, in Poland, no division between church and state. In Russia, no division between mafia and business. In the US, entertainment and reality. Only people without brains think the world's all black-and-white. You're not still worried about legalities?" Messing with her hair and phone, she crossed a double line and pulled onto the 101. "Are you? I already told you we're returning the painting through a lawyer, so it's *legal*. We just fake-steal it from people who are inviting us to steal it, got it? Look, even the queen of England had offshore investments. Panama bananas and all that." She tossed her phone into my lap. "All money's dirty. In a way, we're cleaning it. Everything's upside-down these days. Everything's mixed up. The Roaring Twenties are right around the corner again. Burn, motherfuckers!" Bobby flicked her cigarillo stub out of the car onto an island full of dry grass.

"And the Russian, he has promised you a million?" I confirmed for the eleventh time, as Bobby's stories tended to be mutable.

"Well," she said, taking the exit into Hollywood. "Never trust men's promises. Cliché but true! Unless it's Sleepy, of course. You can trust him." Oblivious to horns, she forced her way through two lanes of cars, over a curb, into a parking lot. "Now, since we have only *one* of the stolen paintings, we won't be getting all of the thirty-five-million reward. Seryozha thinks he'll get ten million for just the Vermeer. He had, like, someone who knows someone who knows someone on the inside confirm it or something. And anyway, I want to be a curator again."

"For the gallery that doesn't exist," I said.

"You're starting to finally understand," she said, flipping off another driver, parking in a loading zone. In dark shopwindows, mannequins posed naked, as if undressed for the night.

We entered a French restaurant, yellow walls busy with unflattering photographs of customers, famous and obscure. Red noses, red eyes, double chins, big smiles. We crossed the dining room and Bobby approached the owner, Bastien, by the swinging kitchen doors.

"Bobbi-ee, *ça va?*" He waved his hands around like French and Italian guys do. Did we want some *soupe à l'oignon?* Some French French fries?

In a powder room adjacent to the toilets, costumes spread on plush chairs, we transformed. In a bra, in a gilt mirror, with a feathery brush, Bobby drew a mole on her chin, then one on mine. She called it a *mouche*.

"I'm not into Marie Antoinette," she said. "Nobody knows this, but she wasn't even crowned."

Crinoline, face powder, tall white wigs. A woman emerged from a stall, staring as we hurried out.

"I'd be more comfortable stealing without this wedding cake on my head," Bobby said, as we left the restaurant. "But it must be done. Let them eat snatch."

She turned the car on, lurched out of the lot, her wig flying into the street. "Fuck, there it goes!" She slammed on the brakes. "Baby, go get my wig."

"Okay, but you said it wasn't stealing," I said, opening my door and gathering my petticoats.

"It's not." She laughed. "You're such a bore. Do I seem like a person who could rob someone who doesn't wish to be robbed? Okay, here is the official story we'll tell anyone who might ask, including the museum people and the German police!" she shouted for anyone to hear as I retrieved the wig.

"Official version: One night I went to a party full of film people and saw this famous painting on the wall. Being a gallerist, I recognized it as *The Lady Waiting*. Being drunk and irresponsible, a typical LA bimbo—I am one, wouldn't you say? Who can deny it? Say '*ja*,' like you're a German policewoman."

I fashioned my face into my best impression of a German policewoman and said, "*Ja*."

"So, I snatched the painting off the wall and snuck out." Bobby sped onto Hollywood Boulevard. "I'd heard about the reward, *und so* I've brought it to you here in Germany."

"We're going to Germany?" I held on to my door handle as she whipped us around a stopped bus.

"*Ja wohl*. Seryozha has a minion who works at the airport or something. Don't worry about it. Anyway, the official story is, I put the Vermeer in my suitcase, with my heels and my dildo-slash-hair-curler, and stupidly checked it in baggage. And it went through!" She let go of the steering wheel. The car veered toward the curb. "What do you think? Unlikely, maybe, but not impossible. That's all that matters. The museum people want the painting back at all costs, or they wouldn't have put out the reward. There'll be no mention of Seryozha either. The house where the party is tonight is owned by an SPC in Dubai owned by an SPV in Malta and . . ."

She talked and talked as we sped west on Hollywood, along what Bobby called the *Walk of Shame*, the trinkets glittering on display tables, stars in the sidewalks flying by. People in line for musicals. Kitsch brings the dead back to life. Embraced by an Elvis, a woman with varicose veins and a visor wept.

"Home of the best-looking homeless." Bobby pointed at some people in a bus stop shelter, sitting atop newish-looking sleeping bags, drinking beers. "Out-of-work actors, evicted last week. Good abs, white teeth."

"Put your helmet on!" the song on the stereo advised us.

We continued on Sunset toward the sunset, and soon it was dark. The farther west we drove, the fewer people, fewer restaurants. The boulevard became impersonal and lush. We took turns and U-turns. We were in the quiet, cliffy streets of the Pacific Palisades.

"Hang on. I thought I knew where it was, but let's ask." She typed the address into her phone.

Following prompts, we drove left, right, left, right again. Palms, houses, driveways, the Pacific, porch lights, white window frames ...

"Shut up, you cyborg bitch!" Bobby screamed at her phone, but we had reached our destination. Bobby parked in a gardenia-scented cul-de-sac.

"There's something wrong!" wailed the song. She turned off the car, and the astronaut floated off into the outer space beyond the end of songs. Crickets filled the sudden silence.

"Okay, put your helmet on," she said.

We put on our wigs.

In a dramatic whisper, Bobby said, "I feel like, when you watch shitty spy shows, they always, *always* know exactly where to go in foreign cities. Even in, like, Istanbul! Real spies use mappy apps."

The moon above the city glow looked artificial. Her large powdered face had some of the moon's sick yellow, and I felt sick with fear, not of anything immediate or familiar, but of some unearthly trouble, something not yet known, not yet imagined, a moonquake during a moon landing.

"Ready?" Bobby took my hand. The rings under her long white gloves had the appearance of swollen joints. "We need to return *The Lady* to humanity. Don't you love humanity?" We stepped out of the car.

I didn't dare ask which house it was. I'd expected a mansion with columns and limousines slinking around a fountain. The houses on this street were nice but understated, medium-sized, where doctors or lawyers might live. Their normalcy underscored the night's uncanny quality. The stucco house Bobby approached was one of the smallest on the street. There was indeed one limousine out front, a pair of fishnetted legs extending from its back door. Two large men smoked on a balcony. One had on a hat with triceratops horns. They laughed and spoke loud Russian.

"I thought there'd be no Russians here," I whispered.

These Russians, bulky muscles jammed into tiny T-shirts, fit a certain pan-Slavic stereotype, only too familiar to a pair of *Polka* bitches. They belonged to a world of spray-painted vulgarities, cars stripped for parts, dislocated jaws, corner liquor stores you learned to avoid. I began to feel a sort of psychic nausea, a feeling of my own provincial origins tracking me down in this cul-de-sac, a scenario from my own forked future—as if my own thuggish brothers, fully grown into petty criminals, had come to visit me in California. Were those *my* future legs, sticking out of the limo?

"I told you," she said, interpreting my queasy face in her own way, "good parties no longer exist. A good party is a myth from the past." She extracted a receipt from her bra, on which were notes in pink ink as well as something like a scribbled map.

"Gh-urls! You want drinks?!" Triceratops yelled down to us, waving from the balcony.

"Ignore them." She refolded the receipt.

"*Suka blyat,*" the hornless Russian said and spat.

The spittle landed in our path, was wiped away by Bobby's dragging skirt.

"Don't talk to anyone, don't look at anyone. If someone speaks to you, pretend you're mute. It shouldn't be hard for you." She pulled a rope and a wooden gate swung open. We walked down a narrow path between the house and a fence. On an inverted bucket, a man with a shaved head and bruised knuckles played a game on his phone. A bow on my skirt brushed his shoulder.

Nurses, witches, discount superheroes drifted in a dim room. The music was French rap. Tables and chairs had been pushed aside to clear space for dancing. No one was, except for one guy in a beanie performing some mediocre breakdance moves. A woman in a tiara and pink elastic stood above him, offering advice: "You suck! You suck!"

Bobby headed for the stairs. Someone behind us yelled, "Get off my pony, *suka*!" "Fucking film him licking it!" someone else was shouting.

Upstairs, two doors faced two doors. Bobby consulted her crumpled map and turned the handle of the first door on her right.

"It's on the wall next to the closet," she said. "Do you see a closet?"

An open window failed to dilute the smell of sweat, smoke, and pine air freshener. She squeezed past an unfolded sofa jammed with crumpled sheets, dirty socks, ketchup-stained plastic plates, and video game consoles. All the room needed was a Vermeer. Cardboard boxes and hoodies and jeans made the floor hard to navigate in our high heels. Behind a closed door, a toilet flushed.

"There's someone," I whispered.

"It's okay. Remember, we're just *fake*-stealing."

There's no painting, I realized, looking at us in our eighteenth-century dresses, bell-jar shapes distended in the belly of an ancient tube TV. Through the bathroom door, we heard the buzzing of an electric razor.

"There's no painting," I said. "Why are we here really?" I was watching myself saying this, a shadow of a queen, star of a film that plays only on screens that are off.

"Oh fuck, there it is!" Marionette-like, Roberta Sleeper as Marie Antoinette pivoted and disappeared from the darkened screen.

I turned and teetered after her, clutching my crinoline. Inside the walk-in closet, under a hanging puffer, propped against an empty hand-dryer box—TRAPS 99% OF AIRBORNE BACTERIA! promised the box—stood a painting inside a gilded frame. A muslin sheet lay crumpled at its base.

"It is it?" I marveled, moving closer.

She was on her knees, cooing, as if at a feral cat. She mostly blocked my view. The painting was less than a meter tall. She could easily have carried it herself. Cooing, whispering, hand on the frame, she was engaged in something like a ritual adoration.

Running water now replaced the buzzing from the bathroom. Nervous and excluded, I stepped over an ironing board by Bobby's side. The painting portrayed a woman in an old-fashioned dress— a simple dress, not from Versailles, and yet seeing Bobby on her knees before it in her own old-fashioned dress, I almost proclaimed, "It's not a painting, it's a mirror!" But I didn't yet possess the confidence to be interesting, to believe in Viva in America, whoever that was. I was beginning to believe in the painting. There it was.

"We have to be so, so careful. It's precious," she whispered. To Bobby, nothing was precious, no object irreplaceable. "Let's go."

She put the painting in my hands, covering it loosely with the muslin, lifting my skirt so I wouldn't trip, and we trundled out of the cluttered room. My hands felt weak and numb, the frame sharp, and the painting frighteningly fragile.

On the stairs, the muslin slipped off. Bobby didn't pick it up, never let go of my skirt. No one questioned us, no one hit on us, insulted us, or offered help. In the front hall, a nurse and a witch traded celebrity gossip. On the strip of grass by the side of the house, the man with the bruised knuckles used a match to clean the tread of his shoe. It was probably mud, but it looked like shit.

At the car she said, "I don't think there's, like, anyone else on earth doing what we're doing right now." Then she started laughing crazily. We placed *The Lady* in the trunk, wrapped in the clean towels and Bubble Wrap.

"Of course, you can't *own* a painting," she said between cackles. "You can, like, physically own it, until it outlives you. Like, right now *I* own it. But who even *sees* a painting these days? We go to museums, our feet hurt, our minds get blurry. We look at each one for less than ten seconds." She gazed at the Bubble Wrapped thing in the trunk with glowing pride of ownership.

"Should we now go and talk after?" I suggested, scoping the house to see if anyone had followed us. A quiet street, no people, streetlamps golden inside crowns of trees, the limo. The legs were gone. We got into Bobby's car and didn't close the top. Electric wires in skeins and tangles flew by overhead.

In her white wig, white powder, scarlet blush, Bobby was a figure from a pre-electric era, from a bad dream about mirrors in museums, old mirrors that once held candlelit courtesans and irascible queens. Burning palaces, rolling heads. She chattered at me as she drove, about value and valuelessness. Faux Marie at the wheel, uncrowned. Real Vermeer in the trunk, really stolen.

8

The safe, located in the walk-in shoe closet off Bobby's "boudoir"—not to be confused with her bedroom, which was in the tower she shared with Sleeper—was wide open, jammed with a massacre of Bobby's lingerie. She clawed the lingerie out of the safe and studied the empty confines.

"*Kurwa!* Look. The opening's too small," she said. "And now I'm exhausted. Put it down for a minute. Let's just look at it."

I propped the painting against a wall, beside a knee-high regiment of leather boots.

"Do you want to get us some champagne?" she said. "And don't wake anyone. After last night, they went to bed early."

The night before this one, we'd stayed up till first light watching Godard films, Lance and Bobby providing so much rambunctious commentary and alternative subtitling that I didn't understand what the films were about. People robbed people, drank coffee in dark sunglasses, fomented communism, lay on their bellies and asked if their asses looked nice.

The house was quiet. No sound from the Sleepers' tower or Lance's room at the end of the hall. Without turning on lights, I crept downstairs to the kitchen. I always kept a bottle in the fridge, because we celebrated often. There was rarely anything to celebrate.

When I returned with the bottle and glasses, Bobby lay in her underwear on the closet's carpeted floor. Her dress had been tossed into the ranks of pumps.

"That dress is so uncomfortable," she said. "I'd have been a shitty eighteenth-century influencer. Take yours off, too. Somehow I can't imagine *her* naked."

In the painting, the woman gazed at her hands. Clustered reddish fruit, like a coral reef, decorated a silvery plate by her elbow. She sat by a window, which let in a wintry light, imbuing the folds of black fabric in the foreground, a coat or a shroud, with traces of blue. Her face had a dreamy suspension to it, an oblivion.

As I took off my dress, Bobby held the champagne between her knees. She peeled the foil, popped the cork.

"No, sit with me," she said. "Here on the floor."

I sat cross-legged by her side. She ran a fingernail along the imprint the dress's zipper had left on my side.

"You have a zipper viper. Its tail's on your hip, and its mouth's in your armpit."

"It tickles."

She moved her hand away. I poured champagne.

"You did *so well* today. Sleeper will be so impressed. Why are you looking at her? Look at me. Drink your champagne." She reached for my glass and pushed it toward my face. Despite her compliments, she didn't seem impressed with me. Her face had that hungry look again, as if her environment weren't enough to satisfy her appetites.

"It's good," I said.

"You should never discuss wine or champagne. Just drink it in silence." Under her gaze, I finished my glass. "Just joking. Speak. Extemporize!"

She poured me another. I finished that, too. If I tilted my head, I could see, in both opposing mirrors in the closet, Bobby and the painting snaking off into an infinite regress of lazing Bobbies and ladies waiting.

"Has he still not?" She took my glass, put it aside, held my chin, and examined my lips. "Poor baby. How could he treat you like that? I know what you're going through. I remember when Łyski invited Sleeper to a party at our house. We lived by the ocean then, in a little blue bungalow way down almost in Redondo. Midway through the party, I told Sleeper he had to come out back with me, to where we kept the wine, because I needed help carrying bottles."

I rested on one elbow, listening to a story like a child.

"He wore a blue shirt. I could hear the waves. Everything was blue and wavy. I was hoping he'd kiss me, but he didn't. I would've given my life for him to kiss me. I would've sold out my whole family and Łyski, shot them each in the head. People don't believe this kind of feeling can exist."

She drew a circle with her finger on my stomach, like a surgeon preparing an operation.

"They hate you for it. Łyski will always hate me, forever-always." It was the first time she'd mentioned Łyski since his late-night visit.

Her fingers slipped into my bra. Her touch on my nipple was practiced, dismissive—a woman about to trim a wick on a candle.

"Later," she said, "when we kissed, like this—" She leaned over and kissed me.

Her kisses were more violent than the kisses of the men I'd kissed but delicately violent. When you kiss a man, you know his goal. But this kiss, missing the primeval desperation of the male, was sorcerous, without projection or trajectory, entirely focused on its own disturbing power. Her face a blur, she smelled of powder, of our rented costumes.

"Don't peek or you'll know it's me. Close your eyes! Pretend I'm my husband, you little thief." She put her tongue back in my mouth, took it out. "Later," she whispered, "he told me he knew I'd wanted to kiss him, out behind my bungalow. But he purposefully didn't. He told me he liked us being on the *precipice of kiss*. He wanted to, like, extend the precipice. The edges of experiences interest him. He hates certainties, plateaus." Her hands were on my belly, my hips. She'd started rolling down my underwear. "The problem is, there are almost no experiences left worth having. They've all been *had* by everyone already."

I was tipsy, still a little hyper from our heist. Within this feeling lived its paralyzing opposite—a weakness that spread through my legs as my underwear and her fingers slid down.

"What are you doing?" I barely said.

"I'm about to give you some fourth-rate cunnilingus. Do you mind?" She pushed me onto my back and my knees open.

Younger readers, don't be disgusted! Understand that fashions change. Oral sex might have had a very brief heyday (1965–2031) in the grand scheme of centuries, but it was never more fashionable than in 2018. When someone said "She licked my pussy," almost no one made a gagging sound.

So she licked my pussy, very unexpectedly. And yet it was, apparently, for her, a natural reaction to the day's events or to some buildup I had missed or understated to myself over the last few weeks. Amazing how misaligned experiences can be, even among people sharing a house. I let her do it. It was easier to submit than to oppose. I didn't want it or not want it.

After a few seconds, she pulled back and looked at what she had been licking. "I feel bad for you, all lonely, masturbating to my husband every night. Do you think about me, too? Do you?" She seemed to be addressing my clitoris more than me.

"What?"

"Oh, don't pretend. I know you think about nothing but him. But am I in your fantasies, too?"

"As far as I know, I'm not that into women," I said in Polish.

"I'm not like other women." She lowered her face and gave me a few random kisses. "But you like to think about yourself as me, with him fucking me?"

"Maybe," I heard myself admit.

"Good. He thinks about you, too, you know. I do, too . . . sometimes. He'd like to do this to you. He's much better at this than I am. Now I'll draw the number three. I think the whole drawing numbers and letters with your tongue is bullshit, but I've read it in, like, multiple blogs and magazines. You tell me if it works, okay?"

Her tongue was moving, soft, inexpert. It was not the technique but the situation—that she was my boss—that aroused me. Her tongue carved clumsy letters and ciphers, a new alphabet decreeing the whimsical laws of a parallel sexual world. Her silent spells transformed her into Sleeper's surrogate. My hand in her hair, I pulled her face against me. Was he upstairs? Was he going to come in? From time to time, I looked at the closet door. In the Vermeer, the woman also waited.

"Okay, wow, that's *exhausting*," Bobby said after maybe two minutes, and sat up. "Men are so much more sexually conscientious than we realize. Everyone says men are selfish in bed, but this is, like, *really hard*. I can't believe they do it for so long. My tongue's about to fall off." She massaged her jaw muscles and drank some champagne from the bottle.

"Did you not do it before?" I asked in English.

"Only in theory. Can you finish yourself off? I'll watch if you want."

"I can't. With you watching."

She put down her champagne and squeezed one of my breasts, not erotically, more curatorially.

"Sleepy's going to love your tits. He hasn't already seen them, has he?"

"No. I never—"

"Good. He loves a perky pair like yours."

"Where is he?" I thought maybe he was about to come in. Maybe it was part of the plan.

"I told you. He's asleep," she said. "I didn't want to wake him just yet. Don't you think a woman should know what her husband is doing?"

"Yes," I said, becoming alert to a possible trap.

"So now if he does it, I'll know. Do you like it this way, with a knuckle?"

After a while, we gave up. Bobby lay on her back in a quiet, atypical mood. I wasn't embarrassed for myself but for her, for having failed the challenge she'd initiated, and then embarrassment gave way to quiet power—the power held by those whose satisfactions don't come easily. Her shoes, the hundreds of them, were inanimate witnesses to what hadn't happened. My usual desire to wear, to own, these shoes was absent. For one long moment, even the painting was less than the sum of its parts. I was beyond objects, no matter how holy. I was elevated by dissatisfaction. I'd discovered the allure of being difficult.

"Don't worry about it," I said in Polish. "You'll do better next time."

The morning after the heist Lance came into my room, a coffee in each hand. "The queen wishes to see you," he said. "Her *rack* has burst as she was trying to dress and it has lost its *screws*."

I looked at the cup he was not drinking from, and he grinned and pretended to drink from it.

"Just kidding. Hey, tread warily this morning, little kitty. I think she's a touch PMS-y." He passed me my coffee, put his on my nightstand, and collapsed into my bed. "D'you mind?" He closed his eyes.

I scanned his face for signs of knowledge of the painting or the fourth-rate cunnilingus. Hard to tell with Lance. His face was sallow, chin even less assertive than usual. Maybe he should grow a beard after all, I thought, sipping the coffee, leaving my room, passing the frescoes, noticing for the first time that paint had peeled and formed white stars in trees and flowers and women and beasts.

I passed the record room, where endless vinyl gathered dust, and headed to her boudoir, wondering if she was about to fire me again. I should've feigned an orgasm. This didn't strike me as outrageous. Though I had a perfunctory sense about boundaries—work not to be mixed with sex, marriages better left uninvaded—I knew instinctively that most pleasures resulted, partially if not entirely, from boundaries' violation. I was unscathed by politics, ravenous for novelty. New experiences and objects, luxury objects, decadent experiences, sex, money—all of this was waiting for me.

I entered the boudoir, that odd little wedge-shaped room with its burgundy wallpaper and oil-black furniture. Men weren't allowed in the boudoir, not even Sleeper. I stepped into the clothes closet, adjacent to the shoe closet. Racks, shelves, bins, and baskets packed with fabric. Weeks ago, I'd begun organizing everything by type and color, but my work had been wasted. Coats already consorted with dresses, dresses wrinkled inside bags, and the stack of neat white T-shirts had toppled.

Behind a chest of drawers, a rack had indeed fallen, both down and apart. Metal bits poked out of the mess like the ribs of a fantastic slain animal whose skin was a rainbow of raincoats and leather pants.

"Bobby?" I said, disrupting hangers as I peered behind the remaining overloaded racks into the bathroom at the closet's other end.

She stood topless by the sink. She addressed me without turning. Or else maybe she was talking to herself.

"The only way to test if a pashmina's real is to burn a tiny piece of it and see if it has a synthetic smell." She gestured at an explosion of ashes and purple cloth in the freestanding tub. "So there it is," she continued in Polish. "It's real! But now it looks like a fucking miscarriage and reeks like a Changthangi goat." She rubbed her eye, smearing ash around it, accidental kohl, and flopped into a chair. Bathrooms in the Sleeper house were rooms with baths, sinks, showers, sideboards, sofas, coffee tables. Despite her toplessness—she wore green fishnet tights that didn't pinch her belly—she didn't have the vulnerability of naked people.

"Miscarriages," she said. "You ever had one?" White-purple

flakes of pashmina blew about the floor as she stood up abruptly. I tried to read her face, but she turned away.

"Just kidding. How about bidets? You a bidet fan?" She took her tights off, revealing a lacy thong, then placed a foot in the bidet and washed ash off her toes. "It's important to be immaculate back there. I had them installed to shock the Americans. First thing I did. Americans would rather have dirty asses than imagine an appliance designed specifically to wash your ass."

"Okay." Complain about Americans—this was something we could do together. This suggested I probably wasn't fired. Sometimes we'd just say "*Amerykanin*" and roll our eyes the American way.

She was back in the chair, which poorly contained her Amazonian dimensions. "Do you want to get some screws for my rack? Otherwise it might just, you know, *stay* broken. Sleeper will drive you. He's running errands in that part of town." Her nose was swollen. Had she been crying?

Her phone rang, and she rose and grabbed it from a shelf, knocking over a box of Q-tips.

"What kind of world is this in which you have to destroy something in order to authenticate it?" she said into the phone instead of "Hello." Who was she talking to?

On my way out, I peeked into the shoe closet. *The Lady* was intact, but Bobby's sentence troubled me. Was she planning to destroy it? Burn an edge of it? Was there something a little wrong with Bobby?

There was little wrong with Sleeper. If things with Bobby were becoming complicated, there was now between Sleeper and me a lovely simplicity of mutually acknowledged attraction. If he'd met

me at a café or a bookstore, I don't think he would have liked me.
Maybe he'd have liked my figure, but my face was unremarkable.
As a teen, I was given a compact and carried it here and there in
my pocket but never looked into its little mirror. I had a face that
belonged in a pocket. He'd have liked me, maybe, if he'd noticed
me. Beautiful men normally didn't.

As I got into his car, I thought maybe he was different. Maybe
he had insight into my *essence*, if there is such a thing—or more
likely my lack thereof, my absence of ostentation, which might
be attractive if contrasted with Bobby's lavishness.

"Off to the appendix of Sunset," he said. He pulled out in one
smooth swerve, the muscles on his forearm tensing as he turned
the wheel. Taiko drumming thudded from the stereo.

"What is appendix?"

"Here." He put his hand under my shirt. His fingers were cool.
My abdominal muscles twitched. I wish there were a drier way of
putting it, but I was promptly wet.

His hands were back on the wheel, his profile a constant against
moving houses, stores, gas stations, sidewalks with women walking with other women, women taking their children to school,
women alone.

Being alone with him—the first such outing since he'd driven
me to my car that night in May—was easy. Maybe not. Maybe it
was overwhelming. I said nearly nothing, though a monologue in
Polish hurtled through my head: "I know things about you you
don't know I know. I saw you sneak out of that restaurant last week
and leave a bottle of vodka by the heads of a homeless couple sleeping between dumpsters under bougainvillea. You didn't tell anyone
about it. You know the names of waiters and they know yours. You

take antihistamines for allergies. It's me who leaves them next to your coffee in the morning. You think Bobby does it. Pink, oblong pills. You sleep with three pillows, one between your knees."

I'd never have said any of this aloud. He considered such disclosures awkward and demystifying. For me these details constituted a small shared life with him, a home in my head.

The "appendix of Sunset," it turned out, was a block that included such landmarks as Fatty's Automotive and Bundy Collateral Pawnshop. The day was unusually cold for June. We bought screws and left the hardware store. I had them in my hand. In the parking lot, he unfolded my fingers and lifted my hand above my head.

"What are we doing?"

"Don't move."

His coat blew open and flapped around me.

"You look like a Roman copy of a Greek sculpture. Plus a handful of screws." His mouth was scornful. He had a photographer's eyes and no camera.

"Why copy?"

We stood a few cars down from ours in wind and dust and noise. We stood across from Fatty's Automotive, but it might as well have been the Trevi Fountain. He bent and kissed the corner of my mouth, then my mouth. Folded in his arms, I shrank—I felt I did—but also inwardly expanded.

The kiss lasted a long time—until a group of guys in hard hats speaking Spanish came out of the hardware store and we had to move out of the way.

"Why copy?"

"Because real beauty"—he brushed my mouth with his finger—"is only ever in the context of, if not a deviation from, an imaginary ideal."

"You are saying I am not beautiful?"

"On the contrary. But if I told you you're beautiful, it'd hardly mean anything. You'd think me an unimaginative clown."

"Bobby is a Roman copy, too?" I asked him.

"She doesn't have a prototype. It's a big problem for her, from which she suffers daily."

Despite my English, I understood his compliment. In the car, his hand on my leg confirmed my place in a history of deviations, of splendor and devastation. My face appeared to shimmer in the wing mirror.

"I have before never kissed a woman," I said, immediately embarrassed, but I felt he understood the woman was Bobby and that I was bringing her into our kiss—to let him know I knew she approved.

"It gets easier with practice," Sleeper said.

Probably Bobby had already told him about last night—the sexual part, not the painting—and now she'd sent him as her surrogate to do better what she'd imperfectly done. And his kisses *were* better. His hand on my leg carried more charge than her face between my legs. This was, I told myself, an introduction. What was next? Would he take me to a hotel?

But he drove home, said goodbye, and went into their tower. I stood in the foyer, paralyzed for several minutes, then ran to my room and started crying, not because I was upset. I don't know why. I sat on my bed in ambiguous tears and wondered, had he really found me beautiful? Had the guys in hard hats thought we were a couple?

That evening, I didn't dare attend spritzatura. To see them together would have been too much. I stayed in my room thinking about them, about how little I knew about them, and that too much of what I thought I knew came from Lance, who presented himself as a source of "reliable misinformation in this Gomorrah of a household."

"Sleeper went to Yale, or so he says."

"You don't think he went?"

"All I know is what he says. He says he's from a long line of San Francisco gold diggers who did the missionary. Never met any of them, though."

This was maybe a week ago. Lance poked the photograph of a redhead in a red dress on the sideboard in the dining room. She fell onto her face.

"That's supposedly Sleeper's mother, but I think it's something Bobby cut from an eighties copy of Italian *Vogue*."

"She is not his mother?"

"Could be. But none of his friends or family made it to the wedding."

"Why?"

"Who knows. Maybe he's actually a redneck from Alabama. Now, Bobby . . . what is there to say about that tart? I taught her everything she knows. Chiefly by virtue of being Canadian, I'm her chief adviser on all things American. She used to butcher all her idioms. 'I *butched* my idiom again,' she'd say. I always saved her a seat in class when we were at USC. She'd wobble in late in high heels, overcaffeinated, daffy. After college, she upset her daddy so much with her profligacy that he cut her off, so she found another daddy, then another. But she's a useful person in my life. She provides booze and shelter. She carries my eyeglasses in her purse when I wear my sunglasses and my sunglasses when I wear my eyeglasses. Once, she forgot my sunglasses! It was horrific. We were shopping on Melrose. She was trying to teach me Polish. I have no interest in languages with declensions. 'I fuck off. You fuck off. We fuck off,' I declined, staggering down Melrose, desert-blind as Paul Bowles. It was the worst thing she's ever done to me. I forgave her, though."

But *did* Bobby approve? Was it a trap I was meant to fall into and then be forgiven? Or fired? Was he bored with her? That seemed impossible. Lying in my bed, no longer crying, I recalled a conversation I'd overheard when I first moved in. They'd had another couple over for dinner. The four of them sat at the dining room table. I could hear them from the kitchen. They had drunk a lot, and the woman playfully asked Sleeper if he was still "in love with his wife."

"I'm in lust with my wife," Sleeper said with conviction.

The woman's husband seemed uncomfortable and made a joke.

I, too, was in lust. I reached for the soft-nosed bottle of nose drops I pressed against my perineum when I was about to come. As if on command, I heard a muffled moan from somewhere in the house. Were they fucking in the tower? Maybe it was Lance watching porn.

9

L ook, a storm," she said. In a string bikini and a blazer, she
sat on the kitchen island watching the gold trim on a china
cup emit sparks in the microwave. They were up unusually early.
"Sleepy made eggs."

Sleeper said nothing. His back, toward us, felt ambivalent to
me. He was talented in the kitchen when he wished to be, pro-
ceeding down its sunny length with slow, precise mastery of its
appliances. Stove, toaster, espresso machine. Squares of bread, precisely browned. Steaming cups of coffee. He wore a khaki suit.

"Here." Sleeper passed me a plate, with a smile but no eye contact and nothing secret in that smile, no trace of yesterday's kiss.

"Where's Lance?" I said and was ignored.

We ate on the terrace, Bobby's legs in Sleeper's lap. They passed
the sugar bowl and butter to each other with small private jokes.
He fed her eggs from his fork.

"Sleeper's a *businessman* today. He has to go to work." She looked out past the terrace, down onto the canyon road. "Seems trafficky."

Indeed, cars floated along at a funereal pace. I tried to look into his eyes. They were like ships, weather-bound.

"Work *is* the curse of the drinking class. Has either of you seen my keys?" he asked, and picked a string of my hair off my face and tucked it behind my ear.

Bobby watched, reactionless. I wanted to kiss his hand. Instead, I ate eggs.

"I don't know how you can stand it," Lance said, appearing in the terrace door. He collapsed into a chair. "Work, I mean. As of today, I'm done with my play. I'd let you read the first act, if you weren't illiterate," he said to me. "Okay, where can a person get a cup of coffee here?" He grinned at me, as if it were my job to get it for him. Possibly it was. Whether my service extended to permanent houseguests had not been clarified. So I pretended not to hear him and looked down at Baggywrinkle in the garden, hard at work on a hole.

"Wear your Phrygian cap, if you wish, fine with me," said Lance, returning to the kitchen.

Sleeper got up to leave, too. Bobby followed him into the house. A long bikini string swung at her hip as she walked. Together they looked for the keys. I heard them go downstairs. I saw them through the open top of one of the terrace windows, framed by hanging senecio. She bent to search a basket of magazines and umbrellas by the door to the mudroom.

"No keys here," Sleeper said, pulling her bikini to expose a triangle of untanned ass.

"Show me again." She turned to face him.

He took her hand, inverted it, and lifted it above her head, then kissed her. I realized he was making her into a Roman copy, minus a handful of screws. I felt betrayed but not. I felt included but not.

"Did she do this?" She placed her hand on his crotch.

"She didn't do that."

"So what did she do?"

"She did this." He kissed her again.

"And then what?"

"And then I go to *work*. But when I return, you'll be punished for last night. Say you deserve to be punished. Say it like you're in a bad nineties erotic thriller."

"I deserve to be punished," she said, "like I'm in a bad nineties erotic thriller."

"That's right. You're going to pay. And now you'll have to wait."

He withdrew his hand from hers, reached behind her, and spanked her once, hard—she had a good ass, better than mine. He snapped her bikini band goodbye. What was she supposed to pay for? Perhaps they'd had a fight about me. The thought thrilled and worried me.

She stood in a spot of light from my window—my shadow was on her, too—with an expression of vindicated mischief and dull desire. She didn't look up.

Then, for a week, I barely saw Bobby or Sleeper. She went to lunches, appointments, spas, sample sales. I wasn't sure where he went. At night, they projected old films onto the living room wall. There was a lazy, languorous conflict between the sexes, in the films and in the house. Women with teased hair and cat eyes manipulated men in wrinkled suits and fedoras. People walked for long minutes down boulevards, beaches. They sat primly in black-and-white living rooms and never dared to go beyond a kiss.

"When are we going to Germany?" I asked her one morning.

Nose to the mirror, she filled in her Cupid's bow with a tiny brush dipped in gloss.

"Soon."

"But when?"

"As soon as Seryozha gets his customs guy at LAX. There's been some delay." She threw the brush onto the vanity and grabbed her purse. "Don't forget the window guy's coming at three."

That they hadn't touched me or spoken about touching me for so long now was a reprieve, though tinged with awfulness, the awfulness of actions left incomplete. The Vermeer had transformed the shoe closet. The lady waited for Bobby to dress. She waited for me when I tried on shoes when Bobby wasn't home. She was the secret only Bobby and I knew. She waited until she was no longer a secret. I was shocked—another betrayal, one of many to come—when, one evening in July, I heard Bobby in her bedroom yelling on the phone.

"I'll send you a check for a hundred dollars if you stop mocking me, once and for all. Mm-hmm . . . I *am* a real gallerist. *You're* a fraud. What? When was the last time you even played a gig? I'm actually a major gallerist. I have, like, a real fucking Vermeer in my fucking shoe closet, okay? Fine, two hundred, but never again." She flew into the hall. We nearly collided. "Are you eavesdropping again? Never get divorced. Ex-husbands are the worst breed of adult children. What time is it? Fuck. I'm late for my hot stones massage. Can you button me up?"

"Was that Łyski? Did you say to him about the painting?" I

whispered, fastening her jumpsuit as she rummaged in the basket of knickknacks by the front door. "You said to say to no one."

"Don't worry. He is precisely that. A no one. Where the fuck are my keys?"

I dismissed a premonition of disaster. I dismissed so many feelings back then. When young, you both overestimate and underestimate your inhibitions.

By late July, the Sleepers were interested in me again. They rarely had guests, but they took me to parties. Glass houses, canyon houses, hillside sprawls. Beach barbecues in Malibu, gallery openings on Abbot Kinney, start-up soirées in industrial spaces downtown, after-parties on upper floors of Hollywood hotels, cocktails in gardens. Sometimes there were famous rappers, actors. Bobby pitied the celebrities.

"They're living ads," she said. "They constantly compare themselves to other people. They're the busiest, most miserable people on earth, with weak egos and strong abs. You should always, always be nice to them." She'd kiss a few on the cheek, call them by their fictitious first names. They clutched their phones. They looked hungry.

Almond croissants. Truffle paste. Anchovies. Occasionally, when I thought Sleeper had forgotten me entirely, he'd bring something I liked, something I barely knew I liked, as my tastes were expanding. Wines with certain dates on them. Cherry-smoked trout. At parties, I ate from his hand.

"Here comes a *whore's divorce* for you," he'd say, feeding me crayfish on crackers, after "rescuing" me from a remarkably good-looking not-famous actor.

"If you want to make the beautiful fall in love with you," he said, "make them feel stupid. It doesn't matter how good-looking you are yourself. Showing them you value intelligence as a currency superior to beauty will make them want to prove themselves to you. It's all about currency exchange. Blue cheese with fig?" With mock discernment, toothpick in hand, he hovered over the cheese plate. "On the other hand, if you want the smart to fall in love with you, don't ever make them feel ugly. The principle isn't reversible. It's also much harder to make them feel stupid. Just stick to courting the beautiful."

"What if I like someone beautiful and smart?"

"This kind of person is too rare to worry about," he said, going for a canapé. "Swordfish with sun-dried tomato?"

But of course I never courted anyone. I didn't want to, and they wouldn't have let me. They "protected" me at parties.

"Are you an actress?" a man with bleached hair asked me. He had such a thick American inflection I could barely understand him. His vowels stampeded at me like bison.

"Of course not. She's with me." Bobby stepped in, red wine in one hand, the other circling my waist. Once, an agent gave me his card and told me it was my "lucky day." Bobby swooped in and plunged the card into a wedge of brie.

"Leave her alone. She's already won the lottery."

When people flirted with me, Sleeper would appear. I grew to expect the feeling of his shoulder next to mine. When in the mood, he'd say something fantastically inappropriate to the hapless flirter—asking earnestly about the guy's "tan-to-education ratio," for example.

Once, Bobby thought the hostess of a party had insulted me. "I'm so sorry, we have to leave," she said. "The music's so bad here, it has ejected my tampon."

"Look at all these false priests," Sleeper said, indicating a group of what they called *industry people*. "You can tell an agent by a good suit and an air of constipated melancholy. Stay away from this type."

Once, I asked Bobby, "If you hate film people, why do you live in LA?"

"Reality's over, haven't you heard? Where else are we supposed to live?"

We were on the rooftop of a hotel downtown, and the twenty-eighth in line to the defunct Ashanti throne of Ghana was performing mouth-to-mouth on the Swedish ambassador, who wasn't unconscious.

"The Swedish ambassador." Bobby yawned.

And then, at the end of August, I had my first non-solitary orgasm ever. In public, to boot.

In a house behind the Getty, Sleeper and I stood behind a column, faces to the window, backs to actors, donors, constipated agents. I wore my stolen gray dress.

"What's that? Down there." Sleeper pointed at the semi-dark, at sagebrush, manzanitas. "Either a deer or a drunk. Speaking of drunks, what do you want?"

"Do they have champagne?"

"All benefits for underserved communities have champagne. I meant in life. You don't qualify as a drunk yet. You have work to do."

He stood behind me.

"Don't answer. I know already."

"What?"

"You want everything. It's not vulnerability or depravation. It's *want*, purified. You're a creature of desire, unpolluted by cerebral qualms. I see how you look at everything. You're the only honest person here. Everyone else is just seething with ambition, while pretending to be altruistic. You want honestly. You're pure. Don't ever change."

He stood behind me very close. I wondered if he included himself in the list of "everything." The music cut off. A woman spoke into a microphone.

"Some noble speech signaling the virtue of the speaker is about to start. It turns my stomach. Time to run." He placed his hand on the small of my back, as if to guide me into the crowd.

I pushed back against his hand. "No. I want something."

"What?"

"Touch."

"I *am* touching you." He had his hand around my waist now. We were a few meters away from others, but they couldn't have been farther away.

"No," I said. "You think I like just being toy?"

"Which one of us is a toy is a matter of interpretation."

"Play with toy," I whispered, my face hot and probably red, though he couldn't see it. He was pressed against me from behind. The column shielding us from other guests was massive, holding up a corner of a glass room. Two tall panes dovetailed in front of us. It felt as though we had been thrust into some pivotal but secret space, like the bow of a ship. Below was a dry sea of sage.

"No one will see," I said. "Not your wife. You will tell her of it later."

"If you insist."

He rested both hands on my belly, then his right hand moved, found its way through the slit in the thigh of my dress, then under my panties from the side. A series of fleeting thoughts: Was I too wet? Did my wetness betray my rapacity? Would he do better than his wife had?

His hand continued, stopping my thoughts. He was hard against my back, but I had no thoughts of reciprocation, no thoughts of the hundred people in the room behind us. I wanted honestly. Violation of social norms played no role in my excitement. I covered my face with my hands. I was immune to context, finally taking what I'd been teased with for months. He was adept and focused. Quickening. The woman with the microphone was still introducing the major donor when I squeezed Sleeper's hand with my thighs and said, "Stop. It is finished." It was remarkable that other men had never made me come, because the whole thing had taken less than two minutes.

We found Bobby outside by a planter, smoking, swinging her metal clutch like a censer.

"Let's go," she said. "Bad party. Aren't they all? The good party . . . Where is the good party? The good party's a myth from the past."

Sleeper had nothing to add. In the driveway, on the red carpet, we waited as cars pulled up, disgorging the post-reality elite. Sleeper didn't have his customary take-it-or-leave-it face on—or, if he did, there was more *take* in it than usual. Bobby studied him and me. I kept my eyes on the little car icon approaching us on the map on my app.

"Maybe this party wasn't that bad for you two after all," she said, holding on to Sleeper's chin.

When the car arrived, we got in with me in the middle. As we drove up and down the winding streets, she pushed my head forward and leaned behind me, whispering in his ear, then pulled me back up by my ponytail and laid herself across my lap, falling asleep or pretending to. He stroked her hair. I wondered if she smelled me on his hand.

I didn't listen by their door that night.

We never went to Germany that summer. Neither did we go to bed together. Each act of intimacy between me and one of the Sleepers was inevitably neutralized by an attendant act of distancing. Weeks passed. We stopped going to parties. Fewer spritzaturas. When we did drink together, they'd finish theirs quickly and walk inside, absorbed by each other, holding hands. Red oak and green maple leaves in the pool. The pool boy was out of rehab but not to be found. I cleaned less. No one cared. In LA, you can't quite tell when it's fall. In English, you fall in love, fall from buildings, fall behind, ill, asleep. I was in free fall, free of will.

And then, as if to complete this general collapse, the Vermeer disappeared.

10

I moved it to the safe," Bobby said when I confronted her.

"But the safe is still open and has underwear and thighs," I said.

"It's *tights*, not *thighs*, unless you're, like, Ted Bundy. I'm talking about a different safe. The safer safe," she said and sashayed away.

For a week, she wouldn't talk about it, or about much at all. He, too, was growing colder. Was their behavior an abuse of power if that power was the very thing that turned me on? Perhaps it *was* an abuse of power. Perhaps abuse of power is my fetish. I have often thought so in the years since losing them, years of failing to find anyone to "abuse" me the way I require. Maybe Bobby was punishing me for my lapse in passivity at that party, for making him touch me. Maybe only my powerlessness turned her on.

When, after that party, no further advances came, I struggled to look in Sleeper's eyes. Soon enough he made it easy. It is easier to look, for a moment at least, at a stranger's eyes than the eyes of a potential lover, and now he gazed at me shallowly, as if I were a transparent layer over other, more important data.

Off he went to lunches, meetings with investors—some guy from Amsterdam, another from Zürich, one from Florida. I heard snippets of conversations: investment-related issues, a new sushi restaurant, an insurance claim, a haircut. Nothing whatsoever about fingering his assistant.

Politely ignored, in my borrowed bed, in my gifted clothes, I paid their bills, ordered their meals, coordinated errands, worried about my future. My mother in Poland had to be moved to a home and my brothers asked me for money. I sent what I made but needed more. Ruined by Bobby's standards, I couldn't go back to my previous life, to a rented studio by the airport. I couldn't teach kids in this language I didn't know well enough; I couldn't go back to Poland and teach. I'd been taught a different, more opulent way of life. I'd been spoiled, and so was my future.

I made lists of questions on my phone. Had Seryozha abandoned his plan for Bobby to return the painting? Had she destroyed the painting? Would I ever get the money she had promised me? Or was it all a game? Should I have resisted the Sleepers' advances? Why was I unable to think about anything else? How shameful was it, if at all, that I regretted not faking an orgasm with her? Or should I have, unashamedly, faked an orgasm with her and hidden one from him? One moment I was sure they were merely busy with other matters, the next I was convinced they were toying with me, the next I was disconsolate, certain they didn't want me anymore. Rage at being undesired leads to rebellion.

But I wasn't at rebellion yet. I wanted their attention back.

One day, I opened my door and found Bobby outside it, bundled in a blanket, pretty, sullen. She dragged her pomegranate nails along the door's edge.

"Don't worry, I wasn't eavesdropping. I was about to knock."

"What's wrong?"

The lamp overhead cast half-moons under her eyes. She pushed in past me and collapsed onto my bed next to the laptop she'd bought me.

Her shoulders shook. Was she crying? She looked back at me. Her eyes were dry.

She said, "You know how you can know someone for years and that one stupid someone is why everything falls apart? Everything. Someone so dumb, the kind of dumb that makes him just stand in his room and hit his head against the wall for days and be, like, surprised he doesn't end up with a million dollars."

"What are you talking about?" I asked in Polish.

"About the million," she continued in English.

"*Our* million?" I asked. "Because the reward is actually in euros," I said in Polish. "I read about it."

"Dollars, euros, *złoty*," she said. "When we first met, I had to force that idiot to shower. He'd forget to eat. He'd sit playing his guitar, the same stupid tune over and over. I sold my earrings to buy him that stupid guitar. I was basically his mother. Well, now he got me good."

"Who? What are you talking about?"

"Łyski. Practice your English." She was scratching flecks of food or dirt off my keyboard. "He took it all. A few pairs of shoes, my favorite deco mirror, some purses, speakers. And he took the painting, too."

My tongue tasted of gin, although I hadn't had a drink in days. "He took?"

"He came in and robbed us, and we didn't even notice."

"The painting, too? The one?"

"Yup."

"But you said it was in the safe . . ."

"I lied. Surprise!"

"But how? When?"

She placed her finger on her upper lip, like a moustache, and mocked me in a cartoonish voice: "How? When?"

"We have to call the police," I said. I felt not sick but very strange. I sat on the bed next to her.

"He doesn't even know what he's taken. He's probably going to try to sell it at, like, the Santa Monica Farmers Market." She found her phone under her leg. "I've called a hundred times, and now it says the number's disconnected, probably because I didn't pay the bill. His phone's still, like, under my name, but don't tell Sleeper. He'd be mad." She moved her phone back and forth on the bed like a child playing with a toy car. "Mad, mad, mad."

"We have to tell Sleeper," I told her. "Also police."

"We can't! Don't you get it? That painting is stolen, and we stole it from the people who, like, stole it."

"You said we *fake*-stole it."

"You always go along with things, and then you play innocent and act all righteous. Of course we fake-stole it. Only that's, like, a secret."

"What does it mean?"

"We fake-stole it from Seryozha, but the police would see it differently, you know? Like, they always have these wrongheaded, simplistic interpretations. They'd think we're involved in *art theft*. Like you, they don't understand complexity, like that we're going to *return* it." She stared at me meanly through smeared eyes, which

I imagined smeared not merely with yesterday's makeup but with paint from centuries of art and carnivals and whorehouses. "The laws," she said, "aren't up to date yet to deal with people like *us*."

Though her head was on my pillow right in front of me, I suddenly couldn't see her properly. Her face appeared remote and blurry like your own face becomes when you look too long in the mirror without blinking. What did I really know about her?

She shifted and brought her knees to her chest.

"And Seryozha, he won't be happy to lose ten million. He's not like us. He's so materialistic. He'd sell nuns to the pope. You should've seen his Bel Air place. Dripping with gold leaf and stuffed with Louis Seize. Do you have anything to drink in here?" She opened my nightstand drawer.

"That's bad," I said. "Seryozha's bad, right?"

In English, I spoke in essentialisms. Good, bad. Simple words squeezed the essence out of reality. The blanket fell from her shoulder, white silk pajamas underneath. She rifled through my drawer—pens, aspirin, nose drops, petroleum jelly—then slapped it shut.

"He's not bad normally, but when he loses millions, he can be very bad."

"Why did you do it?"

"What? You're blaming *me*?"

"Why you have left it in the house? And why did you say to Łyski about it?"

"I didn't *say* to him anything," she mocked me.

"But I heard you. You yelled him in the phone you have Vermeer."

"No, I don't think I did that. I don't ever tell my exes the truth.

Anyway, what do you suppose we should have done?" she asked in Polish. "The thief who stole the *Mona Lisa* stored it under his stove for decades. He was a simpleton, and yet a very effective one." When she was upset, she spoke her posh Polish, pretentiously proper. Could a person in silk pajamas who spoke like this go to prison?

She dropped her face onto my pillow, smudging it with makeup. "Never turn your nose up at a million. I wonder if Mother Teresa was gay."

I got up and paced from the bed to the closet. My new coat's sleeve, caught in the closet door, made me think of a passenger's arm in the door of a train, heading for who knew where, nowhere good.

"Well, as it is, we'll get nothing." She sat up. "The thing is, I don't think *nothing* is acceptable to Seryozha." Her small voice belied her fearless physique, her tall torso, wide shoulders, breasts in a gold push-up bra, solid as a breastplate, pushing through her unbuttoned pajamas. Even her hair seemed bellicose. "He won't even talk to me unless I text him that I have it back. He's a bureaucrat. An apparatchik, really."

I kept expecting her to start laughing and say she'd made the whole thing up. There was no Seryozha. The Vermeer was a "genuine fake," like a purse at the bazaar in Wólka Kosowska near Warsaw. Didn't I like scenarios and games? Ever since I'd come to LA, life had felt like a game, a dumb game for intelligent children.

"We have to find Łyski," I said. I tucked the sleeve into the closet. "Where does he live?"

"That's the problem. He doesn't, like, live anywhere. He couch surfs, and I already called all his loser friends. No one's seen him.

But don't worry," she said in English. "Seryozha wouldn't hurt us. He, like, loves me."

"In America, people shoot people," I said in perfect English.

"In Russia, too. But don't worry. Seryozha can't come here. Remember? Magnitsky list."

"Do you know what for people are on Magnitsky list? For to break human rights. I read this."

"Not Seryozha. He, like, loves people." Thumb in her mouth, she bit off a red crescent, ate it, examined the exposed nail bed. "Do you think shellac is, like, toxic?"

That evening, she decided to tell Sleeper.

"What I hate the most," she said, "is that my one-million-euro surprise is ruined." Apparently dollars and euros were all the same to Bobby. Not to me. This made my loss fourteen-point-three percent more upsetting.

She was at the door to Sleeper's office. I was halfway down the hall behind her.

"Wish me luck. He's going to be really mad." She pressed her cheek to the door, then disappeared inside. The hardwood of the hall smelled of lemon oil, because I'd just polished it. Outside, the gardener mowed in light rain. I expected screams, cries. It was quiet for a long time. I waited twenty long, wooden minutes, then left.

The Sleepers didn't come down for spritzatura. Dinnertime came, and they were still upstairs.

In the kitchen, I found Lance on his knees, licking Huso Huso caviar off the floor, a smashed jar beside him. "No judgment, please." He looked up at me with black teeth. "I hear we're in financial trouble, and this cost at least two hundred bones. It fell out of the fridge when I was reaching for the kefir. You are welcome to partake."

"No, thanks," I said. "Do you know what is happening?"

"A regular cold war. Russia conniving, America asking earnest, hypocritical questions, and Poland ineptly interfering, shedding tears and shaking tits at the superpowers. I mean, this is nuts, isn't it? Bobby planned to negotiate an art heist? Ten million euros? She's never made a penny, but now she's lost ten million? *That's* something. I never suspected Łyski of such chutzpah. Ten million, that's a lot of caviar . . . I dread to think what he'll do with the painting." He looked back at the caviar on the floor. "Hmm. Now that you're watching, I can no longer eat this in the canine fashion. But we certainly can't waste it. Pass me a spoon?"

I fetched him a teaspoon. "What did Sleeper say?"

"Seryozha isn't picking up her calls. Neither is Łyski. What I want to know is, why'd she pick *you*, and not me, for the heist? Booby's a harlot. She must see something in you I've not noticed. Unless she was just trying to keep you away from her man. Or around him." Lance's round head, with its thin, conceited smile, gleamed like a larger version of the spoon he held. Gently, he inserted it into the inky smear on the white kitchen tiles.

"Is Sleeper angry? Does he think it's my idea?" I squatted next to Lance. "They said they will fire me?"

"Poor Viva. Once, when I spilled milk and cookies in my bed, I slept in theirs. I thought they were still in Martinique. At dawn, I was snug in the sheets, and Sleeper confused me for Bobby. It happens. Similar profiles. We all grow to resemble each other. He pulled the sheet off my head to show me his giant peninsula. I whispered to him, 'Are you finally giving me what I don't actively want but would be perfectly willing to accept?' The reaction was immediate. From tilt to wilt. But quite a sight. He was very sprezzy about it. Just put it all back in his shorts. Didn't even rush. You must like him a lot."

"No. I like my job. It is good job. I don't know other people, and I don't want to go home."

"Home. Jesus, right." His benevolent expression suggested I should say no more. It also suggested he assumed I came not from an improving country in the EU but from some hellhole where men raped sheep and women gave birth in ditches.

"Of course, you're in love."

"I am not this."

"Be happy. Love is as rare as a Vermeer," he said. I waited for the customary mocking afterthought, but it didn't come. He had the dismayed look of a comedian who'd run out of jokes onstage. "I've pretty much given up on the idea of exclusivity in love. Like Jesus, I love all men. But I am intimate with only twelve on a regular basis." He sighed and ate a spoonful of Huso Huso. "You don't have to worry. You've made yourself indispensable. It took me a while to figure out a hook for myself. Not that it's such a privilege to live with those two, but it's definitely better than getting a job. Or living with my mother."

Licking the spoon, he waited for me to ask him what his "hook" was. I didn't.

Then his face softened, became almost friendly. "I'm indispensable to their way of life. Biographical, they call it. A *biographical life* wouldn't work without a biographer, you see. My play will have to do. She wants all their misbehaviors romanticized and italicized in stage directions. The trouble is, I write so little."

"What is *my* hook?"

"Well, at first you were a dessert, but desserts are vomitable." He simulated inserting the spoon into his throat and made a few gagging noises. "Now, however, you can put them—or Booby at least—in jail. Of course, why would you? But the sheer possibility adds spice to the situation, no? Not only were you sexually harassed, but they unwittingly made you an accessory to a crime. I wouldn't mention to your future lawyer all the accessories you got out of this arrangement, or that you hankered after the harassment. You're just an assistant abused by unscrupulous employers. I'm their unconscious, you see. I know things they don't entirely know about themselves. Just to spite them, I should paint them as a pair of decent middle-class monogamists! Maybe I'll call it *Three Husbands*. What do you think?"

"Three husbands?"

"Łyski, Sleeper, and Seryozha. Or Seryozha, Łyski, Sleeper, to be chronological."

"She was married to Seryozha?!" I wanted to blurt but didn't, ashamed to disclose how little I knew. Lance threw his spoon into the sink and left the floor for me to clean.

Overnight, the rain and wind increased. At nine a.m., the Sleepers came downstairs, ignored me in the kitchen and each other by the door. I went into the sitting room and watched them through the big bay windows: Bobby in the driveway flapping an inverted umbrella. Failing to fix it, she threw it onto the lawn and got into the car, Sleeper already at the wheel. The umbrella somersaulted after them as they drove off. Hunting for Łyski?

Lance stayed home. Through the half-open door to his room, I saw the devotional bend of his back against the backdrop of a news site.

"World's going to hell. Let me savor it in peace, please!" he barked when I offered him coffee.

My texts to Bobby went unanswered. I roamed the anxious, empty house.

Until now, I had limited myself to spying on the Sleepers in a casual, uncommitted way, within the bounds of my job description: entrances unannounced, cat-quiet lingering in places to which, by structural flaw or architect's whim, sound carried. The bathroom by the billiards room received tidbits of voices from the kitchen. An ear to the swan on the second-floor bedroom's marquetry wall would pick up what was said by the front door. The mouth of the mermaid fountain in the garden emitted engine sounds from the garage.

Now I decided to spy with commitment. In Sleeper's office, I probed his floor-to-ceiling bookshelf, opened books at random, finding not even a photograph or receipt. Most of the books were pristine, unread. Nothing in his desk drawers: no pens, paper, folders, check stubs. In vain I tried to bypass his computer log-on screen.

I ran my hand over his desk's smooth surface. What was I looking for? Old wedding albums? Marriage certificates? A certificate of authenticity for a minor Vermeer? Some proof that what had happened was a hoax more than a crime. That it had been Sleeper's painting all along. Bobby kept no records, had no office.

Sleeper's side of the bedroom was as minimalist as his office. Each piece of his jewelry told time but none the right time. Earphones looped a nightstand drawer's knob. His shirts were folded loosely, not meticulously. On his bedside, newspapers, one folded open to an article on Assad and the Middle East. Next to it, a thick history of the Middle Ages. I opened it to where it was marked, read a paragraph on Ataulf, king of the Visigoths, then looked at the bookmark. It was a fragment ripped from a medical letter.

Dr. Ashok Sivakumar, consultant clinical psychologist, 12 Harley Street, London W1G 9QY, said the letterhead.

The letter said, *I reviewed this charming 33-year-old left-handed gallerist with a number of different symptoms. She reports . . .* The rest was missing, except for a part of a lower sentence: *. . . sensation, like a tiny heart under the skin. The sensor—*

Was the painting a copy, the whole heist a semi-delusion? But Lance had confirmed it. Or was he accessory to her deceptions, even coauthor? I replaced the bookmark, carefully sealed Ataulf and Ashok back up together.

The teenage tenderness I felt for Sleeper's objects, for his balled socks, eyedrops, unflamboyant ties, their object-secrecy, turned into teenage rage on Bobby's side of the bedroom. Envy of her life, its largeness, made me wrench open her drawers. They rattled with manicuring tools sufficient to arm a mental ward or small militia: files, cuticle cutters, scissors, orange wood sticks in glass vials. I cried as I perused the other drawers, finding notebooks full of scribbled, indecipherable entries, dates, places. A travel itinerary? A tear for Rio, a tear for Lugano. Maybe I *would* go to the police.

I kicked a drawer shut, shuffling the salves and sleeping pills atop the nightstand. Dull, disappointed, I read their labels: A retinol cream. An under-eye cream. A glycolic foot peel. WASH OFF AFTER FIVE MINUTES. DO NOT USE ON FACE, read the inscription.

I stopped mid-sob and watched myself with curiosity as I selected a bottle of rose serum and held it and the glycolic peel both up to the light. Each had a cloudy, white appearance. I transferred both into an empty wineglass I found at the foot of the bed, then refilled each bottle with my witchy hybrid, feeling the messy comfort of forgotten childhood malice. Washing my hands, I felt calm, as if, through this probably inconsequential action, my agency in the Sleepers' universe had been restored. Acid on faces, roses on feet. An act of worship, an act of hate.

"Got to stay in practice," said Lance, lackadaisically humping my bedpost. "Anyway, Booby needs your help packing. She told me to tell you. We're going to Italy."

"They know where is Łyski?"

"It seems one of Bobby's passé art friends—a woman I once witnessed sewing two dudes' scrota to another woman's handbag at the Whitney—heard that some long-haired loser has been contacting art whores in Venice, hoping to offload a stolen Vermeer. Of course, Bobby's idiot friend thought Łyski going around flaunting the painting *was* performance art."

"We're going to Venice?"

"*Sì.*"

"Me, too?"

"You, too, I'm afraid."

"We leave when?"

"Few days. Bobby wants you to buy the tickets. Two coach, two business. That's right, poor friends and staff travel with the plebes. They told me to tell you they understand if you don't want to come with—they even had an NDA drawn up, with two months' severance—but then I tickled their vanity and said you were a very excitable lass who wouldn't miss chasing Bobby's exes down the sewagey *calle* for anything in the world, because, like me, you don't have anything of your own going on. Was I right?" He took my hand and held it. "I beg you to come. I *can't* sit in coach by myself."

VENICE

11

S ignora, you cannot enter the EU with a vegetable," said the customs officer, hefting a butternut squash he'd dug from Bobby's suitcase. The squash had a smiley face drawn on its bulging end.

"What is this?" I whispered to Lance.

We stood behind a plexiglass panel in the nothing-to-declare zone of the Marco Polo Airport.

"Oh god, that's one of Bobby's smothered babies," he whispered back. "She gave birth to it last week on the kitchen floor. It happened right after the farmers market, in a bout of mutual arm-chair psychologizing, when she and Sleeper decided her hysteria stems from unexpressed maternal instincts. They took the squash they'd bought, drew a face, and declared Bobby a mother."

With maternal ferocity, Bobby reclaimed the vegetable from the customs officer's hands.

"We packed it by accident. We'll just throw it away," Sleeper told the officer.

"What? I nursed that thing from infancy!" Under the strong ceiling light, her face, swollen from flight, was not un-gourd-like.

"*Signora . . .*" The officer, his own face weary with other people's travel, looked from the gourd's malicious smile to Bobby. "*Mi dispiace . . .*"

"You can't make me throw away my baby!" The officer looked to us for help. She invoked her rights as a tourist, an EU citizen, a green card holder, a mother, and a woman—first in English, then in passionate stumbling Italian.

"It's okay. You can take it." Sleeper pried the squash out of her hands, passed it to the officer.

As he dragged Bobby away, she wailed with an intriguing combination of real and satirical grief.

"*Melanzane, cippole!*" the officers yelled at our backs.

"I hate uninformed uniformed men," she said, bereft and defeated, as we entered a drafty arcade that led to the water-taxi piers.

"*Conformisti!*" she yelled at an innocent group of Carabinieri.

Free from the pragmatism of concrete, of freeways and roads, water-bound places have a certain lightness, a mischief. Along the piers, women, gripping boatmen's and husbands' arms, boarded water taxis that swayed and knocked people against one another. The night, the rippling lights in water, laughing passengers, and boatmen bantering in dialect—this carnival, this buoyancy lifted my mood and Bobby's.

"So long, my Satanic spawn," sang Bobby in the direction of the airport.

A boatman loaded our baggage. Bobby had five large suitcases. We each had one.

"Get in, perverts." Sleeper waved us aboard.

On the lagoon, with her hair blown upward into a mad, undulating crown, Bobby squeezed my hand. On a padded bench, Lance slept. Sleeper teetered between annoyance and amusement, standing in the bow . . . but Bobby's enthusiasms were infectious. By the time we reached Burano, he was standing between us, holding us each by the neck. Our hair intermingled across his wide back. I forgave her her secrecy, forgot her forgetfulness. Her will to dismiss me—if it existed—was suddenly dismissible.

Our entry to the Grand Canal was fast and brusque. Gold lights warped in the water. Except for America and brief trips to Sofia and Brno, I'd never traveled, not even around Europe, so for me the Grand Canal was as stupendous as it is for any lass from Tokyo or Topeka. It made sense, in some nonsensical, purely aesthetic way, that we were coming here to retrieve *The Lady*; she belonged to old stone, to its heaviness and weight, and to these murky colors that seeped from windows, nooks, piers, and hulls like paint from overturned cans.

Pale palaces made of moons and bones, with moldings indicating the aristocratic or merchant order of deceased inhabitants. Fleurs-de-lis in the windows to ward off bad luck. Venice at night— with its moss, mold, stains, its peeling layers—can restore in you, briefly, a childhood belief in curses and charms.

Charms can be cursed and curses charming. Sleeper leaned over and kissed me on the mouth, then kissed Bobby exactly the same; then she kissed me, a shadow of his kiss in the watery dark, a kiss like an offertory, depleted, cold, granted by the patron saint of frivolousness welcoming her acolyte to the necropolis.

On the staircase of a grand old hotel, we said good night, and they kissed me again. It made sense. Venice herself requested it. The

Sleepers couldn't ignore me here. They were even more cursed than I was. My bed was mahogany wood and mahogany velvet. In it I felt a sensation of eerie return, not only to them, but as if all the nights of my life in cheap beds had been but temporary substitutions for this true night in this stunning, ancient bed.

I woke to the splash of an oar in my ground-floor—or should I say water floor—window. My curtain blew open, revealing a gondolier with a worried face, unfree in his jailbird shirt. I'd slept well. My mind was less enchanted than it had been at night. Were they merely teasing me again, or were the rules in Venice as different as everything else? The buildings across the sunny canal did seem vague and illusory, made of crochet, even in daylight. My phone beeped.

Bobby waited for me at the hotel restaurant. In a belted cardigan, in a French window lazy with boats, she sat crumbling toast into her coffee saucer. She had the poise of self-sufficient women who dine and die alone, this woman who could do nothing alone.

"I don't know why we live in LA, when we could live in Venice," she said, dipped toast into her coffee, nibbled it, and dropped it onto the tablecloth. "What do you want to eat?" She passed me the menu. "Continental breakfast?" She waved down the waiter and ordered it for me before I could respond. "No Italian would ever order 'continental breakfast.' But you're as Polish as John Paul. Anyway, I'm going to see Caio after breakfast."

"Caio?" I squelched an urge to ask if he was yet another ex.

"You know, Caio! He was, like, cryptic on the phone, but I'm pretty sure Łyski tried to sell him the painting." Her tone was light, as sunny as the scene behind her. "Caio would never sell a stolen work of art. I've seen him close his eyes on things, like, once or twice. He bought a piece made of bald eagle *and* golden eagle feathers once from these Americans. They're threatened with extinction."

"Americans?"

"No, eagles. Americans are next. All birds of prey are headed for extinction." She sighed.

At the next table, a waiter with a napkin draped over one arm set down utensils soundlessly, with the quiet focus of a music student drawing clefs on a staff.

"The thing about Łyski is, he can't keep a secret from me for long," she continued. "After the divorce, he called me up just to get permission to sleep with some model bimbo. He hates me, but I'm his only friend. He can't survive without my guidance. Just wait, he'll call me soon." She wiped her mouth. "We're meeting a private detective tomorrow. They actually have a detective agency here in Venice, can you imagine? It says on their website they offer cheating-spouse surveillance and hidden-assets investigation, so I called and asked, 'How about a faithful ex, who, like, stole something very expensive?' Anyway, you should have Sleeper take you around while I'm with Caio. Oh, and here's a list of things I need." She passed me a crumpled piece of paper from her pants pocket. "See you later." She licked a silver spoon, slipped it into her purse, and strutted out.

Painkillers, eye drops, eye-makeup remover, eyelash curler, Q-tips . . . The list went on. At the very bottom, in a different color pen, she'd added, *condoms.*

On the Bridge of Sighs, Sleeper held my hand. It felt natural enough. He pulled me through the rowdy groups of tourists, touts selling roses and "souvenirs."

"Coming to Venice is like being the last person to have a great idea," he said. "At least we're sprezzatourists."

"What is this?"

"We didn't come to see the sights, the museums. We might happen to see something others come on pilgrimage to see, but only in passing, by accident almost, on our way to something else."

"We had something that can be in museum," I said.

"You're right. We have the honor of having lost what others here would pay to see. That makes us sprezzalosers. A very distinguished category." He looked at me thoughtfully.

I waited for him to explain his plan to retrieve the Vermeer or to complain about Bobby's recklessness, but he took my hand again and led me off the bridge and into the alleys. He knew Venice as if he had lived there. Not once did he check his phone for directions. His anecdotes had the offhandedness of stories people told about their families.

"The city was built on alder trees. They drove long wooden piles down into the lagoon. In Irish myths, lovers hide in alder trees. Can you relax your hand? You're cutting off my circulation."

"Sorry. I always hold hands like this."

He readjusted my hand on his. "Just do it gently. I promise it'll work just as well."

"Keep saying about your wood," I said.

He laughed. "Alderwood turns hard as stone underwater. Out of water, it decomposes. It needs to stay under the surface."

"Like love affair," I said, immediately regretting it, but an idea of us as a couple had been present in my mind, confirmed in the faces of strangers, who I was sure couldn't differentiate us from countless couples who come to Venice.

"A love affair," he said in a lazy, contemptuous tone—as if

examining the term itself and dismissing it, tossing it into the canal—and he led me over another bridge.

"Keep up," he said, adjusting his pace to mine. "You're so little." He looked at me sideways from under his sunglasses, and I filled with a feeling of melting and narrowing and held his hand tighter.

But then he was dragging me more than holding my hand. His attention came in bursts. I tried to retrieve it with questions. "What happened right here?"

"Here? Nothing. There used to be great parties in that palace over there, but now it's a museum, like everything. They have a skeleton of an *Ouranosaurus*, if *Ouranosauruses* interest you."

"And there?"

"A bunch of people died a slow and miserable death and were buried."

"And here?" I said, stopping in the middle of a small piazza with a restaurant on one side and tree roots uprooting the concrete.

"Some Liverpudlians suffered from indigestion."

"Who?" I laughed.

"Pure conjecture. Revisionist history."

"And here?" The junction of a tunnel and a minor *calle*. Stones the shapes and colors of olives. A shuttered shop.

"This place is still waiting for something to happen. It's one of those historically left-out places."

He faced me and played with my hands, and the melting and narrowing got to the point that I thought I might cry. Somehow, though we'd kissed already, though he'd made me come, the atmosphere this day, in this place still waiting for something to happen, was more charged with firstness, with pre-kiss precipice dizziness, than any preceding moment. But the kiss didn't come. For all I know, that place is still waiting.

He took off his sunglasses and pointed with them past my shoulder, down the *calle*.

"Over there, in the arcades, only a hundred years ago, Luisa Casati walked her cheetah."

He was dragging me again. We turned and turned again, emerged into sunlight. "And there"—he pointed at a vast beige building with a double row of columns—"at the Scuola Grande di San Rocco, two years ago, Bobby Sleeper slept for hours, curled up in her stinky mink in a docent's chair, and nobody woke her or asked her to leave."

"Did she tell you to come here with me?"

"We don't make each other do things. I do what I want, and so does she. We happen to like the same things, and usually the same people, too. Hungry?"

We sat at a table in a restaurant made mostly of glass. On the boardwalk before us, a giant statue of a woman faced the sea. At her feet lay a cloth made of bronze. I didn't know what the cloth signified, but it pleased me, forever discarded, immobile while scarves, coats, and hair of passersby were tousled and turned.

"I like this place," he said, "because the food here tastes exactly like it looks. The pasta scolgio tastes like a tide pool. Know what I mean?"

"Yes," I lied. In the window light, in his white shirt, he was so pretty that truths seemed irrelevant. I sucked a mussel from a shell. Our legs touched under the table. We drank white wine from stemless glasses.

"Or maybe it's the Russians. It's absurd, but since Bobby got us into this disaster, everything's been slightly more intense. Sex, architecture, food. I wonder if this is how men feel before battle. I bet the horse soup, or whatever it was, tasted spectacular the night before Verdun."

"What is this Verdun?" I said, turning the diamond bracelet from Bobby. When he had said "sex," an image or brief waking dream of diamonds, inside my dress, chains of diamonds all over my hips, had ignited in my head.

"One of the bloodiest battles of World War I. A threat on the horizon makes reality more acute. Don't worry," he reassured me, misinterpreting my look, "nothing will happen to us. Bobby creates danger. I keep us safe." Did *us* include me?

"What do you think of Seryozha?" I said carefully, in perfect English.

He looked at me, or rather past me, and I regretted asking.

"I don't know if any man can form a reasonable opinion about his wife's ex. Too many biases. You know, biases? Prejudices?" I nodded. "I guess he amuses me, anthropologically speaking. He's a man who belongs to an older culture than mine, sees things in primary colors. He has no apparatus to understand a woman like Bobby. I don't think she understands he doesn't understand her." He laughed. "Coffee?" He ordered two cappuccinos, stirred some sugar into his, and lightly tapped the spoon against the cup's edge.

He settled the bill. We walked on the waterfront. "All this is why I'd rather . . ." he said, trailing off into another mood, staring off between the dome of Santa Maria della Salute and the orange edge of Giudecca in the mist.

Around us, dozens of boats, hundreds of people, flowed in every direction, around statues and streetlamps, bricoles and buoys, and yet no one bumped anyone, no gondola overturned, no *traghetto* crashed.

"I would like gelato," I said. My tone was purposefully girlish, demanding even, out of sync with the moment. Bobby would have said something witty or poetic. To outshine—or at least appropriate—the environment was her talent.

"And yet, if you look really carefully," he said, putting on his sunglasses and turning from the water, "there's probably, way out there, someone drowning—you know, some dude whose wings just melted."

I didn't ask what he meant.

"Gelato, you said?"

We walked toward a *gelateria*. A large group of teenagers in matching yellow sweatshirts separated us, and as I maneuvered to get back to him, a man passed weirdly close to me, brushing my arm, looking over his shoulder right at me. His head was shaved. On the back of it was a small tattoo of a grinning cracked skull with many teeth. Men with such faces didn't come to Venice, not on holiday, I thought. He'd looked me in the eyes but very briefly. I'd seen him before somewhere.

"Here you are." Sleeper pulled me into the *gelateria* line with him, behind the teenagers. "Again, we're the last ones to have the great idea."

"What idea?"

"Look at this empress of gelato." A woman in a skewed cap filled waffle cones and counted coins. "What flavor, *Mała*?" Sleeper asked me. *Mała* means *little* in Polish.

Nocciola, stracciatella, crema di pistacchio. We leaned over the display. "*Nocciola*," I selected.

Licking, we strolled back through alleys smelling of leather, sewage, and sugar, stopping, because of human traffic, in a narrow passage made narrower by baskets of pink and black candy.

"You can relax around me, you know," he said.

"I am," I said.

"People say it's the eyes that tell the truth, but the truth is, eyes lie. If you're into honesty, look at people's mouths," he said, covering my eyes with his hand. "It's the mouth that tells. Cover your mouth if you want to be inscrutable."

"I am relaxed," I said.

It was like a kiss, his hand on my eyes. I wondered if I had gelato on my upper lip. He pulled me toward him and turned me around, so that when he removed his hand and the crowd moved forward, I found myself under his arm. We walked on like this.

At a pharmacy smaller than Bobby's shoe closet, where there were no shelves and you had to request items at the counter, he helped me with Bobby's list.

"I see you and my wife are trying to seduce me," he said, when he got to the list's final item.

Maybe I blushed. He examined the blue box the pharmacist passed him.

"*Grazie*," he said.

In my room, he sat on the bed. I stood as far away as I could, laughing nervously. He watched me, his eyes large and focused.

He patted the taut sheets. "Onto the bed." He unwrapped the blue box and set it on the nightstand, tossing the cellophane onto the rug. I stepped over it.

He rolled off my tights unhurriedly. The rest followed. No clumsy tugs, just deftly opened clips, unbuttonings, shedding of straps, and yet I felt entirely uncontrolled. The organized chaos of the alleys and canals had arrived in my bed. I lay naked while he, still in his coat, his face far away between my legs, was both a stranger and strangely familiar.

At some point he stopped, removed his coat, rolled up his shirt-sleeves. His hair messy and boyish, he began again. In the dusk that, inside a one-windowed room facing east, had the density of midnight, I stopped being shy. Gondolas slid through the murk. My hips rolled up and down, my figure in the wardrobe mirror refashioned around his head into a jagged, forked S. What made me come so violently, oddly, was a vision of Bobby, surrounded by tall boots and pumps, doing badly what he did so well.

Then he was naked, too, atop me, a smooth, precise weight. The kind of adult sex that acknowledges each body part for its hedonistic potential. My climax, the second one, was first like a cradling, a descent into vague concavity, and then, at the end, a rounding, a closing of a circuit, and the circuit flowed; the water in the window did; we were asleep.

I woke to voices, a door closing. For hours or minutes I'd slept. The canal in the window was blackish-blue. He'd taken a shower and stood in a towel, lifting our clothes from the floor.

"Was someone here, just?" I asked.

"I asked for towels." He put the clothes on the desk and came toward me. I rose on an elbow and pressed my cheek to the damp terry cloth around his waist. His hands were in my hair.

He said, "Bobby made a rez at Harry's Bar. I hate the food there, but she insists on it. Hemingway used to eat there. Not much has changed. They still serve the same veal in tuna sauce, nasty. All the good company's been dead for decades. Care for some fishy meat in fishy company?"

12

"Anal sex is an evolved pleasure, like black olives," Bobby said, lifting her long skirt to walk down the steps of a bridge.

"Therefore, 'the gays'"—Lance wagged his air quotes lavishly—"are more evolved. The further from reproduction, the better." In a chartreuse hood, he hopped off the bottom step, breaking up a group of strolling nuns. "Libertinage abhors progeniture," he said to them politely and, pointing at a pair of leather loafers in a store display, to Bobby, "Oh *no*. Are those better than the ones we bought?"

"Absolutely not," she said. "Whatever I buy for *you* is the best." She spun and said, "Sleepy, aren't your new loafers the best?"

Lance: "What?! You bought us both a pair. Stop *doing* that! Men who live together shouldn't dress the same by accident. My body, my choice!"

Their antic teenage energy made Sleeper and me, walking behind them, the adults. The city, too, seemed older than by day. Our shoes in the alleys and courtyards produced old sounds on old walls, the latest in the carnival of shoes, the shoes of cardinals, merchants, doges, tourists, tourists, tourists, plague doctors, assassins, jealous husbands, angry wives.

Bobby was everything but angry. Occasionally she turned and looked at us with shy excitement, as if half in disbelief that what she'd been concocting half in jest had actually occurred. Lance knew, too, of course. This was the source of their giddiness, this pair of vampires revivified by virgin blood.

"That's what Lisa's thinking about." Bobby gestured at a *Mona Lisa* poster, one of her ironic, moustached reincarnations, partially obscured by ads for gallery shows and concerts.

Lance: "Lisa's thinking about loafers?"

Sleeper: "She's thinking about black olives."

We passed the Vallaresso *vaporetto* stop, turned the corner, entered Harry's Bar, were led upstairs by a waiter with wet spots in his armpits and given a table by a wall. Large mirrors made myriad the intensely local clientele, the husbands old, the wives once young, the clothing both flamboyant and conservative in that peculiarly Italian way.

Over pilaf and cuttlefish, Bobby related, for my benefit, her meeting with Caio. She spoke to me as one does to a partner, not to an inferior. Chewing tuna-sauced veal—not as awful as promised, though far from delicious—it struck me that, in your twenties, it's okay that it's all about your body, if you're lucky enough to have a body of interest. My body was a ticket to inclusion. Vicious thoughts toward her fell away. She was magnanimous. What a confident, admirable woman, I thought, to be not jealous but excited by her husband doing what he'd done.

"—and then Łyski showed Caio the Vermeer on his phone, and Caio told him he didn't want anything to do with it, that Łyski

should, like, return it where he got it. So then Łyski said he'd
gotten it from me . . ." she said to the table, the team. I was as inte-
gral as Lance now, maybe more so. "That's why Caio didn't call the
police. Caio loves me. Once, when I was interning at the Biennale,
we spent a whole night on our knees separating sunflower seeds
from pumpkin seeds for a piece in the Croatian Pavilion."

I listened to her without listening. She was seated across from
us with Lance. She'd granted me her usual place next to Sleeper.

"The good news is, Caio didn't tell him it's a Vermeer. He managed to scare Łyski out of showing the painting to any more deal-
ers," Sleeper said. "So now our bright boy's just cooped up with it
in some moldy hole, no idea what to do."

I felt calm, free from the anxieties new sex normally awakens.
I told myself this was mature, futureless sex, leading to nothing
more but more sex. To be mature was to feel vivacity but never
love. At least, these seemed to be the rules of the arrangement.
Only idiots fall in love at the carnival.

"But what's to stop Łyski from collecting the reward himself,
other than ignorance?" Sleeper was saying. "There's a chance he'll
eventually figure out what the painting is and that there's no need
to look for a buyer."

"I don't think he'd have the balls to approach the museum directly, with his criminal record and all," Lance said.

"It was just a few shearling coats smuggled from Turkey!" said
Bobby.

The waiter brought us limoncello. Sleeper kept looking over
Bobby's shoulder at the door.

"No," she said through cuttlefish-black teeth. "He won't return
it. He knows nothing about art."

I got up to go to the bathroom.

Bobby took my arm. "You're making all the husbands in Harry's Bar crazy," she whispered. "One of these aging trophy wives might follow you into the can and try to kill you."

"That was *such* Hades food," Bobby said, as we walked back north through Castello. Ten o'clock might as well have been two a.m., the piazzas deserted, storefronts shuttered.

"What is this Hades food?" I asked.

"You know, everything that's gray and not fresh," she said. "Gravies, goulashes. Four-day-old leftovers."

"TV dinners," Lance pitched in.

"Yes. Also old-fashioned food. Most Polish meals are Hades food. *Gołąbki*, mashed potatoes. What are you doing?" Bobby asked Sleeper. He'd stopped a few paces behind us; he stared at a street-lamp casting a yolky glow on a section of canal and an old boat covered with a tarpaulin.

"Wait here," he said, walking out of the light along the narrow canal-side ledge. There was something uncanny and out of character about him walking away like that, hands in pockets.

"Is he about to piss into the canal?" Lance asked.

"Sleeper!" Bobby followed him. They stopped briefly, talking, then disappeared around a bend.

"What's going on?" I said to Lance.

"I don't know, but I'm freezing."

Tumbleweeds of fog drifted over the canal.

"We should go to the hotel?"

"Do you remember the way?"

In the distance we heard Sleeper yelling, "Hello! I know you're there!"

Lance: "What the fuck? Who's he yelling at?"

"*Zdravstvuyte!*"

"What the fuck? Was that Russian?" Lance stepped out onto the ledge, then back, pulling his phone out of his pocket.

The Sleepers reappeared, holding hands, and I realized the sight made me jealous.

Lance: "What've you guys been doing? My Honoré de Ballsack's frozen."

Bobby: "Oh, nothing. Sleeper thought someone was following us."

Sleeper: "Someone *was* following us."

Lance: "Who'd be following us?"

"Someone was following maybe earlier, when Sleeper and me . . ." I said.

Bobby: "What?"

"Maybe the man who it was was the same who, when we stole the painting, was cleaning his shoe and today with the *gelateria*," I said. "I didn't remember how I know him. Now I remember."

Lance: "Someone translate this gibberish into lingua Anglica, please!"

In Polish, I told Bobby that the man I'd seen by the *gelateria* might have been the man with bruised knuckles behind the house in the Pacific Palisades.

"Oh, probably one of Seryozha's baboons." She waved her hand. "He has a whole army. Seryozha's such a neurotic. Total control freak. But nothing to worry about, just his dumb KGB habits."

Lance: "What?! He was in the KGB?"

Bobby: "No, why do you say that?"

"*You* said it."

"I said *habits*, not that he was in the KGB! Guys, it doesn't even make sense—"

"Lower your voice," Sleeper said. "If there's someone . . . Anyway, I'll speak to Seryozha. This isn't acceptable."

"Oh, come on, stupids," Bobby said quietly, atypically obedient. "We don't even know it was a goon. Venice is full of creeps. Especially after dark. I mean, look at Lance."

The next day, the private eye came to visit the Sleepers. On my knees on their bedroom floor, I was cutting tags off Bobby's new Italian clothes. Performing my assistant's tasks, few as they were, proved not to be demeaning in the aftermath of sleeping with her husband; on the contrary—my tasks had acquired a sexual edge. Acts of fetishistic contrition, of subjugation to the powerful, powerless wife. Or it was I who was the incognito wife, doing the thankless household chores, while she, the mistress, the impostor, wore what should have been *my* expensive clothing.

The private eye, Fabrizio, sat on the living room sofa across from the Sleepers. I could see their profiles through the bedroom door and hear them without being seen. Curled in a decorative chair, in a red knit dress, Bobby told the story of her ex-husband stealing a painting from her, an account that ignored the whole return-to-the-museum subplot, along with the Russians, and misidentified the painting as "a family heirloom by the Polish painter Kossak."

"All I need—*we* need—from you is basically to locate my ex-husband. We don't need you to re-steal the painting."

The private eye said, "Full name, Damian August Chlebek, no?"

"That's right. But everyone calls him Łyski, like the drink," she said. "But don't look for him in a whiskey bar. He drinks beer, wine, and vodka."

"It's crucial he be located before he leaves Venice," Sleeper added. "As soon as possible. Bobby's family is upset about this theft."

The private eye had an earring, skinny jeans, long hair on the sides, and a few last wisps on top. He wore a blazer over a T-shirt that read: "THAT'S WHAT." —SHE

"I'm going to ask a question. A question, no?" he said.

"Okay."

"Here in Italy, me, my friends in the office . . . often we are under false pretenses hired. Chasing wild geese, as you say. I would like to know that you didn't ask him to steal the"—he consulted his notes—"painting by Kossak."

"Why would I do that?" Bobby yelled, knocking the coffee table with her knee. Teapot and teacups clattered. "Why would I want him to steal from me? It makes absolutely no sense. You're a logical man, aren't you?"

"*Signora*, eeh, it is only to ask. Many reasons." He bent over his notepad. "To hide the painting from your new husband, for example." He looked into Bobby's eyes. "No disrespect, *signori*. I ask always. Or your father? Or extort insurance money, no? People have needs, expenses. I ask."

"Well, you can ask, but that definitely makes no sense!" Bobby shrugged, stirring three spoons of sugar into her cup.

It seemed to me it made some sense. What if Bobby and Łyski *were* running a con, planning to scam Seryozha, escape together with all the reward money, and leave me with Sleeper as a consolation prize? But I liked this idea more than I believed it.

Sleeper cleared his throat. "I can assure you, her ex-husband acted on his own. When we realized he'd taken the painting, I wanted to report him to the police in Los Angeles, but my wife felt bad about having him arrested. I'm sure you understand."

"Why did Damian Chlebek, according to you, steal?" asked the eye.

"Obviously you haven't been married," Bobby said.

"No, in Italy, divorce, fifty percent. Marriage, a bad gamble here. My job, usually, it is to follow unfaithful wives." He lowered his eyes, as if to report on the unfaithful wives' doings was against his professional ethics.

Bobby snorted contemptuously.

"My theory is, Łyski feels bitter and wants revenge," Sleeper said. "Anyway, I don't see how his motivation is relevant."

"To know his psychology, it helps me, no?" The eye wrote something in his notebook. "Any *habits* I should know?"

"Habits? I don't know, what does anyone do?" Bobby said. "He drinks, plays guitar, like gigs or whatever in shitty bars. He takes long walks at night, talks to himself. Posts on social media. Here, I wrote down his account names for you." She passed the eye a folded piece of paper.

"And how do you know he is in Venice?"

"He spoke to a friend of mine here a week ago."

"Can I have this friend's name?"

"No point. My friend left Venice. He wouldn't talk to you anyway. I'm sure you can check if Łyski checked into hotels or rented a place? Do other stuff that I can't do? Not, like, just talk to my friends?"

"Don't worry, *signora*. We'll find him. My friends and I, we like to chase birds. Not wild geese, *signora*. And *not* pigeons. We hate pigeons in Venice."

"Why?" Bobby said petulantly, as if unfaithful wives and pigeons were the groups she most cared to defend.

"Pigeons more even than tourists. We give pigeons contraceptives, put it in the bird food. Even Excellency the Archbishop supports this."

At three pm be in your room, said the first text on my phone. Naked, said the second.

I spent an hour in a mirror.

"Hello, mouse," I said to my reflection.

The great inequality, Bobby had told me, is that a man's face is what it is, whereas a woman's face is a potential, a canvas. She didn't see this as an inequality in men's favor. She was forever improving on nature. Men should learn from women—makeup, heels, shapewear. Some men already had. If she could have it her way, she'd resurrect corsets, bind women and men alike. One evening, back in LA, she'd made up my face with highlighter and bronzer. "*Now* you're pretty," she said.

"Pretty mouse," I said to my reflection. "*Mysz*," I added in Polish. It was three, and I removed my clothes. At three ten, I got cold and under the covers. At four, I put my clothes back on and lay on my back, not to smear my makeup. Tears felt likely.

At four ten, he entered my room.

"Greetings. What's this?" He pointed at my sweater and jeans, coming toward me, and his face had a lovely, lonely look, serious but amused. This is what attracted me to him, among other things: The mix of incongruous moods. Moods folding at the corners. Elegant moods stained with spilled wine and coffee. Agonized humor, blithe seriousness.

"I *was* naked at three," I said into his neck, glad to hide my face, which, I feared, disclosed that I would've waited till midnight and beyond.

"I see." He pulled me on top of him into a chair, pulled my sweater off, binding my head and arms within it, kissing my breasts. "At least no underwear."

He tossed my sweater onto the floor. His belt buckle clinked like a bell. I resisted his weight, then gave in, following primitive protocols, conquest and forfeit, this ungentle gentleman handling my breasts, our clothes all around us like slain men.

It was from atop him that I saw her. The old-fashioned door to my room didn't lock automatically. She peeked at us from around a partition, barely visible except for one hand with burgundy nails, a string of blond hair, one wide-open eye, curious, hungry, odd, unpaired.

I'd never before been observed during sex and was amused to discover it turned me on. I rode on. Bobby's eye made us odd. Two plus one. The third person is a mirror.

She left quietly, as soon as I came. Sleeper hadn't noticed her, I was pretty certain, hadn't known that I was cheating on him with his wife in my head.

One hour after sex, his wife took me shopping. Neither of us had the will to purchase anything, though, so we wandered onto the Accademia Bridge, then back to Campo Santo Stefano for spritzatura. The intensely blue sky above the buildings attacked the ruby of the spritz in my hands. I drank it quickly, and the alcohol burned pleasantly in me.

"I saw you in the room," I said.

She sat next to me facing the *campo*. "No idea what you're talking about."

"When I first started to think of you and Sleeper, I had fantasy," I said. "Like what we did today, but other way around." I added in Polish, "In my fantasy back then, it was me who snuck into the room and you who were, you know, on top." I blushed, from the spritz, from the fantasy, mine, hers, ours, from my sudden audacity.

At first I confused the contraction of her face for excitement. Her bottom lip stuck out when she was displeased, but also absent-minded or absorbed, giving her a babyish look. The lip trembled, protruded, then extended into a malignant smile.

"Wioletta, darling," she replied in her precise, posh Polish, "do you really think I care to know what's in your bird brain? This is my fantasy. *Mine*, not yours." She leaned across the table and pinched the skin on top of my hand with two fingers.

"Repeat after me," she said, holding the pinch. She seemed drunk, though she'd had only half a drink. "The fantasy is yours."

A swarm of barren pigeons passed overhead.

"You're hurting me."

She didn't let go.

"Not all fantasies are equal. What do women fantasize about?" She spoke in English now, in a child's impish voice, a little girl narrating out of the hell of a grown woman's body. "Usually we like a tedious and prolonged foreplay, in which a rakish, promiscuous male adored by other beautiful women teases us, finally fucks us, disrespects us a little, but at the end wises up, drops his mistresses, and becomes a good dad, with a dad-bod instead of the cad-bod he had when he first made you swallow his dick. You have to read some books to make your fantasies more sophisticated. But even then, *even then*, they're all just variations on the same theme. Shall we have something stronger? I'm freezing."

She got bored of her performance. Her voice dropped to its

regular register, her claws relaxed. "I'm sorry, baby!" she said. "Did I hurt you?" She bent down and kissed my hand. "I'm glad you enjoyed yourself with my husband. That's what life's about— enjoying yourself! I hope he made you come many times. Do you want to go and find us some grappa? The waiter's gone some- where."

Hearing her say "come many times," I felt an echo of excitement, as if she were bewitching me back to this afternoon. Purse in hand, I stood up and entered the café. People crowded by the bar, drinking, laughing, and it took me a while to get the bartender's attention. By the time I got back outside, night had fallen. In the *campo*, peddlers had their night products out: fluorescent yo-yos that glowed blue and green when spun, neon rings that soared above the buildings and back into the peddlers' hands. Nobody bought them.

I placed the shots of grappa on the table and sat down.

"Look, there's Sleeper and me in, like, a hundred years." With her grappa, Bobby pointed at a stooped old couple in matching trench coats slowly crossing the *campo*, the woman leaning on a walker. "Men die younger than women."

The couple stopped. The man tucked a lock of the woman's hair under her beret, and they continued their slow journey.

"He still cares about her hair! They're going for a spritzatura. By the time that's Sleeper and me, you'll be pretty old, too. You'll be ugly and divorced and rich from your ex's money."

As the couple cleared the *campo*'s central sculpture, I saw the bald man in the puffer leaning against it, looking at us. "Oh my god," I said.

"Oh, relax," Bobby said, "you have a few more years."

"No. Seryozha's man. He is there, at sculpture. Don't look now."

"Ha! Where?" She looked immediately.

"Don't look."

The *campo* wasn't crowded. A peddler fired his neon ring into the sky, over and over, a halo for sale. The man took a seat on the sculpture's stairs.

"That's not the guy," Bobby said. "All bulky big boys look the same with shaved heads."

"I really think that I am not wrong."

"How can you tell?"

"I just know it is he."

"Let's drink these and go home. It's getting late anyway." She lifted her purse from the back of her chair.

"Should we call Sleeper, and he will walk us?" I placed a few banknotes under the ashtray. She had me carry our "petty cash," as she called it. I paid for all minor expenses. She paid for items that weren't "petty"—shoes, purses, scarves, a cashmere skirt with two leather pockets.

"Why call Sleeper? How's he going to help us?"

"I don't know. He is a man?"

She got up and cinched her red fur coat. "Stay close," she said. She headed for the café door, but then made a sudden right into an alley full of shops. "When we were married, back in LA, Seryozha had me followed a few times. I'm not afraid of his goons."

As we turned the corner, I looked over my shoulder. The man was indeed following us.

"It's he," I said. "He's wearing same puffer!"

"Come on." She grabbed my hand and broke into an awkward high-heeled trot. I hurried after her, past clothing stores, a peeling church, a kiosk full of postcards and porcelain masks.

"What happened when they followed you in LA?!"

She slowed, and we walked down a *calle*, holding hands.

"Christ, my body isn't built to jog." She rested her hands on her knees. "Do you see him?"

We were in what looked like the courtyard of a palazzo. Coniferous trees poked above one of the walls in lit clusters, and against this wall leaned two elderly, local-looking men.

"Should we go to police?" I asked, feeling safer in the presence of these grandfathers.

"And say what? 'We think a man might be walking behind us? Arrest us! We've been *bad*.' Let's sit here for a while." She pulled me toward a bench covered with carved initials. The bench was cold and damp.

The grandfathers eyed us and spoke inaudibly.

"Let me find back to the hotel." I pulled out my phone.

"It makes no sense. Why would Seryozha want to follow me anyway?"

"Maybe he doesn't trust you." The path back in my map app was insanely complicated.

"Nonsense. Everyone trusts me. Especially Seryozha. He knows if I lie, it's for his own good. It's an advanced form of trust. You understand, because you're from the East. My blisters are killing me. Baby, do you have the Band-Aids?" It was cold, and she smoked her own breath, out the mouth and into the nose, what I'd heard her call a French inhale.

"Sorry," I said, "we all used."

"We used them all," she corrected.

The grandfathers detached themselves from the wall and walked away. Some church bells tolled, and a family of four entered the courtyard.

"*Kurwa*," I said, because a few paces behind them, like a relative they'd been trying to lose, came the man with the skull tattoo. "Bobby." I squeezed her hand and whispered in Polish, "He's here. Let's follow this family."

She'd been fixing her shoe. She looked up at the man. The family noticed him, too, and something in his appearance made the German-looking father grab his children and wife by the hands and leave the courtyard.

"Bobby?" I stood up. "Shall we go?"

"I give up. I shouldn't have worn pointy-toed heels. I can't go anywhere," she whined.

Pretending to look at Bobby's shoes, I peered at the man through my hair. He was coming right toward us. No, he wasn't. He'd settled under the palazzo's windows, hands in pockets, looking past us more than at us. A large watch glinted on his wrist, above dark joggers and pristine white sneakers.

"Excuse me, sir?!" Bobby said in a false, mellifluous voice, Marilyn Monroe singing "Happy Birthday" to the president.

"What are you doing?" I said in Polish.

The man didn't react. Perhaps his sharp chin shifted skyward slightly. There are countries in which, I thought incongruously, thugs like this are presidents.

"Excuse me, sir, darling!" she sang.

Did he not speak English? There was no one else in the courtyard, and her voice reverberated: *darling, darling, darling.*

"Okay, I'll come to *you*, though it's not very gentlemanly."

When she stood up, gathering her fur around her neck, I remembered the ripped letter from the psychiatrist in Sleeper's book. Her limping toward the thug was like the missing part of that letter, some testimony of madness, performed instead of written.

"*Dorogoy*," she said in Russian. "*U vas ne budet sigarety?*"

"What you want?" I thought I heard him mumble.

Her laughter was short and jagged. "Could I steal a cigarette from you?"

He looked at her.

"Cigarette. *Sigareta.*" She mimed lighting a cigarette.

From his puffer's pocket, he fetched a pack and passed it to her. She took one cigarette out, handed it to him, and pocketed the pack.

"Tell Seryozha you can poison yourself with something better, *dorogoy*," she said again, which I think meant *darling*. "Now, can you help us find our way back to the hotel?"

"What hotel?" he barked.

"My hotel." She leaned toward him in a way that was strangely intimate. "Really? Do you have to continue this tedious game? So unattractive when a man can't simply tell the truth! *Do svidaniya!*" she told him. "Come here, baby."

I walked to her, and she leaned heavily on my arm, lighting and smoking a cigarette that had a very Slavic smell—of teachers' lounges and the parking lot behind the meat factory where my mother worked when I was a kid. We walked out of the courtyard.

"Hey!" he said, maybe realizing he'd lost his pack. He took a step toward us but stopped, like a dog confused by conflicting impulses. I thought her limping was an act. She kept it up all the way back to the hotel. I'm not sure if he followed us.

In the golden, mirrored warmth within the elevator, she looked haggard. Humidity had made her own hair wild but left Ruslana's relatively smooth. There was something erotic to this chaos. I wanted to mess her up further.

"Please don't tell Sleeper about us talking to this guy, okay?" she said. "It's not like he'll be able to change anything, but it will annoy him. I'm going to order room service."

In the plush silence of the hotel corridor, she inserted the key into her door. "Don't wait up for Sleepy tonight," she said in a prissy tone.

13

When, a few days later, the private eye texted the Sleepers the address of a small hotel near Chiesa di San Lorenzo where Łyski had supposedly stayed, Bobby stealthily deleted the message from Sleeper's phone. She didn't even tell Lance about it. I think she was hoping the two of us could fix what we'd messed up.

"We're going to get our upper lips threaded," she announced at breakfast.

"Why? I love that stubble-in-a-skirt look," Lance said, without looking up from his book, strawberry jam on his fingers. The hotel had incredible jam that came in tiny single-serving jars. I had hoarded sixteen already. "You see it with the eighteen-year-olds lots these days," he added.

Sleeper read news on his phone, dark circles under his eyes. From what—a sleepless night of bickering, tax strategy, sex? Side-lit by looming windows, his irises looked amber, cruel, distant. I watched him butter his toast. He made sure the whole surface was evenly buttered, leading the knife over it one more time, a caressing, unnecessary motion. He didn't look up at me or Bobby. I'd have eaten the toast already, with jam.

"I only said the thing about our upper lips as an excuse," she said as we left the hotel. "If I said we were getting our nails or hair done, they'd notice we didn't. Sleeper would, anyway. He's a nail fetishist. Has he made you spread your fingers on your tits? You still have that pearl gray from LA. The tit thing's better with a dark color, for contrast." I had learned not to respond to such questions.

In the shopwindows, male torsos wore shirts of many colors. Quills lay in long beige boxes in the souvenir shops. On a large display board outside a bookstore hung hand-drawn maps of the archipelago and prints of famous paintings, each wrapped in plastic film. It was early, and the churches laid their shadowy weight on the *campi*, affording only slivers of sun where a few locals stood shivering with their dogs. With no crowds to navigate, we reached Łyski's hotel in under twenty minutes.

After Bobby knocked a dozen times on doors and windows, a woman, presumably the owner, stuck her head out over one of the hotel's balconies. *Sì*, a man named Damian Chlebek had left more than a week ago. Her nephew had helped him move his stuff.

"Where did he go? Did he carry any large packets? Frames? Anything rolled up?" Bobby asked.

"*Aveva una chitarra*," the woman said, kitchen noises clamoring behind her.

"He had a guitar," Bobby translated. "The nephew took him to Piazza San Marco. I feel we're getting close."

"How so?" I asked in Polish. "She didn't actually tell us anything."

She tossed her hair over her shoulder and began walking back to our hotel. "Do you speak Italian?"

"No."

"So you can't know what she said."

"She said something more helpful?"

"Stop speaking Polish!" she snapped.

I followed her in careful silence for a dozen paces. She spun and pulled a roll of tape from her purse and came at me. I ducked back.

"Hold still," she said, ripping off a piece of tape with her teeth. I thought she was about to tape my mouth shut, but she slapped it on above my lip and pulled.

"Oh! Owwwww!" She got one of my nose hairs.

"Well, it *needs* to be a little red. He notices everything," she said, taping her own lip.

The nose hair brought a tear into one of my eyes, and that brought resentment and then an uncharacteristic desire for confrontation. I wanted to ask her *why* she was letting me sleep with her husband every day. She and Sleeper were not in a marriage of convenience, not sexually indifferent to each other, not at all. There was a game afoot, and I wanted to fathom it, not just be a puppet in it. But I didn't ask. I watched our silhouettes on glass and stone, mine smaller than hers, overtaking hers, sometimes blending with it. I wanted to ask her but worried the answer might end the game. Some games are for the naïve, for the uninitiated only.

On the wall of a cathedral, a third silhouette walked on shadow-stilt legs behind ours, disappeared after a turn, then reappeared and kept its usual distance. She ignored him; so did I.

In the following days, Bobby and I searched for Łyski. Like everything else, our search was disorganized, and tended to include places Bobby wanted to eat at or see. Had we found him, would it all have ended not so terribly?

Sleeper and I were afternoon lovers. After sex, each day, for half an hour, we were a couple. We'd lie in bed watching the canal in the window. The building on the canal's far side had a thick growth of moss, with light and darker territories. Gondoliers floated past it, as if across a map.

"I like being with you," Sleeper said, our heads on one pillow. "You have a quality that's very uncommon. You're pretty-sad. Not pretty sad, a pretty type of sad."

"I'm not. I just look. My mouth is down," I said, "and you are not sad," not because it was true, but to deflect his too-hot and too-sharp attention, to alleviate some of the melting-narrowing feeling in my head and chest.

"I'm not sad, because nobody lets me be. There's a conspiracy against sadness in our household, maybe for the best."

Did he mean Bobby, her constant demand that everyone around her entertain? Could there be a touch of tyranny behind the joie de vivre? I didn't want to talk about Bobby. Bobby was all I wanted to talk about.

We lay not touching, closer than touching. Unable to stand it, I lifted his hand and kissed it. There was a white line bisecting his right palm.

"What is this?"

"An old scar from sailing."

"I don't know you sail."

"Used to, long ago." Without letting my hand go, he rearranged the comforter. "Tell me something about you I don't know. You've barely told me anything. You don't speak much."

"There is nothing about," I said, feeling my "nothing" was like his sadness, an archaeological layer under the city in which we lived out our everyday lives. Not every layer is worthy of excavation.

"Good. I'm interested in extremely vapid people." His smile was warm and teasing.

"That's not how I meant."

Someone yelled outside; someone yelled back. Snippets of Italian often came in through windows, cracked open to counteract the radiators that couldn't be turned off.

"How about something from your childhood?" Sleeper said.

"I don't have it."

"You look like one of those people who might have had a childhood."

"Okay." I shifted toward him, onto my side, our faces so close that he was just a blurred presence. "Once, I was twelve, I stole a soap."

"A soap?"

"At Lourdes. We went for pilgrimage, from church. There were soaps in the basket outside, next to stores, like here in Venice, and I just took one, like Bobby takes."

"Soap is needed in places of worship. Especially in the summer," he said.

"I didn't go to church again."

"Right," he said, "and who can be sad in bed with a lapsed Catholic girl like you?" He sat up and drank from a water bottle, his Adam's apple moving.

"And my mother has aphasia," I told him, as if there were a link between that pilgrimage, long ago, and her disease now. Lourdes, Fátima, Rome. Old women with swollen feet and plastic bags in hands, stepping off buses, my mother among them. Aphasia, the very last bus to a forgotten place.

"I don't like to talk to her, because I don't like to see how she forgets," I continued. "Then I feel guilty about." Was it true? True enough, enough of true. It was part of some general opening up: legs, hearts, hierarchies.

"It must be incredibly hard for you," he said, stroking my hand. "Sometimes the thought of forgetting my parents one day makes me even sadder than the thought of losing them. Adulthood *is*, in a way, the slow process of forgetting your parents."

Then he *was* close with his parents. Why hadn't they come to his wedding? Did they dislike Bobby? I didn't ask but asked instead, surprising myself, maybe him, too, "Is it true Bobby can't have a baby?"

I don't remember Bobby telling me any such thing directly. It was more that there was something essentially childless about her, not in the way of women who chose not to have babies because of careers, but in a premodern way.

For a second, a distance developed between us. He closed it with a warm, evasive smile. "Some people don't want to be forgotten," he said.

"Now you say about." I touched his chest, drew back, then made myself touch him again. My caresses were tainted with tentativeness. "Make us not sad. Or say something about you that nobody doesn't know."

"My name is Sebastian Sleeper. I'm thirty-nine. Everyone who knows me knows that," he said.

"What?" It took me a moment to realize my error. English is full of traps. "You know that's not what," I said, faux-exasperated. "Polish, there are double negatives. You know?"

"I know all about double negatives."

"So . . . you tell me something nobody knows," I corrected. "I want to know something from your childhood."

"At this point it's hard to believe in my childhood, but okay. When I was a kid, the same age as your soap-stealing self, my dad left my mother for another woman and had a daughter with her. I became obsessed with the idea that somehow I wasn't his biological son, as if his becoming a father to someone else should retroactively cast suspicion on his paternity. The fact that I was actually suspecting my mother of a dalliance with some unknown man, just because her husband decided to leave her, escaped my underdeveloped reasoning. I still haven't quite put the reproductive process together." He touched my stomach. "So I stole my father's comb, hoping to have his genetic material analyzed."

"Did you do it?" I said, remembering Lance telling me the redhead in the photo might not have been Sleeper's mother. But his mother sounded real, much more than mine ever was to me.

"Nope. I still have the comb somewhere," he continued. "A first-class comb, made in China. So you know, you and I, we're both drugstore thieves. We can't blame it all on Bobby." He kissed the nameless place where my side became my breast. "I like this part."

"I have to say something, too," I said. "Few days ago, the man always behind us . . . the man was talking to Bobby."

"What about?"

"She just asked him for cigarettes, I think. She said not to say. To you," I said, "but I thought it is better to say."

I was betraying Bobby's secret to create my own secret with Sleeper. But it didn't seem to bring us closer. He was no longer looking *at* me, but through me, as Americans say. I could feel the room's window in my midriff, stone walls and green water that could, on some meteorological whim, pour into my room, through the hole between my stomach and heart.

"She said not to say," I repeated, asking for the smallest sign of allegiance from him, against her. "Can you not say to her I said?"

"Sure."

"We will find Łyski?" I asked.

"It's in the hands of the private eye."

"I can ask another question?" I sensed this one would have to be answered. Back then, I still thought sex led naturally to honesty.

"See," he said, his jocularity returning. "I knew you liked to talk. You just needed to be provoked."

I asked, "What am I now?"

"What do you mean?" He was kissing his way from my hip to my legs, his hands on my belly, caressing it, stitching it closed.

"I feel bad taking money." It wasn't true. True enough.

"Don't you need it? For your mom, among others?"

I nodded.

"Take it, then. Like the soap. It makes you neither an assistant nor a concubine. There's no definition for the role you play. All the more exciting for you. These kinds of roles happen only a few times in life. The rest is very familiar, very *definable*. When you're a hundred years old, like me, you'll remember the one role you couldn't name."

"Why do you and Bobby always talk about when you're old?"

"Who knows. Out of immaturity, I guess. Or premature old age."

"Are you *definable*?" I asked. He was pleasantly heavy on my legs. I brushed his hair.

"Oh, there's a definition for me. A sad cad." He paused in thought. "Well, it's the same with fashion, really. What woman wants to wear a thing no other woman would? Of course, *you* seduced *me*."

"I? No!" I laughed. "I didn't seduce you."

"You did. You're always dressing to entice me."

"What?"

"Look at the dress you're wearing now."

"But I am naked."

"Oh, I thought that was just an extra-tiny slutty dress. Something Bobby bought you." He pulled himself on top of me. "Open your legs."

14

Giovanni e Paolo Hospital. Sleeper hurt. I was taking a late-morning nap when the text came, and my eyes were dry and itchy. Through a film of eyedrops, I read the message again and got out of bed.

What? What happened? I texted back. Is he okay?

No response. I called her, Sleeper, Lance. Lance's phone was off. The Sleepers didn't pick up. I dressed quickly in clothes I'd left on the floor. Always picking up after Bobby, I had no strength to pick up after myself. In the lobby, the concierge was giving hushed directions to an older man with a newspaper under his elbow. A receptionist told me the fastest way was by water taxi.

I'm coming, I texted and crossed the black-and-beige checkered floor, playing a game with myself—if I stepped on beige, Sleeper wouldn't be okay. Exclusively on black tiles, I made my way to the canal door, onto the pier. The Grand Canal teemed with people in boats, on bridges, in windows, on walkways, people selling objects, people rowing people, people on the cathedral's cupola—these, on second glance, were gargoyles—all this shimmering, drifting, bobbing, floating to the pulsing rhythm of panic in my head.

"Giovanni e Paolo Hospital, please," I said to an attendant.

"Taxi arrives, *signorina*," he said, scanning me up and down, probably to assess if I was injured or unwell.

Just then Bobby texted. It was as if she were next to me, watching—this intuitive luck, this talent for disruptive timing fueled both her charm and her uncanny control over other people. All good, she wrote. No need to come.

It calmed and angered me. Is Sleeper ok? I knew if I called, she wouldn't pick up.

Already left the hospital.

The taxi pulled up to the dock.

"Sorry, I'm not going," I said to the attendant, smiling at him.

"Are you sure, signorina?"

"Yes, thank you."

Is he ok? I texted again.

I knew he was probably fine, but the possibility that he wasn't troubled me. The taxi bobbed; its captain shrugged at me, then revved and steered away.

I stood to one side on the pier, staring at my silent phone, and from under the noise of motors and bells a private inner noise arose in me, a white noise full of wanting and frustration, violent and pathetic. I opened my notes app: to-do lists, a how-to-improve-B's-house file, a how-to-improve-myself list. Opening a new note, I typed in Polish at the top: *why do I — him list*. I couldn't bring myself to actually list any reasons, or even to write the verb.

I don't know how long I stood there. Finally a new message came from Bobby:

I told you not to tell Sleeper
about us talking to Kostya.

                                    Who's Kostya?

Seryozha's goon.

                                    What happened??

Meet us for lunch at
Trattoria Malebolge.

                                    When?

Now.

I started to type that I was busy now, then deleted it and apologetically approached the liveried attendant again. Normally I'd never have hired an expensive water taxi just to go to a restaurant, even if the Sleepers were paying for it, but I indulged this expense out of spite.

Had my loose tongue caused Sleeper to get hurt? Scenarios flooded my head. He'd had a heart attack. Some thirty-nine-year-olds do, especially ones with wives like Bobby. Spite eclipsed the fear I'd felt, as well as disappointment that the "secret" I'd shared with Sleeper had come back to Bobby so soon.

Green water splattered on my jacket as the taxi sped. To my disappointment, the restaurant didn't have a dock, and my imagined water arrival with the Sleepers watching didn't happen. Instead, I disembarked blocks away and navigated down the narrow streets until I found Trattoria Malebolge, tucked between an antiques seller and a secondhand-books store. I looked around. At least no goons had followed me.

Sleeper, Bobby, and Lance were seated with a man and a woman on a terrace looking out over a side canal, bottles of wine and remnants of food on everyone's plates. They must have been there for at least an hour. Sleeper had a bandage on his left eye. Bobby, a hand on his chin and a glass in her hand, was saying, "—like unattractive men. You see them all balding and beer-bellied and, like, they still have appeal. People assume they must've been handsome crocs in their youth."

"When a broken *bricole* floats in a canal," said the man with an Italian accent, "the Venetians, they call it a crocodile, a *coccodrillo*." He was older than Sleeper, probably in his fifties, balding.

"Dangerous to the boats," said the woman by his side.

Maybe due to the noisy British family at the only other table on the terrace, I stood unnoticed behind the Sleepers in their chairs, the patio heater hissing in my ear, for nearly half a minute. The man and woman with them saw me but didn't react. Maybe they assumed I was staff. Finally, I touched Bobby's shoulder.

"Here you are!" Bobby said. "Everyone, meet our assistant. This is Caio and Chiara, horrible people. We ran into them in front of the hospital. What the hell were you doing there, anyway?"

"We were checking on Chiara's mother," Caio said.

"Something bad?" Bobby asked with barely veiled macabre interest.

"Oh no, it's just she had a small . . ." He mumbled the name of some ailment, as I squeezed around the British family to our table's only free chair. I didn't look at Sleeper, but his hand brushed my knee as I passed.

"Hello!" said Chiara, giving me two air-kisses on the cheeks. She had chin-length hair, silver rings on each finger including her thumbs, and, despite her kisses or maybe *because* of them, an air of superiority. Or maybe I just didn't like other women around Bobby. Chiara's husband nodded at me the way he had nodded, a moment ago, at the waiter.

"I'm Viva," I said to Chiara and Caio, then looked at Sleeper very pointedly, concernedly, girlfriendishly. "What happened? You are okay?"

"Sleeper got into another fistfight!" Lance yelled from the table's opposite end, hiccupped in what was meant to be his comedic pause, and then delivered, ". . . with his wife!" Everyone laughed. I didn't. Theirs was the kind of laughter that follows a running joke that's getting old. "I said to Bobby," continued Lance, "'Not another nosebreak!'"

Sleeper lifted a knife and facetiously studied his reflection. The eye bandage gave his face a sexy, piratical look. "It's possible the memory of my original nose," he said, "has become so idealized that each new nose appears clumsier than its predecessors."

"But who have you fight?" I demanded. Was I the only one who cared about him?

Lance: "Bobby!"

Bobby: "Kostya! He fought Kostya."

And then of course they launched into their usual aggravating giggles. Sleeper only smiled, I guess amused by keeping me poorly informed. Chiara whispered something into Caio's ear. I'd expected an emergency and found a party. At the head of the table, I was bitterly exposed and yet invisible. A waiter passed me a menu.

"She'll have what I had," Bobby told him. She returned my menu and pointed at a pile of empty black shells on her plate. She then ordered the whole dessert menu for everyone to share and asked the waiter to serve it at the same time as my dish. I didn't feel like mussels, but apparently I had no choice.

"But didn't you fight Bobby's ex one time? Back in LA?" Chiara asked Sleeper. "What's his name again?"

"Łyski," Lance said.

"Maybe you fought him again?" she said with a flirtatious air. She had long, pretty fingers she tapped together as she spoke. I wondered what she thought of Bobby and what Sleeper thought of her.

"I wish!" said Sleeper. "But we haven't found old Łyski yet. That, as you know, is why we're here."

"How do you know he's still in Venice?" Caio asked.

"We don't," Sleeper said. "We're waiting on a private eye to tell us."

"I prefer the public eye." Lance yawned, turning his collar up. He was drunker than usual.

"Oh, I know he's still here," said Bobby.

"And how can you know that?" Lance threw a bread ball at Bobby and missed.

"Intuition." She smiled. "Besides, it's important to come here at least once a decade. Not to mention, these two are having such a lovely honeymoon."

"Who?" Chiara said.

"My naughty husband and my great assistant." She placed her hand on my shoulder, and everyone looked at me. "A honeymoon without a wedding. Sleeper's had her many times."

"What?" said Chiara.

"Yeah, they're at it night and day. It's so exciting! Don't look shocked. It's quite a thing, not just with humans. Lance, what was that thing with the grouse?"

"What?" said Lance.

"The grouse that doesn't want to fuck the other grouse."

"Oh, the *grouse*." Lance rolled the *r* the Polish way. "Nerds at Oxford conducted a study on fucking grouse. The male grouse chases the tail of the female grouse. But she's not putting out. Then the grousologists, like, put the male grouse with this hot, stuffed female grouse with extra feathers in her nostrils or whatever makes grouse hot to grouse. Seeing the rival, the female grouse comes running back, knocks the stuffed hussy over, and boinks the male grouse she previously didn't find attractive."

"Right. Except it isn't that I didn't find my grouse attractive." Bobby tousled Sleeper's hair. "But, yeah, that's the general mechanism. Works on birds, cats, bitches."

"Maybe that's enough birds, cats, and bitches," Sleeper said and smiled at me.

She followed his eyes to mine. "What? It's not my fault it works this way! I didn't, like, design evolution. *God* did!" She guffawed. "The stuffed grouse benefits, too. It gets to feel adored and real!"

They all looked at me. The distressed concentration on Chiara's face especially annoyed me; she was studying me, I could tell, re-evaluating a judgment she'd formed earlier. What did she see? My burning, shiny face, my hair in a messy bun on my nape, flaking skin on my nose. I'd left the hotel in a hurry. The Sleepers had been telling me I was so pretty, but I didn't believe them, and now I was allowing myself to be judged by the whole group, these strangers—especially Chiara, who was somehow the final arbiter, being an attractive woman of the world to which I had begun to feign belonging. Her judgment would cement my lack of beauty. My defenses disappeared. I was weak, with love, with this sudden exposure, with my role as catalyst—or stuffed grouse—of my employers' desire, which I understood less the more it was explained. I couldn't look at Sleeper or Bobby or Lance and thought I was about to cry and yet knew that to cry now was to lose, to ruin it all forever; I looked at my hands, the canal, and across the canal a curtain in a window, on which was cast the unmoving shadow of some nameless woman I'd never meet.

There was a change in Chiara's face when I looked back at her. Her brown, upturned eyes, with their thick eyelashes and tiny wings of burgundy eyeliner, expressed something like a conclusion. It was neither compassion nor sympathy. It was admiration, perhaps even marvel. Who knows how we interpret the looks and thoughts of others, but for me this unexpected—perhaps even misinterpreted—look was a salvation. From this look, I was able to construct a new self-definition. Stuffed or not, I was the thing the grouse wife envied. Instead of shabby and underdressed, I felt part nun, part off-duty model, someone ascetic and above adornment, whose religious strictures or bone structure elevated her above the multitudes who spend time vainly preening. I'm pretty sure I even smiled.

"Bobby," Chiara said in an admonishing tone. "You shouldn't joke like that."

"Oh, don't be so narrow! She *has* seduced my husband," Bobby said. "It's the truth. How can you deny an assistant what she desires? One must be democratic!" She reached and stroked my face and said, "Darling." "Darling," she said to Chiara, "don't look so shocked! You want me to believe old Caio never rogered an assistant? How about that Finn girl who worked with us at the Biennale? The one with the big butt, who never wore a bra?"

Chiara: "What Finn girl?!"

"I don't remember anyone like that," said Caio stiffly.

"It's okay, my wife gets carried away after some wine," Sleeper said. "Ignore her, Chiara."

Bobby kissed him on the mouth, with tongue.

Chiara: "I don't know if I think it's right for an employer and employee to sleep together."

Bobby: "Oh, you're wrong. Women should be able to use beds as vehicles to power."

Lance lifted his wine. "Cheers to Roberta, the last hope of feminism."

"You, too, are, as usual, wrong. It's a very, very feminist point. So feminist *I* shouldn't even be making it. Women love power. If a woman wants to sleep her way to the top, it's her right. And death to any sexist pig who wants to stop her." Bobby shrugged, then finished her wine. "*Vino veritas!* Don't pour it into me and then expect me to lie to my friends and lovers!" She opened her mouth, into which Lance poured the last drops of wine from the bottle.

She had said "lovers." Did she mean me? Lance kissed the bottle, with tongue.

The waiter appeared with my mussel linguine and thirteen desserts. Caio broke the tiramisu crust and complimented its texture. Chiara swiped on her phone. I twirled linguine on my fork, and Bobby reached for more wine, her unruly breasts, in their peach cashmere, nudging the edge of my plate. I was mildly shocked to realize I wanted her tied up, naked; I wanted to whip her with something, to punish her until she called me *boss*, to fuck her with the bottle.

———

When I asked Sleeper later that afternoon, he was standing in the middle of the room, hair wet from a shower, bending over a room service cart.

"You want to do what? Say again?" he said, carrying a plate to the bed. "French fry?" he offered.

"Yes to French fry," I said.

He put one in my mouth. Naked, he sat at the foot of the bed, his bandage damp from the shower. I hadn't asked again about his eye. Information was to be gathered only indirectly here. His being hurt was attractive. A man returned from battle.

"You want what?"

"At the same."

"You want me *and* Bobby, together? Am I not enough?" he asked with a comic frown.

I hid my face in the pillow. "You know I can't talk about!"

"You're a good Catholic. You can *do* it but not talk about it."

"No, if you are not the priest."

"Why do Italians always skimp on ketchup?" He got up and searched the cart for condiments.

I admired his broad back and laughed. "I don't know. I just want this."

"But why? I'm very curious." He discovered another ketchup jar under a napkin, placed it on his plate triumphantly, and got back into bed.

"When I am with you—" I started, then started again. "When I was with Bobby, I prefer you. But I can't stop, you know, to think about her. I feel like she . . . she could be here, too." I patted the bed, smiling, as if it were generosity that drove me, though, in fact,

I wanted Bobby in this bed to rob her of the witchy, counterintuitive power she wielded by "giving" him to me, day after day. I wanted to repay the gift, a gift so weighted with potential consequences that it terrified me. Yet this wasn't a fear that inhibited action. This was fear as aphrodisiac.

Indeed, there was movement under the sheet, below his waist.

"See? It agrees! It tells only true," I said. "It doesn't lie."

"What can I say?" he said.

I smiled sweetly at him, terrified. The bed is as good a place for revenge as any. The best place, perhaps.

The envelope was gray, with Bobby's and Sleeper's names written in golden script. It had no stamp. Someone had brought it to our hotel. With a butter knife I found atop the minibar, I carefully unsealed the envelope. The text was in Cyrillic, but the date and time—October twenty-seventh at eight p.m.—were readable. Two days away. Without a Cyrillic keyboard to input the letters, I couldn't use the internet to translate it. It looked, though, like an invitation. From whom, Kostya the goon? He didn't look like he could spell his own name, never mind throw a party. A different Russian friend? Did it have something to do with the Vermeer?

The foreign writing filled me with foreboding. I would go to her and hand her the envelope. Sleeper and I were to meet her at a rooftop lounge in an hour. It was her idea, to meet her out in the city for spritzatura, as if Sleeper and I were a couple arriving together.

I turned on the old-fashioned shower taps and stepped into the shower. I had showered in preparation for school, work, dates, parties, medical examinations, but never a ménage à trois. I shaved more carefully than I would for any doctor—any man, for that matter—and examined myself in the mirror for blemishes. I pinned my hair back like a ballerina, extended my eyes with shimmering eyeshadow I'd snatched from Bobby's makeup bag. I pulled on a strapless dress and studied myself for a long time in the long mirror.

When Sleeper knocked on the door, a queasy feeling hit my arms and stomach, like before a test or performance. I opened the door. He was different, the same. His kiss was less known, less *mine*. He didn't seem nervous. He brought me a single flower. I misplaced it somewhere before we left. Did he have a flower for her, too, in his jacket? The envelope was in my purse. I didn't mention it.

Late, grave, funereal Venice. I held his arm to avoid slipping on damp stones. At the rooftop bar, I ordered white wine and drank it quickly at a table by the railing, in the wind.

"Cold?" Sleeper asked me. Before I could answer, he asked a waitress to turn on the overhead heaters. No need to tell him my trembling wasn't due to cold.

Bobby was late, of course. People watched her cross the rooftop terrace, satin dress under her mink sweeping the parquetry; she appeared to glide like a queen being moved on a chessboard.

"You ordered an escort?" she said to Sleeper in a low voice. "I don't know if my pimp explained, but it's extra for couples."

"Wait, whose fantasy are we in?" Sleeper asked.

She sat across from us. "Tonight you're a businessman, like . . ." She didn't finish. Had she almost said, "like Seryozha"? Ruby lips, rubies on fingers, she reached into the bowl of pistachios. She was drinking, chattering about escorts, pornography, cracking nuts and arranging the shells in a line.

Sleeper watched her, one hand on my leg, the other on his drink.

We ordered whiskey. I was learning about whiskey. Bad tastes taste good in whiskey. Rotten leaves, brass. Autumn on ice. Church bells rang, and a flock of pigeons, small as flies, rose from a scatter of tourists' bread in the piazza below.

"I'm for sale. I'm expensive," she said.

"I think that's right. You're a prostitute in essence. Only no one can afford you," Sleeper said.

"I'll fuck you for a Vermeer," Bobby said. "Throw in a Rubens, I'll fuck your little wife." She looked at me defiantly, lit a cigarette, and propped it against a Murano ashtray. The basilica of Santa Maria della Salute, made miniature by distance, jutted from her shoulder like a weird wing. It had been built, Sleeper told me, to commemorate the plague.

"I like this new vulgarity on you. Very Weimar and velvet," he said.

"Vulva," she said and swept the flotilla of shells off the table. Some fell between rails down into the piazza. The cigarette pack she'd placed by the ashtray fell between her shoes. He bent to pick it up. The cigarettes were labeled in Cyrillic. He knew whose they were. His bandage was off, and the swelling exaggerated the sudden bad weather in his face. She was taunting him in ways that exceeded the rules of the sexual game, that weren't fun for him. She wanted us both to hate her, a little at least. It struck me she might be someone who invited revenge on purpose, knowing the eroticism of revenge.

I remembered the envelope, even thumbed its edge inside my purse, but didn't pull it out; to do so might derail the game, turn Bobby back from escort into wife and me from wife into pumpkin.

Sleeper plucked the smoking cigarette from the ashtray, took a puff. I'd never seen him smoke.

"Cheap," he said, "but good."

The whiskey arrived, and we drank it quickly, like you aren't supposed to.

"Is it hard, having two women to defend now?" Bobby asked him, taking my hand in hers on the table, her eyes faraway, looking right into mine, dreaming through eyeliner—dreaming *at* *me*, if that makes sense, through a black flood. Before he could respond, she said to me, "So, this is what you wanted?"

She wanted my confession.

"I do what you say. You're my boss," I said. I'd become good at the game. Whoever admitted desire admitted to weakness. I played with her fingers, her rings. The winner, if there should be one, would be the more distant, the one with more sexual sprezz.

Sleeper watched with ambivalence, amusement. "You two are wonderful together," he finally said. "Let's go to the hotel."

"Let's go," Bobby said and shivered. "Stupid can't wait to get us into bed. Look at Viva's tits, aren't they great?" she said, unbuttoning my jacket.

"You show your," I said. "Your pimp said I can see."

"Oh no," said Sleeper, chuckling, as I opened her fur.

She pulled away; her arm shot into the air, gold and platinum bangles clinking. The waiter came immediately. Waiters came to her immediately.

Holding hands, we filled the widths of the *calli*. People stuck to walls and walked around us. We had, that night, an energy that insults those it doesn't include. The Russian, Kostya, was following us. I didn't know it until we were in the hotel. Sleeper called the elevator. Bobby pointed through the glass at Kostya lurking by the restaurant across from our hotel.

———————

"Drinks. We need drinks!" Bobby called room service once we were back in their suite.

I paced in the living room, pumps leaving divots in rugs, gliding my hand across a table, the mantelpiece, roundels on the backs of armchairs. Though everyone had been with everyone already, a general nervousness had developed. I stopped by the window and looked out at Venice, at two cities really, one in stone, the other a drunken copy rendered in water by light. The Russian was down there, in the watery outside. He must've delivered the envelope. In my bag on the floor, it was erotic, mine. It was a fetish. Maybe I'd never give it to them. I had the power to disinvite the Sleepers from wherever they'd been invited.

Sleeper sat, used his phone. I sensed him behind me, a hard, silent presence. Proud but self-seeing—but preening, articulate, a hopeful nihilist, a man with money and answers, the last man alive who pulled out chairs and opened doors for women. It will be difficult for my younger readers to fathom my desire for—to even imagine—such a man. But read your history, girls. Men then were publicly opinionated. They didn't speak only when spoken to, and you didn't have to beg them to go to bed. Quite the opposite. Men in my generation agreed to sex willy-nilly, without messaging their lawyer, without even a short-form contract, much less a personal long-form. In 2018, sex was still almost entirely unlegislated.

I faced him, struck by how resigned his face was in the toxic green light of his phone—a wounded man in a medical waiting room, a bankrupt waiting for his audit to begin, a man disinvited from a party.

Bobby put on loud pop music and, waving her dress flamenco style, flashing a gartered leg, blew out of the bedroom. Sleeper's face regained its usual expression of ironic distance. In that distance Bobby and I began to play, to kiss and giggle and undress each other.

A knock on the door.

"Ladies, hey. Go hide in the bedroom. I don't want to depress the staff."

When Sleeper pushed the cocktail cart into the bedroom, Bobby called out, "Who are you? You've come to serve us?"

We were on our knees in a huddle. They were kissing, crushing me between their torsos. A glass of wine, his hand between my legs, her hand and mine on his cock, his face tense. He was no longer bankrupt or sick—a businessman, though, evidently successful enough.

He had a beauty mark on his hip bone I hadn't noticed before.

"I think he's ready," she said after a minute. "Viva's ready, too," she told him.

"You first," I said.

She frowned but pushed me down onto the bed and crawled on top of me, with her ass in the air and her breasts in my face and one of her knees between my legs. When he started to fuck her against me, the full weight of my months of wanting him and wondering if I also wanted her—but certainly wanting her things and her life, maybe wanting them so much I wanted to wreck them—slammed into me. I came from that weight, secretly, against her knee. Her climax, minutes later, was preceded by another frown, one of concentration, as if she were leaning over a nearly completed jigsaw puzzle. Finally she found the last piece, and there it was: a battlefield, an island.

"Fuck, it's hot." She was sweaty, a little indignant. "It's like camp. Not *Notes on 'Camp,'* but summer camp," she panted; he collapsed off her, off us. "Your turn," she said to me.

"Give me fifteen minutes," Sleeper said.

"Are you asleep?" Bobby said. Their room at dawn, emergency blue. A multitone sound, a ghostly singing, came in through the cracked-open window.

"What's that?" I asked.

"*Aqua alta* siren. The lagoon is rising. The city is flooding," she whispered across Sleeper's sleeping form. "That was crazy, wasn't it?"

"Crazy," I said in Polish.

"English," she said.

Sleeper made a small noise of protest, then was again silent, an athlete at rest, his javelin under the bed. You could do anything to him. Cut his hair. Massive between us, he rose and fell.

"Let's hydrate." Bobby opened the minibar and crouched nude in front of the liquor and orange juice, peanut jars and chocolate bars.

"Sometimes I like you so much I want to be you," I confessed, surprising myself.

She returned with two waters. "Well, now we've done it all together. Robbed robbers. Had an orgy. You fucked my husband, you home-wrecker. You don't have to be me. You can just, like, be my friend."

That morning she believed it, as did I.

I reached for my purse, abandoned on the floor with shoes and underwear. I fetched the envelope.

"It came for you," I said. "It was for you at reception."

She opened it and shone her phone onto the invitation.

"Party on Saturday," she said, crumpled the invitation, and threw it across the room, where it landed by an overturned champagne bucket.

"Where?"

"Seryozha's."

"Seryozha lives in Venice?!"

"No."

"He comes about the painting?"

"Relax, he's just having a party. Why would everything be about that stupid painting? Nice of him to invite us." She fastened and unfastened a button on the duvet cover.

"Bobby . . ."

"Okay . . . but at least he's invited us, right? If he were upset, he wouldn't. Don't tell Sleeper yet, but this time for real. I'll tell him right before. If we tell him now," she whispered, "we risk . . . Well, you know how he is." She finished her water and extended her hand for mine.

"Bobby . . . I have a question," I said in Polish, handing her my water. "Why did you marry a man like Seryozha?"

"I don't know why I marry people," she replied in Polish. "I mean, why does anyone? Money? Green card? Just kidding. I was in love. With his money! No, I was in love. Ha. All the nineties movies tell you it's easy to love successful men. He was living in LA then. We met at the Gagosian. Łyski was in Poland, writing bad love songs for me, and could only visit for, like, a few months at a time on a tourist visa, and I was on a student visa. So I figured, marry Seryozha, use his green card and connections to get my own green card, pay my dues as an oligarch's wife, get that on my CV.

Then divorce and marry Łyski so *he* can get a green card. I didn't predict I'd fall in love with Seryozha. At first, we'd just go to parties and occasionally sleep together. It was fun. He was so lavish, so conspicuous, as only people from Eastern Europe are. It's easy to make fun, to call them vulgar nouveau riche, when you have the decadent Western perspective of people who've been so rich for generations they try to outdo each other appearing not rich." She switched back to English. "That's just countersignaling—it doesn't fool anyone. Seryozha had a terrible childhood. He was extremely poor under communism, and then, when an opportunity presented itself, he took what he wanted."

"I understand that."

"Exactly. I know you do. Eastern Europeans still get it. In America, only rappers get it."

Sleeper opened his eyes but didn't see us, or maybe saw us and thought we were in his dream, some dream of nouveaux riches at the Gagosian.

"And Łyski agreed to you marrying Seryozha?" I asked in Polish.

"Oh," she said in Polish, "it was his idea. At least in theory. Someone had to marry someone so the two of us could be in the US together. Not the best idea, but I was young—your age. You make all your most spectacular mistakes then. I probably should've done it the other way round, made Łyski marry someone for a green card, and then later married Łyski," she said. "Anyway, I had my gallery and didn't want to go back to Poland. I've always felt a weird loyalty to Łyski. I have, like, this infantile dream of him onstage in front of a hundred thousand swooning women, strumming his dumb guitar. I thought we could make that happen in LA. Like it was my responsibility. If that could happen, I thought, I'd want him more. I was naïve."

"What happened to gallery?"

"Seryozha paid the rent, but then . . . I was good at art but not math."

We lay on our sides, noses touching, in the cocoon of postcoital honesty. The tension between us had lifted. It seemed impossible I'd ever harbored violent thoughts toward her. She was being honest, eager to answer all my questions.

"And Seryozha didn't care you are with Łyski?"

"At first he didn't know. He was always traveling for business. Then, once he figured it out—well, he's a barbarian, very self-destructive, but I managed him. Tits and tears. Men can't resist them in tandem. Throw them a bone, they grow an *r* on the end of it. I was a good wife, though, to Seryozha, mostly. Best I ever was at being a wife. Probably because I knew I was *playing* at being a wife, you see. Now that I'm a true wife to Sleeper, it's harder to *play* wife."

"What does it mean?"

"Oh, nothing. Just don't fall too much in love with him, okay? You're not at all ready to go places he'd need you to go."

"I'm not in love."

"Remember, you're supposed to love *me* most." She kissed me without lust.

"How long you were with Seryozha?"

"Just a year. That's the maximum time you can be with an unsophisticated man. It will be so strange to see him on Friday."

15

You heteros and your precious adventures. Really, the impoverishment of you people is stunning. Each time you do something *slightly* beyond the normative, you want applause. If we weren't in Venice, I could get a four-way scheduled in five minutes on my phone, with a preview of each asshole's asshole." Lance lapped tea from his overfull cup like a dog. "But whatever, well done," he said, patting my hand.

I had told him, I think, because some events only take on actuality when told. Also, they recharge you with each retelling.

In a *cioccolateria*, we sat by the window, which looked onto a busy alley. Between the window and our table was a raked display containing, curiously, tools made of chocolate. Outside, apparently unaware of us behind the glass, face after face hovered over edible nails, drills, screwdrivers, needle-nose pliers, with expressions of rapturous amusement.

"Just look at these fucking people!" Lance squawked. "Okay, for example, Thomas Aquinas." He pried a raisin from his cookie. "*He* had a threesome with two angels. He rejected a prostitute, scared the poor thing off with a fire poker. Then two angels descended into his room as a reward, and he diddled them sideways."

A group of teenagers approached and photographed the tools. Lance regarded them with disapproval.

"It is not just threesome," I tried to explain. "I feel—don't laugh, but I am maybe tiny bit . . . in love. Not with him, I mean, but to him through her, but also to her through him."

"Exactly. Moral of the story. Don't fall in love with the angels." Lance meowed and waved his teaspoon. "What do you think it is about chocolate tools that makes everyone grin like fools? It's not anticipation of a treat, because you'll notice almost nobody comes in here and buys a tool. Some automatic serotonin response in the brain? The same thing that happens to old women in church and assistants in marital beds?"

"I'm talking serious. Last night was like . . . like I was sand inside the glass hour."

"The fuck? Are you speaking in tongues?" For the first time, he regarded me with worried interest.

"You know what, in Polish it is *klepsydra*."

"Ah, right, we have that word in English, too. Say 'hourglass' next time." He divided his cookie into small sections and ate two of them. "Jesus, don't look at me like that. I'm wearing sunglasses to protect myself from just this kind of incriminating look. Which suit should I wear to the party tomorrow, by the way? The gray one or maybe the new black one? What do you think?"

"The new one," I said.

He checked his watch. "I warn you, it's a murderously ostentatious crowd."

"And Sleeper," I said, "did she say to him whose party it is?"

"Doubt it."

An old man entered the café, sending a wrinkled front page of *L'Arena* out from under a table, across the floor. I wondered if he'd buy a tool.

"So what do you think . . . about Bobby and Sleeper, for me. What will happen?"

"Darling," Lance said, "despite my extensive sexual expertise, my romantic experience is antediluvian. It mainly involves platonic crushes on various straight professors and pedophiliac seminarians. I just don't know. I think to be wanted by the two of them must be very hot. Others can't even get one person to like them. I think what you confuse for love is the power of nonnormativity. It's exciting, to do what others fantasize about." He pointed out beyond the shopwindow. "Look, over there, behind the trash can. It's our lonely Russian friend. What do you think he'll wear tomorrow?"

Kostya, in a woolen hat and striped sweatpants, hovered over a large puddle.

"Hope not these pants," I said.

"Terrifying," Lance agreed. "The Sloppies are shopping right now for a dress for Bobby."

"They went now?"

"See? It's the calamity of odd numbers. One always feels left out."

"It's not how it was last night," I said.

"Don't be fooled," he said, finishing his cookie. "Sex is a *momentary* equalizer."

"I don't like that."

"Birds and beasts. We want to kill and hump. Bobby likes being on top. Her desire to control you will spike again. Your ability to defend yourself, after what you let them do, will dip. Garlic dip. Limp dick. Don't look at me like that. What do I know about love? Do I have a successful love life in your view? Nobody loves me. Nobody even likes me." He seemed genuinely dejected.

"I like you," I said, surprising both of us.

"You do?" He didn't look at me. He gathered the crumbs off his saucer and ate them. "You must have an exceptionally high threshold for monstrosity. There must be something wrong with you."

"You're maybe right. There is something with me," I said.

"Look, he's coming over," Lance said. "I don't think anyone can see us through the glass because of glare or something. Maybe he wants to buy a chocolate gun."

We waited as Kostya checked out the display case, for his face to fill with the apparently universal joy the chocolate tools elicited.

"Doesn't have normal human responses," Lance noted. "Something wrong with him as well."

Cold wind flowed under my dress, though I wore one of Bobby's fur coats. That year was one of the last for fur in the West, but Bobby frowned at "moralizers in synthetic jackets." She had declared more than once, "I prefer to kill ferrets than sweatshop children, thank you very much." She loved children, especially babies. She cooed at them in public places, asking mothers if she could hold them "for just a minute." Then, pressing one to her breast, she'd coo, "Hello, Mr. Baby. Do you want a new mommy?" And the babies smiled at her, liking her offer, and the mothers took their babies back with uncomfortable laughter. I never found out if Bobby had fertility problems, or if she'd ever lost or even tried to have a child.

"This gondola feels like a coffin," said Lance. Bobby and I sat facing him and Sleeper in the low seats.

The gondolier sculled in a cloud of his breath. Facades and piers materialized from fog.

"What are you talking about?" said Bobby. "It's the only way to arrive to the party like a local."

"In what century?" Lance snorted. "If I sniff the slightest whiff of anything bad, of shady behavior on Seryozha's part, I'm out. Don't care if I have to swim back to the hotel and end up like Katharine Hepburn."

"What happened to Katharine Hepburn?" I asked.

"She wore big dude pants," Bobby said. "She's why women don't wear skirts anymore, except for me and bimbos."

"Pants or no pants, she had to dive into a canal here for a role," Lance explained, "and picked up some eye infection from the sewage in the water. She never recovered from it. Her eyes were always watery. Forever after people asked her if she was crying. Ruined her reputation. Christ, do you smell, like, the bathroom in my basement flat in Montreal? Remember that rathole?" He snuggled against Sleeper's shoulder. "I don't want to die tonight. I don't want *this* to be my last smell."

"Relax," said Bobby. "Nothing will happen. Your imagination is too fecund."

Wobbling in a *vaporetto*'s wake, our gondola entered a narrow canal. In the receding *vaporetto*'s window, a lone male figure stood, not Kostya, no one, just that nameless passenger who, any night, on any form of public transport, passes you and has no consequence or face.

"What's wrong with everyone today?" said Bobby to Lance, but really to Sleeper. In a navy coat I'd never seen, he sat watching the water. I tucked my hand in his, and he held it for a moment. Then he placed it on my knee with an avuncular pat. Even his hair, moussed up for the party, struck me as a sign of some new inhibition—he wanted to rein himself in, keep me and Bobby off him. Without the usual strings of hair that fell across his eyes, his features were even more voluptuous and defined but also inaccessible, features that weren't quite his but those of a distant relative, a great-grandfather who arrived at parties in gondolas without pretense or affectation, a man who could never understand us—not me, not Bobby. This man would probably have challenged Seryozha to a duel.

Bobby hadn't told Sleeper the party was Seryozha's until we'd left the hotel. He'd been quiet ever since.

"We'll be in and out, I promise!" she said in her baby voice, playing with her elaborately pinned-up hair. "Sloppy Sleepy, there'll be lots of people there. You probably won't even see Seryozha!"

"The good ol' in-out," Lance murmured, thrusting a pinkie into his fist.

"I can tell *you* don't want to go either," she said, attacking me. "Fuck Seryozha. If nobody wants to go, let's just *not go*," she said, though she did nothing to turn us around. As we entered a wider canal, house music thudded from a palazzo's open windows out onto the water, and our gondolier increased our speed. Motorboats—no gondolas—ejected guests onto the palazzo's dock, into the arms of valets.

"Does he *own* this architectural orgasm?" Lance said as we docked.

"Just rented for the weekend. This will be a bore," said Bobby.

Past the *porta d'acqua*, several girls my age were taking off rubber boots and changing into heels. Canal water covered the flagstones of the inner courtyard. Assisted by valets, guests crossed wooden planks to a staircase.

Following Bobby through a *portego*, I realized, never having seen his photograph, I didn't actually *believe* in Seryozha. In a columned hall, against grisailles of hunting scenes, overly made-up women spoke Arabic and Russian.

Maybe I believed in him the way people like my mother "believed" in a deity—an apocryphal presence, predicated on an absence and a threat. The house in the Pacific Palisades where we found *The Lady* could have been rented by anyone, Bobby even. The Vermeer could be fake. What did I know? But this palazzo . . . who could afford a place like this, even for a weekend? Someone real and powerful had made this happen. In Bobby's universe, you learned about people through their possessions—bought, stolen, rented. Possessions preceded you like courtiers. To be was to have.

"Bar," said Sleeper, possibly the first thing he'd said that night, and we followed him into a ballroom, past fountains flowing with chocolate and vodka, swans of shaped ice, dead crustaceans, and silver salvers full of caviar and blini. Normally Bobby planned her entrances, waiting for a moment of relative silence, a drop in conversation, a temporary dispersal of other beautiful women. Today she acted more like me: stayed close behind Sleeper and Lance, casting anxious glances, pulling down the hem of her short dress.

"Git ten Rolexes in a room together, they all stop, but my Patek's just like my heart. It ain't quit!" said a man in a cowboy hat, his American voice dominating the "*dai*" and "*vai*" of Italian voices in a group beside us.

The line to the bar was full of angular Slavic faces, shaved heads, and suits. I looked for Kostya. The room was enormous, mosaic floors, tables lining the walls. In the center, near a Poseidon statue winged by fish and nymphs, stood a group of older men. They had the expressionless faces of those who think mostly in numbers but lacked the friendliness, the bovine benignity, of their American equivalents. They drank vodka from small glasses and talked with their hands.

"Do you see that guy there, pale as Julian Assange?" Bobby whispered and clutched my hand. The group reshuffled, parted, and a short man with snowy hair and a pin on his lapel approached a much taller man and stood on his toes and kissed the man thrice on the cheeks. "That's Seryozha!" she whispered.

A waiter passed, martinis on his tray, and we each took one. Bobby drank hers in a couple gulps.

"Let's say hello," said Sleeper, sipping his.

Bobby took it from him and finished it. "Wait, let's——" She broke off because Seryozha had spotted us, was walking toward us with extended hands, a priest approaching devotees for a benediction.

"Sebastian," he said to Sleeper, "what a surprise."

I couldn't tell if his hair was light blond or white-gray. He seemed old and young at once. His voice reminded me of willfully aged things: wood, wine, whiskey.

"Hello, Seryozha. Thank you for inviting us." Sleeper shook Seryozha's hand. Then Seryozha put a second hand on Sleeper's, and then Sleeper put a second hand on all of that, and they kept shaking. I'd seen this done by politicians on TV—an explosion of cordiality that meant, somehow, the opposite. They looked like men performing a folk dance or an exorcism. The man who'd just been kissed by Seryozha stood looking on with an approving smile, holding a briefcase.

"*Rybka*, Bobinka!" Seryozha released Sleeper and flung his arms wide, and Bobby stepped into them. She had to hunch her shoulders and bend her knees to embrace him. I couldn't imagine them in bed—couldn't imagine them doing *anything* together. I glanced at Sleeper, who was looking at them with unseeing eyes. This party was a terrible idea. I wished we were at our hotel, in bed. There was something so innocent to the three of us together, in comparison with what was transpiring now—although, ostensibly, nothing was transpiring, just people greeting one another at a party.

Seryozha greeted Lance with zero interest.

Then Bobby said, "This is my friend Viva."

For me, not quite zero. "Are you one of Bobby's art friends?"

"A friend *in* art, more like." Bobby giggled, pulling again at her dress and looking to Sleeper, for approval maybe. It was hard to say. I didn't know this Bobby.

"Welcome to a flooding house. But, as they say, if you don't want to get wet, don't come to Venice." He gave me three dry kisses. Up close, he had a narrow, elfin face. "Bobby she always has the most marvelous friends, I say that always. I say it now. Once, in America, a couple of them, friends who are a couple, they come and stay the night. In the morning, I see them in wedding clothes. I see the woman in a veil. 'Bobby,' I ask, 'did you forget to tell me something, *rybka?*' Bobby she says, 'Oh no, they're on their way to a polling station.' She says, 'That's how they dress to vote.' 'To vote?' I ask. When they come to the polling station, everyone cheers. They say, 'Our guests are waiting but we have to vote!' So everyone cheers more, and they skip the line. Most interesting, clever people!"

"It's the best way to skip a line when voting!" Bobby said. "I've done it myself."

"She's over politics and weddings now," said Sleeper, encircling her shoulder with an arm.

"I'm post-everything." She laughed, strained laughter, strange.

"Not good to give up interests, not even for love. True love." Seryozha held up his hands again—a priest, a civil servant in a city hall. "But she still loves art. I hear this. This is very good. How is your gallery?"

"It's good," Bobby said. "Thank you."

I glanced at Lance. His glass, containing an olive and no drink, was trembling.

"Bobby's doing all she can to make good on her promises to all her patrons and clients," Sleeper said. "I give you my word."

"Very good, very," Seryozha said. His eyes had an unusual, rat-like concentration, at the same time unattractive and superior. Not the shifty eyes of pet rats, but the single-minded eyes of mythic sewer rats that survive nuclear holocaust. His hair was luxurious, nuclear-white.

"As long as we understand each other, I'll even forgive you the damage to my good looks," Sleeper said, pointing at his bruise and smiling.

"Ah, Sebastian," Seryozha said. "Disgraceful. Acts of vandalism, they disgust me most. Acts of violence without sense. In Russia, every day I fight against *Homo sovieticus*—a violent, simple man. I say, debate, don't stab, don't judo. I say, read books! Cultivate! I cast pearls at pigs. All the pearls in the farm! I'm very shocked." He patted Sleeper's shoulder.

Were they speaking in code? Was Seryozha apologizing for, or at least acknowledging, his goon punching Sleeper? More people had gathered around us. Imperceptibly, we'd shifted to the middle of the room, by the Poseidon sculpture. The palazzo had seemed so grand when we entered, a rented museum, but there was something a little too finished about the Poseidon and his fish and nymphs. Perhaps they had been badly renovated; perhaps they were fakes.

A woman Bobby's age, with little silver cobras hanging from her earlobes by their tails, took Seryozha by the arm and spoke to him in Russian.

Seryozha smiled a host's beatific smile, whispered something to a guy beside him, whom he hadn't bothered to introduce, and the guy walked off with the woman.

"I would like to introduce you to my wife," Seryozha said, "but she seems to have disappeared. She always flies everywhere." He flapped his arms. "She is a social fly."

"How is she?" Bobby asked. "Is she still a cosmetologist-novelist-model?"

"Just last week, she got a prize for her book of stories."

"Your wife's a cosmetologist?!" Lance gasped, not because he wished to join the conversation, but because he'd stayed silent longer than Lances can. "That's so great. Hey, in Russia, do they wax men? Like, can you just walk into a waxing place and, you know— because in Canada, there's been some controversy." He looked around to see if anyone was listening.

Seryozha wasn't. He was in a staring match with Sleeper.

"Haha!" Lance said. It wasn't a laugh. "Haha!" he said again. Luckily, a waiter came by with a tray of drinks. Lance's olive was carried away in his empty glass.

"That's wonderful for Lavinia," Bobby said, failing to get a drink, instead pressing her empty glass to her lips, pulling it away, losing lipstick. Bobby and Lance had been losing their sprezz, unlike Sleeper. His mood seemed to have improved since the gondola ride.

"This is a very modest palazzo," Sleeper said. "Business not going well? Or have you turned into old money when I wasn't looking?"

"Ah, Sebastian. Funny. Funny!" Seryozha laughed and wagged his finger at Sleeper's sternum. "But let's be serious for a moment." He took Sleeper's lapels gently in his hands and looked up into his chin. "Are you hungry? Are you thirsty?"

"You're right," Sleeper said, smiling, placing his hands on Seryozha's shoulders. He could lift him, if he wanted to. "Appetites *are* serious."

Seryozha's mouth widened with cordiality, exposing two even rows of neon-white teeth: "Can I bring you anything else to drink? Bobby? What do you drink nowadays, Bobinka? Something to eat? Maybe the chef he prepares something? Your favorite spinach *pelmeni*? One word from you, and he makes what you want. For tonight, I'm here to serve you. I'm your host. For tonight." He released Sleeper's lapels. "This is a very, very nice suit."

"Another day, when you're *my* guest," Sleeper said, still holding on to Seryozha's shoulders, "I'll introduce you to my tailor in LA."

A rolled-up ruble and a mother-of-pearl compact with coke on it traveled from Bobby to Lance, from Lance to Bobby, and then back to Lance. We were sitting in a row on a medieval-looking bench in one of the palazzo's numerous side rooms. A faded canvas full of saints and angels hung at the center of each dark wall.

"I hope this coke wasn't scrounged from a toilet seat," Lance said.

"You're in luck," said Bobby. "The toilet seats have fuzzy covers!"

"No! Not the fuzzy!" Lance reinserted the ruble into his right nostril. "Wow, it's really better through a ruble than a dollar! People in the West have no idea! It's like I can taste the exchange rate." The three of us sat crammed together on the bench, the only seat in the room.

"Leave some for Viva." Bobby took the compact from his hands and passed it to me. I had never taken any serious drugs, but now I obediently snorted a little.

On the floor by the door, some middle-aged Russians and Italians played spin the bottle.

"The Russians are friendly people," said Lance, retrieving the ruble and the compact from my hands. "Aren't they? I was so worried about coming here, but now I feel at home again. It reminds me of our Bel Air days. Oh, did you see our thug? He looks so hot in a pinstriped suit. I saw him by the bar, gorging on kielbasa."

"That wasn't kielbasa," said Bobby. "That was Russian who-knows-what. But yeah, I think everything is okay, isn't it? We should've just confronted Seryozha from the beginning. Should we go find him and do a line with him? But I need to pee. Where's Sleeper?"

"Well, he's not in here." Lance looked from side to side.

"I don't know. Whoops, I lost my husband. Where's our boy toy?" she whined at me.

I felt separated from their gaiety, alert and anxious. The bottle on the floor spun. I stood up and went where it pointed, out through a door, down a hall. I reentered the ballroom. Here was

Seryozha, eating herring from a small plate by a window, surrounded by people, Sleeper not among them.

In another room, people were speaking English. "There are opportunities for real-estate-backed debt, especially in Yalta," said an old man in shorts and a baseball hat.

I carried on, unnoticed, my timorousness replaced by a feeling of jubilant, cokey autonomy. I, like everyone here, was safe, because I wasn't an *actual person*, just an outline of one, and nothing bad happens except to actual people, and how could I be one of those if I was a guest at this party? I didn't have to worry about Seryozha or look for Sleeper. He wasn't real either. He was also a guest at this party. He was safe, somewhere in the palazzo.

I looked down at the flooded courtyard from an inner balcony. The air was damp and sweet from algae and boat fuel. Open-flame heaters, suspended on chains, cast gold and blue jellyfish into the courtyard's water. Valets at their leisure, everyone having arrived hours ago, drank bottled beer and kicked trash into the canal, their backs to a few drunken guests wading in rubber boots in the courtyard shallows. Next to me two men, ties loosened like forgotten nooses around their necks, spoke in hushed voices. They were safe, too. Their executioners had departed for the night.

"Hullo," someone said. I turned. Kostya the goon stepped out onto the balcony and looked over the edge.

"Hi," I said, unreal, unafraid.

We watched a woman who, directly below us, wobbled in the courtyard's water singing a quiet Russian song, her soaked dress dragging behind her.

"Cigarette again?" he said.

"Yes," I said, "*spasiba*."

I don't smoke now and didn't then, but I took a cigarette, and he lit it for me. I imagined, cokebrainedly, that he'd mistaken me for Bobby. Lance was right: Kostya looked different in a suit. He wasn't an actual person either; he couldn't hurt Sleeper or anyone else. He was just an outline, too, and so was the taste of the cigarette, just a dry and dirty ring inside my mouth.

"Good party," he said.

"Good party," I said.

16

Sleeper had been calmer since the party. Perhaps he thought he understood his opponent. Perhaps something more had transpired between them that night. The private eye reported from Rome that Łyski had stayed one night in Testaccio. Seryozha was promptly informed, and the Sleepers bickered over whether Bobby should still be the one to return *The Lady* to the museum and collect the reward. Sleeper thought Seryozha probably no longer wanted her involved. Bobby flaunted her expertise at "talking to lawyers." December twentieth, the Gemäldegalerie's deadline to return the painting, came up constantly. The subject of my cut came up never.

The eye returned. He hadn't found Łyski in Rome, but there'd been a few new sightings here in Venice: a man fitting Łyski's description playing John Lennon's "Imagine" on the public piano in Ca' Pesaro's hall; a "Polish dude with long, unwashed hair" sneaking around San Polo; a musician from Los Angeles buying shoelaces at a cobbler in Mestre.

I was no longer allowed Sleeper alone. Our sex, now including Bobby, was performative—like an anecdote told with confidence at dinner, like a long, digressive joke successfully brought to a hilarious end.

Days of rain. Raining blue light on the sheets. Bodies complete, as if built from blueprints. You don't see how beautiful beautiful people are until you see them with your hands.

"Viva has the best ass," Bobby said. "And good calves."

I liked to squeeze in between them, holding on to Sleeper, Bobby on my back.

"I have a perfect belly button," she said. "That's the most perfect thing about me."

"The most perfect thing about you," Sleeper said, "is your self-regard."

"Sleeper has beautiful hair," I said.

"Sleeper has beautiful everything," Bobby said. "Let's take his hair, my belly button, and your ass and make a baby."

"A perfect surrealist monster. Many-handed, many-headed, with my hair, her ass, and André Breton's nipples," Sleeper said, sliding down past our hips, a boy in a candy store.

Sometimes I watched the two of them together, sometimes one of them watched me with the other. One night, about a week after the party, when Sleeper was in the bathroom, Bobby said, "How about you two fuck without a condom? Sex is *so* bad with condoms, and we don't have any diseases." She had the condom box in her hand, her arm held back as if she was about toss it through the window into the canal.

"No, Bobby," I said. "That's one thing I won't. I won't have your baby."

"What are you talking about? How would it be mine? You're

crazy." She placed the box back on top of the nightstand and laughed and laughed.

That night I found her awake again, naked at the desk near the bed in front of her computer, watching something. It looked like a film of the side of Basilica di San Marco, shot from a camera on a crane or a drone. Other than a few collapsed café umbrellas, the gray piazza was empty. At its center was a rectangular puddle, as if someone had dropped a long mirror.

"It's a live feed. They have cameras all over Venice. It's the only way to see San Marco without all the tourists. The perspective is better, too." She spoke to me quietly over her shoulder, trying not to wake Sleeper. "When I watched you two together tonight, I remembered how I felt when I first met him in LA."

I wrapped myself in a cardigan and sat down beside her.

"We drove up to Yosemite and stayed at the Ahwahnee. We couldn't stop fucking, you know, like now. So *hot*. There was snow everywhere."

All this was ostensibly a compliment, yet her tone and body language were defensive. She was repurposing their love story, making me into a surrogate performing a simulation of her past.

"What is this Ahwahnee?" I asked, my tone neutral, negating the reality of all experiences outside this Venetian room.

Maybe she sensed my resistance, or maybe the memory wasn't shareable, trite when told.

"Just an old hotel. I think they renamed it. We should go there."

I was so thankful for this noncommittal invitation that a bitter, doomed love feeling came up from my chest into my throat.

"I want to go somewhere snowy," she said. "I'm sick of this damp place. Let's go to Switzerland. Maybe St. Moritz."

"I'd like to go there with you," I said.

"There's a great hotel there, by the lake. Hotels are so fucking great. Everyone just sleeping and fucking in rented beds. In a way, I can only feel at home in a hotel. This one's not bad."

"I've only been to this one," I said. "Only, you know . . . motel before."

"Has this one disappointed you yet?" She didn't wait for an answer. "Have you noticed everything is, ultimately, a disappointment? Everything's like shopping. The best part is when you're at the cashier," she said, sipping a glass of last night's wine.

With her flaking mascara, smeared lipstick, and under-eye circles, she seemed, as well, last night's. She looked like an exhausted guard hunched over her endless feed of security footage, hoping for a bit of street drama. Her impossible breasts impossibly sagged. *Marx and Engels,* Sleeper called them sometimes. *Romulus and Remus.* They had names for body parts, for people. Everything, everyone, had to exceed the sum of its parts, be supernumerary, polyonymous, polyamorous. I wondered if I was *too few* for them.

"I'm sorry you feel things are disappointing," I said in Polish.

"Do I? I mean, just because I said it, does that make it true? Sometimes I just feel like I'm full of shit," she said in English. "Like, if someone takes a black-and-white photo of you, it doesn't mean you're in the past." Her face had a canine sadness, tiny wrinkles around her eyes I'd never noticed before. I saw her in the future, in ten years, after many more winters, beds, hotels.

Suddenly, I felt pristine, intact, my skin terrific, breasts ideal. "Here," I wanted to say, "they're yours, take them, take my youth, devour the fourteen years between us," and as I articulated this generosity in myself, the glossy, mercantile, volatile nature of our

affair became apparent to me—mercantile not because it was defined by money, but because it depended on an exchange of qualities as definite and countable as money. Freshness, youth were my
denominations. Sleeper's were stability, sanity, authority. Bobby's
were experience, vivacity, mystery, pride.

In that moment, lit by San Marco's lamps on the screen, Bobby
appeared a little demystified. I knew her body, her face, their
slight imperfections that in ten years would be flaws, in twenty
the end of beauty. She slouched, unselfconscious, without her stories, makeup, clothes. I felt a tenderness for her, for which she
would've hated me, had she known. Had she hated me, it would
have helped, rebuilt her in my eyes, as hatred is a way of shoring
up, of cultivating mysteries.

She yelped, as if stung by my thoughts. She moved her face
close to the screen.

"What?"

On the laptop, the image froze. An ant of a person crossed the
piazza. He stopped by the rectangular puddle, took out his phone,
and aimed it in our direction, photographing the basilica.

"Never mind." Bobby sighed, picking up Sleeper's T-shirt from
the floor and pulling it on. She took a bottle of calvados from the
desk and, with two fingers, tried to remove the foil. "I thought it
was Łyski. Don't laugh."

"I laugh?" I took the bottle and removed the foil, unscrewed the
top, and poured the calvados into our dirty wineglasses.

"You laugh with your eyes," she said, placing her hand on my
eyes, an imitation of Sleeper's gesture a month ago, a month that
felt like a year. "Łyski and I came here for our honeymoon. We
did everything wrong. Our honeymoon was the worst part of our
relationship. We fought so hard about, like, the disaster of the wed-

ding. It was on the beach in Venice, California. Łyski had a sort of breakdown, took off somewhere in the middle of the night. So the rest of us, Lance and other guests, went skinny-dipping in the ocean. We were wasted and, like, dropped our clothes on the beach, and someone stole my shoes, these expensive shoes I had. The only person who didn't see me naked on my wedding night was my husband. He didn't even sleep in our room. I actually believe *he* stole the shoes."

"Łyski?" I said. "Why?"

"Oh, he was obsessed with possessing me, or anything of mine. He'd always storm off, leaving suicide notes. Then he'd be back in time for lunch. Once, I found him eating steak in the basement, even though he claimed to be, like, vegetarian. One night, here in Venice, Italy, we had a fight and he stormed off, and was gone for hours. Then he called and told me to go to this website." She pointed at the screen. "He knelt there, in the middle of the piazza, and asked me not to ever fight with him again. So melodramatic!"

She was beautiful again, with her betrayals, thefts, half-truths. San Marco was, naturally, just an altar for Bobby the bad bride, the bride-not-to-be, losing shoes, husbands.

"Things were better between us for, like, a week," she continued, braiding her hair, sipping calvados. "And then back in LA, I saw Sleeper again. I couldn't resist him—you know how he is. And the problem with Łyski is, he needed constant taking care of. What if I want to be taken care of? Łyski was my teenage boyfriend. But that means very little by the time you're in your thirties. Anyway, I know it's stupid, but since we've been in Venice, I keep thinking, though he might not feel like calling me or texting, he might sense I'm looking at this site and come to the piazza and, like, give me the middle finger at least. After all, he's already had his revenge. It's not like he knows how to monetize the Vermeer anyway."

"And he's not scared of Seryozha?"

"He hates Seryozha more than Seryozha hates him. I think hatred makes you forget fear. Seryozha has a bigger life than Łyski, so it's normal that Łyski hates him more. Łyski's so, I don't know, *unexpressed*. He can't find a girlfriend, can't get his career going . . . can't pay his bills. I feel like I shouldn't have told Łyski the painting was Seryozha's. I think it gave him additional motivation not to return it."

So she'd spoken to Łyski about the painting more than once. "You did as you are thinking was right," I said. "Are you crying?"

"No," she said, wiping her nose and eyes with Sleeper's shirt. "Sometimes old emotions catch up with me, and I have to, you know . . . even seeing Seryozha was weird. It's just that each person carries with them, I don't know, a whole life. People say an orgasm is a little death. I think divorce is one, too. Or worse, it's a little apocalypse."

I didn't feel sorry for her at all. But then I'd never been married. I'm eighty-four and have never been married.

November nights in Venice—the knocking on my door had the morose regularity of Morse code. I heard it in my sleep as if from across the sea. Almost asleep, I opened my door.

"Is Bobby here?" Sleeper walked into my room.

"No."

"I texted you."

"I was sleeping. Come in."

He followed me into the room. "I haven't seen her since lunch," he said. "She's not picking up her phone."

I cinched my robe.

"Do you know where she might be?" he asked, pacing from bed to bathroom and back.

"No," I said. "Did you check Lance's room?"

"He's out for the night. Hasn't seen her." Sleeper was disoriented, anxious, out of character.

I took his hand and pulled him toward me. He sat on the edge of the bed, letting me wipe droplets of rain off his coat. The bruise around his eye had paled, but areas were still gray-green. I looked at his face, and after a few long moments, maybe because we were alone at last, its familiar shape collapsed into new pieces, so that I was overwhelmed by swirling fragments of feeling, random and intense. Fury, ache, desire, hints of memories that had never happened, pieces of imagined life. The two of us, a summer evening in a city somewhere. A ride home along the sea. In a car, pulling up the top against the rain. Two, not three.

"—and what worries me is, Kostya's not around," he was saying. I understood almost none of what he said. "Not that he ever hangs out by our hotel at night. It seems we're all equally bad at this, whatever this is. Are you sure she didn't mention anything about tonight? Party at the *marchesa's*, maybe?"

"She didn't say nothing," I said. "Bobby never goes alone." Bobby was only ever *taken places*.

"I'm going to talk to the receptionist again," he said. "They must've seen her leave."

"I go into your room and look." I took the key from his hand.

"Look for what?" he asked but didn't wait for me to answer.

From the Murano chandelier in their suite hung three pairs of stockings. A lion of lapis lazuli and brass had two bras on its neck and bobby pins on its tongue. I picked up her clothes, folded them, placed them in suitcases. In the bathroom I ran water over her tubes of foundation, cleaned her eyeshadow palette with a Q-tip. Each eyeshadow was named after a colorless concept, written in gold: RENEGADE, EGOIST, LOVER.

Sleeper appeared behind me. "What are you doing?"

"I thought I will clean a little." I wasn't sure what I was doing. Readying the room for her disappearance. Moving in. "Did they see her in lobby?"

He shook his head. His shoes left wet prints on the floor as I followed him back to the living room.

"I'm going to make you a drink," I said in perfect English, knowing the sentence by heart.

The stupidity of the minibar calmed me. I poured him a whiskey. He took it, didn't drink it, set it on the table by the hotel stationery no one ever used.

"Do you know Seryozha's cell?" he asked me.

"No."

"So I'm that guy now."

"What guy?"

"The one who contacts his wife's exes to find her."

I'd been wiggling toward him stealthily on the sofa, and now we were almost touching. I'd let my robe fall open.

Seeing his eyes on my breasts, I said, "What about your *little* wife?" The sentence slipped out, a half joke, half admonition. My hand on his leg. "Do you want we make love?"

"What?" His face had a sardonic sneer verging on cruelty. Judg-

mental eyes, the brown of pulpits and lecterns. He didn't even with-
draw my hand from his leg.

"It was joke," I said. It cost me a lot not to close my robe.

"Even if we went to the police," Sleeper continued, "we'd just sit
there for hours explaining and translating. And no crime's been
committed that doesn't also implicate us . . ."

I pointed at the pink edge of her laptop on the coffee table,
under a pile of magazines. "Did you look at her email?"

"I couldn't find her computer." He almost smiled at me with
appreciation. I jumped up, grabbed her laptop, letting the women
on magazine covers slide onto the floor. We sat huddled together as
he opened it. Galaxies of dirt mapped where Bobby's continuously
creamed and re-creamed wrists rested to either side of the mouse
pad. The fan sighed and an image of a giant strawberry, revealing
itself on second glance to be a woman's tongue, glowed under the
detritus of her desktop. There were no passwords. She was too lazy
for protection, too vain.

In her inbox, under heaps of luxury-clothing junk mail, was an
email from a company called Servizi Discreti, dated this morning.
It contained an address in Cannaregio and explained that Łyski
had been seen there two days ago.

"I don't get it. He's always supposed to email both of us," he
said, apparently referring to the private eye.

"She deletes. She lies, and she hides, and she lies." Something in
his voice had allowed me to say it.

Again my intuitions were wrong. He stiffened and shifted slightly
away from me—we were once again people who'd never touched,
people who'd never touch again. I looked at my breasts, sisterly and
useless. To close my robe would mean to expose myself further.

"Get dressed," he said. He copied the address.

"We should take something to protect," I said, as we got up.

"What are you talking about?"

"I don't know. Knife?"

"If I can hold my own at fisticuffs with Kostya, I can wrestle a painting out of Łyski, don't worry." He faced me with the thinnest smile, maybe a sprezzy smile, but it wasn't enough. He was supposed to tell me everything was okay, we could stay, have sex, and Bobby would just turn up later, smug and victorious, canvas in hand, complaining of the effects of damp weather on hair and seventeenth-century art.

"Let's take this, at least." I lifted a butter knife from atop the minibar. "If Kostya is there."

In the window, a motorboat skidded by, carrying a blur of sequins and a hoarse, drunken "O Sole Mio."

"A butter knife? Don't be ridiculous," he said. "Unless you want to destroy someone with irony. I'm afraid that would be lost on these orangutans." Nevertheless he slipped the knife into his pocket and, as if my still-bare breasts had lost all meaning, ceased to scream their ancient messages—"touch me, make me pregnant, let me feed you and your children!"—pressed my shoulder in a gesture of comradery. "Get dressed."

In the simplistic grid of Los Angeles, you can turn a corner and see all the way to the sea or the hills. Venetian *calli* have the labyrinthine architecture of a human life, with its setbacks and dead ends. Liquid copies of us crossed the puddles, mine thin, Sleeper's hulking, hands in pockets. What else was in those pockets besides the knife? *Vaporetto* tickets, coins, a Bobby bobby pin or two.

"Why she will not send text at least?"

"Because," he said, "Łyski has an unusual psychological grip on Bobby." He was reading a stack of street signs the color of bad teeth: ALLA FERROVIA, PIAZZALE ROMA. "At some point I even put a small amount of money aside, call it a medical fund, because Bobby was worried Łyski would get mouth cancer like his dad. Łyski smokes, and of course doesn't consider it important to get health insurance. Bobby feels responsible for him." In his voice, anger and amusement balanced each other out, created a sort of plateau.

"It's sad she can't have children. She would be good mother," I said, trying on a small outrageousness. I had become convinced my theory was correct.

He laughed, without registering the meanness of my sentiment or maybe because of it. Secret motivations, slips of tongue, small aggressions cowering behind seemingly innocuous statements were always immediately apparent to both of them, therefore ineffective.

"You're right," he said. "I can't decide if Bobby is a narcissistic egoist or simply a monstrous altruist. Those two aren't as far apart as people think. Did I tell you last year she emptied our account sending a seventy-thousand-dollar check to an animal shelter? She said it was 'for the puppies.'"

Was seventy thousand dollars enough to empty their account? Perhaps just one of them? I had acquired from them, along with a taste for luxuries, a certain shrewdness, a rich person's attitude toward money, though I still had none. But now, as we hurried through an unlit tunnel, the difference between what seventy thousand dollars meant to her and meant to me brought back a resentment I hadn't felt since we left LA. I guess it had been crouching, waiting in unlit parts of my brain, along with other moods, mundane horrors, snippets of emails from my brothers: need money for mom . . . you left us, the least you can do is send . . . doesn't feel well, today she forgot Marcin's name . . .

We crossed a courtyard, passed a stone Venus seasick with moss. I shivered and wondered if I had the onset of a cold.

"There," said Sleeper, approaching the narrow entrance of a red-shuttered building. The lamp above the door was broken, the bulb exposed.

"Wait here," he whispered. His breath smelled of strawberry, as usual; he disliked artificial mint and used kids' toothpaste.

"If you don't come out?" I said.

"What do you mean?"

"I want to go with you," I said. I meant, "I want to go away with you." I clung to him, his arms opened, and we kissed without intending to—and it was back, the fruitless hope, the possibility that had been plucked, stubbed, snubbed. A sudden summer flooded through my kissing head. Us together somewhere, just us, in a house as much mine as his.

"So hot. Put a hand down the front of her pants," said Bobby, emerging from a nearby gate, military in her black raincoat, and I was moved aside, and he was holding her by the shoulders, not softly, asking her where she'd been.

"I'm right here, stupid." Giggling, she kissed him, and I had to look away. There were baby clothes hanging from a clothesline between two balconies. I began to cry but without tears or sound.

"Where the fuck have you been?"

"I tried to fix things. And I did! Don't be mad. I wanted to make you proud—and just, like, get the painting back. And guess what? I fixed everything. Łyski's here, and he's agreed to give us the painting. It's in Poland. He left it with his aunt for safekeeping, the idiot. He only came back here to boink this Bulgarian waitress he met in a laundromat."

"Okay. Let me talk to him."

"He's up there," she said, pointing vaguely. "Do you two want to kiss again? I can go back into the dark over there and you can pretend I'm not watching."

She pulled me to her, tucked me under an arm, pulled Sleeper by his belt buckle. As we stood in this complicated three-way embrace, my misery sharpened, the slick material of her raincoat pressed my face, confirming I needn't ever hope again: she was indeed synthetic, indestructible. Even today I sometimes believe it. After all, dead people might as well be simply absent, and the absent simply dead.

The damp wind that rose then had something to do with the dead as well. It was an absence set into motion, blowing at us from the cemetery on the Isola di San Michele, brushing past our faces as she pushed them even closer together for a three-way kiss, in which there was something wrong, beyond the usual clutter of too many chins and noses—she was restless, fidgety, and I realized the kiss was not for me and not for her but a ploy to distract Sleeper from going into the building.

"Ladies," Sleeper said as he disentangled himself, "duty before pleasure."

The front door of the building opened, and the stripes of Kostya's tracksuit flickered in the entrance above a pair of bright white running shoes.

"So all my wife's friends are here already," Sleeper said. He stared at Kostya's shoes.

Kostya tilted his chin at us and lit a cigarette.

"You know he follows me everywhere," Bobby said defensively. "Do you think I *want* to be followed?"

Kostya walked past us and stopped by the canal. There was an ugly hint of complicity between him and Bobby, something more than the goal we all shared—as if Bobby had switched teams, betrayed me and Sleeper. Maybe this was just my jealousy; maybe it wasn't true, or maybe it was and didn't matter. The sensation remained, though, as Sleeper led us up the stairs, past muddy envelopes on floor mats, past umbrellas, prams, and a dozen doors.

"Guys, we should be celebrating, honestly! We found him, at last," Bobby said, overtaking Sleeper on the fourth floor and blocking one of the doors with her body, making an X of her limbs in the doorway. "I'm your Vitruvian woman, perfect proportions."

"Nice try," Sleeper said and rang the bell by the opposite door.

"Oh, whoops!" she said. "I'm a dumb blonde. How did you know which door it is?"

"I have the address. Curiously, I found the private eye's email in my trash," he said in the facetious tone he used when listing her transgressions.

"I didn't touch your email. Maybe Viva did." She pushed past him and pushed the unlocked door open. "Maybe she fondled the hell out of it and sucked it off all night. Email molester."

"No," I said to him. "I didn't touch."

We entered the apartment.

"Hello? Łyski?" Sleeper called into a lightless kitchen.

"Shush. He's probably fallen asleep." She overtook Sleeper again, and we followed her down a hall, into a living room cramped with old, eclectic furniture draped with plaid and floral blankets. Above the sofa, an expressionistic mural turned out to be, on second glance, an elaborate growth of mold. A bottle of vinegar, on its side, had leaked onto an already-stained carpet. Dry fusilli crunched under our feet as we maneuvered around an upended chair. Bobby kicked the bag of pasta under the coffee table, atop which was an over-turned bowl of chopped lettuce.

"What happened here, Bobby?" Sleeper said.

She stopped in front of a half-open door. "Łyski's always been messy," she said, then added, with a guilty giggle, "Okay, there was a mini-blini altercation. Kostya was, like, impatient . . . You know, Łyski's so stubborn. He's in bed, back here."

A low voice, speaking Polish, came through the bedroom door: "He back? Get him out. I told him everything."

"Relax. It's just Sleeper," she responded in Polish.

"No, thanks. Don't feel good."

"Łyski, it's me . . . it's Sleeper. May we come in?"

There was a silence.

"Okay, but just you," Łyski said in English. "Not Seryozha's *przydupa*, and not Bobby."

Sleeper looked at Bobby, who sighed and shrugged. He pushed the door open, revealing a corner of a rose-patterned rug. The rest was dark.

"Coming in," Sleeper said and closed the door behind him.

"Unbelievable." Bobby threw herself onto the sofa.

I picked up a chair and sat on it. "What happened?"

"What happened?" she aped. "Nothing happened. That fucking detective sent me this address, so I came. I thought it was yet an-other false lead. Fucking Kostya followed me, and then there was, like, drama. Just like always with men."

"What's wrong with Łyski?"

She fussed on the sofa, kicking off some dusty blankets. "Can you imagine living in a dump like this, even for a week?"

It was marginally better than any flat I'd ever lived in.

"But what is *wrong* with him?" I asked.

The church bells tolled, dividing her silence into sections.

"I think his rib might be broken," said Sleeper, coming back out of the bedroom. "He needs to see a doctor." He got a glass of water from the kitchen and took it back into the bedroom.

"Did Kostya kick his ass?" I whispered in Polish. "Did Łyski refuse to tell him where the painting is?"

"Speak English, please" was all she said.

Sleeper came back. "His chest hurts on the right."

"Right side's better than left!" said Bobby. "He probably just ate too much. He had, like, two pizzas for dinner. I saw the boxes in the kitchen."

"Roberta, he was beaten up," Sleeper repeated. "His lip is cut."

"Kostya barely touched him. Barely! I know because I saw it."

She often spoke about her love for "the demimondaine." She'd wanted to live in a seventies film, the kind in which men lounge in smoky rooms and femmes fatales commit boozy acts of self-sabotage. Can-canning her legs in the air on the sofa, she seemed unmoved by Łyski's injuries. Had she somehow been involved in inflicting them? I'd seen her slap Sleeper before, once or twice, playfully, but with real force. She didn't believe in violence, and somehow that convinced me that she was more capable of it than other women. Any violence she might commit was performative, a trivial expression of what everyone already knew, didn't they? That being hurt by Bobby was basically black olives, BDSM.

"We're going to the hospital," said Sleeper. "He might have internal bleeding or a concussion."

"But we've been to the hospital on this trip already!" she whined, clutching a filthy pillow to her stomach. "God, how many ER visits were there during our marriage because Łyski *thought* he was having a heart attack?"

"You could've gotten hurt, too." Sleeper's Adam's apple jerked when he said *hurt.*

Was Kostya going to come back up here? Was he still outside? We were three against one—four counting Łyski—if things got violent, but that seemed unlikely. It was all a Bobby story. It didn't even feel true that Kostya had roughed Łyski up. I didn't understand what Kostya was. I'd been told he'd physically fought with Sleeper and now Łyski, yet the Sleepers saw him daily and paid him little attention. Lingering behind fountains, around corners, in cold and rain, he'd become almost a part of our group, our own dejected satyr playing games on his phone while we dined and shopped. At Seryozha's party he'd been almost cordial, to me at least. But was it possible he'd hospitalize Sleeper next, or Bobby, or me? Was this a game, and if so, what were the rules? The Sleepers refused to explain it.

"Me? How could *I* get hurt?" Bobby laughed loudly, unnaturally. "These thugs aren't feminists. They'd never actually hit a woman. You have to believe a woman your equal to hit her, no? These goons know women are physically weaker, so they'd never dare to, like, punch me. What? It's true. Don't look so outraged," she told Sleeper. "When I was—"

"Oh, shut up, Bobby." It was the first time I'd ever seen him speak rudely to her. She opened her mouth and looked at him with amazement, then chewed her glove, probably plotting her counterattack.

"We need to get him to the hospital," he said, "and then get tickets for Poland, for tomorrow. And, of course, explain it all to Seryozha . . . Have you spoken to him yet?"

"I'm so sick of everyone telling me what to do," she said. "You all just boss me around!"

Tears—not of hurt but of indignation—turned her eyes glassy, and I knew she was about to have a tantrum. She could forgive big betrayals but not small slights, and she was determined to punish Sleeper for his small outburst of impatience. A prolonged and vicious fight would ensue, complicating our progress toward recovering the painting.

"Sleeper is right," I said loudly. "We need to call Seryozha now and say to him we are his friends. The painting is safe in Poland? It doesn't get damaged?"

"We *need* to call Seryozha?" Bobby's face scrunched up with vicious delight. She'd taken the bait. I'd stopped the fight between them by directing her malice onto myself. "You know my ex-husband better than I do? I know you're trying to know my *current* husband better than I do, but that's an indulgence on my part. Don't leave the room when I'm talking to you!"

I'd gotten up and walked to the kitchen, and Bobby was following me. Good, I thought. Now Sleeper can call Seryozha or the paramedics.

She tapped my shoulder as I opened a sideboard to get a glass. "You're just a little whore, really. It amuses me to watch you fantasize about being me," she said. "The saddest thing about you is your self-esteem. You're pretty, but you'll never, ever know it."

I felt my mouth open to defend itself, but no words came. Łyski slouched into the kitchen.

"It hurts here," he said. He seemed diminished in size. A sharp sweaty scent wafted from him, with unpleasant culinary under-tones. Vinegar, I realized, noting the brown stains on his shirt and remembering the toppled bottle. Maybe he'd been punched while making salad. Lifting his shirt to reveal a lattice of broken vessels around his ribs, he lowered himself carefully into a chair.

Then Kostya came into the kitchen.

"Oh fuck," said Łyski, not getting up. "Bobby, get me something to beat this *skurwiel* with. Get me a bottle." He closed his eyes.

"Seryozha," Kostya said, holding up his phone. "He wants I put on *gromkaya svyaz*." He winked at us, the wink of a sleazy, clown-ing uncle at a reunion to which he'd not been invited.

17

B obby, Bobby, Bobby. *Rybka, dyevochka.*"

We all stood over Kostya's phone on the kitchen table, which was on *gromkaya svyaz*, that is, *speakerphone*.

"But it's good news, Seryozha!" Bobby yelled. "Like, nothing really happened, we just have to go and get it. There's still time to do the original plan. Łyski didn't understand it was yours, you see. He thought he was, like, playing a prank on me."

Łyski nodded, lankily slumped in his chair, looking half dead, Christlike, but with alert eyes trained on Kostya, eyes that weren't unlike the eyes Baggywrinkle made when, by the end of dinner, still no morsel had been given to him. I wondered how Baggywrinkle was doing at his doggy hotel in Hollywood and found myself wishing we'd never left.

"You're a funny girl, Bobby. That's what I like," said Seryozha, his voice distorted by the *gromkaya svyaz*. "A woman who knows how to tell a joke. How about the one about a Soviet tractor?"

"I don't remember that one," she said in her baby voice, resting a haunch on the table.

"A man calls *Vsesoyuznoye* radio, communist radio. He says, 'Is it true that Vasya Pupkin was caller number one thousand nine hundred and seventeen and won a tractor in the radio competition?' 'Hello,' says the radio presenter. 'It is true.' 'Wonderful,' the caller says. 'It is true,' the radio presenter says, 'only it wasn't a tractor but a wheelbarrow, and Vasya didn't win it, it was stolen from him.' Good communist joke." He paused. "But now, we be serious. Look. Sebastian."

The atmosphere was strange, solemn. Sleeper placed a hand on Bobby's thigh, an ordinary, orthodox moon in the window behind him. Kostya stood with crossed arms, regarding his phone on the table with pride and amusement.

"Seryozha. It's Sebastian." When Sleeper said his first name, he looked different to me, incomplete. The air smelled of burnt food and vinegar.

"Sebastian! Hello. Welcome. Bobby she is my ex-wife, but she is your wife. I like her, I like she does this and that, I like she tells stories. I like suspense okay. Sometimes, for a woman I like, I wait. But it's enough, Sebastian, it's enough. I'm tired. There are people in this, transactions you don't want to know. Some of them I won't invite to dinner, you understand? Old friends of FSB friends, impatient friends. For now, I say to them, 'Have a rest, have some good wine, forget about this.' But for how long? How long till they make an action against you? Days? Weeks? I'm not their boss, you see. 'Have a rest,' I say to them. But they don't have a rest. 'Where's my picture?' they say. 'If you will go without a tsar in your head,' they say, 'it will cost you.' What costs me, it costs you. It costs you,

Sebastian. Me, I don't wait for good weather by the sea. I give you one week. You go with Łyski and get the picture from his aunt. You get the picture from his aunt in Poland and give it to Kostya in Poland on December first, and Kostya he takes you and the picture to Germany, and Bobinka you talk gallery talk with the museum people, the lawyers in Köln, you collect the reward—"

Łyski's shaggy head popped up off the table. "Reward?"

"—and Kostya he gives you wire instructions, and maybe I even give Bobby her part, even though she makes trouble. Bad weather in Poland on December first," said Seryozha, "but Sebastian, give Kostya the picture, I'm happy, Bobby's happy. Let it rain, no matter. Let it storm."

"I understand you, Seryozha, very well," said Sebastian Sleeper. "I'm interested in efficiency myself, and I like having no debts, and I appreciate you honoring your agreement with my wife if she delivers. Now that we know where it is"—he looked at Łyski over his shoulder—"you have my word you'll get it back safely and on time."

"Good words, Sebastian, wise. You give the picture to Kostya, Kostya takes you and the picture to Germany. Bobby does her job. We meet and celebrate. You two come, visit me in Cayman Islands, we drink, we scuba, we feed stingrays. You married a good man, *dyevochka*. I say this now. But if the picture goes missing again, another boyfriend, off he goes to Bangkok, Ashgabat, you will be a sad girl, telling crying stories, *rybka*. There are crying stories I could tell you all night. Soviet stories and even sad stories of before."

"Seryozha, *nu zhe*," Bobby said, "how can you say things like that to your *rybka*? We were married, we are friends!" She sounded genuinely distraught and looked at me. I deliberately looked away.

"Disgraceful," said Seryozha. "I'm ashamed. Marriages and man-

ners, they are funny. Important funny. Marriages cost fortunes sometimes. Manners are worth something, not everything, maybe a million euros. What do you think?"

"I hardly took anything from you in the divorce!" Bobby stamped
her foot like a child.

"That's why my manners, for you, cost a million, maybe two.
For you, I'm a gentleman. But no more than two, *rybka*. To everything a price. No man he pays ten million for manners or he calls
himself a fool."

At my door, I said coldly, "Good night," but Bobby followed me
into my room.

"Do you think Łyski will be okay all alone at the hospital?"

"Listen to what doctor said," I said. After some X-rays, the doctor had declared Łyski essentially unharmed. They were keeping
him overnight in case of concussion. "I'm tired. I'm going to sleep
now."

"No, no sleep for you." She grabbed my hand and said in her
pleading, tyrannical voice that tolerated no opposition, "Come
with me."

She dragged me into their suite. In their bedroom, she pulled
down my pants. "Sleepy's really mad at us even though we might
just have made a million euros."

"He's not mad at *me*." I resisted as she tugged at my panties, but
to resist completely would be against the rules. We all knew our
roles.

"I'm mad at you," she said, and to Sleeper, "See? She's sorry."

He'd been watching us, a little wearily, standing by the window,
in which dawn was near.

"I want to see *you* sorry," he said to Bobby, coming over to us, pushing her down on the bed.

She was giggling, a little falsely, unbuckling his belt. I helped Sleeper step out of his jeans. I gathered Bobby's hair and pulled her face away from his. Her insults, out of bed, hurt me badly. In bed, they added fuel.

Between those two hard, stubborn, reckless individuals, I felt neutral, capable, but also calculating, secretive. Switzerland in the map of the bed. I thrived and got rich on the war around me.

Around seven, I left their room. Outside mine, I found Lance vomiting into the planter.

"Is the queen awake?" He wiped his chin. "I wanted to go in and do the lobotomized flapper."

"Do what?"

"The lobotomized flapper. It's a dance." He wobbled to his feet, gyrating his hands and legs, gaping his mouth, shaking his head.

"We had a hard night," I said. "We found Łyski. We are going tomorrow to Poland."

"Not me." His glasses sat crookedly on his nose.

"What does it mean?"

"I'm going back to Canada! Return of the prodigal son. Time for some mother's milk."

"You're leaving?"

"Booby texted me the whole saga," he said, and I wondered when Bobby had had time to text him. "I'm not made for the life of crime. Too weak. Too risk-averse. No Russians for me! Leaving in a few hours. There won't even be a last supper! Not even a last breakfast. How come nobody paints *that*?" He tried to stand up, reaching out to prop himself against the wall, but he misjudged the distance and collapsed.

I helped him up and back into his room, onto the bed. I sat on its edge.

"I had a wild night, too," he said. "Empty sex with empty people. How is poor old Łyski?"

"He got punches but the doctor said he's okay. He comes to Poland with us tomorrow."

Lance rolled onto his side and dry-heaved a couple of times. "Can you pass me that trash can?"

"I think Bobby hates me." I brought him the little can, empty save for a lonely chocolate-bar wrapper.

"Bullshishkabob." He hung his head off the bed, over the can.

"But I'm serious."

"She's way too self-absorbed for that."

I sat by his feet. "I will bring you a towel for your mouth."

In his bathroom, wet towels covered the floor. I found a semidry one on the back of the door, wet it, and wrung it.

When I got back his glasses were off, his face bare, unfamiliar. He said, "Did you know that doges used to throw rings into the sea, in a ritual marriage to the sea? Doges married the sea! Rubies and sapphires, off they went with the squid. Did you lose your ring?"

I wiped his mouth. "What ring?"

"Your ring of G."

"What?"

"I'm not referring to your G-spot, or whatever you girls think you have up in those hells between your legs. The ring of Gyges! You know, of invisibility."

"I don't know this."

"So there's this gangster, G, and he finds a ring that makes him invisible, or, actually, he's a woman, V. V's been dallying with the royals. Lending a helpful hand, so to speak. So one very boring night, after she's binged some series about vampires or housewives or women's prisons or whatever, V gets her ring of invisibility on, sneaks down the hall, and peeps into the royal bedroom, where she sees the queen fucking the king. The queen learns about it because V can't help but boast about it in court. The queen summons V and says, 'You've committed a crime. You saw me fuck the king. Now you have a choice: either you kill yourself or kill the king.' V kills the king, marries the queen, becomes a queen herself, and fucks the queen every night with, like, an obelisk or a goat's penis, whatever they had in ancient Greece before the invention of rubber. Get it?"

"No."

"What I'm saying is, throuples don't last. Not even in antiquity, not even in parables. Peeping Vs either get their asses punished, or they take what they want by force. That's it. Just imparting the last of my wisdom before I go. These stories are always true. That's why everyone today has learned to ignore them." He took my hand and held my thumb. "I'd take you with me, but how would we support each other, like, financially?"

I almost told him about my one hundred grand but thought I'd better not.

"Do I smell?" he continued. "Normally, I'm a nosegay."

"What?"

"Sniff me. Do I smell like vom?"

"You don't smell."

"Hey, can you set my alarm for noon?" He squinted at me for a moment, like some character from a children's book who needs his glasses to keep his eyes open. They closed, and he let go of my thumb.

I set his alarm, plugged in his phone, covered him with a comforter, picked up his glasses from the bed, and placed them on the nightstand, where I rearranged his water glass, his glasses rag, his glasses case, a vial of pills. I checked the closet for leftover clothes and found his passport in the nightstand drawer. I put it on his suitcase. Perhaps I'd been an assistant for too long.

We took the *vaporetto* to the airport. At each stop, a boatman looped a rope around a bollard, his face peevish with old-world knowledge, mudbanks, currents, shallows . . . the Sleepers' faces peevish from bickering. They'd been at it since we'd left the hotel. Bobby offered us a mini bottle of Irish cream liqueur. Sleeper waved it off, but I'd learned not to refuse anything that came from her.

"Tell him not to be upset," she told me.

"Bobby said you to not be upset," I said to Sleeper.

"Tell her I can hear her and don't need a middleman."

"What did he say?" she said.

"He can hear you and don't need a middleman."

She pouted, sucking on the bottle I passed back to her.

As Venice diminished behind us, I had a superstitious thought: What had happened between us was connected to the city and could only exist on water. This relic city, this receptacle for other people's pasts, contained our past now, too. Irretrievable, therefore trite. (And yet, I just read that the Chinese are going to build a replica above the sunken ruins, so maybe it isn't irretrievable!) One past of many, one past too many. I didn't have the strength of personality to infect them with my melancholy, and anyway they were already in two separate bad moods. I was just a link between her emotions and his taciturnity, my own sadness small, secondary, the sadness of deliverymen, midwives, messengers, postmen. An assistant sadness.

"Let's make a tour of this shitty boat and see if Łyski fell off," she said, getting up and taking Sleeper's hand. He let her hold it, but reluctantly. "Rude of him to disappear after we took such good care of him the other night!" she said, her own involvement in his beating apparently forgotten. "If we're not back in five, it means we fed ourselves to the seagulls, like Hitchcock fed his cock to the birdies."

"I'll pass," Sleeper said. "Take Viva. I'll be here watching the bags." In this gray morning light, the bruise now only a shadow around his eye, he looked pale and delicate. This delicacy was a secret, I thought, a facet of who he privately was, or once had been, before Bobby: a young man in a bookstore, a film student hunched over celluloid spools. Had he had to betray some undisclosed integrity to be with her?

"Whatever, crank." She dropped his hand.

We entered the enclosed passenger area. Łyski, feet up on the seat in front of his, listening to headphones, drew shapes with his finger on a fogged-up window.

"Hi. We're going to the back to feed Viva to the birds," she said, smacking his knee. He gave her a thumbs-up without removing his headphones. Bobby had told me that Łyski harbored great and unrequited feelings for her. In reality, the two appeared fraternal at best.

She shrugged, sighed, "Men!," and headed aft. I followed her. For a while we stood against the railing, each in a separate lagoon.

"I hate Venice," Bobby said. She wasn't getting enough attention from her men and had to blame someone, if not another woman, then a city.

A dozen people on the aft deck. Italians, some Danes playing cards. A card blew off the boat into the sea. A hearts card would have been appropriate.

I said, "Lance said doges threw rings in the sea."

"*Lance*, that diaper rash. I can't believe he just abandoned us."

"They'd throw and it would be for symbolic marriage to the sea."

"Yeah, I know that story."

"Yeah. Good story." I made sure not to glance at her. I thought she might do it. She wouldn't. I wanted her to, just to prove I could manipulate her. She couldn't do something so awful, though.

Or could she? She was looking at her rings. "Well, I'm good at getting married. Just ask my husband or ex-husbands."

Our eyes met, and maybe I said with my eyes that I knew she wouldn't; maybe that's why she rotated the diamond on her middle finger, then pulled the ring off. Its flight was brief, disappointing even. The diamond glinted once, dissolving somewhere between water and air.

"For better, for worse, in sickness, in health, don't mind if I do!" she chanted, with fake laughter, proud boredom, joining the lineage of doges, popes, celebrities who've wasted resources for the sake of stupid, extravagant gestures. The ultimate act of admiration is that of destruction. She wanted Venice drowned, Vermeer's work lost, all rings and husbands at the bottom of the sea. I, with my middling passions, my working-class concern for waste, found her, in this moment, spectacular, like a massive crash you pass on a freeway.

"What are you doing?" Sleeper said, appearing behind us. His amused tolerance for her mischief, which irritated me, was absent.

"Oh, hi," she said.

"She threw a ring into the sea," I said.

"What the fuck's wrong with you?" he asked her. "Which ring?"

"Not my engagement, don't worry." She took off her emerald engagement ring and held it over one eye, like a monocle. "I do," she said and giggled. How many mini liquor bottles had she consumed? "Don't mind if I do." She winked at me through the ring and backed up a bit closer to the railing.

"Don't taunt me, Roberta," Sleeper said in a firm, flat tone. His features had hardened, as if he'd aged ten years since I'd seen him ten minutes ago.

"Oh god, do you really think saying *that* will work? Look, everyone!" She pointed at some travelers on a bench—a teenage girl and her purple-haired boyfriend or brother, sharing chips from a bag. "Daddy will lose his temper!" She cackled at Sleeper.

The cardplayers looked up. Purple Hair licked his chippy fingers, reached into his pocket, and aimed his phone at us.

"Please, no videos," said Sleeper, in Italian, but the kid kept filming.

"No videos! Daddy has spoken, and he's mad!" Barbaric in her big fur coat, Bobby screamed in her most perverse baby voice, raised her arms, and made a high-pitched sound, neither laughter nor a growl, a siren yawn to send sleepy sailors and jet-lagged businessmen down to their deaths. A boat passed behind her in the mist. She herself seemed on the verge of evaporation.

"Roberta, if you have any respect for anyone . . ." Sleeper was close to her now, not touching her. I'd been intimate with them in nearly every way, but I'd never been here. I felt sick, out of place.

"Daddy wants me to be quiet or he'll lose his temper!" But it came out weak, self-conscious, her hysteria a failing act. Hipshot, posing for the video, ring in her fingers suspended above the sea . . . she was a bad actress after all.

"You *will* regret it this time," he said sadly, quietly.

"I already do." She turned to the teenager filming. "Did you get that, or should he repeat his line?" She placed the ring on her tongue. "My holy communion."

"Spit it out, Roberta."

"I can srow them all into the sea if I want, and you can't do any-sing," she slurred and spat the ring into her hand and extended her fist out over the water. "It'll be my fourth marriage." She was laughing but her makeup was ruined by tears.

I felt sorry for her. She didn't want to lose her engagement ring but was imprisoned by the demands of her performance. The kid, face scrunched with professional concentration, was on one knee, filming her from a low angle. A couple of people, Łyski among them, had gathered behind the kid to watch.

"Bobby. You don't have to," I whispered in Polish.

Sleeper leapt at her so suddenly that onlookers gasped. He grabbed her wrist. She fell deliberately, letting her legs go limp, her weight pulling them both down. He pried at her fist, which she un-successfully tried to hide under her belly. On the deck they writhed, a four-legged hermaphroditic beast with two snarling heads. To anyone else, I realized with horror, it must have looked like some psychotic had just attacked his wife out of the blue.

When, at last, he pried her hand open, the ring fell, skittered across the deck, and—how could it not—rolled into the sea. The irony was, I don't think she ever intended to drop this particu-lar ring.

A boatman stepped between their kicking legs, yelling in Italian, pulling Sleeper's jacket, while the kid went in for a climactic close-up, still snacking, sprinkling Sleeper's hair with chip crumbs.

"*Lasciami!*" Bobby shrieked at the boatman, who was bellowing about *polizia* and pulling Bobby's sleeve, which she ripped free with a howl. He looked with disgust at a handful of fur in his hand. She seemed hardly human there, on all fours on the deck in her mink.

"It's okay. No need for *polizia*." Sleeper got up, patted the boatman on the shoulder. I felt so bad for him, so much for him. He had the face of a man sneaking out of a bar after losing a fight. Someone applauded.

"Get up." His hair was wild and sprinkled with crumbs and paprika. He offered her a hand, and she crawled toward it, like an animal about to nuzzle it, and—maybe because she knew no limits, but more likely because she did have limits, secret ones, and out of guilt, solidarity even, wanted to protect him from being perceived as the male aggressor, to take the blame by appearing completely insane—she bit his index finger.

He roared and cursed. The kid hovered over them, yelling encouragement, getting his best shot yet.

It was awful to watch. It was the death of sprezz.

ELSEWHERE

18

After the death of sprezz, there's still the rest of life, which is not always terribly long. A bandage, purchased at a Venice airport store, spotted with blood, was messily wrapped around Sleeper's finger. He held the wounded digit upright against a window full of early winter sky, looking like he was about to use it to dismiss an argument. He'd been expressionless and silent since takeoff.

Bobby's hair extensions, dislodged in the fight, looked like a cocker spaniel's floppy ear pinned to the side of her head. Under her nose, lipstick masqueraded as blood. On her lap, her mink, inside out, had a rip in its lining. They'd done nothing to clean themselves up, each punishing the other with their miserable appearance.

Unheeded—not even a "hi" or a smile—I continued past them, back from the WC, to my cheaper seat and sat with my unasked-for traveling companion.

"They're nuts," said Łyski, or rather, as we say in Polish, *popier-dolony.* "Takes a chick like Robcia to throw a ring overboard." His hair was up in a bun. "Sell it if you don't like it. Monetize! People buy anything on the internet, package it right."

I couldn't help but feel some sympathy for him. With his straightforward emotions, simple sentiments, he reminded me of myself—my former self. He flailed his arms as he spoke, nearly overturning my water cup.

"Man, I need another tomato juice. I'm all fucked up," he continued in Polish, hand on ribs. "'Scuse me, dude," he said in English, waving down a female flight attendant. "Can I have another 'mato juice, like, with two pepper packies though? Thanks, man, appreciate it." He smiled at her. "Man, I'm all fucked up," he said to me in Polish. He never spoke English to me.

"From the beating?"

"That was nothing. Should've seen me six months ago. Delivered these guitars to these dudes in Albuquerque and, like, two guitars went missing. One got lost in my garage, a Gibson with a beautiful neck. Man, it fitted my hand like holy Maria. But before I can explain, five dudes on top of me. There was one woman with them, some dude's sister. Guess she didn't like them all ganging up on me, like found me handsome maybe. Some chicks do, dudes, too. She pulled me right out from under them all, by the legs. I'm always getting saved by women."

The flight attendant brought him his tomato juice and a packet of pepper.

He dumped the pepper into his juice. "Shit, man," he called after her, "I said two peppers, yo." She ignored him. "Jesus Maria," he said to me, "what do you have to do to get a little spice in this world? What was I—ah, women, right. Oh, dude, I'm telling you this in confidence because I can tell you're a solid babe . . ." He narrowed his eyes at me. I produced a benign smile.

"Robcia thinks I'm giving her the painting back because I'm scared of Seryozha. I'm just doing her a favor. Do I need Russian mob millions burning a hole in my ass? I thought it was worth, like, twenty grand. I've got, like, at least six dudes more dangerous than Seryozha out to get me. Curse myself to God if I'm lying. Anyone who thinks I'm scared of Seryozha ain't been in this beautiful world for long."

"Who are these six dudes?"

"Guitar dealer from Albuquerque. Club owner from LA. Fucking plumber from Kazimierz. Cut his wife's tongue out for flirting with another dude. I've known dangerous dudes in my life. You live, you make enemies. When all I really ever wanted is to make music." He drank his juice and played some air guitar—not facetiously, but with sincere feeling. "*You live, you make enemies. You live, you die . . .*" he sang in falsetto. "Fuck, I've known dudes. Especially in Gliwice. I don't seek them out. They come by themselves. Not a week goes by without hooligans attacking someone with axes. They wait for you and chase you into the woods. This one dude, paranoid. He thinks I have his kilo of mephedrone from, like, twenty years ago. What would I do with mephedrone? That's why I can't tell anyone I'm home." He pulled his jacket over his face. "I'm traveling incognito, as they say."

"But you did tell your aunt we're coming? The one who's storing the painting for you?"

"Oh yeah, sure. Auntie Dorota. Man, I don't trust anyone. But my auntie Dorota, she's fearsome like holy Maria. During communism, she stole from the commies. She's a smart woman. Taught me everything I know, almost. But, hey, I don't like *knowing* things too much. I'm into feelings." Jacket still over his face, he tapped his chest. "Dorota always says, 'The wolf's always got to return to the woods.' She's right. I don't trust him."

"Seryozha?"

"No way, these Russian bosses, they eat from my hand. Sleeper's who I don't trust."

"Sleeper?" I laughed.

"Yeah. Never liked him. Always quiet. Always *thinking*. What's he thinking? I tell you, I don't mind seeing him this way . . ." He pointed up toward their seats. "All messed up, finger gone to the dogs, hair a bit this way." He pulled his rubber band, letting his own hair down. "What kind of dude wrestles his wife over some ring? Jesus Maria." He stretched his rubber band as if to fire it off above the seats in front of us. "Buy your wife another ring! He has money. Where's all that money from? Something's just off about Sleeper. Overheard him one time just, like, whispering all these super-long numbers into his phone, like covering the phone with his hand. But you know Robcia has fucked-up taste. She was normal when I met her, curse myself to God if I'm lying. Sweet girl, loved movies. Then one day she went crazy, marrying a Russian big shark on the side and not even telling me, buying all these clothes. America burned her heart. But I loved her. I forgave her.

"Then, at *our* wedding, she fucking stuck her tongue into her bridesmaid's mouth right by the altar. That hurt me. Not that I'm a hater of women who go for women. Won't stop anyone from doing the scissors or whatever you call it. But it was our wedding! A man has feelings."

"I don't know her well," I said. "I just work for them."

The pilot announced we were about to land.

"My advice," he said, "don't get too close."

Gliwice was a mining city less than a hundred miles from my hometown. Today it no longer exists, I guess because of the birth rate crisis. Already in 2018 it had a sadness, a foretaste of dissolution. Most of the mines were closing or closed. We drove to a boutique hotel on the Adam Mickiewicz Park. In the taxi, Sleeper announced he'd be staying in a separate room. Bobby pretended not to hear him. Łyski produced a hiccup of surprise and looked at me. I pretended not to see him.

We pulled into the hotel's porte cochere. "I like how squares and streets in Poland are named after poets," Sleeper said to me as I paid the driver. "America hates poets." His voice had a softness unlike the tone he'd been using with Bobby.

"I've been doing some writing myself," Łyski said to him in English. "Maybe I'll play you my new song. Wrote it in Venice one dark-soul night. We can make a little gig in my room, unplugged. Nine p.m.?" Everyone ignored him.

Sleeper's thoughts about poets and Polish parks reminded me of something Bobby had once said: "When I met Sleeper, he had this intensity about him, like someone who'd do great things, like invent a vaccine or move us all to a different planet." Instead, he'd stopped making films—stopped doing everything, in fact, except tending to his investments enough to keep Bobby in Bobby style. And he'd continue doing nothing. As I watched him pick their suitcases up from the sidewalk—the hotel had no porter—it hit me: It was because of Bobby that Sleeper would amount to nothing. Bobby, who found all effort unbearable and no success impressive enough. Another woman might still push him to be something, but for her, only wasted potential had appropriately radioactive glory.

In the evening, I ran into Bobby in the hall. She'd taken a shower, pinned her damaged extensions into a chignon. She wore a gray sweater and matching pants. I'd rarely seen her dressed so simply.

"Are we going to Łyski's aunt?" I asked.

"Not until tomorrow morning. She got delayed on her way back from Zakopane, where she was doing god knows what. I'm going to see Mama and Tata for dinner," she said and walked away.

I assumed Sleeper would go with her, and was surprised to see him, an hour later, in the door of my room with a roll of bandages and a bottle of rubbing alcohol.

"Open the door, quick. Unless you're in the mood for Łyski's recital," he said.

"No!" I said, laughing, letting him in, my heart beating swiftly.

"I escaped after two songs." Brushing past me, he entered the room. "The man has taken a liking to me. He wants my *input*. It's a mystery. Will you be my nurse and change this bandage?"

"I will wash my hands," I said, happily retreating to the tiny bathroom, running the tap.

In the mirror, I saw him sitting on the bed, unwrapping the old bandage from his finger. I felt such an ache of tenderness, I opened the "why-do-I — him" list on my phone in my head: *Hair curling on the back of his neck. He rescues a small bird trapped under table in a restaurant. The way he settles bills, never spending too long with the numbers. Knows math. Polite.* My list had been growing. It had been growing because my — was not reciprocated. People who are loved back don't have time to make lists.

"Maybe we should do this in the bathroom," Sleeper said, joining me by the sink. He placed his bandages and alcohol on the bathroom shelf and showed me his wound, a scarlet ring of little tooth marks—a wedding ring, I suppose, on the wrong finger.

"Maybe it is infected," I said. "Not very, but. Maybe the doctor."

"Oh no, I'm not going to a hospital a third time on this trip. I wouldn't know how to explain to a Polish doctor what happened, even if I spoke the language."

"You say . . . a bitch bit you."

He didn't smile at my joke. "This should work just fine." He handed me a tube of antibiotic cream and sat on the edge of the tub.

I opened the alcohol and poured some onto his finger, holding it over the sink. He hissed.

"It pains?" I said.

"It pains," he said.

There was a hesitation, something like shyness, between us. He embraced me with his other hand, and I sat on his lap.

"Have you missed me?" he said.

We'd all slept together just the night before. I knew he meant something else.

I nodded, squeezed a globule of cream onto each tooth mark.

"I'm not exactly at liberty to visit your room whenever I want," he continued.

"I know," I said, flattening each globule with the tube's silver mouth.

His mouth was near my ear. "You do? You know about the visiting permit I occasionally receive from the BIA? That's Bureau of Intermarital Affairs. Well, right now I'm here without a permit." This was unusual. Though an open secret, he'd never discussed it. I was his freedom, dosed, legitimized, controlled.

I looked up at our reflections in the mirror. He had on his

facetious face. Underneath, there was a softer layer of understanding, friendship even, and under that, a layer of jest that was a facet of acceptance of trivial things, of dead-serious things, of marriage and its illiberal liberties.

"Bobby's generous," I said.

She could be. Maybe he would be, too. Since he'd brought up what we'd never dared discuss, I thought I might confide as well. As if my family had sensed my return to Poland, I had another email from my brother, asking for money, this time with what seemed like a real invoice from my mother's care facility attached. He was in debt, and the treatment cost a lot, and I'd not sent money since we left LA.

Slowly, I unwrapped the bandage from its roll and began to wrap Sleeper's finger.

"When we fake-stole the painting," I said carefully, "Bobby promised me I also get. A hundred thousand euros, she promised. A million for her."

No reaction. Had she never told him?

"Please make sure the bandage is tight," he said.

"Do you think I will still get it," I said, careful not to look at him in the mirror, "when the painting is given to Germany? If we get it tomorrow from Łyski's aunt?"

"If Bobby gets hers, you'll get yours," he said a bit curtly.

I struggled to secure the bandage, then feigned struggling, smoothing its surface. Something unpleasant had settled between us, and I waited for him to defuse it with a joke or deliver one of his world-weary theories that cleansed money of guilt, restored its purity, its purely functional value. I could have explained my situation better, but I was overwhelmed by its smallness. My pride

balked at being a person in need. Such people don't inspire desire
or love.

"Thanks," he said, and left the bathroom, and I thought perhaps I'd hurt his pride by referring to the reward money. It must
have been hard for him to yield to another man's will, to see his
wife accepting orders and maybe soon money from Seryozha. I followed him into the bedroom. I'd been yielding, over and over, to
Bobby's will, to his, but I had learned I often liked to yield. To
yield wasn't in Sleeper's nature, though.

He stood by the bed, in the gray light of Poland, looking out the
window at the park. Early winter dusk had long fallen, followed by
an early snow. It fell on roofs, the park's trees, the statue of the poet
nobody but schoolchildren read. I wanted to tell Sleeper I understood him, his ugly situation, but telling him would make it uglier;
it was too late for confidences, so I just approached him and embraced him from behind. He was tense at first, then relaxed, put
his hands on my arms. I began to unbutton his pants. He stepped
out of them with a somnambulist's obedience, still looking out the
window. I took off his shirt. I was dressed, and he was naked, the
reverse of our first afternoon together. He didn't adjust his pose
because of his nudity and didn't seem more vulnerable because of
it . . . like a person alone on a secluded beach without a self-
conscious thought.

Finally he turned, reached with his unbitten hand, pulled me
into the bed, and I let myself be pulled and stretched, self-consciously
playful and cold, a snow angel in the sheets. His mouth on mine was
an objection to the world's petty austerity, the disappointments. His
one hand undressed me with surprising swiftness. He was like an
injured sculptor. Even his errors had deftness in them.

"Do you have a condom?" he asked, condoms being one of my professional responsibilities.

"It's okay," I said. "I take a pill."

"You've been on the pill this whole time?"

"Yes."

"Are you sure?"

"Yes, sure," I murmured into his shoulder. "I don't have with anyone else."

There are different types of nudity. There is shadowy nudity, hidden nudity. Nudity ashamed, proud. There's matter-of-fact nudity, viewed and unviewed. That winter afternoon his nudity was luminous. It belonged to me. He did. It was summer again in the bed.

And yet, though my feelings for him were more sincere than ever, though he did everything right, I was unable to come, perhaps because there was too much tenderness between us. Emotion dampens sexuality for some. Bobby often made a distinction between lovemaking and fucking. What we three had been doing was fucking. Now, with just us two, engaged in the most intense and fateful lovemaking of my life, I didn't want to make excuses or explain myself, so I ended up faking an orgasm.

Twenty, thirty minutes later, we woke up in the northern afternoon night.

"You're lovely," he said, unpretentiously, without metaphors or comparisons.

"You and I could be together in different life. We will never fight and you will be bored," I said. "I will never throw a ring in water and we can—"

"I'd love to be bored," he interjected, before I said what could be—what could have been. "I'd marry you just for that."

Facetious confession is confession nevertheless. An old, sentimental song, familiar to me from high school dances, came through the window from a car on the street below. In its simple rhythm we were married, if only for an hour, without rings, a dress, a priest, a party, without consequences.

I knew something was wrong when they didn't come down for breakfast. Texts unanswered, I sat at a table looking at a parking lot and ate a bowl of cereal. The dining hall was empty except for a woman with huge hoop earrings speaking to her boyfriend in a low, troubled tone. The air outside was the color of lead. A man in skiing gloves was clearing snow from his car, parked near the window. Our eyes met in the glass and parted without exchange. I had a heavy, nervous feeling in my stomach, and the institutional coffee made it worse.

I ran into Łyski by the elevator. His eyes were puffy and his breath beery.

"Where's breakfast, dude?"

I pointed him in the right direction.

"They have pancakes?"

"No pancakes. See you in the lobby in"—I looked at my phone and stepped into the elevator—"forty minutes?"

He saluted me and traipsed toward the dining hall. "No pancakes, fuck, man . . ."

The corridor stank of stale cigarettes and bleach. I knocked on Sleeper's door and, getting no answer, knocked on Bobby's. Sleeper opened it and let me in. I was disappointed to find him in her room but told myself I didn't care. I glanced into his eyes in passing: no acknowledgment of yesterday, just the impervious eyes of a stranger in a hurry.

The room was significantly larger than mine. Trays with tea things everywhere. Bobby in bed, the comforter piled so high I could see only the tip of her head propped up on the pillow.

"Bobby's sick," Sleeper said.

"Baby, I have the plague," she said in a small voice. "Come and give me a kiss."

She extended her hand, and I came to her and sat on the bed. A damp towel had been placed on her forehead, her face a spectacular red. The skin around her eyes and mouth seemed to have loosened and wrinkled. She looked ancient, a dowager queen on her deathbed.

She played the role perfectly: "Don't kiss my face," she said, "kiss my hand." She extended it to me, and I gave it a peck.

"It's some sort of allergic reaction, or else it's from stress. She's been through a lot," devoted Sleeper said, her badness forgotten. He sat on the other side of the bed, took her other hand.

"I've lost my looks, my hair, and my skin, and Sleeper still loves me," she said, reading my mind with malicious precision. She picked up a detached section of extension and threw it at my face.

"Look, even Ruslana's dead!" She laughed insanely.

I flicked the extension off my shoulder.

"I'm like that mermaid from the story," she said, watching me carefully, "the one who gets turned into an ugly human. You know, the one who was insanely in love. The cruel Polish version of the story."

"I like a woman with a flaking chin," Sleeper quipped weakly. "I guess I'm taking her to the hospital. We're just waiting on her parents to confirm their doctor friend is working."

"I understand," I said. "I know how it is for with hospitals in Poland."

"What if it's bubonic plague?" said Bobby, smiling. "It's not extinct. It still, like, lives in damp, old places. Venice is damp. Look . . ." She showed me her phone, her photo gallery full of gangrenous-looking pustule close-ups. "The one on my cheek looks like a bubo! My head is on fire!"

"Viva," Sleeper said, "can you put more cold water on her towel?"

I removed the towel from her head and took it to the bathroom.

On the counter was a pack of tampons and various creams and ointments—among them the rose serum, a finger-length less full than when I'd filled it. I can't say I'd forgotten what I'd done, but nevertheless it surprised me to see the bottle. I'd cloistered it in a bubble of denial for weeks, but that didn't make it any less undeniable right here, out of my head. Its petty truth had come to pass. Bobby must have used it more than once. Her face had already been flushed and flaking slightly yesterday. I picked the serum up but lacked the will to throw it out. I ran the water, wetted and wrung the towel, returned to the room.

Sleeper stood by the window, texting. I sat on the bed, reapplied her towel. I felt no guilt. The way she'd spoken about the mermaid, the sight of her now, ripping tiny spiderlings of skin off her face and placing them on a model's face in a fashion magazine, above a headline exhorting the women of Poland to GET WHAT YOU WANT— it all made me wonder if this was just another provocation. Bobby might well know I'd switched the serums. They often joked that she was an alchemist, with her jars and potions, her search for immortality. Skin was her battlefield. I imagined her sniffing the serum, smelling highly concentrated acid, guessing it had been tampered with, becoming inspired: it might be worth it to endure a little temporary peeling if it meant arousing Sleeper's sympathy. She probably knew he'd been to my room. What could be Bobbier than to punish me by allowing my plot to complete itself?

"Don't pull the skin off your face," I told her in Polish.

I was surprised when she clutched my shirt—the rough clutch of the dying, of the senile, of babies pulling at your shirt to get your breast—and pulled me so close I could smell her slightly sour breath.

"A punishment?" she whispered in Polish.

"What do you mean?" I said in Polish. Was she asking me if I had punished her, or threatening to punish me? Was she about to laugh hysterically in my face? To bite me?

"Punishment for me," she said, tears running down her burnt cheek. "Yesterday, at my parents', I didn't want to tell Tata about the stupid fight, so I told them Sleeper was sick. I couldn't stand it if he ever got sick—like, really sick. I love him so much . . . And then today *I* woke up sick."

Relief—she didn't know I was the culprit. Poland, parents, burns, all this had made her revert to childhood superstition. It was jarring and unpleasant to witness. She'd always been so fearless.

"What if it *is* bubonic plague? I mean, weird things do happen." She embraced me, draped her arms around my neck. "I don't want to die."

"You won't," I said in English.

I could have said something about the glycolic, made up some half-truth that would have led her down a reassuring path. But part of me enjoyed her like this, helpless, superstitious, irrational, in my arms. Then I thought, if she actually believed she had the plague, was she now making sure she'd infect me as well? She breathed heavily on my face, hung heavily on my neck, and my eyes came to rest on her phone on the comforter. On it, some anonymous man with blackened wounds was really dying of plague, dying as a reference, dying for the rest of us.

"If I die, can you tell my *tata* that—" she whispered.

"Okay, it's all settled," Sleeper said.

I never learned what Bobby wanted me to tell her dad. She withdrew her head from mine and tried to compose her face.

"What is settled?" I asked, a little nervously, while Bobby watched me closely with her shiny eyes.

"I'm taking Bobby to the hospital, and you're going with Łyski to meet his aunt. Kostya will meet you there. He's probably lurking somewhere outside our hotel anyway."

"No," I said. "No, I can't go alone with myself."

"We're all alone with ourselves in the end," lamented Bobby.

"Don't be silly," he said, brushing my hair behind my ear. It was a tender gesture, but tenderness was not its intention. It was a bribe. "You're perfectly capable. I don't speak Polish anyway," he said. "You don't have to do anything yourself. Just make *sure* Łyski gets the painting and gives it to Kostya."

"But it is safe?" I said. "I can't go alone with Kostya."

"Łyski will be there."

"Sleeper, no . . ." I thought about crying. It worked for Bobby.

"Do you want to get me more tea?" she interjected, uninterested in my safety, uninterested in art, in oligarchs, in ten-million-euro rewards. "My throat feels weird."

Sleeper took my spot on the bed, feeding her a spoonful of tea from a cup on the nightstand.

"What if I stay like this forever?" she said between sips. "Will you still love-love me?"

"Always," he said in a gentle voice.

"You will?" she cooed. "I will always, always love-love-love you, too."

It nauseated me. I didn't want to stay here listening to them cooing at each other. And I truly didn't want to go anywhere with Kostya and Łyski. But what I wanted mattered not at all to anyone but me. Of course, if I didn't go, who would make sure I got my hundred thousand euros?

Part of me hoped I'd get hurt, not badly, just a little abused, a not-quite-black eye. I wanted the Sleepers to be worried, to overlook the damage no one knew I'd done to Bobby. And maybe I was pleased to be sent on a mission alone, proud that Sleeper trusted me, thought me capable. I was starved for compliments, for recognition. Without another word, I walked to the door.

In our last moment together—no one knew it was our last—there was no communication between me and the Sleepers. They were grossly engrossed with each other. I might as well have been hotel staff, unregistered by them, unremembered.

"I'm so cold," Bobby said to Sleeper. "Can you bring my stinky mink and cover me?"

As I closed the door, I saw him drape the fur on her and say, the way one might to a sick little girl, "My lady."

19

I still had twenty minutes before meeting Łyski, so I lay on my bed, scrolling through messages, texting no one. I hadn't told family or friends I was in Poland. I didn't know I'd be leaving again in a matter of hours. On the TV, Polish politicians—accused by a commentator of undermining the judiciary—waved their arms, decrying immoralities.

I woke up, realizing I'd fallen asleep. The watch on my phone showed ten forty-six, six minutes past when we were all supposed to meet in the lobby. Had the Sleepers told Łyski the new plan?

I took the stairs. He wasn't in the lobby or the dining hall. When I got to his room, the door was open. His guitar case and a pair of grimy socks on the floor—around which the cleaning lady gingerly stepped as she tended the bed—suggested he hadn't fled. I mumbled something about looking for my friend. My hands shook as I drafted a text to Sleeper: Łyski did not come. I didn't send it until after I went to reception to ask if they'd seen Łyski. The receptionist informed me the gentleman from room thirty-four had bought a toothbrush but she hadn't seen him leave. I returned to my room to see if he was waiting for me there.

I finally sent Sleeper the text, standing by my window. Outside, in the concrete morning light, Mickiewicz the poet also stood, forlorn and massive, unromantic, unrefined. All canonizations are absurd. They say more about the canonizer than the canonized. The Sleepers, too, were heroes of the working class. Who says? I do. After all, they made me rich.

Yes, texted Sleeper. Łyski left with Kostya. They're going to his aunt. Please meet them there. Again, he texted me the address.

On my way, I texted back.

Sikornik was a complex of communist apartment blocks, what Americans might call a *housing project*. Concrete cubes of flats repeated like a brutal chant about utility and unity. In an apathetic nod to individualism, each cube was painted a different, faded underwear color: gray-white, dull red, brown-pink, lint blue. In a playground covered with snow and slush, children hung from metal rug-beating racks, watching me with feral detachment. Under their gaze, my mission to retrieve one of the world's masterpieces from a guitar thief's elderly aunt struck me as so incongruous that I briefly forgot my fear. I looked around for the kind of showy car Kostya might drive but found only Škodas and worse. I texted Łyski again: In front of your aunt's building. Are you here?

The lock on the building's main door was broken. I walked up a humidly odorous staircase to door 5A and rang a few times. An inch ajar, this door looked broken, too. An elderly woman in a faded leopard bathrobe opened the door. She had that weird, clipped 1980s hairdo that remained so popular into the 2030s among aging women of the former Soviet bloc. She pointed a steak knife at me.

"Hi," I said. "Are you Mrs. Dorota?"

"Kamiński's boy is right downstairs," she barked, looking over my shoulder suspiciously. "He's a strong boy who does that mixed martial arts, where they fight for money and you can do anything except this." She hooked a finger in her cheek and pulled. "He beat ten boys last month in Tarnowskie Góry. Tell your friends that!" She brandished the knife.

She seemed distressed if not deranged. If she attacked me, would I have to fight back? (Today, an old crazy myself, I'd have no qualms tackling a fellow octogenarian.)

"My name's Viva," I said. "I'm supposed to meet Damian here."

"So he's back already! What's he want? Money for gas? It's a long way to Sucha Beskidzka, ha! Tell him if I see him again, he better run where pepper grows." Again, she looked into the dark staircase behind me.

"Oh, no," I said, intuiting the situation. "I'm not with him. He stole from my employers. I'm just here to recover what he stole."

"Recover from here?! He steals from me, from his mother, God burn brightly above her soul." To my surprise, she stepped aside. I hesitantly entered the apartment. "A fig with poppy seeds, that's what you can recover from here after what they did," she grumbled. "Come and see for yourself!"

She led me into a dim living room. Drawers hung open. Framed saints, potpourri, potted ferns, table linen, and folk dolls in embroidered dresses lay strewn among the toppled furniture. I sensed she'd let me in because this trauma demanded a witness.

"This is terrible," I said, my sympathy both feigned and genuine. "What happened?"

"As you say! He's a thief! When he doesn't steal, he loses. Sieves for hands." She put the steak knife in her bathrobe pocket, gathered a pile of TV magazines, and placed them on the sofa. She moaned at a broken crystal bowl, surrounded by spilled fruit drops. As she fussed over a dented lampshade, I experienced a double déjà vu—first of the room where we found *The Lady*, then of the epic messes I'd cleaned in Bobby's boudoir. All happy messes are more or less the same. This one wasn't happy, though. This one was brutal and upsetting.

"So you said Damian was here already?" I asked quietly.

"There's not a decent person left out there, my dear, not since they let the immigrants in." Dorota sighed. "I was still in Zakopane when Kamiński calls me and says two Russian riffraffs are vandalizing your apartment. Such riffraffs, he says, like we don't even have here in the *osiedle*, not since they closed Bar Pod Kogutem. Even if some of those boys do nothing but sniff glue and kick cats. This will take a week to clean." She looked up at me from the wreckage of what certainly had taken decades to accumulate.

"I feel terrible this happened to you."

"You're a nice girl," she said distractedly, picking up the pieces of a smashed clock. Could Kostya have done this? Had one of the other Russians involved sent his own goons?

"I'm so sorry, but I have to ask again," I said. "Damian was supposed to meet me here at eleven to return a painting he stole, and my job depends on getting it back. Was he just here? Did you already give it to him?"

"So you're not the cleaning girl," she said. It struck me she was possibly a little senile. "Wróblewska said she'd send a girl because she herself can't come and help me. She can't come, she says, her bunion hurts, she's making *gołąbki*, and not even with kasha but rice, so I tell her, 'Fine, don't come, but save your rice for your daughter's wedding,' her daughter, you see, being not so marriageable. 'Save your rice,' I say to her. 'Save your bunion so it won't hurt at the wedding that will never be!' She says, 'I'll send a girl to clean,' the same girl who came to clean when her niece left the hamster cage open and the hamster ate the upholstery, shredded the carpet, got into Wróblewska's dresser, and bit a large hole I will never say where."

"I'm not the cleaning girl," I said gently. "I'm—"

"Friends! I should've known! I'm old. I had a great friend once, my dear, until one day I came home early from church and caught her serving strudel to my husband. In her slip. He's dead now, may God burn brightly above his soul." She flailed her arms. "But what a mess. What a mess!"

"Was Damian here just now? Maybe half an hour ago?" I tried again.

"Damian! One thing worse than friends is family! I should've beat him with a rod on bare ass instead of good morning," she said, picking up a spoon with a fish-shaped handle and placing it on a rickety chair. "When he was a youngster, I beat him with a fly-swatter, a kitchen rag, nothing more. He was a bad, lazy child, but I had a soft heart. I should've known then. Who treats his own aunt like this? Who destroys his aunt's apartment, the few possessions that have not been stolen from her? And then comes and asks for favors the next day?"

"I don't understand," I said. "Damian demolished your apartment?"

"Not Damian, but his *Ruski* buddies. But who else other than Damian sent them, when Damian, he comes here this morning, all innocent-acting, but with him a Satanic-looking *Rusek* with a big, bald head, all 'Good morning, ma'am,' speaking Russian to me, asking about my health—who says I don't remember my Russian from school! So I said back to him, '*Prosim. Spasiba.*' But all I wanted was to flick his nose and ask him how his mother raised him. But I did much worse. I cursed him. I erected three crosses of black pine in my heart just for him. At Damian, I didn't even look, didn't even scold him. I had them wait outside the apartment, in the corridor, pretending it wasn't them who destroyed it. I wasn't going to give the satisfaction." She laughed without amusement, gathering her folk dolls. "Beware people from the East. Who keeps company with the wolves will learn to howl." In the ruined room, holding a family of dolls, she looked like a wartime orphan grown old.

I had a feeling she still wasn't sure who I was but welcomed my presence. She required a sympathetic ear for her complaints.

"I feel terrible this happened to you," I kept saying. "But I have to ask—did you give Damian that painting he left with you? When you just saw him?"

"He was a rotten seed all along, my sister's fault. On the day of his baptism, she gave him a bath. 'You'll wash the holy water off,' I said to her. She didn't listen. Look what he's become."

She was of that stubborn breed of women who, though power-less, had learned to retain power by never responding to questions. In that respect and no other, she reminded me of Bobby. I stood awkwardly amid the wreckage. What was happening? Could Kostya and Łyski have double-crossed everyone? An unlikely alliance, but what did I know. Perhaps Łyski was taking his revenge on Bobby after all.

"All men are cheaters," she said, slapping a TV magazine. "This one has a beautiful wife, two children, and yet he goes astray with a floor mat. Of course she's his sister. But he doesn't know it. Doesn't mean he doesn't sin." She clicked her tongue. It took me a moment to realize she was now disparaging not her nephew but a character from a soap opera, presumably played by the actor grinning at us with white-hot veneers on the magazine cover.

I began to feel a little panicky. I wanted out of her apartment. I glanced at my phone. No messages from Łyski. Even Sleeper had stopped responding. In my last message, I'd asked him for Kostya's phone number.

"People come and go like it's a train station in Warsaw, without any respect for me and my property. Who are you?"

"I work for Bobby Sleeper. Your nephew's ex-wife. She's a gallerist now. I'm here to oversee the return of the painting to those it belongs to. It's really, really important and time-sensitive and involves many important people."

At first I thought she hadn't heard me. She was putting Christmas ornaments back in a cardboard box, but then she said, "Robertka, that darling. How is she? She always remembered me. When I had my kidney stones, she visited the hospital. She always brought me my candy, even if my doctor said it's bad for my teeth. She'd say, 'Dorota, if you lose a tooth, I will buy you a new one.' And then I lost it, not on a candy, but when I bit into a *pączek*." She opened her mouth and pointed at a gap from a missing canine, a tiny black door to the mean world I'd escaped, a world where you're reduced, one indignation at a time, by cheap dentists, expensive priests, needy parents, treacherous children.

"But by the time I lost it, Robertka was gone. That baboon, my nephew, scared her away. He didn't treat her right. She came here with beautiful, shiny shoes on, and Damian drags her through the mud. We had bad rains that October in the *osiedle*. Everything was flooding. I remember coming back from church and seeing old Pankracy's prosthetic leg floating in a giant puddle like it's Noah's. 'Carry her over the mud, baboon,' I said to Damian. 'Don't you see you got yourself a lady?' I never had a chance to speak to her after they broke up, but she's a nice girl. Too good for my nephew."

I was surprised Dorota liked Bobby. But then Bobby had apostles everywhere. I am her last.

"Well, Bobby needs this painting back." I decided to try one last time. "As I said, your nephew stole it from her."

"I bet he did!"

"And now she's being threatened by these Russians. They might hurt her if the painting isn't returned. I—"

"If not the *Ruskis*, then the *Schwabs*, if not the *Schwabs*, the Jews and atheists. Muslims, ecologists, the gender homosexuals . . ." she said crazily. "Not a decent person left. Damian's hands have always been sticky. He lived with me since he was twelve, after his mother died, Lord shine on her wayward soul, and every day I thank Jesus those years are over." Polish women of her generation tended to prefer Jesus to God, and their sons to their husbands. Apparently not nephews, though. "He treats my cabin as a hotel and my cabin shed as a storage," she said, leading me into the kitchen.

"Is that where the painting is?" I exclaimed. "In your cabin shed?"

"You're a clever one." She looked at me sharply over her shoulder.

The kitchen was in a terrible state. Plates—cheap white ones and older ones with a trim of bluebells, probably family heirlooms— were shattered all over the shelves and countertop. On the floor, green packets of spice lay like cards in a game that had ended in a brawl. A flush of thyme, a straight of marjoram. She walked over them, opened a cupboard, fetched a bottle of homemade kirsch and two unbroken glasses.

She opened the kirsch, licked her fingers, and poured. "I once found twenty fake purses in that shed. Another time, a bag of marijuana in my wheelbarrow. My nephew is a Judas."

"Where's the shed?" I asked, accepting my glass.

"Sucha Beskidzka." She grinned and drank. "I did find the painting." She poured herself another. "Rolled up, wrapped in a blanket. At first, I thought it was a kitchen cloth my mother embroidered during Gomułka's era. I needed space for potting soil, so I brought the painting back with me. I was going to tell Damian I did, but when he showed up with his *Rusek* this morning, I told them it was still in the shed! These boys with nothing but tripe in their heads."

"So they're on the way to Sucha Beskidzka?" I sipped my kirsch, awful. "And the painting's still here? They caused this much mess and didn't find it?"

"I'm not one for giving favors to people who destroy my property. When Kamiński called me to tell me some *Ruskis* trashed my apartment, I knew my nephew dipped his fingers in it."

My phone began to vibrate in my pocket. Texts from Sleeper: Did you find him? Did you get it? What's going on? Three missed calls. My phone must have hit a patch of bad reception.

"I said to myself, 'Oh no, not this time,'" Dorota continued. "'You won't let yourself be taken advantage of.' I've suffered enough in my life. I had three miscarriages. My husband died of cancer when I was forty-one. My second husband died of a heart attack when I was forty-nine."

On her right hand, the one with the glass of kirsch, she had three wedding bands. Some widows wear their husband's band atop their own. I'd never seen it done with two dead husbands. Who was I to judge? Three, together for eternity.

"So you still have the painting," I said for the eighth or ninth exasperated time.

Dorota had about her the contrarian bravado of women like my grandmother, countryside women defined by elemental brutalities. Crops frozen overnight. Chicken heads flying off. People dying in the fields.

"They will get there and find potting soil." She giggled, poured herself another glass, and drank it. Her tongue poked through the gap in her teeth. "You're a good girl, I can tell. You should come over sometime and try my gooseberry, early carrots, maincrop carrots. No grocer has dill like mine. May I see your ear?"

"What?"

"Your ear. Let me see it."

"Why?"

"Let me see it."

I pushed my hair behind my ear. She reached for me across the table. Her breath smelled of kirsch and bacterial breakdown. More than I, she was defined by deficiency, by poverty that was generational. She touched my ear with thin, cold fingers.

"As I thought."

"What?" I laughed, loudly and unnaturally. I had a superstitious thought that she'd been reading my mind, siphoning my brain through my ear like a witch from childhood stories. My friends and I, little girls, feared witches, never imagining we'd become them.

"You have good fleshy lobes. People like my sister and nephew don't have good, large lobes. Their ears connect directly to the head, like hyena ears. Don't ever trust people without large lobes. Demons have small ears." She pronounced "demons" under her breath, as if she were embarrassed to go that far. "Because your ears are good and you're kind, I will sell you the picture." She looked at me now in a new, canny way, a marketplace face, not a senile face. "How much is it worth? Must be a lot for the *Ruskis* to trash my apartment."

"It's worth a lot," I said.

"How much?"

"A lot," I repeated.

"How much?"

"Four thousand złoty," I said, not daring to look at her, looking down into my kirsch.

She whistled. "No wonder those Ruskis raised hell. I'll sell it to you for four thousand six hundred."

"Four thousand two hundred," I haggled, scared that if I didn't, my ruse would be less persuasive.

"Four thousand five hundred," she said. "Who will pay for my dishes?"

"Okay. I think Bobby will be fine with that."

"I've worked my whole life. Do you know how much retirement I get? One thousand złoty. And Damian gives me nothing. When will I get my gratitude for all the years I labored raising him? Holy never, that's when. I have arthritis, hypertension, and gall-bladder." She poured more kirsch into the glasses, and raised hers. "To a deal well done." We clinked glasses and drank. "Cash first," she said.

I opened my purse and took out my laptop case, unsnapped the outer flap pocket, and pulled out my passport, folded in which were the petty cash złoty Bobby had given me at the airport. With shaking hands, I counted four thousand five hundred. "Where's the painting?" I handed Dorota the money.

"In my car," she said delightedly. "Those boys didn't think about that! Their ears are too small for their brains to chop an onion." She counted the cash twice, stashed it in her robe's pocket next to the knife, and took her car keys from atop a cupboard.

Her Maluch was parked among other cheap cars by the *osiedle* dumpsters. She struggled with the old key lock. I looked in a frosted window and amazingly—but really not when you consider everything else—there was *The Lady Waiting*, face up on the back seat. Who knows what had happened to the frame. Dorota climbed into the front, reached into the back, retrieved a cardboard tube, and handed it to me. There was a peace symbol sticker on the lid. Of course, it was all a joke, a practical joke at my expense. Everyone I'd ever met was about to jump out from behind the dumpsters, yelling and laughing.

"Here's your painting," Dorota said. "The *Ruskis* could've made me a nice offer, like you. For them, ten thousand, but they can afford it. I'll never understand men. Not for communist China, I won't!"

"That's the painting," I said, pointing the tube at it. "This is just a tube."

"I meant here's your tube for the painting," said Dorota, not fetching the painting.

I stepped around her, climbed into her car, and carefully gathered the canvas. In the gray Silesian light, in that plebeian parking lot, Dorota and I stood side by side, regarding the Vermeer. I held it up. The lady had aged in waiting, her forehead diagonally creased. Otherwise, no visible damage. Scared it would snow, I rolled her up, wondering if one rolled up famous paintings. She felt soft, insubstantial, an outdated map, a map of nowhere. I enclosed her in the tube.

"So much commotion for a dearie looking out the window," said Dorota.

20

It was barely past noon, but the overcast sky seemed already to
tilt the day toward nightfall. I sleepwalked into a taxi. Car
lights behind a row of bare trees, the cold air, the tang of coal
smoke in it, these summoned a distant emotion I couldn't place: a
solemnity of something forgotten, maybe childhood walks to midnight mass on Christmas Eve, back when the legendary and quo-
tidian blended—three kings, three neighborhood boys smoking by
the church, dogs that seemed on the verge of speech. The world
otherwise silent and snowy. In church, only old women and young
girls believed.

I told the taxi driver to take me to the hotel. His unshaven face
had the spent quality of an old banknote. Through the back window, I kept checking for Łyski or Kostya or people who maybe
looked like Russian goons. More than a few pedestrians did.

I don't recall ever having any explicit intention of stealing *The
Lady.* I was taking it back to the Sleepers. My actions, not my in-
tentions, betrayed them. Some primitive force, original greed, had

enchanted my mouth, my hands. My hands, holding my phone, the phone I hadn't looked at since touching *The Lady*, felt alien, dead, male—poet's hands cast in plaster in a museum, holding an object that belonged in a museum. Texts from Sleeper: What's going on? Why aren't you picking up? About to go to the aunt's address. Worried. A few from Bobby: Hey bitch. I'll live. The doctor said I overdid it on retinol. Baby where are you baby? The last message said, Are you okay?

Why did my hands not move to open these messages? *Are you okay?*

In my window, people of Gliwice rushed in and out of store-fronts, huddled and bent, as if ready to dodge collapsing roofs, collapsing skies. A man sold pretzels from a cart. Tired mothers pulled their children by their backpacks away from the danger of the street. Disco polo beeped and thumped out of the taxi's radio. Baby where are you baby?

"Actually, sir," my dead mouth said to the driver. "Can you drive me to the train station?"

I didn't mean to get on a train or even out of the taxi. It was yet another outrageousness I was trying on, like Bobby's clothes or husband. I was on my way back to them, to our hotel. I hadn't texted them, because of my hands, my hands that were primitive, weak, illiterate.

The driver pulled into the station. I paid with Bobby's petty cash and stepped onto the curb, clutching the tube. My taxi left, but there were other taxis waiting. Any of them would take me to the Sleepers. I felt both observed and immaterial. I looked around for Kostya. Nobody was obviously following me.

A new crazy thought: If nobody followed me, it was because I'd already returned the painting to Kostya and forgotten it. There was a gap in memory, in time. I'd fallen through ... into the train

station. A loudspeaker announced arrivals and departures. As a
child, I'd heard a story about a woman who'd fallen under a train.
Her hair turned white as her body was split in half. People, I remembered Bobby saying, no longer kill themselves for love. Or had
she said *sell* themselves for love? People passed in all directions. I
gazed at the timetable with a bad student's dullness. Panic at the
blackboard, hand dry with chalk, names of cities as mysterious as
the names of minor saints.

It was time to return to the hotel, return *The Lady* to my lovers,
explain that Kostya had been sent to Sucha Beskidzka in vain. It
was time to go to Berlin. Bobby's lawyer was in Köln, I recalled,
but the Gemäldegalerie was in Berlin. There were numerous lawyers, Bobby had said, who specialized in such transactions. Time to
show Bobby that I could do what she alone claimed to be capable of
doing.

It was time. The train station clock showed half past twelve.

I joined the line at the ticket window. People smelled of unlaun-
dered coats and exterior air. Women in fur-trimmed puffers on
their way to visit relatives, stooped-shouldered students, two drug
addicts begging for change. The board reshuffled, dropping the top
destination as a train departed.

I leaned close to the opening in the glass to speak to the ticket
clerk, half expecting a hand on my shoulder, a bag over my head,
almost longing for violence to relieve me of what I was doing.

"There's a train to Berlin in one hour," said the clerk. "You'll
have to switch in Opole."

"I'll take a second-class ticket," I said, restraining laughter that,
had it come out, would have sounded unhinged.

So I had a ticket in my hand. A lucky one, as Bobby would say.
What about my clothes at the hotel? I didn't need them, as I wasn't

really going to leave. Were my clothes mine? I walked to the platform, along its edge. Suicide was nowhere in my head but, then
again, the category of the possible had suddenly burst open. My
hair would turn white. Like Bobby, I would lose my hair, my skin.
I laughed, loudly, alone at the end of the platform. There was no
madness in my family—only forgetfulness.

One can have a ticket but not board the train. One can board a
train but not stay on it. Leave on it.

On the train, I had a strong sensation of error, as in a dream
when an irreversible awful thing happens. Your tooth is now
broken. Your mother is dead. Your mother is not dead but has forgotten everything, even herself. Her mouth is full of teeth, her
clothes no longer hers.

When the train moved, it was as if the whole Eurasian Plate
had shifted. The great earthquake the Californians were all waiting for had found me, impossibly, in Poland. *Are you okay?*

Through the city outskirts—apartment blocks and offices gave
way to walls festooned with black and blue graffiti hearts, cocks,
tits, and names of soccer teams. Abandoned structures of red brick
blurred in the now-falling snow. I twisted the hippie lid of the ten-
million-euro cardboard tube pressed to my tits, my blue heart. The
ticket collector collected my ticket.

I would collect the reward and return to the Sleepers with the
money.

"I always suspected you had a hidden talent for subterfuge,"
Sleeper would tell me.

There would be anecdotes, spritzes, white wine, white sheets,
white lies, a big new bed, a grand hotel with beautiful women in
the bar, but everyone's eyes on me. I am illuminated by my epic
act. I wear something subtly extravagant. We make love, Sleeper

and I, and Bobby blends into the background, the towels and luggage benches, the bedroom air. In the expensive silence of the mind's hotel room, I'm the wife, protagonist, and solo mistress.

The fantasy of my victorious return was hampered by the squalor of this old compartment. Cigarette burns on the seats, pink cushions of gum under peeling upholstery. I'd gone from sleepwalking to sleepriding. The wheels below me rattled on the rails. If I returned with the money, I realized, they'd make me return it to Seryozha. Then what? My relationship with Bobby was already fraught. The future seemed repulsive, unimaginable. Back to California, folding Bobby's clothes, paying her bills and compliments, in love not in love with her husband, with her, with them, with neither, each as an aspect of the other, all of it defined by jealousy, incompleteness, reflectivity, and capriciousness . . . I'd have perhaps one hundred thousand euros in the bank, or invested, with Sleeper's help, in something safe, government bonds in a stable, predictable country. That was hardly enough to buy my freedom from Bobby's wicked kingdom. I'd still be an assistant, subordinate to two individuals and their marriage, forever sentenced to the sidelines, forever at their bedside, beside them in their bed.

In the nineteenth century, governesses went mad. What about twenty-first-century assistants? Where do they go?

Berlin.

21

In Berlin, on the platform, I finally dared to look at my phone. Twenty-five missed calls, as many messages, some from an unknown number. So Kostya and Łyski must've gotten to the shed in Sucha Beskidzka and found potting soil instead of the painting. The top message on my phone, sent three hours ago from an unknown sender—Kostya?—said, hore. The simplicity, stupidity, of the misspelled insult was powerful. It was like seeing one of the graffiti slurs I'd passed, only with my name on it.

Messages from Sleeper: Please, let's talk. They are dangerous people. I'm worried about you. I don't know what you're doing but I'm worried. Your safety matters most. I hadn't read all of them. His last was just one word: Mała...

Regret chased love in my head. I could never betray him. No one had witnessed my thoughts of betrayal—I'd technically not betrayed them yet—but even contemplating doing so had marred the purity of my emotion for him. I had never known how pure it was until it wasn't.

Maybe everything was still reversible. But somewhere on the rails between Poland and Germany I had lost the possibility of return.

In the station, Germans flowed around me in goal-oriented patterns—this organized hive of tall, neat men with briefcases and women with ballerina buns and kitten heels, exiting and entering trains and elevators on their way from offices and meetings. Sensible women who had learned that the world runs on numbers, not love, not even sex. My dead hands woke up and typed unpoetically into my search bar: *hotels near train station Berlin*.

In front of the two-star hotel, new asphalt had been laid, smelling of burnt feathers. I took the last free room. I placed the tube on the bed, washed and dried my hands, removed the lid, unfolded the canvas, and held it aloft.

I shouldn't have rolled it. I guess that had begun with Łyski. The crease on the woman's forehead was puffy, like a vein. The frameless flimsiness of the canvas terrified me. Would someone really pay millions for this distressed piece of painted fabric? I laid it carefully on the bed, sat cross-legged by it, and stared. The fruit on the lady's plate was redder in the hotel's dark light, almost burgundy, the foreground drapery a dusk-to-dawn rainbow of blues. Bobby had said if you live with a painting long enough you eventually *see* it, the face of it. After an hour of staring—I didn't know what else to do; it was late; heavy feet stomped up and down the stairs outside my door—I *saw* it. Maybe not the painting's face, but the face of its subject. The lady now embodied the opposite of the qualities I'd originally attributed to her. She wasn't a woman of ideas or mystery or beauty; rather, she was plain, ordinary, like me.

Much later I learned *The Lady* wasn't a portrait—almost none of Vermeer's women were. They were *tronie*: studies of expressions, physiognomies, stock types, produced not to commemorate a particular personage but to represent anyone who fitted the type, to be sold on the free market. I lay on my side at her feet.

At midnight, I woke to drunken baritone singing in the next room. The painting was gone. I turned the light on. It had slipped onto the floor. Finding no new damage, I placed it on the closet floor on a towel. Damage. Would there be? *They are dangerous people.* Would the Sleepers be beaten by goons? They'd find a way to repay Seryozha. They would "liquidate their assets," a mellifluous and mysterious phrase, almost a chant, I'd heard them repeat. I didn't think they were worth much more than ten million. So they'd be in debt, poor for a while, never as poor as I'd been—the once-rich find ways to be rich again.

Was I in danger? Even if the Russians pressured the Sleepers, they had no way of tracking me down. We'd never had a contract. I was paid in cash. My surname was painfully common, and the Sleepers had never asked the name of my hometown. I'd received no bills, left no traces of identity in their house. I'd long since sold my car; my laptop was with me. Receipts? I'd never used my credit card for anything involving the Sleepers. I didn't exist.

I drank a bottle of German water from the minibar, opened my laptop, banished my anxious thoughts again and again, and started looking for law firms in Berlin whose specialties included "art." I studied their websites, judged their attorneys by their faces. Each face had a very different mixture of two ingredients: arrogance and friendliness.

I overslept and missed breakfast. I dreaded checking my email. Too scared to use my phone—lest the Sleepers, who paid the bill, find the numbers on their statement—I used the room phone to contact the few firms I'd researched. I spoke haphazardly, in a trembling voice. Kiraly Rechtsanwälte couldn't see me until late January. Sylvia Durchenwald and Associates was booked until spring. I was dismissed by their assistants before I could explain my case. "All of our internship positions are taken," said the receptionist at Ziemssen, in heavily accented English.

"But I have a famous Vermeer, right here I have, on my floor!" I finally told a receptionist at SVB, a law firm I'd found on a list of "famous art lawyers" on the *Le Chat Noir* art magazine website. On the SVB website, two lawyers, Andreas Gutherzig and Zhi Liu, were photographed against an industrial wall in unostentatious clothes, as if on their way out of some warehouse party.

"Please repeat. I do not understand you, *madame*."

"I have a Vermeer. It is for millions for the reward, but the reward *expires*—do you understand me—on December twentieth."

She wouldn't say if she understood me, but she took down my hotel's phone number and my room number. I stood over *The Lady*, projecting my helplessness onto her. Maybe Bobby was right that you needed special skills or connections to pull off such a transaction.

Like someone tentatively approaching a room full of betrayed and resentful lovers and relatives, I dragged my finger on my mousepad and opened my inbox. Unread mail, black bold letters, mostly threats and demands from Bobby. Her most recent ones had subject headings in all capitals: FATHERLESS UNEDUCATED SZMATA. I remember that one. There were several from Sleeper, with more demure language. For those of you born after 2040: with email, we could read the first line of each message without opening it. I found it morbidly intriguing that my inbox was entirely messages of hatred. My brothers didn't even know the Sleepers, but they'd sent me messages so brutal and despairing, messages that mixed with Bobby's so seamlessly, that I told myself this was not my inbox but my spam box: Dear beloved, we find way you enlarge your penis. Dearest, you steal 10 000 000 euro you will die. Blessed beneficiary, I hate you go to hell in peace. We the US Department of Justice is contacting you regarding your funds. CONGRATULATIONS YOU WIN! Please provide following information, your phone number, your location bitch and scan of your green card.

I never opened any of them.

I called reception and inquired about room service. There was no room service. I thought about using the delivery apps on my phone, but they contained Bobby's information, and the details of my order would appear in her inbox. This thought triggered a new paranoia—would the Russians hire a hacker, track my phone? I removed my SIM card and broke it in two. It hurt me to do so. Unlike Bobby, I didn't like destroying things.

Now I had no food and no phone. My stomach growled. I lay on the bed, gazing at one of the world's masterpieces, feeling like some shipwrecked aristocrat of yore, perusing her jewels, lamenting their inedibility. Finally I took a shower, dried my hair, put on my smelly, only clothes. I was about to look for a place to hide the painting from the cleaning staff when the phone rang. The receptionist said something I didn't understand, followed by another voice saying another something I didn't understand. After many back-and-forths, I realized it was Zhi Liu calling me from SVB, asking me to come to their office that evening.

My heart sped as I hung up. I was full of apprehensive joy, joy I checked immediately with a series of cautious, inhibitory thoughts.

This could all still lead to nothing. Or German prison. The reward might be much less than advertised. It might not be available to just anyone who brings the painting back. It might require presenting paperwork showing the painting's provenance. The painting could be fake. There was a crease in it. Could I go to jail for damaging a painted face?

Still, they wanted to see me. Lawyers weren't in the habit of wasting time.

You had to know how to speak to lawyers, Bobby always said. You had to know how to look when speaking to them. "Hello, mouse," I said to the bathroom mirror. Eyes, nose, mouth— everything in its usual place. Who wouldn't trust this unremarkable face? "I'm here to return a precious work of art. It came into my hands by accident," I said in Polish, then used my laptop to translate the sentence into English.

After prolonged deliberation, I stashed the painting in the closet, hung a DO NOT DISTURB sign on the doorknob, then called reception and asked that no one enter the room for the next several hours. I needed sleep, I said, and snuck out of the hotel with a scarf covering my face.

In the first place I could find, I devoured two kebabs, better than any meal I'd had in weeks. Satiated, walking along an arcade of shops, I had a sensation of having entered a shadow life. Spoken German around me was shadowy, extended, a night language trailing behind me in long choral vowels. It began to snow, and my attention fell to the Christmas lights lining the store display windows. The chaotic scrum of holiday shoppers rekindled my paranoia. Someone worse than Kostya was following me, had flown in from Moscow to stake out the Gemäldegalerie.

Doppelgängers of the Sleepers peopled the streets. I bought new sunglasses, a burner phone, a hat. As an act of faith in the painting's value, I spent two hundred euros on a navy-blue suit. The less money I had, the less I'd waver in my resolution to keep the entire reward.

At a cosmetics counter, a man with sparkling eyelids did my face—nothing like the face Bobby liked to paint on mine, but an unfamiliar, aggressive face with feline eyes and a stubborn, mercenary mouth. I licked the lipstick off, wandering the department store. Mechanized toys saluted me. I bought tape, scissors, Bubble Wrap. At my hotel, I asked reception if they had a cardboard box. They found me one that said VORSICHT GLAS on it. I cut it up and packed the painting into a neat parcel, put Łyski's nutty tube in the trash, and washed my face.

In my new hat and sunglasses, I took a taxi to the offices of SVB. The packaged *Lady* rode beside me on the seat. I paid the driver in euros from Venice and carried my parcel across the snowy street toward a large white building. Then came a fluttering feeling, half chest pain, half back pain. A few huddled figures stood outside the building's revolving door. One of them had Kostya's bulk, a hood. He started toward me. His approach possessed a mythical quality. I think I stopped mid-street. My ears muffled my head, my heart turned to chalk. I was the only creature in a bleached world. I felt my bladder loosen but not let go. But he passed me, wasn't Kostya, wasn't anyone to do with me, just a German with a bored expression, shoes forming a line of Vs in the slush.

The SVB office was just as I imagined it—a large room with modern furniture, minimalist light fixtures—except for the art, which was not abstract but figurative. Paintings of horses, horses in motion, galloping, rearing, boxing the air with their hooves, their flat eyes made fuzzy by the madness of combat. I was deposited in a conference room by a receptionist. I stashed *The Lady* underneath my chair.

Many muddle-headed, anxious minutes followed. In a mirrored panel on the wall, I saw myself, a ridiculous figure in a hat and sunglasses, perched behind a giant table. I removed the hat and sunglasses just in time for the receptionist to return and introduce a woman in a suit far more expensive than mine. She wasn't Zhi Liu but Frau Schmitt. Short brown hair, cut straight across her forehead like a clipped phrase: "That's enough." Her whole slim figure had a quality of preventive measure.

Introductions were brief. She was familiar with both the theft and the reward. They'd worked with the Stiftung Preußischer Kulturbesitz before, she said.

"Now," she said, "please explain how you came into possession of the painting. Attorney-client privilege obligates us to secrecy," she said slowly, her words easing into my fearful silence.

"What does it mean?"

"That I'm required by law not to reveal any information you share with me if you retain us. Are you retaining us?"

"Okay." My heart would not slow down. I'd always been easily led. I was brave at parties, after a drink, in a tight dress. Offices frightened me, as did demands for professionalism, for direct, clear answers. I began, eyes on fingers, fingers on knees, ankles pressed to my parcel on the floor.

"Now," she said again, like a recording of herself, "please explain how you came into possession of the painting."

I had not prepared for this. I started by telling the truth. "I was in America," I said. "I worked for one couple, man and woman, in

Los Angeles, for their assistant." The truth began to sprout small feathers. "One night she showed me a painting. She got it from her ex-husband. She had many ex-husbands but one new husband. The one from she got the painting, it was her first ex-husband."

"Your employer," asked Frau Schmitt, "did she know the painting was a stolen work?"

"No, I don't think so. She never said."

"Very good. Continue, please."

"I worked for them. Then, for a goodbye gift, they told me, 'Pick one thing,'" I said, suddenly inspired.

It was a detail lifted from my previous job in Chicago: The night before my employer put her head into the oven, she'd asked me to choose one item from among her belongings as a gift. I had picked a silver cruet—"a family heirloom," she'd said, "extremely valuable"—only to find out months later, when she was bones and the outer layer had peeled from the cruet's belly, that it was silver-plated copper. It was on my little table in my room in the Sleepers' empty house, forever lost and worthless, in Los Angeles. It had beautiful curvature, though. The woman in front of me was defined by straight lines and right angles. She sat straight-backed across from me, the table immaculate and empty between us.

"Why did you pick that painting as a gift?" she asked.

"I didn't want a gift too expensive. They kept it in their luggage room and didn't care. Some time after, I watched a movie. There were many movies. My employees were filmmakers but retired."

"So they were older."

I didn't deny it. I hoped not to have to reveal who they were. They were older than I, after all, and Sleeper *was* "retired."

"The movie was about Vermeer. It was actually a video, online—anyway, they said Vermeer always painted women by windows. They showed the painting, my painting. They said it is called *The Lady Waiting*. I couldn't believe it. I ran to look at it for the whole night and searched the internet."

Indeed there was a video like that. I'd seen it.

"So it was luck." Frau Schmitt's face was accommodating.

"Luck," I confirmed. I couldn't get rid of the word. "I was in Hollywood," I added, nonsensically, as if defending a role I had landed. Of course, she didn't believe my story. I felt ill and began to draw mental lines from her bangs to her notepad.

"Very good," she said. "Can you provide me with a form of identification?"

"What does it mean?"

"Your passport or ID."

"Oh, yes." Why did they need my passport? Calm. I forced myself to search my purse methodically. I found it and slid it across the table to her.

"*Polen?*"

"Yes. But I don't live there."

"Miss Nowak. Let's make a pause. Would you please wait here a moment?" Frau Schmitt held my passport in a germophobe's two-fingered grip and pressed a button on an intercom console I hadn't noticed, a touch screen embedded in the table to her left. She said something in German to the console, stood up, smoothed her blazer, and disappeared behind a pair of polished wooden doors with my passport. She would return with a policeman. He'd be more polite than policemen in the US or Poland. I saw myself in my new navy suit in a very polite German prison.

The door opened, and Frau Schmitt returned, along with a man who announced, "Andreas Gutherzig. Nice to meet you." His presence imbued Frau Schmitt's movements with a deferential, almost apologetic quietness. She whispered the door closed and herself down onto a chair.

Not in his photo on the website, but in life, Gutherzig resembled the paintings on his office walls. Most people compared to animals don't actually look like them. This man was an exception. The paintings were a conscious choice, I felt, dignity through acknowledgment. Sitting here with Gutherzig, you wished you, too, looked like a horse.

"So the situation is this," he said. "You were given the painting, a gift. Still, the painting had been stolen. Our job is to prove you acquired the painting by what we call *adverse possession*. In short, we show you didn't know it was stolen, which you didn't, as my partner tells me, until you knew and came to us. See, this is just—" He spoke to her in German. She was the bad doctor and he the good doctor. She diagnosed the cancer, he treated it.

"A precaution," he said to me in English. "The truth is, the foundation doesn't care if you're the thief, which you're not. The authorities are not involved. It is in both parties' interest—yours and theirs—that it stays without authorities. All they want is a peaceful exchange, with minimal questions. Once the authorities are involved, the artifacts are in danger. Burnt, damaged, shot at, ripped. In the past, thieves have done this." During all this, he sat down and stood up a few times, always gesturing with his hands, pantomiming a peaceful exchange, a gun, the ripping of canvas. "Baumann, the president of the foundation, he is desperate to get the painting back. All he cares about is the art. He won't ask you anything. Only . . . there is public opinion to take care of. The public needs a story. The foundation is not allowed to reward a thief. Not in Germany. In America, maybe."

"Okay," I said. "I'm not a thief."

"Precisely my point. There's the advisory board." He smiled. "They are the ones who meddle."

"We will have to give a few names," said Frau Schmitt, "to confirm the story."

"My employers are . . . so private. They didn't know anything of the painting. I don't like to get them involved."

"What about your employer's ex-husband? The one who gave her the painting."

"I think it's not a good idea. He's a Russian . . . uh, businessman."

"*Ja*," they both said and nodded, as if more than enough information had been provided.

"Anyone else? Anyone who could confirm the story?"

I thought briefly of Lance, then dismissed it. Lance would never lie for my benefit.

"They will actually be questioned? Or is it just . . ."

"No one will be questioned, not initially at least. But we need to provide at least one name. We want to protect you. See, you could easily be turned into a victim, or worse, a defendant. That's how it works, the press. The foundation board is very *uncurious*. But the advisory board sometimes doesn't understand how it works, the world."

"The advisory board," Frau Schmitt echoed.

"You're doing a great thing for culture in Germany, a heroic thing. Heroes should be rewarded and not punished." He paced and stopped, paced and stopped. Had he leapt onto the table, demonstrating German heroism, I'd have accepted it.

Frau Schmitt's eyes, narrowly set, appeared to organize an assault on her nose. "Also," she said, "Baumann knows if you hold the painting for another twenty-one years, the Stiftung Preußischer Kulturbesitz will technically, according to German law, lose their right of return. *Technically.* Of course, there would be appeals."

"*Ja*," said Gutherzig. "We're obligated to inform you that, under German law, the owner loses rights after thirty years. The painting was stolen in 2009. Again, if you were given the painting without knowledge of it being stolen, by 2039 you would acquire ownership. The law works similar to occupiers, yes? In houses they do not own. But we do not advise holding it for twenty-one years. First, you are here. One might argue you already know the painting is stolen. Besides, the laws could change, the painting might get damaged, if not preserved correctly."

"I can't wait twenty-one years. I want to do it now," I said.

"Wise choice," said Frau Schmitt. "We have a partner that provides excellent investment advice. Of course, it's all a process."

"The deadline is December twentieth . . ." I said. "Do we return immediately?"

"The deadline is just for contact," Frau Schmitt said. "Completion and return can happen after."

"You have already retained us, yes," said Gutherzig, "but after you sign the agreement, we can act on your behalf. Full service for a ten percent commission."

"You can take a vacation," Frau Schmitt said.

"And how much will be the reward?" I couldn't look at them when I asked the question.

"Thirty-five million euro," Gutherzig said, "is the number for the group of stolen paintings. The final number for *The Lady Waiting*, it depends on the board. I speculate perhaps ten."

"We have also a branch that provides tax planning strategies," said Schmitt. "Where is your residence?"

"United States."

They produced the same sullen faces they had when I announced Seryozha was Russian.

"Is it not good?" I asked.

"Bad planning for you," said Gutherzig.

"Why?"

"There are tax considerations. US person status. But this is all for later. Maybe you no longer live in the United States. Where is the painting now?"

"It's here."

"In Berlin? Wonderful," said Frau Schmitt.

I lifted the parcel from under my chair. Would they laugh at me once they saw it?

"Ah, *here*! Wonderful. May I unpack it?"

I nodded, and Frau Schmitt cut through my tape with the point of an SVB pen.

"Interesting." Gutherzig said. They lifted the painting and placed it flatly on the table. "It will have to be authenticated. X-rays, chemical paint analysis, radiocarbon dating. Part of the process."

I searched their faces for doubt or derision, but they gazed at the canvas with corporate calm. Like an insecure woman whose only confidence comes from lovers' compliments, the painting seemed to gain value from their mute but apparently affirmative assessment.

"Very good," Frau Schmitt said and left.

"Now, Miss Nowak. Tell me the whole story again." Gutherzig perched on the table's edge, the snow spiraling in the window behind him.

This time, I spoke with more assurance. Like a cuckold accepting an obviously fraudulent account of his wife's night, Gutherzig accepted mine, supplying suggestions, strengthening links, our voices becoming more intimate and hushed the more we spoke, inverting the rickety narrative into one acceptable to all, a bedtime story in which infidelity and falsehood fall asleep. I gave the Sleepers' names. In silence, I signed the documents provided and was given back my passport. I shook Gutherzig's delicate hand and left *The Lady Waiting* in their vault.

Out on the frosty street, my Byzantine mood began to melt. The Sleepers would never confirm my story. I wandered down Unter den Linden. What if I emailed them, promising I'd split the money? But then I'd have to read their emails first. I was in love with Sleeper. I hated Bobby. I loved Bobby. But, as Seryozha had taught us: to everything a price. No woman, she pays five million for love or she calls herself a fool.

Besides, if I managed to pull this off, I told myself, they'd admire my opportunism, the entertainment it would provide. Perhaps, impossibly-possibly, they'd even wanted me to steal the painting. Anything else would be a disappointment, a wrong move in an intricate game of inverted values, where selfishness was generosity. Mine was a sprezzy theft.

Ahead, a Christmas tree glowed over the entrance to an office park. I stared at its stars and ornaments, made of recycled cans, and realized that, though I was unaccustomed to power, at last I had some, maybe even a lot. Of course the Sleepers would confirm my story. They had no choice. If no one's story matched anyone else's, there might be no reward. Given Seryozha's threats, even a chance of recovering part of the money was better than total loss.

They'd have to trust me. Maybe I'd offer them what Bobby had initially offered me.

Maybe I'd wait until they were broke from reimbursing Seryozha, maybe even broken up. I'd call them: "Come live with me in the Riviera." With one call, I had the power to reverse it all. We'd be lovers again, only this time I'd support them. Slowly, Sleeper would gravitate toward me, and Bobby would do things for us. Little things, like making coffee and picking up laundry. We'd be happy. Now and then, for diversion, I'd let her into our bed. I'd tease her, torture her, deny her pleasure, make her come. Sometimes I'd pretend to doze off and let them fuck each other. They were married, after all. All this would happen with tenderness and mischief, a part of a sensual power game. On occasion, on nighttime beach walks, Bobby and I would confess our weaknesses, misdeeds, our ruthlessness and loves. We'd be more intimate than lovers, more understanding than sisters. But we'd always return to our game, because that's what we enjoyed above all. We'd be two parts of the same horrible, confused, majestic person. We'd be happy.

I crossed the street in front of an approaching tram and entered a restaurant. White wine and white fish. Looking for cash in my purse, I found the key to the Sleepers' house in LA. Look at me, I thought. I've become like my father, who got up from dinner one night with nothing more than his keys and a jacket, absconding forever. For the first time I understood him.

22

I couldn't spend another night in the dreariness of the two-star hotel. My bravery needed luxury, and I had enough money saved from wages to live in style for a few weeks. I woke many times in the uneasy dark. In the morning, as I filled a buffet plate with waffles and smoked salmon, Gutherzig called. Nearly neighing with satisfaction, he informed me that the various boards weren't demanding anyone's testimony to confirm my story. They were too eager to retrieve the painting. The transaction could be completed in a month or so without obstacles, once the painting was authenticated by the state lab. SVB would receive the reward and hold it in escrow until their anonymous client was ready for disbursement. Gutherzig recommended delaying my reception of the money, so I'd have time to give up my green card and settle, temporarily, in Belize, Andorra, or the Cayman Islands.

"How much will I get?" I said, my voice trembling.

"The board hasn't decided yet," he said. "It will be a good number."

"How good?"

"Tall seven figures," he said. "Sorry, *high* seven figures."

"I think I want to keep my green card."

"May I ask why? It will cost you in tax, not only on the reward, but in interest, forever."

"Because," I said, "I won it in the lottery."

I'm no longer sure why I chose St. Moritz to wait for the transaction to close in Berlin. Gutherzig wanted me in Europe for the next few weeks, in case they needed signatures, or if the board wanted to "put a face to the hero's name," which thankfully they never did. Maybe because Bobby had promised to take me to St. Moritz. She'd gone to school in a nearby village. I was tired of imagining Kostya on every corner, and he wouldn't know to look for me in Switzerland. I can't remember all my reasons now.

Having grown up in the mountains, I was a decent skier. In a brand-new pearly ski suit, I went down the piste, blurring into meditative speed. I'd checked into the Palace. Women with boots furry as Pekingese spent their winters here or at Courchevel, summers in St. Tropez, at clubs that required letters of introduction from bank presidents to join.

Though my new German account was about to receive seven million two hundred thousand euros—the number at which Gutherzig and the museum board had arrived, after fees, before taxes—my American balance was dwindling, depleted by restaurants, equipment rentals, lift passes, clothes. After two nights in style, I rented a room in a cheap chalet at the other end of town, returning daily for tea or a drink at the Palace. I was trying on being rich, a sort of spiritual discipline. I thought it might help my personality cohere with my predatory actions. How many aristocratic families began with one thug taking another's land by force?

One night, at the hotel bar, I met a party of guests: an asthmatic restaurateur, a bitcoin investor with goggle-shapes of untanned skin on his sepia face, and the daughter of a Scottish politician who was apparently quite well known for being in jail. They assumed I was a fellow guest. I let them believe it.

One day, as we waited for the gondola, she pointed to a family removing their skis by the lodge. "The Wilsons," she whispered. "The famous actor-athlete family."

"Do you think he's cheating on her?"

"The better question is," I said, adapting something Sleeper said, "are the Wilsons talking about *us*?"

"What do you mean?"

"I have a rule," I said, the gondola lifting us over the trees. "Only gossip about people who gossip about you."

The daughter of the guy in jail was impressed. I almost laughed, I was so pleased.

I'd introduced myself as Larissa Hansen-Silva-Baciu, a name as ridiculous as my new pan-European, indeterminate accent, accomplished simply by frenchifying my *r*s. In a bored voice, interjecting an occasional Bobby or Sleeper quote, I spoke of Carnival in Rio, sled dog racing in Kamchatka, eating-disorder clinics in Zürich. Because I'd mentioned vicuña wool and lotus-flower silk, they concluded I was a textile heiress with semi-Eastern origins. When I realized this, I had a photograph of an obscure Prussian baron printed on photographic paper, and, after dunking him in tea and drying him on a radiator, introduced him as my paternal

great-great-grandfather. I dyed my hair red, then blond, got con-
stellation earrings, and told everyone I slept with both women and
men.

In truth, I slept with no one. St. Moritz boasted 322 sunny days
per year. Within my first fourteen, even before the money came, I
came to inhabit my creation. The daughter of the guy in jail, the
restaurateur, or the bitcoin investor paid for most of my meals.
Around dessert, I usually made a pained face and ran for the bathroom, where I went as far as to simulate bouts of bulimia for
anyone present. My nausea, though, was genuine, especially in the
mornings. By the time I returned, they would usually have paid the
bill. I spoke about taxes with authentic, indigestive melancholy. It
turns out it's not so hard to be rich. I was rich, even if seven million
was, in the era of billionaires, relatively paltry wealth, even if I
didn't have it yet.

I skied in the afternoons, ruminating in my helmet—the painting might still turn out to be fake, the mountain collapse on my
back. The emails kept coming, mostly from Bobby, eventually from
Seryozha, too, and even Kostya. Sleeper had apparently given up.
There was one in Cyrillic from I don't know whom. I read the subject headings and first lines but never opened any of the emails. At
last came one from Lance. The heading was: SLUT!

I deactivated my account and opened a new one. Now my only
emails were from Gutherzig. I printed his documents, signed them,
and returned them by mail. A friendly concierge named Roberto
let me use the printer even after I'd left the Palace. I printed the
last batch of paperwork and pocketed his pen.

"Could I please have my pen back, please?" he said to me.

"Sure, though pens and penises are public property and should
be shared," I said, quoting Lance. Roberto didn't laugh. I was em-

barrassed, worried he thought I'd been crassly hitting on him, and I felt like a fraud.

I would often feel fraudulent in those early years of wealth. Yet my documents confirmed my "truthfulness," my identity, my willingness to accept money and, upon its arrival, invest it, with the SVB wealth-managerial team's advice, in corporate bonds and mutual funds. A small portion in venture capital: apples that don't go bad, hearts that don't stop, brains that don't forget. I ended up making a fortune on a memory drug in the late forties. You're probably taking one of its children. Turns out what people want most in life is to remember.

On the day the transfer finally came, I was in my favorite bar at the Palace. A newly arrived group of men from Oman stood by the floor-to-ceiling windows, looking at the mountain in the last sun. At my table, with comparable awe, I was looking at my bank account on my phone. If you've been poor, been told you'll always be, the moment you receive a seven-figure wire, even if you've done nothing to deserve it—and who *deserves* anything, really, anyway?—is a stunning one. It's better than an orgasm or five, better even, perhaps, than love.

Like love, the stunning feeling fades with time. With time, money, if well-managed, grows. I couldn't stay in Switzerland indefinitely on my Polish passport. Afraid to return to America or Poland, I chose Paris because Bobby had promised one day she'd take me. "But not to the Louvre," she had said. "It's full of thousands of people who can't stand other people in the Louvre. We'll eat cheese in the Luxembourg Gardens instead."

I rented a modest flat in the Latin Quarter. My investments had not yet begun to pay out. I veered between ostentatious spending and uneasy thrift. Lovers, in the omnipresent scent of piss that blossoms in Paris with spring, paraded down the banks of the Seine.

Below the blackened walls of Notre Dame, I sat alone in a café, drinking sparkling water, fighting with a waiter who wanted to move me from a four-person table to a two-person table with no view of the terrible damage, though the café was empty.

"Do you always fight the pregnant?" I said to him. I refused to learn French. I still had enough trouble with English. "Do not you know the pregnant are dangerous people?"

He gawked at the folds of my loose linen dress. My belly was still very modestly sized, despite me being in the second trimester. I barely believed it myself.

"So sorry, *madame!*"

Ever since I'd received the reward, I'd been winning petty spats like this—with waiters, drivers, flight attendants. Had I already acquired the entitlement so prevalent among the females of my acquired class? Was it just my pregnant brain? Or are the rich and the pregnant equally annoying to everyone else?

I remember getting up from the table, tossing a banknote onto it scornfully—a useless gesture, as the waiter wasn't there to notice—and waddling out and down along the river. People practiced salsa in an amphitheater set into the esplanade. Tired from my short walk, I sat on one of the stone shelves surrounding the dancers and checked my phone. Emails from my lawyers, my wealth managers, one from my American accountant, one from my mother's nursing home. (The neurotech that was to make me genuinely rich did not arrive in time to save my mother.) In my new life, I had no friends, only providers of services. I knew better than to get an assistant.

Between an email advertising traditional Italian footwear and a newspaper listserv email boasting the discovery of exoplanets, I saw two search alerts. Before leaving Berlin, I'd set up alerts for the names "Roberta Sleeper," "Sebastian Sleeper," and even "Lance Millwood," but all they ever sent were a few links to bootleg sites where Sleeper's old films were listed. There had been no results for months. I'd forgotten about the alerts.

But these two were both links to the Interpol website. One hears about Interpol. One doesn't quite imagine they have a website. They do, and on it was a photo of Bobby, its corner labeled YELLOW NOTICE. I stared at it without comprehension. The other link showed Sleeper, with the same label. They had been classified as missing persons, last seen in Russia, in Tolyatti, on January 15, 2019. For her photo, Interpol had used a detail of her face from a full-body red-carpet shot that had stood on the mantelpiece in her house, taken at the premiere of Sleeper's *Master of the Large Foreheads at the Edge of Time*: silk gown, silk eyes, looking exceptionally fatale, exceptionally present and cosmopolitan. Not like someone who'd one day go missing in the backwaters of Russia. The photo of Sleeper I'd never seen before. In a suede jacket, in front of a rocky landscape, he gazes at the camera, self-possessed, a little absent, a little sad. Where was this photo taken? On his way to some mountaintop? The father of my child, he looks the same in the announcement of his disappearance as the day we met.

People always say, when asked to describe their reaction to horrible news, that they have "no words." I'd say the cliché doesn't go deep enough—it's not words but *thoughts* that go missing, just like the Sleepers. I experienced a complete absence of mental activity, more cavernous than sleep. Unless it was like the dreamless part of sleep, the part we are not built to remember.

When I finally registered the environment around me, the sun was low. Sunset cruises had begun their saturnalian parade down the Seine. One skilled couple in dirty sneakers and ripped jean shorts had taken center stage on the dance floor, others having joined the crowd of watchers in modest defeat. Passersby stopped, clapped, then walked on. People held phones, held hands, kissed, drank beer and wine. These simple social behaviors suddenly seemed callous, incredible, ill-intentioned. I couldn't get up, couldn't go home. "*Ça va?*" someone asked me. I nodded, head in my hands, and looked at the stranger through my fingers.

Finally the salsa stopped, the dancers and walkers dispersed, and I got up and stood alone by the river. Catholic prayers had gone the way of childhood toys. What had happened to my stuffed animals? I went back to my flat. It was night. I was more awake than ever. I scoured the internet and found only two short articles: LA DIRECTOR AND WIFE MISSING and MYSTERIOUS DISAPPEARANCE OF DIRECTOR AND GALLERIST. The articles briefly described how the Sleepers had lived in LA and had, an anonymous witness reported, last been seen in Russia at the Tolyatti Museum of Local Lore, looking at old maps of the Russian Empire.

What were they doing? Where was Tolyatti? It was a city by the Volga. Images of a cathedral with golden, gleaming domes. Post-Soviet buildings. A strange park full of decommissioned tanks and fighter jets at rest on supernaturally green lawns. The detail of them looking at old maps rang true, I thought. Sleeper had always loved maps, especially old, flawed ones. In their house, there had been a poster for one of his films, *Forget What Country*, composed of impossible maps: the Pacific Ocean enveloping Africa, the West Indies in the Baltic, Brazil abutting Bulgaria. Who had seen them in the museum? Who was this anonymous witness who had reported that specific detail to the newspapers?

I began to read whatever there was on the two of them, old posts from before I'd met them, announcements about Bobby's gallery. It had been called Bby. Abstract paintings and sculptures made of plumbing supplies. A photo of Bobby in an embroidered caftan, hands folded on her chest, proprietary, regal. Old film festival photos of Sleeper holding microphones. Photos from sets. I recognized some of his film posters from their house: the one for *Imber*, with an image of women, hands linked, standing in rain that looked like falling necklaces of amber. The poster for *Master of the Large Foreheads at the Edge of Time* was a detail from *The Way to Calvary*, a 1510 painting by the unknown painter known as the Master of the Large Foreheads. *The Indistinct Dead*: an old man at a wooden table, his face melting into a cup in his lap; beneath it, in red letters, WRITTEN AND DIRECTED BY SEBASTIAN SLEEPER. It was that little line, that acknowledgment of his work and possible posterity—in which he'd never believed—that finally made me cry and then made me stop crying because my tears, in this context, indicated he was dead. He was not dead. You're not dead unless others say so.

He could, of course, be worse than dead: imprisoned, scared, hurt. If so, it would be my fault. Seryozha must've kidnapped them. Barefoot, I stood in my kitchen, staring at floor tiles, thinking this happened so I could have all that I have—these tiles, these ugly tiles that aren't even mine. I fitted a foot into a tile, my other foot into another. Define *fault*. Untangle the chain of cause and effect. The whole plan, from the start, was Bobby's idea. And how could I know that she hadn't done something else to piss off Seryozha or who knows who else? As Sleeper liked to say, life's a violation of safety standards.

Would I be contacted by Interpol? By American, German, or Russian police? Found to be an art thief? An accomplice to kidnapping? Sent to prison? Before meeting Bobby, I'd never thought about going to prison. In Los Angeles, Venice, Poland, Berlin, I thought about it often. In Switzerland and France, I stopped. That fear came back now, a hot fear in my stomach, and it struck me that my pregnancy was starkly real, as real as Interpol.

Finally, around one a.m., my anxiety got so intense I began to worry it would harm the baby. I decided to contact the one person who could perhaps provide answers. I wrote him an email, which bounced immediately. I tried, in vain, to find him on social media. Had he gone missing, too? Was he in hiding? Finally, I looked him up in the Canadian yellow pages. There was a Millwood Pet Spa in Sackville, Nova Scotia, also a Millwood Elementary in Halifax. Ellen Millwood lived on Dorothea Drive, and Jim and Nancy Millwood lived on Lavender Walk.

I wrote the last two numbers down, put on a coat, and went down to the phone booths by the Métro station. I didn't want to call from my French mobile phone, in case Lance should try to give my number to, I don't know, the Canadian police. I was too scared to make a new Skype account and use that, even on public wi-fi. Who knew how one could be tracked? I was determined not to talk to any authorities. I had nothing to share about the Sleepers that Lance couldn't have told them anyway. But I needed to know if he had, and if so, what.

Ellen Millwood didn't pick up. The phone rang and rang. At Jim and Nancy's, an older female voice said, "Millwood residence."

I hung up. Feeling stupid, I redialed. "Hello." I hoped they were the wrong Millwoods and no Lances lived there. "I—I'd like to speak to Lance."

"May I ask who's calling?"

"Lariss— Viva."

"Just one moment."

Someone had scratched *merde* with a needle or knife into the phone console.

"Hello," said Lance and cleared his throat.

"Hi," I said.

"Who is this?"

"It's Viva," I said.

"Oh," he said.

There was silence, and I felt like vomiting, nothing dramatic: one often feels like this when pregnant.

"Awkward," he said. "Thirty-three. France, huh? Let me guess. Paris?"

Why was he asking me this? Was Interpol listening in on the call?

"What made you think to go there?" His voice rang with its usual mockery, and I was relieved. You're not a criminal, I told myself. You don't need to feel like one.

"I didn't have no place to go," I said.

"I see your English hasn't much improved."

"What happened to Sleeper and Bobby?"

"What happened to Sleeper and Bobby?" he echoed, and again, I couldn't tell if he was mocking me or asking me in earnest. Maybe both.

"You have talked with Interpol?"

"Interpol," he said. "I did have the pleasure of talking to them. Did you?"

"Me, no."

"Intriguing. Well, they'd like to talk to you. They knew, I assume from Venetian hotel staff, that you all had been rogering. They asked all about you, which caused me to realize how little real information I had. They weren't happy with me at all, but hey, don't ask, don't tell, as I always say in military situations."

"Why are they asking for me? I wasn't in Russia."

"No, I guess you weren't."

"It's just about them missing? Nothing else?"

"Nothing else?" he mocked.

I wanted to tell him I never intended Bobby and Sleeper any harm, but he'd have only found that bitterly amusing.

"What happened to Bobby and Sleeper?" I asked.

"Tell me one thing. In your rural Polish childhood or whatever, when frolicking in pigpens and barns, were you ever hit on the forehead, right above the nose? In the ventromedial prefrontal cortex? Damage to that area can cause psychopathy."

"I was not hit."

His tone lost its satirical sting and became very flat. "What do you want?"

"I already said. What happened to them?"

"Nobody knows what happened to them. I thought *you* might know what happened to them."

"It was Seryozha?"

"I don't know. Yes? One can only guess."

"Do you think maybe"—as soon as I said it, I felt ridiculous—"they were, what do you say . . . agents of secrets? Maybe for Russia?"

Perhaps I even said it to amuse him, to dilute his evident disdain.

As I expected, he laughed. "Maybe I'll come up with a ground-breaking mathematical theorem or discover a new element to-morrow, between lunch and snack. Maybe one day your English will be fluent. Everything is, in theory, possible, right?"

"When you spoke to the Interpol, did you tell of the painting?"

It sounded like he was shuffling papers, stuffing envelopes.

"I'm only telling you this because I don't want you making more trouble for me personally," he finally said, in a tone both mean and muffled, maybe covering his mouth with his hand. "Soon after your treason, Bobby called and begged me never to tell the police or anyone about her having trafficked the painting. She seemed . . . uncharacteristically concerned about the law. I gave her my word I'd be as quiet as a pubic louse. She said she was work-ing out a deal with Seryozha after all. A few months later, they went missing. Draw your own conclusions. I prefer to imagine them in witness protection in Palm Springs than dismembered in Siberia, but I want nothing more to do with this affair. I'm not fond of Seryozha, or the roly-Interpoly chaps, and inaction remains my creed. But if it turns out the Sleepers are dead, even if it's twenty years from now, I'll call the Gemäldegalerie, the Berlin Polizei, *and* Interpol and tell them all, 'Guess what, the woman who anonymously returned *The Lady Waiting* stole it in Los An-geles in 2018 on commission for the Russian mob.' You little dis-posable fucktoy."

On the Parisian street, while Lance soliloquized, a group of drunk men shambled by. One of them smacked the window of my booth and grinned at me, and somehow this playful but menacing action blended with Lance's words, the face in the window be-coming a face from a bad dream, mouthing "disposable fucktoy" out of sync.

I felt disposable, indeed, and sick. I thought maybe my baby was dying. I thought this often but never reached into my panties to check for blood. I reached into my panties. No blood. I began to cry.

"God, are you crying?" Lance asked. "Are you in trouble, stupid?"

A little sympathy at last. "Yes," I said. "Much trouble. I'm pre—"

"Good," he cut me off. "I want you in trouble. I want you to cry."

"You don't understand what happened," I sobbed. "I didn't want to take!"

More envelopes scrunched in my ear, and I couldn't make out Lance's words. "—after Łyski escaped to LA but then was kidnapped at the New Year's party—" he was saying.

"Łyski was kidnapped?!"

"Yes." Then Lance hung up.

There were very few phone booths left in the world, maybe only one with a crying pregnant woman in it. It wasn't until the next day that I suddenly remembered Baggywrinkle. Had the Sleepers made it to Los Angeles to pick him up before they disappeared? Even if they had, what happened to him after? Other than Lance, they didn't really have close friends. I called the dog hotel. A dog named Baggywrinkle, property of Roberta Sleeper, had indeed been left behind and, per policy, after several failed attempts to contact the owners, given away to a local dog shelter. Was I going to cover the bill for the weeks he'd overstayed? I called the dog shelter. They couldn't locate him. After five days, someone called me back. They were really sorry, but a dachshund named Baggywrinkle had been put down several weeks ago.

23

You can "get over" almost anything. It just happens, chemically, in your skull. You don't have to do any work. You have to wait or have a kid. Experience has taught me people are this way, unless, as Lance implied so many years ago now, I'm a psychopath. I don't believe I am. I love babies and small animals. For the longest time I couldn't think about Baggywrinkle without crying. But who can say? The brain does what it can to defend itself, and psychological borders are much thicker than their political cousins.

Łyski was as "guilty" as I was. He'd robbed Bobby, too. Yet, of us all, he seemed the most naïve. I entered his name on the Interpol website. There was his photo, too. He gazes at us, at the future, perhaps a bit too hungrily, like a prophet who could really go for some kielbasa.

He'd gone missing before the Sleepers, in December, last seen in Venice Beach. Still, I imagined them all together, stranded in the endless East, beyond Tolyatti, Łyski in a stained shirt, playing guitar to the tired couple. They didn't have me to entertain them.

I moved to Manhattan, legally changed my name to Larissa Baciu, and my baby boy was born. My guilt about Łyski and Baggywrinkle faded swiftly. There's something frightening about new mothers. If you've ever held your baby in your arms, you know there exists, from time to time, a state of complete maternal absorption, and in this state, what horrors have happened to others before, or are happening now, are so far away.

But I didn't get over the Sleepers. In my new hormonal state of caring only for my son, they loomed even larger. It was as if Bobby and Sleeper had fathered him together. Terrified of Interpol and Seryozha, I was nonetheless obsessed with finding out what had happened to them. If Lance's witness protection theory was correct, I supposed I never would. There was no information about Bobby's parents online. I remembered Bobby, the last time I saw her, wanting to tell me something to tell her father in case she died of "bubonic plague." She never finished her sentence. Did she even have parents, in Gliwice or elsewhere? I opened an email account with a fake name and contacted the journalists who'd written about the Sleepers' disappearance, but they knew nothing beyond what they'd written.

My plan was to look for them after my son was old enough to fly to Tolyatti, but soon after he was born, the pandemic of 2020 struck. New York was all locked doors and fear and sirens. Millions died. And then came the Russo-Ukrainian War, and the West cut its ties with Russia. I could no longer safely go there, not on my Polish passport, and my son is American.

Slowly, I began to accept that the Sleepers were permanently missing, in some interstitial space between absence and death. I thought of this space as *beyond Tolyatti*. Perhaps it was merely beyond money. Maybe they were bankrupt. Money is a fiction, but one we're all forced to believe in. Perhaps the Sleepers were a similar kind of fiction, except they'd lost all their believers.

Beyond guilt is not beyond fear. I realized, at last, that nobody was coming after me, but I worried about Lance, the one link to my past. I'd scour the internet for his name. Nothing new, until, in 2024, my old search alert produced an article announcing the premiere of Lance Millwood's debut play, at an off-Broadway black box fifteen blocks from where I lived with my son. The play was called *Agents of Secrets*. I knew I shouldn't go and that I absolutely would.

There were only five nights in the run. I figured Lance would attend the premiere. I bought a ticket for the second night.

Before leaving for the play, I hugged my son as if I were off to my own execution. He was on the floor, taking my sunglasses carefully out of their cases and putting them on his stuffed rabbits. I inhaled the pure smell of his neck. As if he could sense my anxiety, he asked me to wait, went to the kitchen, and came back with a bar of chocolate.

"I'm going to share my chocolate with you," he said with Sleeperish melancholy, holding the bar out to me in his little hand, "because yesterday it broke, and now I know it's possible to share chocolate. Before, I didn't know."

Half the chocolate in a napkin in my coat, I took a taxi to Midtown. I didn't bother to alter my appearance. Beyond the alterations caused by the last few years and my pregnancy, I looked almost the same. No one would have trouble recognizing me. Perhaps I wanted to be recognized. Part of me wanted to tell Lance I was no longer afraid of him. If he decided to tattle on me, he'd still be implicated in the Sleepers' scheme—not to mention for having kept his knowledge of me, the connection between their disappearance and the painting, secret all these years.

November New York in a taxi window, blurs of pouring water and reflected light, wet-haired people in colorless clothes, huddled under awnings. My arms and legs began to tingle, not from fear but from excitement. I had to remind myself I wasn't here to see the real Sleepers as I stepped into the small crowd in front of a door between a gym and a smoothie bar. I went directly in, downstairs to a room with concrete stanchions and a stage, four rows of chairs on each side. I picked a seat in the last row, beside a fire extinguisher, and kept my eyes on the entrance.

A sparse audience filled the seats in front, making me unexpectedly conspicuous. An usher in fuzzy boots closed the door. The stage lights went on and, amid a few scattered coughs, *Agents of Secrets* began.

Three body bags lay center stage. A man in thick glasses and a knockoff suit, one of Lance's multiple doppelgängers in this play, began a drunken narration: "'American Mermaid Beached on Russian Shore Near Sochi.' Well, the tabloids were wrong, but not about the dismembering. She wasn't American! We all love a good dismembering, it helps with remembering . . ." The narrator humped the air. Long, swaying, idiotic thrusts. "The tabloids and socials all said it was either the ex or the husband who sawed off her arms and legs. And then the boys stabbed each other and bled to death. Well, this is the story of what *actually* led to them all getting killed."

The narrator stumbled and collapsed. A bunch of actors in drab gray stockings ran onstage and pulled the body bags and the narrator offstage. Someone in the audience giggled. Did Lance know something I didn't? If the Sleepers had actually died, and in such a horrific way, surely I'd have learned by now. Also Lance would have probably told the police about me. I toyed with the idea that this was Lance's way to toy with me, but he couldn't have known I'd be in the audience. I doubted he even knew I lived in America, much less New York.

The actress who played Bobby—or Trudi, as her character was ludicrously named—was too polished. She looked and sounded like an influencer. That old-world edge, that shimmering, mysterious discombobulation that linked Bobby to long-dead divas, old Hollywood heroines, flappers—all this was missing. Her assistant, Vera, was too pretty, too tall, too poorly spoken, too Polish, though the actress's accent was worse than Meryl Streep's in *Sophie's Choice*. Lance also gave some of Bobby's more egregious misbehaviors to Vera.

For example, it's Vera who talks Trudi into stealing a painting—an obscure, unnamed Renaissance masterpiece—from a small American museum. Vera's toothless brother then sells the painting to a Russian gangster named Bitchslapov. Vera, Trudi, and Trudi's even more absurdly named husband, Napper, romp around Europe with a bag full of cash. Vera manipulates the couple and seduces them, first separately, then together, in a series of embarrassing scenes that veer between cloying and gynecological. I felt bad for the actors, fully nude except for genital prostheses that looked like they were falling off.

Trudi is stereotypically crazy. When, in Naples, a waiter refuses to let her use a bathroom, she lifts her skirt and releases a truly equine stream of urine onto the floor, which gets mopped up morosely by Harry, an underdeveloped Łyski.

Napper is played by a pretty-boy actor without charisma. His character is vague, a ghost of a person, a man dragged by his nose by his idiotic wife and yokel mistress. His occasional witticisms, lifted from real-life Sleeper ("To lose one parent is a tragedy. To lose both is to get rich" or "Unlike everyone else, I like my beer Italian and my painting English"), make Napper appear at once overly mannered and unwittingly brutal.

Of course, it's the couple's best friend, Lancelot, who saves them repeatedly from Konstantin, another Russian, Trudi's evil ex-husband. I did like the performance of the guy who played Konstantin.

Trudi, a technological whiz, unbeknownst to other characters, installs hidden cameras in homes and hotel rooms, recording all manner of sexual activity and incidental blather. These recordings play on mute on screens above the stage, distracting the audience.

The body bags from act one reappear throughout the play, and the characters, unaware of their destinies, trip over their cadavers and use them as furniture. In act three, Konstantin invites Trudi, Napper, and Harry on a yacht jaunt on the Black Sea. After a rebuffed reach under Trudi's skirt in the yacht's cockpit, Konstantin dons a fencing mask and stabs everyone to death with a pen.

The play is awful. It makes no sense. At the end, I found myself wishing for a fourth body bag for Lancelot.

"This demented love child of Chekhov, Buñuel, and Tarantino should never have been born," said one of the reviews. "The characters are insufferable rich idiots, drowning in self-absorption, greed, and privilege . . ." "The assistant, a meager reincarnation of *Vanity Fair*'s Becky Sharp, is everything but sharp . . ."

I decided to walk home and muddled up Madison Avenue in an unsettled mood. I wasn't frightened; the play was not incriminating. Lance had often joked about taking revenge by making the Sleepers middle-class and boring. He had not, but he'd betrayed their memory nonetheless.

Arriving at my townhouse, I reached into my pocket and found a very cold piece of chocolate.

Agents of Secrets had a sobering effect. It cured me, for a while, of missing the Sleepers. What it didn't cure was my curiosity. Quite the opposite: though its title was the play's only direct reference to espionage, it awoke my old conspiracy theory that the Sleepers had been sleeper agents. The idea was so ludicrous it almost seemed plausible. Who would suspect a couple named Butcher of a spate of grisly murders? Could Sleeper have worked for a government? Maybe. But Bobby? She once said her father had been suspected by the communists of spying for the West. But what an awful secret agent she'd have made. What government would have wanted *me* to end up with millions of euros?

Unless . . . Was it her job to get me to return the painting? But the details didn't add up. She couldn't have known I'd switched the serums, couldn't have timed everything so that I'd have met Dorota on my own, couldn't have known that Dorota would lie to her nephew and sell me the painting. Unless, of course, she'd had cameras installed in each room, as in Lance's play. That way she would have seen me switch the serums, at least.

During quiet evenings that winter, as snowflakes spun and fell in the window, I found myself chanting "*Śpij, śpij*" to my son. In Polish it means *sleep, sleep.*

"*Spy,*" I sang to Sleeper's sleeping son, "*spy . . .*"

It all seemed so far-fetched but not impossible. Not that Bobby was technologically skilled—she could barely format a document—but I could see her having a fancy security system installed in the house. A belated embarrassment spread in me at the thought of having been spied on during my most intimate moments—or, worse, when I thought I'd been the one doing the spying.

Also, in *Agents of Secrets,* Trudi is not Polish but Russian. Was it possible that Bobby had been Russian, too? Was that why she never wanted to speak Polish? She did speak it, of course—very well, in fact, perhaps a bit too well, too properly, with her pan-European, Maria Callas accent. Could it be she'd gone to school in Poland?

"*Spy,*" I sang and watched him sleep and watched the snow. I still didn't see why the Sleepers would have put on such a charade for me, unless their whole life was a charade from which they were to be awakened for some specific political purpose. Perhaps the Sleepers were the exact opposite of what they'd seemed, their blitheness a cover for secret discipline, their apolitical jadedness for political involvement, their *sprezzatura* for extremism. Did Lance know all this? Was that why he hadn't reported me? Then again, if Bobby had been Russian and *not* a spy, wouldn't she have told me? I'd met her years before traveling-while-Russian became such a liability. And if Bobby hadn't been Russian, why would Lance have bothered to change her nationality?

I closed my son's door silently and wandered down my dark wood-paneled hall. The realtor had told me that this flat had briefly belonged to Henry Kissinger. Maybe the walls had infected my brain. The war had turned Westerners anti-Russian. Probably

Lance had just wanted a bit more of his favorite gelato flavor: *scandalo.*

Baroque, ridiculous, my espionage theory made sense only at night. Still, when it did, it sent phantom ants down my spine. Why couldn't the Sleepers be sleeper agents?

One memory in particular haunted me. During my first week in their house, as I was passing by the Sleepers' bedroom, carrying a basket of Bobby's bangles and bracelets to detangle, I heard Bobby behind the door, speaking to someone in what at first I thought was Polish. I was so curious about her then that I drank the old whiskey in a glass on the console table by their door, pressed the glass to the door and my ear to the glass.

She was speaking not Polish but a different, less rustling Slavic language. It was Russian, I realized, and she spoke it in full, elaborate sentences, even though later in Venice, on the phone and in person, with Seryozha, she appeared to barely speak it at all. Then a man's voice responded in a terser way, less expertly maybe, but still, he was speaking it, maybe on speakerphone, maybe in the room. I understood only two words—*ochi chernye—dark eyes—* because these words were close to their Polish counterparts and I'd heard them in an old Russian song as a kid.

At the time, having no knowledge of Seryozha, I thought nothing of it—she spoke French and Italian, too—and soon forgot it. But the *ochi chernye* came back in Kissinger's flat and refused to leave me alone.

Bobby's eyes were blue. Could the man have been Sleeper? In my resurrected memory, he sounded like Sleeper. I'd heard Sleeper yell in Russian, once, in Venice, but he didn't speak Russian. Did he? Desperately, I wanted their story to be neater, more sensational. I needed something to eclipse the too-intense events I'd brought

about. I wanted an improved beginning, middle, end, clear moti-
vations, explanations of each action, but the story wriggled like
Baggywrinkle whenever he was picked up by anyone other than
Bobby.

And I woke up the next day, over and over, as most people do. I
sang my son to sleep, out of childhood. I was close to accepting
unknowability, incompleteness, when, in 2029, I saw Sleeper. This
time it wasn't an actor playing him onstage but him as an actor,
playing nobody, on-screen.

24

The island in the window was not the green of American money or lawns or eyeshadows or green chiffon or the Polish forest. It was a supersaturated, shocking green I hadn't seen before. As the plane began to descend, pink, yellow, and blue roofs cascaded by briefly, like luggage that had fallen from the sky and landed at random angles in the jungle. Then we were back in the green. We landed. The airport was pink and yellow and blue.

"Dominica's total area is two hundred ninety square meters," my son recited as we left the plane. "Its languages are English and Dominican Creole French." He was ten and finding his place in the world through data. He memorized lists. Minerals, elements, capitals, stars. Muscovite, feldspar, fluorspar. Sirius, Procyon, Wolf 1061. Moscow, Freetown, Roseau.

"Population of Dominica is eighty-one thousand," he continued at the baggage claim.

Small compared to the United States or Poland. Large if what you want is to locate two people, or one.

"Watch for the bags." I pointed at the conveyor belt.

Some thirty passengers waited. Locals, ambiguous vacationers, digital nomads.

"Dominica's constitution, 1844," he said. Not "Yes, Mom, I'll do that." He excelled already at mild dismissals of his mother.

When we stepped out of the tiny airport, waiting in the sun, I began to feel ridiculous, like a person pretending to practice an extinct religion. I looked at my son. All he knew was that it was spring break and his mother was meeting a friend.

Halalati Alexander emerged from behind a group of taxi drivers. We had only ever spoken on the phone, so we approached each other with hesitation, pointing to each other awkwardly and laughing.

"Thank you for picking me up. You didn't have to, really," I said. "I appreciate your doing this."

"That's no problem anyway. I like people from outside, from elsewhere. It makes my life less boring."

"Well, I hate to trouble you."

She shrugged. "It was on my way."

"That's my son, Sebastian," I said, and he shook her hand with adult seriousness. He had become as serious about meeting people as he was about his lists. Was he writing their names down somewhere?

We walked to a small parking lot and located her car. The humid island air had a presence. I felt it on my skin, on the nape of my neck, like a hand, or less than a hand—like brushing against a stranger's sleeve.

Halalati was a fearless driver. We climbed a potholed road with dense vegetation to either side. Cars and buses rushed at us from

behind blind curves. She had a way of tucking the car against the
road's shoulder. Felled trees and houses with ripped roofs flashed
by. Sebastian took in everything with interest. Soon, I thought, he
was going to start asking questions. He was always a little shy with
strangers.

"Hurricane Lisa," Halalati said, nodding at the damage. "Been
a year, but . . ." She waved her hand.

"Were you . . . was your house affected by the hurricane?" I
said.

"I'm lucky. My sister's house, no, all gone, nothing."

"I'm so sorry."

"You get used to it." She grabbed her braid and tossed it behind
her. "I was going to bring the files to your hotel room, but there
were too many. Some were also damaged in the hurricane."

"I don't have much hope of finding my friend," I said. When I
said "my friend," it sounded fake. I wanted to tell her I was looking for an old lover, but that kind of showiness embarrassed me. I
didn't understand why this stranger was helping me.

"You shouldn't have much," she said, swinging to the right as a
van appeared from behind a curve and drove us onto the shoulder.
A large frond swept our windshield like a scrubber at a car wash,
briefly blocking our view. We were back on the road. I looked over
my shoulder at Sebastian. Face pressed to the window, he appeared
unfazed, eyes on the jungle.

Halalati's fatalism pleased me. She had a smooth, high forehead.
She must have been a few years younger than I was. I'd been introduced to her by the Japanese producers of the film with maybe-
Sleeper in it. The film was a Japanese–Kazakh coproduction. My
emails had sounded batty: I just watched your film, *The Great Dala*.

There's a café scene, set in a jungle-like environment, and one of the extras sitting in the background, a white man in a linen shirt, reminds me of a person I know, Sebastian Sleeper. He was reported missing years ago. I realize this sounds strange, but it's important, for me and his family, that you help me find this person. I enclose a screenshot of the man in the scene. Please, if there's anything you can tell me, his address or email . . .

The Kazakhs ignored me. But the Japanese put me in touch with Halalati, the location coordinator for the part of the film shot in Dominica, which included my café scene. Halalati had also assisted with local casting. They had shot in Dominica for only a week.

We agreed to meet later at her office. Halalati dropped us at our hotel, which consisted of bungalows on stilts, the bungalows connected by little rope bridges that swayed over the jungle. Mosquito nets cocooned both beds, and Sebastian ran in and out of them, boxing at the gauze. I stood in the window, fighting the urge to play the clip of the café scene on my phone for the hundredth time. I'd seen *The Great Dala* as a part of an Asian cinema showcase at Lincoln Center a few months ago, and later had had Sebastian pirate it and email me the clip. Sleeper hadn't changed. His hair a little thinned. He was leaning over a cup of espresso. It was he. It wasn't.

"Strange thing is, I watched the scene a couple times, even showed it to my friends at the commission, who worked on the film. No one remembers this guy," Halalati said.

We were in a ground-floor office with filing cabinets, two desks, piles of film equipment, chairs, and a life-size cardboard cutout of a woman in a coconut shell bra, which Sebastian frowned at disapprovingly and then ignored.

"But the shoot was two years back," she said. "We had two hundred local extras. Lots goes on in two years. Maybe Lisa has erased our memory."

"Are all hurricanes named Lisa here?" Sebastian said.

"No. For example, in 2017 there was Maria," Halalati said. "Maria destroyed almost every place on the island."

A man in a Brazilian flag shirt came out of a back room and welcomed us.

"Please meet John. He also worked on *The Great Dala*."

"Nice to meet you," I said, shaking his hand. "Thank you both for helping me."

John nodded, then went out again. He came back with two boxes and began to heap contracts onto the desk. "Glad I didn't use these for barbecue starter," he said.

"How do we do this? What're we looking for?" Halalati asked. "We're looking for this name, Sebastian Sleeper? Because I looked before, when you emailed me, and didn't find no—"

"I'm Sebastian," said Sebastian from the back of the room, where he'd been tracing the beaked shadows of palm fronds on the floor with his foot.

I watched Halalati regarding my son and found myself fearing and hoping her eyes would betray recognition of my situation. Her eyes remained neutral.

"He might have changed his name. That's why I'm here, because I'd like to, ideally, call all of the extras," I said, feeling guilty and bothersome. "I can take these files to my hotel and return them tomorrow or the day after."

I worried Halalati would protest, or even laugh, but she nodded. "We can divide them and each of us call."

"The only thing is, I'd like to talk to them myself in case . . . in case I recognize his voice," I said, my face growing hot.

"Okay, let us show you people who *aren't* the white guy in the café scene," Halalati said.

"Most of them we know," John said. "Most of them are not Sebastian."

"I'm Sebastian!" Sebastian came and grabbed a few contracts and marched to the other end of the room.

"Come back and give those back right now," I said, looking at Halalati and John apologetically.

They didn't look judgmental. They observed us with practiced Caribbean sprezz.

"I am Sebastian!" said Sebastian, his voice rising.

"I'm giving you first warning." I extended my hand. "Those are important documents, and they don't belong to us."

He held the papers in both hands, as if he were about to rip them in half, and ducked away behind a pile of film and hiking gear. "I want to see the jungle," he said. He was acting seven, not ten. He knew something was up.

"We'll go and see the jungle later. First I need to do my work," I said, rising from my chair, walking over to him. "This is second warning."

His disheveled hair poked out above the pile of gear. He looked tiny and lost. Finally he emerged, ignoring my extended hand as he passed me, and gave the papers to Halalati.

"I'm sorry—he's tired," I murmured, returning to the desks.

Clouds of watered ink on the contracts had rendered some of the writing barely legible.

"These are for sure not Sebastian," said John, who'd sorted the contracts into two stacks. "This other stack is people I don't know."

"Let me see." Halalati took the unknowns. "You know Lucien Joseph. He went out with Selma when we were in high school."

"I don't know any Lucien."

"Yes, you do," Halalati said. "You drank with him at graduation."

"I don't remember drinking with no Lucien at graduation."

"That's proof you drank with him. He's quiet, half-Kalinago, half-Trinidadian. He runs that little crab cart by the Rainbow Bar in Calibishie."

"I never go up there."

As they debated a few more people in this manner, Sebastian settled on the floor in the middle of the room with his reading tablet. His sulk dissolved as he became absorbed.

"I feel bad involving you in this goose chase," I said, and Halalati waved a hand at me like one shoos a fly.

At last, only a few contracts remained. Halalati dialed the numbers and let me speak to each of them. Two were French guys, long gone from the island. Some couldn't be reached, or their voices in their voicemails made it clear they weren't Sleeper.

"That was not Sebastian," I said after the fifth dead end.

The room was filling up with the electric green light of the rainforest dusk. Wind knocked a bamboo screen against the door. I'd forgotten any guilt I might have felt about abusing the hospitality of these strangers. We were deep in some surrealist game, scouring the population of Dominica, deeming everyone "not Sebastian." It felt strange to refer to Sleeper by his first name, each "Sebastian" darkening the distance between me and my son's lost father. With each Sebastian, my son lifted his head slightly. He, too, felt a game was being played, perhaps at his expense. He might even have thought we were teasing him, but he'd lost interest in the cruelty or stupidity of adults. Finally, head on his tablet, he fell asleep.

"I have an idea," John said, stretching his arms and leaning back in his chair. "Let's put the scene up on the big screen and see who sits next to this guy. Maybe we can find that person, see if they remember something."

Halalati got up, cleared some clutter from against a wall, revealing a projection screen. John switched on the projector, and we all turned our chairs. The already shadowy room filled with more shadows, as the film's hero, Alikhan, galloped across the Kazakh steppe.

"It's a bit further," I said. "At two hours twenty-three."

"I never got why Alikhan goes to Dominica in this movie," Halalati said.

"He doesn't," John said. "Parts shot here are dreams."

"No, they are not," said Halalati.

"Yes, they are," said John.

"Well, I've never in my life dreamed about no café," Halalati said.

The scene began. Palms bent in slow motion. Alikhan sat in a chair, eyes closed, asleep in his own dream, and the camera passed by other tables, catching faces in profile, faces with eyes closed, and Sleeper, near the end of the shot, looking down at his cup. As the camera passes him, he lightly taps the spoon against the cup's edge. Each time I'd watched this, I'd received it as a silvery signal, specifically for me. Never had I felt this as intensely as when I watched the scene with John and Halalati. Oddly, at the same time, being in the presence of strangers who'd been part of making this film made me doubt my certainty. Half the people I know tap their spoons. It was a wide shot, and it had been eleven years since I'd seen my son's father.

"*The Great Dala* again," came my son's sleepy voice from the floor. The shadow of his shaggy head popped onto the screen. "I hate this movie. It's *so* boring."

"I'm sorry," I said. "He's tired. I'm going to have to bring him back to the hotel soon."

"He's right. *The Great Dala* is boring." Halalati yawned.

John said, "We worked on it, and never watched it all."

We all laughed, but I kind of liked *The Great Dala*.

"So can we go talk to the guy who was next to him?" I asked.

"No," said John.

"Why not?"

"That guy was from outside, from elsewhere," Halalati said.

"I'll show this scene to my father-in-law. He's a retired policeman. He knows everyone on the island," John said.

"You should also ask him if he knows a woman named Bobby," I said. "Bobby or Roberta Sleeper. A tall, blonde, beautiful woman . . . She was . . . she's Sebastian's wife."

I thought Halalati looked at me strangely, but maybe it was just the reflection in her eyes of Alikhan turning coals in a firepit.

In our bungalow, Sebastian got a second wind, not unusual after a nap.

"Mom, look." He squatted in front of my laptop, perusing the National Hurricane Center website. "They have lists of hurricane names they came up with in 1953, and they rotate and recycle the lists every six years," he said, "and there's a list of Atlantic hurri-

canes." Then he recited, "In 2033, there will be Ana, Bill, Clau-
dette, Danny, Elsa . . ." I got him into bed. "In 2034, Alex, Bonnie,
Colin, Danielle, Fiona, Earl . . ."

The wind beyond the window was loud, not hurricane loud,
probably normal for the island. I brushed my teeth in the bathroom,
and still heard his voice behind me: "Arlene, Bret, Cindy . . ."

I turned off the light and got into the bed beside Sebastian's. Lit
windows in neighboring bungalows flickered as palms blew in
front of them. Wind, the rustling of fronds on the thin metal roof,
swept us to sleep. *Margot, Nigel, Ophelia. Bobby, Viva . . .*

My phone woke me up. It was past midnight. At first I couldn't
place the voice on the line.

"John showed the café scene to his father-in-law, Big Henry."
Music and voices in the background. Halalati sounded drunk. "You
know, Big Henry? He says go to the bar where they shot."

"Oh, okay, thank you," I whispered, not wanting to wake Sebastian up.

"I should have thought of that. Big Henry says the guy behind
the bar in the scene is actually the real guy Magistrate, who still
works there. That bar's up on the mountain north on the way to
Morne Diablotins. It's called Caracolis. Not many people go there,
just who grow the weed and good-for-nothings." She seemed excited to provide that information. "Did I wake you?"

"Do you think a taxi driver can take me there?" I said.

"We will go there tomorrow."

"I feel bad imposing on you like this," I said.

"You see this hand?" she said.

"I mean, no." I laughed.

Next to me, Sebastian spoke in his sleep.

"Well, this hand," she said. Someone screamed in the background. "I know this hand like I know this island. This island is my hand. Bore me to death. Same ten fingers. I'm so tired of this island. You be my entertainment for the weekend."

From Halatati's car stereo, walls of damaged sound crashed into copies of themselves. It was as if someone had built a whole wall of guitars and then attacked it with a jackhammer. The vocalist, shrieking "*Hey!*" over and over, sounded like he'd inhaled helium.

We'd been driving for forty, fifty minutes, ascending the volcano. "StabYou!" Halalati yelled over the music. "Do you know them?"

"No!" I yelled back.

"Finnish death metal. Best in the world."

Mist surrounded us and the ferns and trees. Leaves left slimy tracks on the windshield as the road narrowed. I raised my hands to my ears. In the back seat, Sebastian did the same. Noticing this in the mirror, Halalati turned the stereo off, but not before the next song, full of cries of kittens skinned alive, had begun its assault. "Well, sorry," she said. "I drive alone. This is my music for the jungle. Hate this jungle."

The absence of music coincided with a ravine opening on our left, no rail, no shoulder. One slip of the wheel and the car would tumble down.

"We're here," she said, and turned the engine off.

"Aren't we in the middle of the road?"

"This isn't a road."

"Don't customers drive up here to the bar?"

"Nah. Nobody comes here. If they do, they come on foot." She shook her head and tightened the laces on her sneakers. "Hell to get the *Great Dala* crew up here. All these trucks stuck in the mud back there. The director was crazy. Crazy. There was one Kazakh actress afraid of heights. I led her on this here path blindfolded. She was crazy, too. Preferred to maybe trip and fall than be safe and see."

"Get out on my side," I told Sebastian, and we opened our doors, having to push them against vegetation.

We followed Halalati down a narrow path, onto a makeshift bridge over a swamp.

"Who comes to this shithole? Poachers and growers, crazy white people, that's who." Perhaps she wasn't finding our company as entertaining as she'd hoped.

My clothes, hair, and face were damp from sweat and mist. Green water in the pools below us hissed a little, and the wood of the bridge was rotten and moldy. Even if Sleeper *was* in this film shot here years before, he wouldn't be here now. I felt depressed, laughable, and crazy as a Kazakh actress.

"Everything's in ruins. You stay on this island, it kills you. Whoever you're looking for, it probably killed him already," Halalati said, reaching the end of the bridge. She fetched a yellow package from her pocket. "Gum?" Sebastian accepted the gum without a thank-you. I decided not to scold him. He was mute with awe, swinging his head to take in the swamp and unusual cries of insects and birds. At least, I thought, I have taken my son somewhere he likes.

Beyond the bridge, we took a flight of stone steps down to an area even more violently green than where we'd been. A roof of feathery thatching emerged from between two mossy thrusts of rock, like a giant bird that had been crushed there.

"Here's your Caracolis," she said almost antagonistically.

"I was wondering if I could perhaps compensate you for your time somehow," I said.

"Keep it, lady," she said and laughed, but not unpleasantly, in fact with sympathy. "Nothing to spend it on here."

We entered Caracolis through a squeaky door engraved with the letters W.C. The bar was nothing more than a wall with a roof and a counter. Most of the tables shown in *The Great Dala* were now crammed together, decked with chairs turned upside down. Spiderwebs, moss, rotten fruit, and leaves were woven through their legs and backs, joining them together into a shape like a ship, wrecked in the woods, a few torn tablecloths for sails.

The roar of a distant waterfall blended with that of retching. We followed the sound and saw, half-concealed behind a canvas partition, two grizzled men playing a board game. I couldn't tell which of them had made the sound. Two glasses and an unlabeled dirty bottle, half-empty, stood by the board between them. It was a very masculine space. A StabYou soundtrack wouldn't have been entirely out of place. Instead, some seventies American rock came quietly from a small blown speaker on the floor beside their table.

I stepped closer to Sebastian and put my hand on his shoulder and waited by the bar for Halalati to approach the men.

"You Magistrate?" She walked over to their table and stood over them, arms akimbo.

"To all who are guilty," said one of the men. He had a tiny, pinched cone of a nose, the result of an injury. I hoped Sebastian wouldn't stare at it. Around his neck, Magistrate wore a brass medallion the size and shape of an egg.

"Big Henry sent me." Halalati didn't seem intimidated by his standoffish response. "But I know you. We met. We did *The Great Dala* here."

"You here to pay for my fan they broke? It's still up in back. Still broke."

"We're looking for a missing guy," said Halalati. "He was in the scene they shot here with you in it." She opened her purse and fumbled inside it.

"They came for you at last," said the other man—the one who wasn't Magistrate—to Magistrate. He had a straw hat and a sunburnt face that contrasted with his straw-blond hair. "After they made that movie," he informed us, "Magistrate here, he went down to Roseau, bought a tux. Only no one ever called him up to go to all those movie parties in a limousine in France."

Magistrate nodded. "That's right. I got myself a suit."

"You never wore it."

"I wore it."

"Where did you wear it?"

"I wore it here," he said. "Hard work. Look nice."

Halalati had taken her phone out and was trying to pull the clip up on it, cursing at it. Sebastian had wriggled away from me and now approached their table, so I followed him and said a quiet hello.

Between the table and the bar, a tattered carpet had been spread over the mud, and its flowery designs had real roots growing through them, crowned with moss.

"I know this game. Why do you play with real money?" Sebastian pointed at the crumpled notes strewn all over the table.

"Jamaican dollars. Monopoly money," said the man who wasn't Magistrate. "Hey, you ever had a *grenouille* that tastes like chicken?"

Sebastian looked over his shoulder at me.

"*Grenouille*'s a frog," I said.

"Frogs don't taste like chicken," Sebastian said to the man.

"Here they do. They're called *crapauds*. You can eat them. You can stick a straw in their *culs* and blow them up if you prefer."

Sebastian looked at me for translation.

"*Crapauds' culs* are *crapauds'* asses," said the man. "Your mother should teach you."

Sebastian looked from him to me, uncertain if he should laugh or frown.

"He speaks enough languages as it is," I said, noticing a shotgun propped against a diesel drum behind the man. .

I put my hand on Sebastian's shoulder, making what I hoped was a bold but also dismissive face at the man who wasn't Magistrate. The man stood up, and to my mild surprise he bowed and took his hat off, placed it on a chair, and pulled another chair out, maybe for me or Sebastian to sit. I didn't sit. And Sebastian was too busy studying the Jamaican banknotes.

"Got it, finally. Here, you, Magistrate, watch this clip," said Halalati, and she played the café scene, and as she played it, I couldn't believe that the scene I'd watched a hundred times in Manhattan had been shot right here. It was as if the reality of this location was more fictitious than the film. Insects droned around my ears. In the corner was what looked like an open compost bucket. A large beetle made its slow passage from the bucket along a long plank leading into the swamp with a gossamer shrimp shell attached to its horn.

"That guy? Never seen that guy," said Magistrate.

"That's you sitting right beside him," Halalati scolded. "Look again."

"I looked again."

"The white guy with the coffee," said the man who wasn't Magistrate. "I know this man well."

"You *know* him?" I sat on the chair he'd pulled out and looked into the map of ancient sun damage that was his face.

"You didn't even look at the screen," said Halalati, and sat on the edge of the table and played the scene again, this time pointing her phone at the man.

"Yep. His name is Bass."

"Bass?! Se*bas*tian? Is his last name Sleeper?" My face went hot. I felt dissociated, saw in my head myself at the table with two men, a woman, a child, figures in a rainforest scene in a painting in a museum, a painting someone had stolen and lost in the rainforest.

"No. Just Bass."

"Is he American?"

"Born here, this island."

"You know *this* guy? The guy in this movie?!" I demanded, disbelieving.

"Yes, *madame*. I know him. He drinks Kubuli and he likes to fish."

"Is he still here?" I said, ridiculously gesturing at the swamp.

"I couldn't tell you that. He used to come here and drink, back in the eighties. Had all sorts of drinking theories. Liked to be drunk, but not too much, was working on keeping it smooth, not deep. 'Horizontal drinking,' he called it. I myself do the vertical drinking. I like it to reach all the way, the liver, the heart." He pointed at his fern-green shirt, which might not have been changed or washed since the eighties. "Bass. I know him well. He is a *philosophe* of drink."

I was excited. "Horizontal drinking" sounded like something Sleeper might have said.

"If he was here, and you were in the movie next to him, how come you don't know him?" Halalati demanded of Magistrate. A weak, hot wind came down the volcano and fluttered her black skirt onto the game board, moving a stack of money.

The man who wasn't Magistrate slapped his hand down on the stack. "The bar was under different jurisdiction then, before Magistrate's time. Davide Priest ruled here then. Pierre knows. He was always here."

"Who's Pierre?" I said.

"Pierre is I," said the man who wasn't Magistrate. "Nice to meet." He extended his hand, and I shook it.

"I'm Viva," I said. It slipped out. Halalati, who knew me as Larissa, looked at me, as if she was also expecting to be introduced.

"Well, I don't know him," Magistrate said. "Never heard of him."

Halalati waved a hand and looked annoyed. She got off the table and brushed her skirt.

"I don't know any Bass," said Magistrate, knocking over a bunch of red houses on the game board. "Never met him, never heard of any." The medallion dangled in the vee of his mostly unbuttoned shirt. It had on it an image of the Virgin.

"Hey, hands off my colony!" Pierre said to Magistrate.

"Does Bass still live here, on Dominica?" I said.

"He comes and goes," said Pierre.

"Does he have an address?"

"Keeps no address. He's private. More private than any of us."

"But he was born here, on this island?" I said.

"Yes, born here."

I'd never been able to locate anyone from Sleeper's family, not even his mother, the redhead from the photo. Most families named

Sleeper came from New Hampshire. None I contacted had known Sebastian. Could it be he was really from here, from Dominica?

"Is there anyone else in town who might know Bass?" I said, leaning close to Pierre. I could smell his herbal, alcohol-infused breath.

"I don't think so. *Pas possible*. He's private. More private than me and Magistrate."

"I'm not private," Magistrate said. "I nightly serve my people!"

"And you're certain that's Bass?" I said, showing Pierre some other photos of Sleeper I'd saved from various film websites onto my phone.

"That's Bass," he said, "and that's Bass and that's Bass. He's always been *jolie*."

"What about his wife? Do you know her?" I said, showing the Interpol photo of Bobby.

"Looks like an angel," said Pierre, and tears began to flow from his eyes.

I was surprised. Tears didn't seem to belong to those hard pupils, those red-lined eye whites.

"Why are you crying?" Halalati said contemptuously. She'd been pacing around the table, sometimes glancing at Sebastian, who was examining a pile of old postcards in a box beside the diesel drum.

"Because I'm a man," said Pierre, which made Magistrate chuckle and refill his glass and drink what he'd poured.

"That's his wife, Bobby," I prodded on. "Are you crying because something has happened to her?"

"Something happened to his wife?" he asked me. It occurred to me he might be not just drunk but in the eighth day of a bender.

Halalati sighed and rolled her eyes at me. My hope began to

wane. Magistrate extended a hand and surreptitiously snatched a few banknotes from Pierre's side of the game board.

"They are both listed as missing on the Interpol website," I said. "Do you know anything about that?"

"No. Do you?" Pierre said, raised his hand, and scratched his sparsely whiskered chin.

"So you knew this woman, his wife?" I persevered.

"No, I never met this angel," he said. "Bass had many wives," he said, but then I thought he'd said *lives*, not *wives*. "Here, he always came alone."

"When was that, exactly?"

"Late eighties, early nineties. *La belle epoque!*"

"That's impossible," I said. "The man I'm looking for was born in 1979. That means he would've been my son's age when he came here and supposedly drank with you."

Hearing "my son," Sebastian looked up from his box of treasures. He looked at me and then at the board on the table. He's still thinking about why they're using real money, I thought.

"Who knows," said Pierre. "We were all young then. Especially Bass. Decades went by and nothing touched him. Not a wrinkle. How do you do that? I keep asking him. Known him for years. My whole life. Goat's milk. He kept a goat in his backyard, washed all his hair in the milk. In the seventies, we sailed Panama to Indonesia. Bass, he took the goat with him and drank straight from its *tétine. Tétines de chèvre.* Amuse the sailors. But the goat died, so we ate it. In 1960, the National Army was after us . . . Want to hear how we escaped the Congo with a diamond up my *cul?* That was a *bordel!* Bass was a practical man. Diamond's still in there, by the way. *C'est vrai.*"

I remembered Sleeper had a scar on his hand from sailing, but I knew it'd be an absurd thing to ask about and the answer equally absurd. Behind Pierre's back, Halalati twirled a finger by her temple, whispered something that sounded like *sinfulness*, and gestured at the door, eager to go.

"Is there anything else you can tell me that will help me find him?" I said to Pierre.

"*Après lui, le déluge*," mumbled Pierre. He drank directly from the bottle.

"And you," I addressed Magistrate, "you're sure you don't know him?"

"Never met him," Magistrate said, his face in his hands. "Never, not once in all the years."

Sebastian came back and sat on my lap. The sun had found its way through the dense foliage, sending little rays, like flickering question marks, onto his face.

"So you don't know anything more tangible about him?"

"Never heard of him," Magistrate said to the mossy carpet between his knees. Then I saw he was reaching for another banknote, probably Pierre's, that had blown under the table.

"Anyone else who might know him?" I said, dejected.

"No one knows him but I," said Pierre. "*Seulement moi.* He comes and goes, but he's always, always lived on this island."

"What did you whisper to me when I was talking to Pierre?" I asked Halalati as we drove backward down the narrow road.

"I did?"

"You whispered something." I repeated her gesture, twirling my finger by my temple. "It sounded like 'sinfulness.'"

"Close," she laughed. "I said 'syphilis.' These old syphilis guys make me sick," she said.

"How do you know they have syphilis?"

"Did you see the nose on Magistrate? It's gone from their privates up to their heads and faces. They all have it. They're all crazy," she said. "It's time for them to die. They are poison to the island."

I said nothing. I was depressed but also strangely relieved.

"I'm hungry. Are you hungry?" she asked Sebastian. I think she liked him much more than she liked me. "How about lunch and swim?"

"Yes to both," he said.

"You seen a black-sand beach?"

"No." He'd unbuckled his seat belt and was leaning with his arms on the front seats. I reached over to touch his soft hair and didn't scold him.

Often still, so many decades later, I remember that afternoon on Dominica, driving down from Caracolis, down Morne Diablotins, emerging from jungle into the sun and driving west to the beach. I remember Halalati's black skirt floating as, knee-deep in the ocean, we three ate fried conch from a greasy bag.

We walked on the obsidian sand, my son and I, a family, small but happy—my mother, by then, was dead and my brothers estranged—and Sebastian told me his most recent piece of gathered knowledge. Did I know Dominica was called *Dominica* because the man who'd found her had sailed by on a Sunday, but before that, in Kalinago, her name had been different and meant *tall is her body* because of her mountainous terrain?

I remember him saying this to me, Sebastian son of Sebastian, and, within this memory, walking the beach and remembering Bobby waiting for me on the 101 and later, in the car, telling me she'd almost been named Dominika, because it meant *Sunday* in Latin, because she was lazy. She was a Sunday child.

This suspect symmetry has been my small consolation over many years. It's turned with time into a sort of key, not like the key to the house in the Hollywood Hills, that real key I still have in my jewelry box in New York, but a phantom key, a clue to the riddle. In the lifelong dream of the answer, there has been no door. But still, beyond wherever that key fits, Bobby is Dominika, and Sleeper has always lived on this island.

2079

New York